INTO DARKNESS

INTO DARKNESS

ELYSIUM'S MULTIVERSE | BOOK 7

Ranyhin1

Podium

Cover design by Nate Artuz

ISBN: 979-8-3470-0390-7

Published in 2026 by Podium Publishing
www.podiumentertainment.com

INTO DARKNESS

CHAPTER 1

The purple sun hovering over him burned with a rich light, fueled by sin that had repeatedly pulled on the link between himself and Gluttony during his stay here. It hadn't been long since Allie left after chewing him out for what he considered to be a massive overreaction after her quick ascension and departure, but he had his own life to play out. And Allie wasn't a little kid anymore—he couldn't be expected to hold her hand.

Though he did worry about Kathrine. Based on what Allie said, the vampiric princess was in trouble. He didn't know Kathrine all that well, but most people from his homeland in the Blood Moon Requiem were less than savory. She'd been a fresh light in that darkness, and he hoped she'd come out all right—for whatever it was she was going through after being kidnapped. Yet again, he was stuck in a situation where there was nothing he could do about it—Lillith had already sent the archdemon Tre'Zix of the Purple Claw to get her back—and now Allie was apparently going to intervene somehow as well.

It just sucked being left in the dark about it all, and his demons weren't too happy about the recent exchange. Athela was furious, Fay looked like she'd had her feelings seriously hurt, and even the titanic flame demon Azmoth was grumpy at the sheer disrespect. Thankfully, Narg the beholder demon and Genua—Riven's elf thrall—were rather uncaring about the whole ordeal and just kept silent, not wanting to intervene between two royal siblings who just happened to be the reincarnations of two original sins. It was, in Narg's words, out of their comfort zone to talk about—or even have opinions about.

"Hey, Riven. You don't look so good," Nora, in her human form, said, sitting down next to him as he pondered the insights he'd obtained on this level. Frowning and brushing her hair behind one ear, she looked out over the half-destroyed room with a frown. "I wouldn't take what Allie said to heart. My Others are telling me that, for a mortal bound to Wrath, she did quite well to contain herself. They were surprised she didn't outright try to kill you and everyone else here, and I'm sure that over time she won't be as aggressive or angry about things."

Riven, for his part, sat with his arms folded in front of him, cross-legged on the ground. His cloak, made from shadows and bloodsilk, slowly flickered in the purple light as his body remained motionless. Messenger's ivory jaws rumbled across his chest where more bloodsilk was woven in between patches of thin plate armor. Red and black eyes stared out at the sun created from sin, and he had to say that he was somewhat disappointed with the results so far. Nora had become something of a badass, and Allie had become Wrath's reincarnation. How was he supposed to beat them to obtain the points for Chalgathi's quest line? And if he failed to fulfill his side of things and his mother's warning about not finishing first came to pass, what then? Would he really need to abandon Panu after the apocalypse beasts wreaked havoc? Should he even trust his mother?

Just how much faith should he put in the woman who'd abandoned him as a child?

"I'm all right," Riven eventually said, closing his eyes with a soft hum. "I don't blame Allie too much. Though I am going to make her apologize to Athela, Fay, and Genua when she's in her right state of mind. She can be rude to me all she wants—we're siblings—but it wasn't acceptable what she said about them. Especially to Athela."

"Or Kara," Nora said, head-bobbing over to the sulking dark elf archer who was pretending to sleep not far from them. "That was ruthlessly mean of Allie to say, especially when Kara hasn't had an easy life. I mean, think about it: Kara was betrayed by her own countrymen, robbed here in the abyss, basically made to do a long walk of shame, and she wasn't allowed back into her family by her father unless she made it past Floor Forty—which would have been an impossible task prior to your intervention. She was destined to die, or return in humiliation for what she'd considered a worse fate after ties with her family would have been cut. If you ask me, Kara has had it the worst. And just when she finds you, who is both powerful and nice enough to try and help her—your sister, Allie, comes out and says absolutely terrible things about her, without even knowing her, before flipping you off and walking away. If I hadn't been in my other form, I probably would have cried on Kara's behalf after seeing her face during the conversation. It was heartbreaking."

Riven raised an eyebrow in Nora's direction. "What did you do instead, since you WERE in your . . . eh, Insane Asylum? With your Legion—so to speak? I still don't really grasp what it is you've become."

Nora grinned, and the smaller, older Asian lady punched him in the shoulder. "Neither do I. The voices keep their secrets even now. It isn't really a hive mind, but it's . . . similar? And demonic in nature. I'm still figuring it out for myself. Anyways, I just wanted to come and tell you that you did the right thing in helping Kara out, and that you shouldn't feel guilty just because your sister is in a piss-poor mood. For the record, I don't think you were flirting with Kara, either. Athela and Fay know you love them, but maybe go talk to them and make sure they're okay, too. Genua's too far gone down the road of losing her mind as a thrall to care what Allie says, so that's good."

"I wouldn't say that's a good thing."

"Riven. You murdered her husband and oldest daughter. Of course it's a good thing—she wouldn't be able to cope otherwise."

"That was in self-defense. It wasn't murder."

"Kind of, but kind of not. But you're the reincarnation of an original sin! Why should you care? You're the bad guy according to multiversal standards, right?! Either way, I'm not here to lecture you on whether what you did all that time ago was right. I'm just saying that, from her perspective, it's a good thing that she became a thrall. Otherwise she'd still be struggling with a lot of mental anguish that she can now push aside rather easily due to what she is, and from what she's told me, that's why Genua agreed to become a thrall in the first place: so that she could finally get past it all. It was her decision, was it not?"

"It was."

"Then don't think about it anymore. If she wanted to be a thrall, then you have nothing to worry about, because you could have let her stay the way she was. Plus, you'll have a lot of time to make it up to her by taking care of that kid, or kids, plural—if you include Len."

"Did you come over here just to fuck with my head?"

Nora cackled, slapped him on the back, and began to stand. "No. I came over here to let you know that I'll be heading back to Chalgathi's trials." She raised her hands to stop any protests he may make. "No, Riven. I think it's for the best. And let me tell you why. As time has gone on, I've owed quite a bit of my progress to you and your friends. Bringing me here has already helped me beyond what I ever thought possible . . . and has reconciled a long-standing fear I've had with the voices in my head. Literally. So . . . as a way of thanking you, I'm going to go back to Chalgathi's trial and do you a solid."

Riven furrowed his brows and stood up, brushing dust from his robes with a huff. "How are you going to do that, exactly? Color me interested."

Nora's expression became savage, and she put her hands on her hips, where her bone-crafted blades rested. It was her second set after her first had been eradicated along with most of her original clothes on her ascension into whatever she was now, but Riven had brought multiple spares for everyone just in case something like that happened. "Well, Riven—I intend to go hunting. Hunting cultists . . . If I can stop them from finishing their event quests regularly, I can make sure they don't get the ten thousand points needed to leave the Altars of Despair and Hope event before you get there. As it is, this descent has taken months. If you complete the Abyssal Descent to make the number one placeholder when compared to prior descents, you'll get another three thousand. But who knows how many points the others have acquired in the time you've been gone? If need be, I'll even kill other noncultists to make sure it's you who gets the title, since you're stuck in here for a while."

There was a short silence after that as they stared at one another.

"That . . . would actually be very helpful. Thank you, Nora." Riven slowly nodded and prompted the screen displaying his old quest to appear before him. It felt like he'd been here forever; these quest-within-a-quest scenarios were really a bit much at this point. He needed to get Lillith, finish first, and get the hell out of here so he could go back home to Panu. Just thinking that he was within a dimensional pocket within the Abyssal Descent and he'd gotten there by traveling through another dimensional pocket in Chalgathi's trials after having originally left Panu—it was just mind-numbing at this point.

[Riven's Quest 2 of the Altars of Despair and Hope:

A piece of the multiverse, taken out of the Narwali sector of Universe 16, has been transported to this territory. Inside it you will find one of a few portals here in these Chalgathi trials that lead into the Abyssal Descent, and three ticket holders who are waiting to enter. You have obtained the necessary tickets and have already entered the descent.

The Abyssal Descent, a monumental event that only happens every three hundred years, is being hosted. It is meant to help forge the lattice meant to transcend into E-grade and help give insight into the way of ascension.

Young elites of numerous factions across the multiverse still within the F-grade will be able to participate, as long as they hold true to any subpillars associated with the Unholy foundation. Use your status page to find the option to teleport in. You will be escorted via Elysium's own power into this trial within a trial where only those touched by Unholy power may be found. Death in this trial will not result in permanent death despite being hosted on an outer world, but will disallow any reentering of the descent at any time. Successfully completing the Abyssal Descent will result in fifty event points. Completing in the top one hundred contenders will result in three hundred event points. Completing this event in the top five contenders will result in one thousand event points. Finishing first will result in three thousand event points. Any other cultists of Unholy affiliation who enter this trial within a trial will also have a 1,000% damage boost increase when attacking you or your minions.

Unlike other participants in this outer trial, you will be able to come and go between the Abyssal Descent and the Altars of Despair and Hope at will via your status page.

Total event points already accumulated: 39]

He cringed when he saw the total points at thirty-nine, and Nora gave a bellowing laugh when he showed her the notification.

"More reason for me to go!" she said with a shake of her head and an amused sigh. "You'll have a lot of catching up to do when you get back. The Chalgathi trial was supposed to be about a year, if I recall, and you've spent months of it here. Even if you get the full three thousand points, it won't be worth it unless you manage some major breakthroughs with your soul lattice. They're not all created the same, or so I'm told. So get it done fast and I'll see you on the other side."

She held out a fist, and they fist-bumped.

"All right, Nora. Catch you later, homie. Just tell the others so they know what's going on."

"I already have," she said with a thumbs-up. "You're the last one I've told. See ya later, bud! Regarding the whole Genua thing and morality about murdering Ethel, you're still the man who saved my life on the pyramid when we were first integrated. That backstabbing elf played you like a fiddle to the tune of her own death, not because you wanted to do it. And I think you're great, so keep your chin up. You have a lot going for you. I have faith that you'll come out ahead."

With that, Nora contacted the system administrator. It was certainly different from how Allie had left, when his sister had been portaled out to a specific location on Panu. Here, Nora flashed and was gone—though based on the quest details she could probably reenter the descent if she really wanted to. However, he didn't know if she'd teleport back to his group's location or if she'd reenter here should she decide to return.

[Unlike other participants in this outer trial, you will be able to come and go between the Abyssal Descent and the Altars of Despair and Hope at will via your status page.]

But he doubted she would be back if she really intended to wreak havoc on the other Chalgathi participants. Those poor suckers had no idea what they were in for after her change, and a grim smile touched at his lips. So far this descent really had done wonders for his party. His original three demons were all now archdemons, Allie had ascended into Wrath's reincarnation, Nora had become a crazy overpowered psychopath of some kind, and even Riven had become far better at fighting after the brutal training sessions back in Gluttony's church. What else he and the other remaining members had to gain remained to be seen, but he was excited to find out.

Turning back to meditation and attempting to keep his mind calm despite ongoing events, he reentered a state of bridging enlightenment and focused on building his soul lattice as connections continued to make and break themselves across the inner world of his core and pillars.

* * *

Mara coughed black blood onto the cavern floor when a large spear skewered her all the way through, and she gasped in pain as Kathrine sobbed while curled up in the background.

"I ONLY NEED ONE OF YOU TO SHOW ME THE WAY! Do not push your luck, ghoul!" Crendir sneered, sweat accumulating on his brows beneath shallow cuts and a long gash over his singed head. His armor was cracked and even shattered in various places, and he had wounds that even vampiric regeneration could not entirely heal after having barely escaped the demon pack pursuing them with various protective talismans—but they all knew that he was walking a tightrope here in the underdark.

It would only be a matter of time before Tre'Zix caught up to them again. Hopefully, anyway, and despite the agony Mara was in right now, she reveled in the memory of those clicking sounds the mantis demons made as they tore apart the traitors that'd accompanied Crendir down here. Those banished demons from the ancient wars were machines of pure malice and murder, and they had curb-stomped the F-grade elite vampire traitors of the Blood Moon Requiem like they were toddlers wielding squeaky toys for weapons.

Only Crendir and one other vampiric soldier were left. All the others were dead.

"I told you, Crendir—" Mara gasped, grunting with a wince as the vampiric spear was ripped out of her gut. Thankfully ghouls could take a lot more punishment than humans could. "It was this way! I am not lying!"

"YES, YOU ARE! We have been going through these tunnels in CIRCLES, YOU LYING BITCH!" Crendir screamed, raising his foot and smashing his boot down onto Mara's face.

The bones in her skull nearly cracked, and she was pretty sure her jaw became unhinged in that moment.

The other man, a bearded vampire whose armor had taken a lot less damage in the recent attack, glanced down at the whimpering, shackled princess with a shake of his head. "This was a mistake, taking this job. I don't care how much it pays if we're dead."

"SHUT UP, FARAS! You came here just like I did, and you're in it for the long haul whether you like it or not!" Crendir snapped with an accusing finger. "We either succeed or die. Those are our only options, and if we don't stop circling around, then we might as well kill both of them now and just go looking for it ourselves!"

The other man shrugged. "Sounds like a plan to me. I say we just kill them and be done with it."

Mara's heart sank. Despite all that she'd said and done, she was still afraid to die.

And the heavily armored man guarding Kathrine seemed very serious about this proposition to kill them.

She didn't want to end up like Nin and Vin.

Crendir seemed to seriously consider the option for a while, burned face contorted in contemplation, then bent down on one knee and violently yanked Mara up by her black hair to meet his red eyes. "One more chance. Just one. If you two can't put your heads together and get us on the right track in the next five minutes, then I really will just cut off your head and bleed Kathrine dry."

"P-please!" Kathrine sobbed, face half covered by brunette hair and body sporting wounds made from silver antivampire blades. "I don't want to die! I d-don't want to die!!!"

Her voice came up in a high-pitched squeal at the end before she started crying again, and Mara felt a lump settle in her throat.

As far as Crendir knew, Kathrine knew where this tomb was. But Kathrine hadn't actually been there. Mara and the survivors of the first expedition had reported to her, before Allie had left, but she didn't actually know the way down. Those other expedition members besides Nin and Vin had also had their names hidden for safety purposes, so Crendir hadn't known they even existed when he'd abducted the two of them. Neither woman had actually said this in case Crendir decided to kill Kathrine for being useless, but Mara was the only one here who truly knew the way to the tomb.

Thus, Mara held both of their lives in her hands.

And time was now ticking.

She had to gamble here. Did she want to risk letting Crendir get a hold of the fallen god's blood? He wasn't a pureblood himself, but if he'd come this far, then he certainly had a means of procuring it anyway. Some kind of work-around, or a vessel to capture it for transport. She'd felt the awe-inspiring power it held even as a ghoul, and couldn't imagine what a vampire would do with that kind of energy. Yet, if she didn't say anything now, she was sealing both her own fate—and Kathrine's fate, too. And she knew that Tre'Zix was on the hunt . . . he'd already caught up to them twice. With serious casualties on Crendir's team alongside major protective talismans needing to be used by the traitor as a result. How many more escape and protective treasures did he even have?

Hopefully not many. If he didn't, then she could potentially risk telling him the truth and leading him down the right path . . . and would need to hope that Tre'Zix could catch them before Crendir got to the pyramid and tomb.

Above all else, though, Mara was just scared. Plain and simple, scared to die. The torture was becoming unbearable as well, even for a ghoul with diminished pain receptors.

Would Allie be mad if she gave in after weeks of torture?

Mara hoped not.

She'd tried, and now Mara was at her breaking point.

Letting out a sob of her own, Mara began to point a shaky finger down the tunnel in the opposite direction they'd been heading. "There . . . three miles down and through a lava pit, we'll come to an abandoned vampiric city. That of native vampires. After we arrive, we will be able to direct you to a new tunnel system where the elder god's followers, vampiric precursors, have started to terraform the tunnels with runic symbols within a labyrinth."

Crendir stared at her for a time, red eyes flaring with light, and he seemed to use some kind of system power on her as a wave of energy coursed over her—as if trying to detect a lie. He nodded in satisfaction, smiling for the first time in a while, and let go of her hair, dropping her to the ground with a thud. "There . . . that wasn't so hard, now was it?"

"UMPH!" she wheezed, getting a swift kick to the gut wound that still bled black, before she felt her body being pulled across the ground with inhuman strength by the long chain attached at her iron collar.

"Come on, Faras, we have a fallen god to harvest," Crendir muttered. "And we've already wasted too much time. Those fucking demons will be on our trail soon, and I'm not sure we'll survive another encounter."

CHAPTER 2

The skill fractal clicked into place on her soul pillar, beginning to churn out power in the form of divinity—the faith-based energy, similar to how mana was used for magic and stamina was used for martial arts.

Her eyes snapped open with a wide smile on her pitch-black lips. Athela had done it!

She'd finally mastered the Body Fusion technique!

Cackling evilly to herself, but not loud enough that Riven or the others filtering into the twenty-first Abyssal floor would hear, she sneaked around the room's outer perimeter to where Genua was seated. She moved like a ghost in the shadows, only able to be matched in stealth by Fimrindle—and perhaps Nora now that she'd gone batshit crazy in between bouts of sanity. Though Athela couldn't say that she minded the change—because at least now the woman was useful and not deadweight.

"Do you have more of Riven's vampiric venom?" Athela asked, sitting down next to the other schemers with a huff of satisfaction. "Did you get it?"

Fay nodded sagely, pulling out a small glass vial with clear, viscous fluid inside. "Absolutely!"

"How did you manage to do that, anyways?" Genua asked curiously, still knitting baby clothes like Athela had taught her to do with the balls of bloodsilk. Her pointed ears drooped as she pooched her lips and looked up at the other women. "Because I know you haven't told him that you took it."

Fay rolled her eyes and gave Genua a playful wink and tipped her witch's hat at the elf thrall. "You'd be surprised at the things I can do with my tongue. I basically massaged it from his teeth."

"No, I'm very aware of what you can do with that tongue of yours. Though I don't think Riven approved of it when he found out you were requesting such things of me, nor do I think he'll approve of this should he find out what you two are scheming now."

Genua gave them a knowing look but kept knitting.

Athela, for her part, drooped her eyelids and gave the elf thrall a blank stare. "Do you disapprove? I thought you liked this idea."

"Oh! I do," Genua said with a laugh, but shot Riven a brief glance across the room where he was meditating under the sun made from Sin. "But you're definitely going to make him angry if you do it. Just don't throw me into the mix if you two get in trouble for this."

"He'll appreciate it in the long term. Plus, there are genuine reasons to do this."

"Which are?" Genua inquired.

"You know just as well as I do." Athela narrowed her eyes more. "Genua, do you even realize who you're talking to right now? We are DEMONS. We make deals with mortals for their SOULS, Genua! Didn't you grow up in a culture where you elves were deathly scared of demons? We're creatures of evil! We are not the good guys. This is what we do!"

"Can't disagree with that," Genua muttered.

"Exactly!" Athela laughed, slapping Genua's thigh. "And now, with Fay's insight complete and her new . . . rather useful ability at play, it makes it all the easier! Plus, Gluttony wanted this . . . and he personally asked us to do it, because Riven has yet to expand upon his bloodline and he's been a fucking VAMPIRE for well over a year and a half. We'll tell Riven after the transformations are complete . . . and what he does with them afterward is up to him. If he doesn't want them, we can just kill them then! Or he can give them to us!"

"This is still a serious breach of trust," Genua scolded. "That's where the problem lies, in my opinion. It doesn't hurt Riven and even benefits him, but you're going to be put in the doghouse for not letting him know."

"It's a white lie! And he wouldn't let us do it unless it was already done by the time he knew!"

"Mmm-hmm. Debatable. However, I won't deny, I will enjoy having the load of labor taken off my shoulders. To have more free time with Len will be nice, and right now I only get to communicate with her through the Blood Mirror technique I've mastered. How did you abduct them, anyway?"

Fay raised her hand. "That was my doing! My illusions replicated Elysium's portals quite well when they attempted to leave, and with the insights I gained into my new alternate prison ability from the Depravity subpillar, as long as they're equal to or less than my own level, I'm able to hold up to fifty souls. It'll solve a lot of Riven's food problems as we build up his blood farm, especially when you're worn out or need a break."

Genua grumbled slightly, rubbing at her neck where a fresh set of fang wounds was still only very recently sealed shut. "I am pleased to serve the master, but yes. He does go overboard sometimes, to the point where I even get lightheaded. Unless he's on one of his hunts—"

"His hunts?" Fay asked curiously.

Genua raised an eyebrow, stopped knitting, and set the half-finished baby shirt on the floor. "You don't know?"

"Obviously not, thrall. That is why I am asking you."

"Mmm-hmm. I see. I think that's a discussion you should have with him, then."

Fay's features darkened. "I am to be his wife one day. Remember who you're speaking to. What are these hunts you speak of?"

Genua stared at the younger woman for a time, shrugged, and nodded in acceptance. "You're right, so I suppose it wouldn't hurt to tell you after all. Ever since binding himself with Gluttony entirely and becoming the reincarnation, he's needed to kill and eat enlightened beings—not just drain them of some blood. He's been doing so behind your backs so that you wouldn't think less of him."

Both Fay's and Athela's eyes widened in shock.

Genua continued when she realized they weren't going to comment. "If he doesn't, he gets very . . . grumpy. Acquires painful debuffs. He tried feeding on me more often to make up for this neglect at first, when trying to forgo the hunts Gluttony requires, but he only became more violent and ended up hurting me in one of his mood swings. He apologized afterward, and I know he didn't mean to do it, but having a ravenous vampire come after you, even as a thrall, is rather scary. He gorged himself on me, and I would have died if not for him using Voodoo Doll to keep me whole."

Athela's eyes fell to Genua's pregnant belly. "Was the child okay?"

Genua nodded. "Yes. Gluttony and Riven made sure of it, but it was a close call. Ever since then, he's never missed a weekly hunt. Usually he kills people he feels deserve death, but sometimes he has fewer options, such as when we had just entered Chalgathi's pocket realm for the Altars of Despair and Hope. He sometimes has to kill a random person because the urges become too much . . . but he doesn't like to talk about it. He's not only embarrassed, but gets aggressively angry with himself over the fact that his urges to feed are beginning to control him. Here in the descent, he hunted various participants up in the main city whenever he could get away from Lillith's training regimens. The urges to feed are getting worse as he grows more powerful and deepens his bonds with Gluttony. But what I meant to say earlier was that when he goes on these hunts, he's usually rather gentle when feeding on me throughout the rest of the week. But not always—and I would very much enjoy having some fellow thralls to take some of the load off."

Fay and Athela continued to stare.

"Why has he never told us of this?" Fay whispered. "He's such a kind person. That must be so hard for him to bear, dealing with Gluttony's urges."

"Is he?" Genua asked with an amused smirk. "I'm not so sure I'd consider him kind, but he is a good master to have. He did, after all, sacrifice an entire city of innocents to get Athela back. I wouldn't say that is kind, I would say that is even somewhat selfish—but his priorities are right, I think. For the record, Athela, I'm glad he did it."

Fay scoffed, obviously irritated that Genua would imply otherwise concerning Riven's kindness. "You have no idea what other warlocks out there are like. Usually, for demons like me that started out weak and too afraid to try our own hand in the hellscape wars to boost our power without a contract, warlocks are utter bastards. My first master was truly a monster to me. Riven is the opposite of that."

"That old criminal underlord guy you briefly contracted with when we were having a feud was nice to you, too," Athela pointed out lazily. "Didn't he try to set you up with his nephew?"

Fay wrinkled her nose in disgust. "Yes, he did, but it never went anywhere . . . and yes, he was a kind old man. I don't count that as a true contract, though—he never once ordered me to do anything. It was more of a time away from Panu. Let's not talk about that, though. I don't like dwelling on bad memories."

Athela shrugged, leaned back, and cast her gaze on the ground between them. "As much as I wish it were Kara, she has no interest in becoming a thrall. And Riven feels sorry for her, so I don't think tricking her into this or abducting her like the others would be a good idea. But, as Gluttony has said, vampires gain different resistances and unlocks by regularly drinking the blood of varying races. It grows their bloodlines stronger, too. So adding two other drow to the menu wouldn't hurt, especially since Riven has no liking for the two people we took. Even if he does get a bit miffed, it's better for him that he does take the gifts. I mean, seriously, what kind of vampire over a year out actively tries not to feed and has yet to expand his bloodline even once? It's an inherent part of being a vampire! Now that I have also mastered Body Fusion, it'll be even easier to get the two prisoners to cooperate—as I know you didn't want to try now that you have a baby, Genua."

Genua nodded absentmindedly.

Fay and Athela exchanged a look.

"Want to go visit the blasphemers? Those who dared irritate Gluttony's reincarnation?" Athela asked with a wicked smile. "Perhaps I won't have to use any tools of torture this time now that I have my interrogation method sealed."

"Yes . . . and I would prefer you didn't torture them while I'm present. It makes me queasy," Fay muttered, brushing her long white hair off her shoulders and straightening her sitting posture with a yawn. Tail slapping against the floor, she intertwined her fingers with Athela's and squeezed her lover's hand. "They've already been waiting an entire day since the last dose of vampiric venom, so we should probably get going!"

They shared a giggle.

Closing their eyes simultaneously, the two demonic women entered a trance—their minds leaving this plane to enter into another as Fay activated her newly acquired ability through the insights of the Depravity sun.

When Athela opened her eyes again, she and Fay were standing up—but still holding hands—in a mindscape very similar to the nether realms their families still resided in. It also skirted the lines of what was allowed by common laws of magic and miracle, as they really weren't sure whether the ability copied their bodies to bring them here. Same could be said for items they brought into this place. This realm was far smaller, though, only a couple hundred feet across, and had the distinct feature of allowing mortals to enter into it.

Such as the two victims that they'd captured from Kara Blackbow's homeland. Zafima, the dark elf enchantress who'd conspired against Kara for some reason or another, was an utterly vile person through and through. Numin, on the other hand, was Kara's old teammate-turned-traitor after he'd been paid off by Zafima, the end goal being that Kara either died here in the descent—or that she returned in shame to be disowned by her family after not reaching Floor Forty.

Riven had thought he'd let them go back home despite wanting to kill them—because Kara had asked him to let them leave—but his minions had other things in mind for these two. If they were going to create a blood farm for their master, they might as well start here now that Fay finally had an ability that allowed for such a thing. Why create a blood farm in Riven's manor when they could have a portable one?!

Chained to the ceiling and hanging from iron manacles only inches off the ground, both Numin and Zafima had been strung up like animals.

[You have entered Fay's Dreamscape Dungeon, a resting place for damned souls. Current prisoners: two of fifty. Prisoners must be weaker in mind, body, and cultivation than the wielder of this ability to be kept here.]

Candles resting on skulls by the dozens illuminated the prison with dim firelight. Athela's bloody tools of torture were strewn about on wooden tables, and empty metal cages were lined up against the abnormally smooth stone back wall—where antienergy runes had been carved by the ability itself to specifically target any prisoners kept here. The manacles they had on were around both prisoners' feet and wrists, their clothes had been left in tatters to reveal shallow wounds that'd been stitched together with Athela's threads, and each of the dark elves looked absolutely miserable. Perhaps miserable was even an understatement.

Depressed?

In denial?

In pain?

Athela couldn't tell, nor did she care. But they both initially had faraway looks in their eyes, which quickly turned to terror and rage when they saw Athela and Fay approaching them again.

"You lying bitches!" Zafima coughed with wide, bloodshot eyes, flailing around and dangling on her chain in the dim light. "Your master said he'd let us go! So let us go! This has gone on long enough!"

Numin, for his part, merely let out a whimper and closed his eyes tighter upon seeing the vial of venom in Fay's free hand.

"Shut up, whore," Athela lazily replied, letting go of Fay's hand and giving the succubus a kiss before walking over to the enraged and battered drow enchantress—smacking her across the face with a satisfied smirk. "Or I suppose it was your mother who was the true whore? You're just her peon if I remember correctly, is that right? This wouldn't go so badly for you two if you just accepted the venom and drank it like good little mind slaves. I promise, it won't be nearly as bad for you after you actually become thralls. Genua loves it! She told me to let you know that she even highly recommends it! And that actually isn't a lie."

"I WILL NOT BECOME A VAMPIRE'S PET MONSTER!" Zafima screeched, flailing against her chains yet again like a fish caught on a hook, as if a renewed effort would somehow get her out of this mess. "I REFUSE TO BECOME A THRALL!!!"

"Please let us go . . ." Numin began to beg, his voice catching in his throat. "I have a family—"

"And I don't care." Athela cut him off with a level gaze, pointing one finger at the man's bare chest and extending a claw. The thin black blade that her finger had turned into carved a shallow bleeding line onto his skin as he hissed in pain, and she withdrew her finger with a wicked grin. "You weren't worried about how Kara Blackbow's ending would go when you betrayed her for this haughty bitch who thinks far too much of herself, but now you expect me to care about yours? Actions have consequences. We like Kara, we don't like you, and our master needs a proper blood farm. You two will be the first, but I'm sure you'll be joined by others as time goes on."

Athela gave them a playful wink and stepped back, redirecting her attention to the still flailing drow woman, who was snarling and spitting in Athela's direction. "And you know what's funny about all this? You have repeatedly told me that Riven didn't want us to harm you two . . . but if that was true, my minion contract wouldn't allow me to proceed."

Something of a twist of the truth, a gray area, but neither demon was about to say that.

Athela's grin widened into a full-blown malevolent smile, showing bright white teeth from ear to ear in a crazed, manic display. Her hand ripped another piece of the once-ornate golden dress that still clung in tatters to Zafima's side. "And my Riven gets what he wants. Fay, bring the vial!"

"GET THAT AWAY FROM ME!" Zafima screamed, lashing out with a frantic kick—only for Athela to whip out one of her arachnid limbs from her back to skewer the drow woman's leg just above the shackled ankle.

Zafima's scream of pain grew more shrill and high-pitched.

"I said no torture," Fay grumbled, producing the vial of Riven's venom that she'd procured from the man in their last snuggle session without his knowledge. "If this is going to be his Christmas present, we need to make sure all the prisoners are in top shape. Which gets me thinking . . . Now that we've learned Riven actually needs to consume people for Gluttony and not just drain them of blood, perhaps we should be a little bit more aggressive in how often we capture people and bring them here? That way, Riven won't have to do this at random and he can just come and pick a person to eat! How nice!"

"That's a great idea!" Athela exclaimed, slamming an open palm against Zafima's thigh. "Hold on just a moment, I want to try Body Fusion on Zafima now that I finally have the skill. My ability to sneak around is great, but this should be a great interrogation method even if my faith isn't that high!"

"Good for interrogating weaklings, perhaps. But yes, I agree." Fay nodded. "Go on, then, show me what you've got."

"Yes, Breasts. I will obey."

"Don't call me Breasts! I've told you I don't like that nickname!"

"What about Horny Breasts, because now you have bigger horns, too?" Athela raised a teasing eyebrow, and then over the continued screams of the dark elf enchantress, Athela's body began to warm. She turned into a writhing pool of blood, coiling around in the air as the place where her palm had been began digging a shallow hole through Zafima's skin. Athela poured her own thoughts into Zafima's mind, her own body into Zafima's flesh, and the chained woman began to convulse while drooling out the side of her mouth. Athela's mass shrank down to nothing, absorbing into Zafima's blood vessels as the captured woman's eyes turned a bright red—her skin showing black patches with occasional white areas similar to Athela's own skin. The soft muscles of the enchantress became toned and smooth, and it looked like she was being zapped by lightning over and over again by the way her muscles contracted against the chains.

Eventually the convulsions stopped and the drow woman lowered her head—and opened her mouth.

"That works a lot better than force-feeding it or pushing it through an open cut," Fay murmured, and popped the cork of the vial before letting half of the fluid drain down the drow's throat.

In an instant, Athela ripped out of the shallow area she'd entered into and the wound was sealed shut with bloodsilk.

"AH-HAAA! IT WORKS!" Athela squealed, spinning around and yanking Fay into a tight hug to bring her around with her spin.

"PUT ME DOWN, ATHELA!" Fay laughed.

But Athela ignored her and continued to spin three more times with the succubus in her arms before dropping the other woman and planting a firm kiss on Fay's lips. "I can't believe it worked so well! I was able to read her thoughts, although only briefly, and I could control her movements after overcoming her own resistances! This is an AMAZING ability to have!"

Numin gawked in horror in the background, staring at the two demonic women and then glancing back to the other drow prisoner—where Zafima was gagging on the vampiric venom she'd been forced to drink. She looked sickly and pale, and her breaths came shallow.

"Now it should only be a few more months of regular venom before they become more subservient," Athela said with a self-satisfied smirk, putting her hands on her hips and setting herself in a wide stance. "Hee-hee! This is great! Now, let's do the same thing with Numin and get back out of here. It may only look like we're in deep meditation, but if we stay here too long, Riven will get suspicious. Can't have that until the job is done."

Fay nodded her agreement and followed Athela back over to the dangling, chained man. "Yeah. But we need to find more variety for Riven's bloodline to bolster. Gluttony said that we should have multiple races and varying species in order to have the best chances to unlock more traits, so if we could get some obsidian orcs, Greed-affiliated demons, or Unholy draconics while we're here in the descent—those races would be hard to come by back on Panu. Let's just keep that in mind and be on the lookout, and then whatever extras we manage to capture in battle can be for him to actually eat."

CHAPTER 3

The continent of Umbra had been conquered under the banner of the Thane Necropolis, but at a cost—the disappearance of Chancellor Mara Tovane, who'd been heading the kingdom in the temporary absence of Allie and Riven. With her and the vampiric leadership of the Blood Moon Requiem now gone—their whereabouts unknown to the public—it was now up to Gurth'Rok the orc chieftain and Dr. Brass to lead the country, while taking counsel from Gaia, General Bruner of Chicago, and various members of the banished. Unrest was prevalent in the recently taken territories in the north of the continent, as well as the elvish kingdom of Tereen, which was being held as a vassal state, and new wars continued to rage on the other side of the world as nearby factions took note of how aggressive the undead kingdom was becoming when claiming land. Whether or not the land grabs were intentional or simply reciprocation were up for widespread debate, with many conspiracy theories running rampant. Preemptive strikes had been launched against Chicago and the cities in what was previously known as the Romanov Empire, which were now all under necropolis control after the head family had been wiped clean. There were plenty of neutral factions after they'd seen that humans of Chicago were still left intact and weren't forced to convert, but true allies were hard to come by, as there was a very real and palpable fear of what the Thane Necropolis represented. For the citizens of Chicago, they'd been saved by Riven's actions when the Azag Hive Cluster had nearly used their population as fertilizer for breeding eggs. But not so for the rest of humanity outside the Death-attuned continent.

Thankfully, though, most of the population of Umbra itself was rather fond of their new existence. The Golden Bull sect, the second-largest faction on Umbra, had willingly given themselves up to necropolis rule without a hiccup—adding numerous cities and towns to the banner that benefited from trade and military bolstering. The dwarves of the underdark, surprisingly enough, had adapted very well to necropolis control, too, primarily blaming their previous king for putting them in poor conditions to begin with, and the undead patrols that now marched through their lands and caverns did a good job protecting them from occasional ratkin raids. The blighted ratkin themselves had either scurried away into the far deeper regions of the underdark, well out of the way and into unknown regions, or had become something like plague-spreading pirates after they'd tried to betray Riven. Despite efforts to reestablish negotiations with the ratkin warbands, success had been elusive.

The humans of Dawn had mostly become a variation of undead called death-touched enlightened, which encompassed the majority of what the enlightened races had chosen to be upon the Scythe's blessing with Allie's original ascension. Variations of white, black, teal, and silver hair had been commonplace—with gray or pale skin and neon-teal eyes. Funnily enough, though, a popular potion that'd been invented by an alchemist in Dawn's multilayered capital city, Mandon, was now going around. It was so popular, in fact, that it'd become a household item across the entire kingdom—with the primary purpose being that it reverted your looks to what you'd been like prior to becoming undead. Herbalists had also been extremely profitable with selective breeding to create plants that were Death-attuned to survive in these environments on Umbra, but they made sure these plants also bore color, leading to large patches of the cities within the Necropolis having gardens that sported various greenery. That was a stark contrast to the usual coloration of Death-attuned plant life, which was usually a mixture of gray, black, silver, teal, and occasionally red.

With these changes came a wave of what could only be described as relief, as a semblance of normalcy was brought back to the otherwise drastically changing lives of the civilian populations, or at least that was the case for most.

Because now, as was being broadcasted daily on the Panu live-stream feeds, there was an absolute plethora of migrants stemming from three different places.

First and foremost were the undead of Retesh's homeland in the far north, where they were exiting by the millions to flee toward Umbra as Judith Marcina hunted them down to the last child. She had changed her tune about the Thane Necropolis entirely, calling it a bane to the natural order, and had employed dozens of mercenary armies from off-world at a discount cost through Elysium's tipping of the scales to put the conflict on more even footing. A few strongholds still remained, but with Retesh temporarily gone in pursuit of greater power and Judith's followers becoming rather fanatical in their genocidal efforts—even going as far as to call this the next great Holy crusade with commonplace references or comparisons to Jerusalem by scholars—it was a good guess that soon Judith would make the official call to attack Umbra itself. Only fear of the Thane siblings had stayed her hand so far, but her power was growing—as were her forces. An understanding with many of the naga and merpeople had also been reached concerning the migrating undead, and although there was a lot of mistrust between them and the new-age crusaders, given that nobody really knew what the sea dwellers were up to concerning World Quest 6: Drums in the Deep, the sea peoples had taken a quick liking to sinking migratory fleets and attacking the undead as they fled for their lives toward Panu's greatest undead kingdom on the continent of Umbra. If the sea peoples or crusaders went too far, legions under the Thane banner easily stomped out any pursuing forces that trailed their new would-be citizens. War hadn't been officially declared by either side yet, but dozens of small-scale battles had already happened near Umbra's coastline as tensions rose.

The second source of incoming migrants was from hell itself. Negrada specifically had opened up its borders to allow its citizens access to Panu to get them out of the way of the wars being waged against enemy dungeons, with hundreds of thousands of demons spilling in to make new homes for themselves. Elysium did not allow anything aside from F-grade demons to come into the integrating planet, but Negrada was a rather weak hellscape dungeon anyway and only had, at best, some E-grades in its upper echelon of minions and citizens. Dozens of different demonic species could now be found on Brightsville's streets, with even more spilling in when news of Riven's ascension to Gluttony's reincarnation caused many to go into a religious fervor. They incorporated rather easily into necropolis society, being incredibly respectful of the laws and even setting up a very large Church of Gluttony in downtown Brightsville, where most of the demons had settled in. They brought with them knowledge of various crafts and enchantments that enhanced Brightsville's economy tenfold and increased their value and reputation with the original citizens by a lot as the capital city grew rapidly.

The third source of migrants stemmed from the rest of the planet as they fled persecution. With a very large divide forming between the living and the undead, racism and acts of violence had surged, with videos being plastered on the cortex daily. Practicing the arts of the Unholy foundational pillar had even been outlawed in many countries, and public executions or lynchings of necromancers or demonic summoners of any kind had been on the upswing. Many undead were killed on sight regardless of sentience or not, which in turn had caused an uproar among the Thane Necropolis—resulting in retaliatory assassinations, arson, and acts of subterfuge in areas the different adventuring guilds of the Thane Necropolis could manage to reach. Not all areas were accessible, but a lot of the most vulgar acts posted to the forums were from countries bordering Chicago, where fear was most prevalent—meaning that monster hunting and mercenary guilds from the heartlands of Umbra were opting to go hunt down religious fanatics and violent racists like it was their day job. This further increased tensions between the necropolis and its neighbors, but General Bruner failed to do anything about it, as he'd publicly stated during diplomatic meetings that these instances were the acts of individuals and not the state. Funnily enough, he didn't bother investigating these acts of retribution, either—and kept unusually silent and smug whenever accusations were brought up about brutally murdered individuals in neighboring territories who'd taken up Judith's ideals.

Overall, though, life had calmed down around Brightsville and the central regions of Umbra, and the area was relatively safe as long as you stayed near the cities and towns. Any dungeons found in their lands were marked and regularly cleared to make sure monster swarms didn't get out of control, and any nesting feral undead that became too much of a problem were put down by the military or the guilds it regularly sent out contracts to. Rebuilding from the initial onset of the integration was on a dramatic upswing, the Rippenvire invaders who'd originally launched attacks on different parts of Umbra had completely left the planet in utter defeat with all other invading factions having avoided the continent entirely for now in favor of easier targets, and regular military patrols of native-born and Blood Moon Requiem battalions kept the population pretty safe. Industry was booming, research into different types of magical and technological advancements was at a high pitch, and people were creating new companies and trading organizations to help spread goods across the continent, thus increasing their quality of life. With only the impending war against Judith's allied forces and the World Quests as true threats in the near future, optimism was starting to build.

Thankfully, most people didn't know where the Thanc siblings had gone. Many thought them to be in secluded isolation to try and ascend into E-grade, or perhaps they'd gone to explore the underdark—but it was all guesswork and conjecture for the civilian side of things. Regardless, their king and queen were still at the very top of the rankings board. They weren't dead, and that alone was enough for most of the necropolis to not question it any further.

Janice was twenty-four years old, having just graduated from college before Earth had gone to shit and magic had become real. She was the first of her very redneck family to ever get an advanced education, but in the end, she'd been glad that she came from a gun-toting, cowboy boot–wearing family of hardened men and women.

Because her entire family had survived the integration thanks to the sheer volume of shotgun shells at their disposal. And after the Riven's Eye Wormhole had opened, she'd gone through to apply for a job at one of the news agencies in Chicago, where she'd successfully gotten the position and had come back not long after.

Her eyes still shone a brilliant neon-teal color. Very pretty, in her opinion, and they were her favorite aspect of the change into being an undead, but with the potions from Dawn she'd been able to revert her gray skin and white hair to her previous brown and more healthy, tanned complexion. She'd always liked her dark-brown hair color and would have paid whatever it took to get it back from the ghostly white, even if her friends had taken a keen interest in their own changes and hadn't reverted their looks back like she had.

And right now, she was filming a nature documentary with some scientists who'd hired her news crew to go along with them, alongside a couple of hired flesh golems and undead orc guards from one of the guilds. It was very relaxed, in an area only a couple miles south of Brightsville beyond the Elysium altar that they could still easily see from their current position, and better yet, the show had been a massive success. Her face was plastered on TV screens across the kingdom now, much to her parents' amusement, and she always got comments about being a celebrity whenever she went home to eat some of her mother's famous apple pie.

Though those apples certainly tasted a bit different from when the fruits had been life-attuned. Now they had an unusually sweet aftertaste—which wasn't necessarily bad, but a noticeable change. She wondered if normal humans would feel the same way or whether they'd find the pies disgusting? Did her change into a deathtouched cause her taste buds to change, too?

Probably.

But she hadn't really tried to figure it out yet, because she simply didn't care. She had other things to worry about, like getting a good shot of the undead fleshweave wolves, per system naming shenanigans, that now roamed these woods to document their behaviors. They were a rather odd species of undead—unlike many of the normal ghoul wolf variations out there, they had unusually long tails made of strands of muscular flesh instead of fur and were far smaller than their canine counterparts.

"There!" Janice said to the camera guy and scientist next to her, who were lying on their stomachs, pointing over the hill to where a few of the majestic-looking, relatively tiny wolves were playing with their young amid a large swath of silver berry bushes. "You better get that shot, Ted! Or I'll wring your little neck! And damn it, they're cute!"

Ted, the cameraman, rolled his eyes but continued filming—with the scientist rapidly taking notes.

"How did I get stuck filming dogs when my friends all get to go film the wars near Chicago?" Ted grumbled under his breath, keeping the large camera steady on the hill's edge. "Now that we're undead, they don't even get scared about being shot or stabbed! Not unless it's to the head, or a bomb goes off that tears their body apart. We're almost invincible now!"

"Quiet! You'll scare them off with your ugly man voice!" Janice said, snapping her pen against the back of his head with gusto. "And you know that's not true. Our people die all the time over there. You should be thankful you're not in any real danger here."

"Yeah, but most of those that die are from the Chicago side of the kingdom."

"That's not true! And I said quiet!" She smacked him hard with her pen again, getting an approving nod from the scientist as he continued scribbling down notes.

Funny that they still needed to use cameras like this. Usually Elysium would do the streaming through their own vision, but it wasn't as clear-cut or stable as a camera could be, and so most news stations continued to use the old Earth technology even to this day. Not just in the Thane Necropolis—it was the same with numerous other Earth-based factions across Panu.

A sharp gasp came from her right, and Janice peered over her shoulder to where one of her news crew was sitting on a small boulder under the shade of a teal-leaf oak. The girl, who was barely eighteen years old, wearing short-shorts and a pixie cut, had just taken her first class as a Truthseeker, and she was usually very quiet. But right now her eyes were wide in shock, and she scrambled over the boulder to where Janice was now lying down—much to the irritation of the scientist.

"You need to see this! It literally just happened!" Ashley, the younger woman, frantically whispered while jabbing a finger at one of her hologram system screens. "Super important! Take a look, fast! If we report on this now, we could—"

"You're going to scare off the wolves, you idiot!" the scientist chastised her, adjusting his glasses and glaring at the younger deathtouched with a scowl. "This had better be worth it!"

True to the man's words, Ashley's exclamation had certainly startled the small pack—and their ears had all perked up. The undead animals all quickly scampered away after that, rushing into the dark underbrush without another word after the older ones had picked up their youngest by the scruff of their necks.

"Gah!" the scientist yelled, throwing his pen and clipboard down onto the hillside. Getting up, he cursed loudly numerous times and began marching away to cool off.

But despite Janice's cold glare, Ashley was still frantically pointing at the hologram screen.

"You need to report on this NOW! It happened only SECONDS ago!" Ashley exclaimed, raising her voice now that the jig was up anyways—and she snapped out a pointer finger in Ted's direction. "Get set up for an interview, fast! We need to make this quick to be the first!"

Janice raised an eyebrow and brushed a hand through her brunette hair with a groan. Adjusting her vest, she got to her knees and then stood up while brushing off the dirt. "This had better be good, Ashley. Those wolves were hard to track down, and the guildies over there charge by the day."

"IT IS IMPORTANT!" Ashley screamed. "LOOK! JUST LOOK!"

This time, Janice obliged. Coming around and staring at the hologram information, her eyes narrowed—and then went wide when she saw what Ashley was pointing at.

[With the coming update in following months: Rankings will soon be REORGANIZED to include both external, off-world threats present on Panu, as well as new arrivals that are not natives, in order to better represent the power dynamics on Panu. Twenty-five billion current participants have been analyzed. The ranking categories are as follows: Apex rank (top 10), Paragon rank (top 1,000), S rank (top 0.0001%), A rank (top 1%), B rank (top 15%), C rank (top 30%), D rank (top 50%), E rank (bottom 50%)]

[Current Top 10 Native Participants:
1. Allie Thane, Level 201 Angel of Wrath—Ultimate Undead/ Bastion of Death, Apex rank, Hero of Death, Reincarnation of Wrath
2. Riven Thane, Level 200 Pureblooded Vampire, Apex rank, Warlock Devastator, Reincarnation of Gluttony
3. Judith Marcina, Level 212 Divine Human, Apex rank, Angelic Fallcaller, Light's Beacon
4. Aren Hrall, Level 207 Snow Giant, Apex rank, Frostmange Berserker
5. Retesh Vorath, Level 200 Corpse Lord, Apex rank, Elder Lich
6. Nora Lang, Level 200 Cursed Human of the Insanity Lineage, Apex rank, Asylum Legion Keeper
7. Netithi Bluskish, Level 200 Naga, Apex rank, Champion of the Kraken, Apostle of Greed
8. Chitter Teh-Sneaker, Level 200 Rat Man, Apex rank, Dark-Blade Assassin, Poison Master, Sneaky Sneak Sneaker
9. Nithkik Brutishvase, Level 199 Dark Elf, Apex rank, Depthdweller
10. Thorman Bame, Level 196 Human, Apex rank, Hammer of the Mountain]

Allie had taken the top spot. But not only that, she'd made level 201—meaning she'd made it into the E-grade. And her titles . . . Were those what Janice thought they were?

Then two more notifications appeared. This time they weren't Ashley's doing, but rather, they were from the system itself. And the results were both shocking and very similar to what had happened when their king had first transcended into Gluttony's reincarnation.

[Multiversal System Notice: To all creatures across Elysium, let it be known that the return of the sins and commandments is at hand. The next original sin, Wrath, has been unleashed from its prison. Other sins and commandments will be released from the abyss over the course of the next ten years. Let the eternal war between the hells and heavens begin again, as the origins of angels and demons clash in the cosmos—unshackled, and unrestrained, seeking to return to the power they once had.]

[Planet-Wide System Notice: Allie Thane has returned to Panu, and with her come the banished demons of the eternal war that were most loyal to Wrath in eons past. As the primary target of World Quest 7: Eradicate the Angel of Death, the prize for killing her has

increased dramatically. The quest name has also been changed to <u>World Quest 7: Eradicate the Angel of Wrath, Allie Thane</u>.

If she is killed before the five-year integration time limit is up, the killer will inherit her fledgling divinity in the form of the killer's choosing, allowing ascension and the start of a path into future godhood. Not only this, but immediately upon killing her the killer will also be given an additional one hundred combat levels, an immediate escape to a safe location of their choosing, and one billion Elysium coins.

Killing Allie Thane within the time limit will also remove the Scythe's blessing on Umbra and return the land to a more natural state.

Guild mercenary options will reflect an even lower cost to acquire off-world Holy warriors in pursuit of this crusade, as long as the guild owner is not undead and the intended target is perceived to truly be Allie Thane or the Thane Necropolis by Elysium's administrator. Guild mercenaries are now able to be hired at an 80% reduced rate from their asking price, with Elysium covering the remaining amount, and there is no longer any distance fee when hiring off-worlders.]

When had their queen even left Panu?

She'd been gone?

How'd she left the planet, and how had she come back?!

"Oh shit! OH SHIT! TED! GET THAT CAMERA UP HERE!" Janice quickly adjusted her hair, tidied her suit jacket, and nodded frantically to the camera guy. "Are we ready?! Are we ready?!"

BOOM

The sky immediately overhead thundered with a massive explosion of energy that swept across the landscape like an aura of hate and dread. The shock wave sent tree branches snapping and made Jannice fall to her knees with a gasp. Clouds and mist were swept away, revealing a large, shimmering portal in the sky, from which a four-winged, six-armed undead woman of unnatural, ghostly beauty stepped out to hover far above.

Dozens and then hundreds of smaller portals began to appear around her—transforming the daytime sky into a black-speckled tapestry of Unholy power that continued to build as demons of all shapes and sizes started crawling out of the abyss and into their world.

Janice's heart nearly stopped as she took in the awe-inspiring sight before slowly getting back to her feet with mouth ajar. "Ted? Are you filming this?"

"Get up, Ted, you incompetent buffoon!" Ashley kicked the man into action, and he scrambled to get an angle beneath Janice that also captured the oncoming wave of new arrivals to their planet.

Janice took in a deep breath and fetched the microphone from Ashley while steeling herself and trying not to tremble underneath the waves of power.

The news crew gave her a silent signal before another thunderclap and residual purple-tinted illumination of the deadlands surrounding Brightsville made them almost forget to start rolling.

"IN FIVE!" Ted yelled over the building storm of darkness ripping the sky above. He held up his fingers, then began to count down as Janice prepared herself with the microphone—sealing her surprise and grimace at the whipping winds that rattled the trees around them.

Four fingers.

Then three.

Two.

One.

Streaming.

"Hello once again to the Thane Necropolis, and to all others currently watching this live-stream here on Panu. My name is Janice Gildy, a reporter with the Chicago Scriptmakers, and what you are now watching is very likely the return of our queen. When she'd left and where she'd gone are both questions that many of you likely have, just like I do, but it appears that just as the system notification has informed us all across the planet, she has not come back alone. It also appears that she has reclaimed the number-one spot on Panu's leaderboard from her brother. A truly momentous occasion indeed. All hail Queen Allie Thane of the Thane Necropolis—all hail the newly crowned reincarnation of Wrath!"

CHAPTER 4

[Insights have been obtained into your Path of Red and Black, and into the inner workings of your class. Blood and Shadow have been incorporated. Death, Infernal, and Unholy have yet to fully incorporate. Sin is now the primary backbone for your soul pillar connections. Sufficient connections between the Shadow and Blood subpillars have been established. Soul lattice is ready to solidify. Do you wish to proceed, or continue expansion?]

Continue expansion.

[Option to delay passage into E-grade has been confirmed. Based on your construction so far, it appears that you are wanting to continue in one of two directions. Please pick so that Elysium may assist you:
- The beginnings of a secondary demonic form and class, with modification of your current class.
- Dual souls, allowing you to split yourself into two bodies at once.]

He'd already discussed this with Gluttony at length. Riven would continue down the warlock's path and specialize in long-range casting combat, while Gluttony wanted to pursue a more hands-on approach. The training he'd been given by Lillith and the other demonic instructors back on the first floor of the descent was completely based in magical casting, which suited Riven's style more. He was very gifted with controlling mana and magic, even a prodigy, but his hand-to-hand combat was thoroughly lacking despite the training he had gotten. So it made sense that he'd continue down a caster's path, while his counterpart, who had eons of experience in fighting hand to hand, would take over the other half of things. Neither he nor Gluttony wanted to divide their souls into two separate bodies quite yet, but it might be an option further down the road when they became more powerful. Right now, that could end in tragedy should one of them die without the other present—as it would result in both of them being ended right there and then. Or so Gluttony said.

[You have selected the first option. Secondary demonic form and class are now under construction. To finish these items, please continue to pursue insights within the Abyssal Descent and expand your soul lattice further before going on to E-grade. You will now be given an option for upgrading your Warlock Devastator class.

Please note that E-grade class selection is much different and more impactful than your F-grade class upgrades may have been. Just like how your soul lattice will be the foundation for your future growth in cultivation and expansion of your soul realm, your E-grade class selection will be the foundation of your future specializations—and coming off this path will be far harder to do than it was in the F-grade. Your base class after Level 200 will not be able to be changed without significant setbacks to your cultivation, with most advancements only offering additional titles and divergence paths instead of entire class replacements. Choose wisely.]

[Level 200 Class Upgrade Options:

- <u>Warlock Soul Singer</u>: The Warlock Soul Singer is a divergence from the path of the class Warlock Devastator. You will lose your on-hit bonus damage equal to 1% of your full mana capacity; instead you will gain the ability to possess enemies. You will also unlock a new skill tree of mental capabilities based on the Unholy subpillar. You will gain +1 additional demonic minion slot with this class. This class comes with two class traits. <u>Class Trait 1 (Unholy Possession)</u>: You may turn into a wraith at will, without mana cost. Possession of enemies can occur, while overpowering them to successfully possess your target depends primarily upon the Willpower stat. <u>Class Trait 2 (Ghost Flight)</u>: While in wraith form, you are unable to be targeted by physical attacks and gain a 130% speed boost with the ability to fly and pass through unenchanted solid objects, but magic and miracles do additional 25% damage to you.

- <u>Warlock Blood Warrior</u>: The Warlock Blood Warrior is a direct upgrade from the class Warlock Devastator. This class is for those who wish to continue down the path of close combat as a warlock, choosing to center yourself and focus your power inward instead of outward. You will acquire a 100% bonus for heavy armor and melee weapons with this class, and it comes with two class traits. <u>Class Trait 1 (Devastator's Reaping)</u>: All physical strikes are naturally imbued with bonus Unholy damage equal to 19% of your current total mana pool, not costing any actual mana, with the most passive damage being done at full mana capacity. Killing enemies absorbs their blood and adds a protective layer of blood barrier around your skin that slowly fades over time. <u>Class Trait</u>

2 (Empower Thyself): All body-enhancement buffs see a 400% increased effect and cost very little to maintain, but at the cost of halved power output for long-range offensive spells.

- Warlock of the Malevolent Storm: The Warlock of the Malevolent Storm is a divergence from the path of the class Warlock Devastator. You will lose your on-hit bonus damage equal to 1% of your full mana capacity and will expand upon your most common fighting style of utilizing mana storms. This class further improves your Path of Red and Black, increasing your damage with Blood and Shadow by 20% and reducing casting time dramatically. This class also comes with one trait and two spell upgrades. Class Trait (Malevolent Storm): When you manipulate your aura to create mana storms while intending to do true harm at high power output, the mana storm expands into a true force of nature without additional input from you. Thunderclouds affiliated with the Path of Red and Black will form, creating spontaneous Black Lightning strikes that target enemies within your domain. Rain will fall from the darkened skies as droplets of needle-sharp blood on your enemies but will heal your minions. Twisters may form protective bastions around minions and empower them while cutting through enemy defenses. Lastly, blood frost will take hold on your environment and freeze your surroundings at a far faster pace than it has previously. Spell Upgrade 1 (Bloody Razors → Storm Razors → Gluttonous Storm Razors): All your Storm Razors will acquire stacking gluttonous afflictions upon impact. This affliction slowly eats away and corrodes your enemy over time as Sin damage unless dispelled, and the affliction can stack. Should you decide to detonate a selected razor, that detonation will burn through the nearby afflictions as fuel for an additional burst of Sin damage. Spell Upgrade 2 (Blood Lance → Sniping Profane Blood Lance → Critical Storm Lance): Your third evolution of Blood Lances are now wreathed in double the amount of Black Lightning as they previously were, have twice the flight speed, travel 50% farther when imbued with Snipe, and leave trails of lingering Black and Red storm energy in their flight paths that can strike out at enemies for a short time should they get too close. Chance for armor-piercing strikes and critical strike damage are both drastically increased with this evolution.]

Riven gawked. "Are all the E-grade classes this much better?!"

"Of course," Gluttony said matter-of-factly with an internal nod, as the two of them went over the text three times in a row, just to make sure they didn't miss anything. "Every upgrade has a significant power advantage over the previous grade. For F-grade to E-grade, it manifests in the class. That won't always be the case in the future, but as the notifications tell you, this is setting the base layer for all future class expansions. Once you choose, it will be far harder to walk a different kind of path."

"And I'm the only one picking, yeah?"

"That was the agreement. You choose for this class, and I choose once we finish the soul lattice and acquire our second class."

Riven paused, though he was very excited about the prospects. All of them were amazing, frankly. The Soul Singer class and possession relied on Willpower, which he had a ton of—and it would give him the ability to fly without using Messenger. Then again, he didn't see himself getting rid of the armor anytime soon, so it probably didn't matter that much, but the 130 percent speed boost while flying would help tremendously. It also gave him one additional demonic minion slot, but he was fine with the current makeup. Narg the beholder was still in a trial run, but it'd taken Riven months to even get that far after the serpent Yattazi had ditched him when she thought he'd been indefinitely incapacitated. That had left a sour taste in Riven's mouth even to this day, and though he felt no ill will toward the demonic basilisk, he had closed off his walls to an extent. Especially now that everyone knew what and who he was.

The second class was nothing to scoff at, either, but had a catch. The Warlock Blood Warrior was nineteen times more powerful as a passive when it came to on-contact, close-quarters combat, and it would have been a great choice if he'd been wanting to stay a solo-class hybrid. That being said—he was going dual class soon due to Gluttony, and Gluttony preferred close-quarters combat himself. So it was kind of redundant, despite the tremendous boost to power it had at face value.

The third option was what called to Riven the most. Warlock of the Malevolent Storm was essentially an upgrade to the way he'd been fighting the most in all aspects. His aura creating mana storms, his Storm Razors he used in swarms to home in on targets, and his high-powered kicker—the Sniping Blood Lance. All three were buffed with this pick; he already used all three nearly every fight. Not only that, but his mana storms when using his aura and raw power would have the ability to heal minions with blood rain and even buff them with twisters—which he was pretty excited to try out. Minions even included Genua, which meant that she'd finally be able to participate in battles with some layer of protection outside of her own skill set—which was a worry he'd had for quite some time now, as she didn't respawn like the demons did.

Passive afflictions using the Gluttonous Razors could stack on high-powered opponents over time, slowly eating away at enemies with a slow burn, while the Critical Storm Lances were a needed answer to a twofold problem. One, he was trying to get to a fighting style that kept him at range, per Lillith's advice—and although his Sniping Blood Lances were great, he wanted something that reached farther, if possible. But he hadn't had anything that could reach beyond that kind of strike's distance up until now. He also tended to wear down opponents with barrages of attacks rather than clean kills, basically beating them to death by sheer volume of attacks, but critical strikes had the potential to solve that. If he got a critical modifier in the ballpark of seven times the hit of what a Blood Lance could do, that'd be absolutely crazy powerful. Critical Storm Lances would travel faster, farther when he utilized Snipe by a good margin, and hit far harder—even having trails of energy leftover that'd leave obstacles and potential remnant damage after the fact. If he sent off five, eight, twelve, twenty, fifty, or even a hundred of those lances? That'd be that many more trails of energy that would remain in the path of each Snipe that had potential to lash out at any passing enemies.

Lots of questions rang through his head as he considered just what the aura storms would look like, but he had to pick it first in order to see.

Which he did.

And he was about to damn well use it as soon as possible, too!

[You have selected Warlock of the Malevolent Storm as your new primary class. Congratulations! You have not gained any additional demonic minion slots. Four of four demonic minion slots are in use.

Warlock Devastator's stat applications have been changed from +3 Strength, +2 Sturdiness, +2 Willpower, +4 Intelligence, +2 free stat points, -5 base Charisma, -1 Charisma per level.

Warlock of the Malevolent Storm now applies +3 Strength, +2 Sturdiness, +2 Willpower, +14 Intelligence, +7 free stat points, -200 base Charisma, -2 Charisma per level.

The Malevolent Storm class trait has been acquired. Your mana storms and passive aura now conjure true forces of nature to heed your beck and call, buffing any minions within the storm while simultaneously dealing severe damage to opponents. Spell upgrade acquired: Storm Razors have become Gluttonous Storm Razors, adding stacking damage debuffs that can be used for additional burst damage when nearby razors are detonated. Spell upgrade acquired: Sniping Profane Blood Lance has become Critical Storm Lance, adding speed, power, reach, trails of reactive Blood and Shadow mana, as well as drastically increased chances for piercing and critical hits.

There are no additional item bonuses to be applied for this class.]

"Thank god for mana potions!" Riven said, sweating and heaving heavy breaths as he continued to experiment with his Critical Storm Lances one by one—sending them at blinding speed to crash into the far wall ahead of them. Fay would create an illusory target and he'd nail it a split second later with pinpoint accuracy, given how the zoom function on his Snipe ability had become better. He downed another bottle of blue liquid, wiped his mouth, and went on for the eighth hour that day as his other minions and friends stared curiously while he worked.

Unfortunately he hadn't been able to summon his aura's mana storm quite yet, as that'd probably count as an attack on everyone else in the room—and would doubtless result in his banishment from the descent. Or worse.

Prince Narzkal Rantali waited on the sidelines with his small group of vampires. They were to proceed with Riven as a partner group for the upcoming floor, as told by the previous notification upon entering this particular area:

[Floor Twenty-One: the Unholy Throne, is now open to you. As promised, by passing Floor Twenty, you are now permitted insight into one of your paths. You may mentally connect with the Unholy Throne whenever you deem yourself ready, choosing any single sun of those available here for a free insight, and when all your party members are done, you may pick another team for a joint operation for Floor Twenty-Two: Ocean of Wrath. Merely notify Elysium when you are ready to proceed to Floor Twenty-Two. Elysium will protect you while on this floor, and no harm may come to you or your possessions while here—so as to not disturb your meditation. The majority of identification information will continue to be unavailable until Floor Forty.]

"How'd it go, big guy? Get anything cool?" Riven asked when he saw Azmoth get up and lumber their way.

Though it would have been hard to miss. The gigantic, armored demon was the size of a gods damned building now, a large one, and the four enormous Shengari Shields reflected the light of the suns as the brutalisk held them in each of his clawed hands.

If one were to cut a kite shield in half and put razor-sharp blades on the outer edge of each shield, you'd get a Shengari Shield. Riven didn't know how or why it became a cultural weapon of the brutalisk species, but it was apparently a favorite, so he didn't press the situation despite thinking a war hammer or something like that would be more beneficial.

Riven put the target practice to rest for just a second and looked up with a friendly smile. "Athela won't tell me why she got the Body Fusion technique, while Genua and Fay are tight-lipped because they want it to be a surprise—whatever that means. Kara is embarrassed to show me for some reason, but at least Retesh was forthright. Our lich friend got a trait that allows him to create bones to use for minions out of dirt or rock—pretty nifty, in my opinion. He'll never lack minions, that's for sure. Narg over there is passed out from exhaustion, but he managed to expand his soul lattice twofold. How about you? Don't tell me you're going to stiff-arm me as well. It's not fair if I'm the only one that's going to show off what I achieved."

Azmoth knelt, and with a surge of hellfire that erupted like pressurized gas, he and the shields he carried shrank down to normal size. Or more normal size, anyways. He was still far taller than Riven, but at least he wasn't an absolute behemoth.

"I increase soul lattice like Narg, not get ability like your hoes one and two," Azmoth said slyly, shooting Athela and Fay a sharp obsidian grin.

Athela gasped and pointed a finger at the brute. "YOU DARE! I am no ho! Don't lump me in with Fay! And which one is one, which one is two?"

"You are one. Fay is two. Double breast size means double ho."

"Shut up, you ugly-looking gorillas!" Fay quipped with a flip of her hair and a humph, clicking her feathered boots together in the act. "Azmoth, the only reason you're still a virgin is because you can't get any."

"I am NOT a gorilla!" Athela declared, aghast yet again and putting a hand up against her chest. Then she winked. "Though I can be for you, babe."

Azmoth's two serpentine, eyeless jaws clicked and hissed from where they extended over his wings and back on either side of his spiked obsidian head. "I only a few years old. I not need women for five hundred years. Five hundred years of peace and quiet is what Retesh say! I not mature until then, no offspring until then."

The lich casually got up, pretending not to have heard, and left before he got dragged into this.

Fay, meanwhile, glared after the undead caster. "Makes sense considering you have a peanut brain. It correlates."

"Fay. You say more words, I throw you across room like I did in dragon's dungeon—punt you like football into one of suns! Riven not protect you! I may not succeed in protecting poor innocent Riven from your groping finger claws, he never wore chastity belt I gave him, but I can always throw again and correct his bad decisions!"

Athela raised an amused eyebrow. Fay grumbled something under her breath, but didn't retort this time upon the memory of being flung across the dungeon chasm like a tossed ham sandwich.

Riven merely grinned good-naturedly but otherwise didn't intervene. Even if Azmoth did end up throwing Fay into one of the suns, that was between them. She'd certainly survive, as the suns weren't meant to harm the participants here; she'd just get a little singed is all—or maybe a shock to her system. Despite Fay being one of the two women he loved and one of his three original demons, his minions were close enough that their little jabs and insults with one another were usually friendly and in good fun. And it'd be sort of funny to see Fay get launched again anyways, as long as those suns didn't burn up all her belongings.

On second thought, he may have to intervene to make sure her grimoire and boots survived should Azmoth actually go ahead and do it.

"Are you guys sure you don't want to share? Kara? Genua? Fay?" Riven asked for the umpteenth time.

Kara clutched the bow he'd made for her to her chest and hastily shook her head, avoiding eye contact and even lowering her hood in what he could only assume was embarrassment. Why that was, he had no idea.

Fay giggled. "Nope! Sorry, it's a surprise for later!"

"Just like what Athela said . . ." Riven muttered.

Genua, on the other hand, reconsidered. She was sitting next to Retesh in a meditative position, hands clasped ahead of her as the headdress of her formfitting priestess outfit clung to her protruding belly. Red eyes fluttered open, and she bobbed her head from side to side before eventually giving way.

"Before this floor and the insights it gave me, my priestess class had a slew of different abilities," she began, letting the words drift thoughtfully out of her lips at a monotonous pace. "It is a ritualist class and allows me to interface with the Blood God's clergy. There's even a ranking ladder. Do you remember?"

"I do," Riven replied. "Though you haven't talked much about it. Honestly, all that Blood God stuff I'm not too familiar with, I just know that he gave us both that ability to call on Blood Legionaries—which are pretty handy, but I don't know his agenda at all."

Genua grunted her acknowledgment. "Yes. Aside from Legionaries of the Blood God, I can use Body Fusion to merge myself into other minions or people, Sanguine Smite as an offensive miracle, Blood Oath—which is the brief invincibility I gain by shifting damage to you—Transfusion Zone, which heals allies and damages enemies, and Sanguine Possession, which requires ritualistic sacrifice to employ. However, I recently learned that Body Fusion can more or less control a person, too . . . but only in very brief intervals."

"Seems redundant to have them both."

"Yes, I'd agree. Which is something that I talked to some of the other clergy about. Apparently, the other priests and priestesses were saying that Body Fusion could potentially be used as a poor man's version of a possession, but it would only work on weak-willed people and comes with a risk of backlash should the soul strike back during the fusion attempt." Genua shot Athela a stern look, but the demoness merely whistled and ignored the thrall. "While Sanguine Possession can be used to control stronger opponents for far longer. Still . . . I've never used Sanguine Possession before, and as you said, it is still somewhat redundant to have. What I ended up doing with my insight under the Blood sun was I used the soul fractals for Sanguine Possession and Transfusion Zone, destroying both abilities. I used their energy and remnant patterns to create something else. Something similar but far better, as a passive trait linked to my aura. I no longer have Transfusion Zone or Sanguine Possession fractals, but whenever I flex my aura, it doesn't require any activation and passively heals anyone I deem as friendly, while passively causing enemies to bleed. I merely need to stand to let them be within my vicinity. My aura trait also grows more powerful the more I sacrifice souls to it, up to once per day."

Riven paused what he was doing and lifted his eyes in surprised approval. "Wow. That's really good! Why didn't you want to tell me about it?"

"Because I wanted to be what Athela called a groupie by joining in with the not-telling-Riven clause," Genua replied smugly.

Riven's eyelids lowered and he gave Athela a shake of the head. "That demon is rubbing off on you, Genua. In more ways than one. She's a terrible influence."

"Am not a TERRIBLE influence! I am a PRINCESS!" Athela stomped her foot down and harrumphed before hoisting herself up on all six arachnid limbs that protruded from her back with a flash, letting her hover over him in the air. "And I do what I want."

"Oh yes, we're very aware of that." Riven chuckled, sending a blast of Crimson Ice her way as she shrieked and—an instant later—was frozen solid. She probably could have dodged if she'd really wanted to, and probably could even break out now, but instead she resorted to muffled screeching from within the ice as Fay dramatically rolled her eyes.

"We probably shouldn't keep Prince Rantali waiting too much longer, Riven. You've been at it with your new spell all day and he's been very patient!" Fay sat down in Riven's lap with a thud, facing him nose to nose, and wrapped her long, toned legs around his waist. "Plus, I want to finish this descent and get back home. I'm very much missing a cozy bed and the manor right about now!"

Riven grinned, seeing her tail sway back and forth behind her, and put his hands on her hips to draw her just slightly closer. "For reasons?"

"Definitely. For reasons! And you owe Athela and I another date—one for all three of us! Remember?! I hope you've been planning something big, because we're not letting you off the hook that easily. Even if you are ridiculously cute!"

Upon this proclamation, Athela took no time in breaking out of the ice coating she'd been encased in.

"He owes me a solo date as well!" Athela called out, scowling back over her shoulder and prying off more red frost. "And you never came to see my clan in the nether realms! Don't make me remind you again, twerp, but you're having dinner with my mother soon, whether you like it or not! You wouldn't BELIEVE the amount of HARRASSMENT the clan gives me over not having had Gluttony's reincarnation back home to meet the fam already! The Sojavi succubi-incubi clan had their turn, and now it's mine. Okay, Mr. Big Shot?! Plus, my brothers are all really excited to meet you after all the stories I've told them, and as a princess, I have a reputation to maintain!"

CHAPTER 5

Despite his girlfriends teasing him about it, Riven had been feeling a bit guilty having not taken them out recently. But when did he ever have time?!

He had to prioritize them more whenever he left this damnable descent. Maybe get them some flowers and take them to a scenic vacation spot somewhere on the coast. That'd be nice.

But it was time to go, and he could dwell on such things regarding his relationships later. Athela and Fay were already ready to leave and telling bad jokes nearby, helping Genua pick up her various garments, different dyes she'd been staining the baby clothes with, and balls of thread. Azmoth, in his smaller form—which was still larger than Riven by quite a bit—stood by with arms folded and in a wide stance as his wings blazed with cinders. Retesh had finished creating dozens of large skeletal wyrms out of dirt, built to travel through almost any environment. The wyrms were each two feet in width and twenty feet long, with serrated spikes, spines, and rows of teeth imbued with death mana in a circular mouth. With Lillith trapped on Floor Fifty, Nora hunting down cultists in Chalgathi's trials, and Allie and Fimrindle having gone back to Panu, that only left Riven, his core minions, and the lich Retesh from their original group. Then there was Kara Blackbow, the dark elf archer who was acting unusually embarrassed whenever she was around Riven, ever since Allie's accusations about Kara, and she very quickly averted her eyes or turned her hood down whenever Riven caught her looking. Lastly, there was Riven's newest minion—the beholder demon Narg, who'd only just woken up after passing out due to the insights he'd received.

"Doing okay, buddy?" Riven called out to the drunk-looking beholder, and the large collection of eyeballs grunted an affirmation before floating upward in his direction.

"Yes, Master! I am ready to go!" Narg replied, wobbling in the air and promptly faceplanting into the ground after a quick lurch forward.

Riven frowned down at the demon and snapped his fingers. "I'm not mad at all, but you need to rest, man. Go back to your nether realm and only come back once you're in top shape. Okay?"

The beholder once again grunted, this time muffled by the ground he was lying on, and ripped open a portal to disappear in a flash of light. Riven and the other vampiric prince standing nearby exchanged glances.

"Welp. That's Narg, Athela, Fay, and Kara now who have received insights yet won't tell me what they are," Riven muttered under his breath.

Prince Rantali grinned and shot a look Kara's way. "I can at least understand why she doesn't want to say it."

"Oh, so she told you and not me?! I didn't realize you two were friends before this, like that enchantress bitch, Zafima."

"We are not, though she did tell me for reasons that are her own to disclose. Can you blame her after what your sister, the new incarnation of Wrath, said?" Prince Rantali gave Riven a knowing look with folded arms. "If I had been called out like that by a primordial entity's reincarnation, I'd want to crawl into a hole and never come out."

Riven chuckled and shoved his hands into his pockets with a nod. "Touché."

"But she doesn't want to leave your good graces yet, either," Prince Rantali continued. "It'd truly be a fool's choice to leave now when she was offered a spot on yet another reincarnation's team. A once-in-a-trillion-years opportunity. If she can get on your good side and stay there, it's a ticket to the very top."

"You put too much faith in me. Is that why you're still around?"

"Of course it is! My mother simply won't believe it when I tell her that I befriended a high-ranking prince of the Blood Moon Requiem who just so happens to be Gluttony's reincarnation!" Prince Rantali wore a brilliant, genuine fanged smile—blond hair slicked back more than usual after having recently applied a thin gel. "I have a hard time as it is making any friends at all! Being a prince means that most people only want to talk to me for my connections and politics. I hope I don't come off as rude, but I'm rather glad that you're not someone who looks up to me! It's rather refreshing!"

The two men laughed.

"At least you're honest. So tell us a bit more about the next level of the descent," Riven eventually said, clasping Prince Rantali's hand in a firm grip as everyone finished gathering their things. He pulled up the old floor notification.

[Floor Twenty-One: the Unholy Throne, is now open to you. As promised, by passing Floor Twenty, you are now permitted insight into one of your paths. You may mentally connect with the Unholy Throne whenever you deem yourself ready, choosing any single sun of those available here for a free insight, and when all your party members are done, you may pick another team for a joint operation for Floor Twenty-Two: Ocean of Wrath. Merely notify Elysium when you are ready to proceed to Floor Twenty-Two. Elysium will protect you while on this floor, and no harm may come to you or your possessions while here—so as to not disturb your meditation.

The majority of identification information will continue to be unavailable until Floor Forty.]

"Of course! Of course. I am happy to hear you're ready to go! I've been rather excited to proceed!" Prince Rantali shrugged his shoulders to loosen his joints, cracked his neck, and adjusted one of the pauldrons of his gaudy golden armor. The other vampire snapped his fingers at one of the three soldiers accompanying him, and the big red-eyed man drew out a scroll that he unfurled and presented to the two princes with a bow.

"Ahem. To confirm, this floor has nothing to do with the sin of Wrath—before you ask. Don't ask me why; I'm not the one that comes up with these naming schemes." Prince Rantali took the scroll and began to read. "'Floor Twenty-Two: Ocean of Wrath.' This floor is one of the constants over the eons of the Abyssal Descent's existence; it has a number of different obstacles to pass through before exiting out the other side. This is primarily a pillar-oriented floor. As vampires, we should have an advantage. First and foremost, there is an ocean of blood we must pass through."

Prince Rantali gave Riven another knowing look as Riven burst out laughing. "Yes, I thought you'd find that funny. But let me continue with the scroll, ahem . . . Ah yes, here we are! Secondly, there are three different sacrificial altars to collect gifts from. Each altar has the opportunity to give greater gifts if you sacrifice others of your team through blood ritual magics described on the altars—and we're talking a value of many times the initial prize."

The vampire looked over Riven's shoulder to where Kara had been when Riven last turned his back. "We could always sacrifice the drow girl since she's not an original member of your team, if you wish . . . as I said, I didn't know her before this. Her life may be worth—"

Riven's face hardened, and Prince Rantali immediately shut up.

"That's an absolute no," Riven said coldly, eyes narrowing as a sudden hostility bristled out from his aura—and the floor beneath him started freezing with black sparks radiating off his skin. "Absolutely no harm befalls her. I don't care what the prize is. Kara may be new to the group, but we all like her and she isn't going to be some kind of sacrificial nugget just for another grasp at passing power. Understood?"

Azmoth slowly turned his head, gradually beginning to unfurl his wings.

Prince Rantali seemed taken aback by the sudden surge of hostile energy directed his way, but gave a small smile as he once again glanced over Riven's shoulder. "As you say."

Riven, for his part, looked confused, but heard a heartbeat behind him rapidly pick up. He turned around and saw that not only had Kara been watching them, but she'd certainly overheard them, too.

Had Prince Rantali intentionally done that to get a reaction from Riven while Kara overheard?

Why would he do that?

But that's the only thing Riven could come up with as he stared down the furiously blushing and oddly smiling young woman at his back. She then averted her eyes once again and pulled her hood down to wander off in the general direction of Fay and Athela, the bow he'd given her grasped tightly in her hands.

"You did that on purpose," Riven said, his aura evaporating.

"Correct. I wanted to show her what kind of person you were, as she was feeling rather in the way and unwanted after your sister's display," the other prince replied with a self-satisfied sigh. "I was just doing her a favor."

Azmoth's wings began to retract, and he once again took his guard back down.

Riven gave a small smile of his own, nodding in approval. His opinion of the other prince just went up by a lot, as it seemed that there was more to the strange man than what appeared on the surface. He had some semblance of compassion, something Riven could appreciate given who they were. As a prince, the man likely didn't need to be kind at all to get the things he wanted. There was no ulterior motive to show kindness to people like Kara. She wasn't even a vampire, and from what Riven understood of vampire societies, most looked down on mortals like Kara as just common cattle to be used for entertainment, drained for blood, and then used for eating before being replaced.

It's why his changes to House Wraithtide concerning his Sarak slaves on the planet Luteski had brought on such a violent reaction from the vampiric nobles and populace there. Treating slaves like they had rights was very . . . unusual.

Perhaps Riven had found a kindred vampire spirit?

His eyes then fell to the chained bald man Prince Rantali had brought along with him through the descent—the only other one in Rantali's group who wasn't a vampire and outfitted in tacky golden armor. The slave had been bought on the second floor—he'd essentially paid off his gambling debts with his life. The man would have died otherwise. So why was there still a very faint lingering feeling in the back of Riven's mind that this was wrong?

And was this so different from what he'd done with Genua?

"Riven?"

Riven snapped out of his trance, coughing into a fist and waving Prince Rantali's concern away. "Don't worry about it, just deep in thought. Sorry."

"What were you thinking about? You looked lost."

"Eh . . . Honestly? I was thinking about whether or not I was becoming something of a monster."

Prince Rantali blinked, then burst into laughter with both hands clutched over his stomach. "Are you being serious?!"

"Hey, man, don't judge me! Let's get back on topic. What else goes on in the next floor—aside from swimming through some kind of blood ocean and visiting a few sacrificial altars? Why do we have to pair up for this event?"

Prince Rantali calmed himself down with a few wheezing gasps, wiped tears from his eyes, and shook his head. Rolling up the parchment, he handed it over to the vampire knight who'd originally presented it. "We just survive for twenty-four hours. Blood-oriented creatures born from the abyss will attempt to eat us, but considering who and what you are . . . I doubt that you'll have much of a problem defeating them. As for WHY we're paired up . . ."

The prince straightened, smile widening once again. "The reason is two-fold. First is that each altar will tempt us to try and kill the other as we work on surviving—and I trust you not to kill me for the same reason you didn't kill that drow woman Kara. The second reason is that other pairs of teams will have the opportunity to rob us of gifts we acquire from the altars. It's generally not hard to pass through the next floor, but there is a catch."

"Is that so? And what's that?" Riven asked.

"The catch, my friend, is that Elysium allows outside viewers to buy in and see our progress if you allow them to do so. They can communicate with us, buy us bonuses and boons from the altars that we can take into the next floor. Elysium is very particular in who it allows to watch, but it is very likely based on past experiences that family and close friends are those involved. For me? It will likely be broadcast across the realms my kingdom controls. For you? That remains to be seen."

[You have entered the pocket realm of Floor Twenty-Two: Ocean of Wrath. You have been designated team leader of Team DEEZ NUTZ. Your objectives are simple: survive the monster attacks for at least twenty-four hours while traveling over or through the ocean of blood. Acquire gifts from the sacrificial altars, where opportunities to enhance your gifts will be presented to you should you decide to take them at the last altar, where contact may also be established with outside entities to help to further your goals at a price. You must touch all three altars from Floor Twenty-Two in order to proceed to Floor Twenty-Three. The majority of identification information will continue to be unavailable until Floor Forty.]

[You have touched two of three sacrificial altars, accepting two Blood Tokens to be used at the very last sacrificial altar without having taken the opportunity to sacrifice any of your party members. You have seventeen mandatory hours left to spend on this floor.]

If this floor was supposed to be a challenge, Riven didn't agree with the setup. They'd blazed through the entire thing like it was nothing, in large part due to Riven's Blood subpillar being fed a nonstop cannon of ambient mana.

Athela let out an excited scream, up on her tiptoes at the front end of their craft with arms outstretched and a bottle of blood wine she'd stolen from Prince Rantali in her hand. "WHOOOO!!!! FASTER, RIVEN! MAKE THIS THING ZOOM!"

WHOOSH

Excited, hooting laughter roared in Riven's ears as they flashed over the crimson ocean together in a yacht created from similarly crimson ice. He didn't actually have an engine to propel the boat, but the MASSIVE amount of blood mana permeating the surroundings invigorated him like a drug. The sky overhead was laden with quite large, brilliant stars that speckled the darkness, and occasional waves would roll up against the boat from distant battles between groups and other monsters—though everything stupid enough to get too close to the impromptu yacht was eradicated quite thoroughly with one of Riven's new Critical Storm Lances, which left long trails of crackling red and black under the illuminating starlight before evaporating whatever it was Riven had been targeting. The swarm of bone wyrms that Retesh had created also acted like watchdogs, spread out in a large perimeter in the ocean beneath where they occasionally battled squid-like Blood-affinity creatures, and the wyrms informed the team whenever anything came too close or broke past their formation.

This was more like a vacation than anything else.

It was even kind of nice.

"You sure?" Riven asked Gluttony one more time with an internal side-eye. "What about Greed's assassins?"

The original sin once again gave the affirmative. "There is nothing to fear on this floor. They are not here, I am certain—and I will continue to keep watch. Take some time to relax and spend it with your friends. Your demons are growing on me, and it is rather nice to have companions such as these that don't see me in a religious light. It very much reminds me of how Lillith and I often were in our younger days, back before the fifth universe came to be."

Riven could tell, for the very first time since bonding with the Great Maw, that Gluttony felt a tinge of remorse at those words. "Is it something you want to talk about?"

There was a pause, their internal silence in stark contrast to the laughter, dancing, and even the music that two of the vampires from Prince Rantali's kingdom of Garth were playing on strange silver flutes.

"Not yet" was all Gluttony said.

"Fine. Let me know when you're ready, bud. I'm here if you need me."

There was no response.

"RIVEN! RIVEN, GO THERE!" Athela jabbed a finger in the direction of a large sandy island, one of many that they'd passed but with a long alcove on one end where red ferns and trees grew. "THE LAST ALTAR ISN'T FAR, WE ALREADY FOUND IT, AND WE HAVE TIME TO BURN! LET'S GO HAVE SOME FUN!!!"

"A picnic!" Fay yelled over the commotion, large breasts jiggling as she jumped up and down. "But with lots of drinking!"

"DRINKINGGGGG!" Azmoth bellowed, already tipsy after having chugged five entire gallons of hard liquor from Riven's storage space. He reached up with massive, muscular arms and clawed at the sky. "I WISHHHH TO PLAY PONG OF BEER!"

"Shit, son, you can't even say it right, you're so plastered!" Riven cackled, but turned the yacht in the direction of the island anyways. "Fine! Let's go have some fun—but I'm staying sober while you guys do it. I'll be the designated driver of this group."

"Nooo!!!" Fay moaned, pushing past Athela on the front of the ship and hiccuping before tripping and falling face-first into Riven's chest. She pushed off, cheeks bright pink, and giggled before falling over to the right. "No, you've got to have fun with us Rivennnn . . . . Palheeze?!"

"Jesus Christ!" Riven said. "Maybe I'll drink just a little bit—but here, let me help you up. And ATHELA! PUT YOUR SHIRT BACK ON!"

"NO! LET ME FLY FREEEEEE LIKE A FLAMINGO!"

"HOW DO YOU EVEN KNOW WHAT A FLAMINGO IS?!" A bra smacked Riven in the face to shut him up, and another gleeful giggle from the front of the ship saw Athela spinning around rapidly while chugging another bottle. Looking at her go, as happy as she was with her long black hair flowing in the wind, Riven couldn't even be mad. Plus, it was certainly a good look on her, in his opinion, even if he did get slightly jealous from the way the other vampires were staring at her or shooting quick glances.

Ten minutes later, the boat was parked. Azmoth was lighting a bonfire and slabs of meat were being stacked alongside squid they'd killed on the ride over for cooking. Genua was getting out spices and preparing various breads. A large perimeter of Retesh's undead, Fay's illusions and traps, and defensive wards provided by Prince Rantali were all set up, too, as chairs, tables, and more alcohol were produced for the lot of them.

"All right, Rantali, welcome to beer pong! These are the rules . . ." Riven said, shirtless, pale, defined musculature riddled with occasional strange black tattoos that glistened in the firelight. "We have to get these little balls into one of those red cups filled with wine on the opposite side of the table, and THEY have to do the same with theirs—but we take turns!"

He gestured to the two giggling women across from them—who'd obliged Riven's requests to put SOME clothes on, but remained half naked in their white bikinis that Riven hadn't even known they owned. Fay and Athela had apparently gone shopping together back on Panu—the uncomfortably tight spandex swim gear he now wore was a testament to their thoughtfulness when it concerned him, too. They'd bought it all as a set.

"Come on now, boys!" Fay said, licking her lips suggestively and taunting them with the ping-pong ball in her hand. "Don't keep us waiting!"

"WE DUN GONNA WIN!" Athela screamed, absolutely drunk off her ass as she jumped up and down and dodged invisible enemies side to side. "We were BORN champions of the PONG!"

"We next!" Azmoth yelled back with a hand patting Genua's head.

The elf thrall swatted the clawed hand away with a scowl. "I can't drink while pregnant! That'd be irresponsible!"

"Then I get KARA!" Azmoth declared, not dismayed at the rebuttal as he pointed two of his other clawed hands in the dark elf's direction.

Kara, who'd been absentmindedly sipping on a glass of her own while listening in to Retesh talk death magic theory to one of the guards who'd taken an interest in the pillar, perked up. "Me?!"

"YES, YOU!" Azmoth roared, slapping a large squid onto the billowing flames. "WE DOMINATE IN THE GAME OF PONG AND BEAT THE OTHERS!"

Kara gave him a half smile and laughed nervously.

"Um . . . . If you're sure . . ." she replied uncertainly, but smiled up at the large demon with a friendly nod of thanks. "I'll do my best."

Athela gasped and pointed at the drow a second later. "KARA! WHY AREN'T YOU DRESSED FOR SWIMMING?!"

"W-what? These are the only clothes I—"

"CHANGE!" Athela demanded, stomping over to her own bag of holding and pulling out a spare white swimsuit—an exact replica of the bikini she currently wore. "You're literally the ONLY person that isn't outfitted right! Come on, girl, don't be a buzzkill! Azmoth doesn't have clothes on, the slave doesn't have clothes on—even GENUA is outfitted properly!"

Kara caught the two-piece bikini with a furious flush and wide eyes. She took a look around. Azmoth looked like he usually did, and despite his plated body, he technically wasn't really wearing any clothes. Genua was in something more modest than Athela and Fay, but it was still a swimsuit nonetheless, putting on full display the Blood God's tattooed crimson runes all over her otherwise tanned skin. Riven, Prince Rantali, and the other vampiric knights were all shirtless in variations of boxer-short swimsuits, and Prince Rantali's slave still had his rags and energy-suppressing shackles on—though he was chained to a stake in the ground nearby.

"W-well, what about Retesh?!" Kara tried to argue, stuttering and fumbling with the quite revealing pieces of clothing in her hands. "He isn't swimming, either!"

The lich eyed her for a moment from underneath his robes and scoffed. "I am above such things as swimming . . . child."

He went back to discussing magical theory a second later.

Athela gave her a bland look as Riven continued to explain the rules of beer pong to Prince Rantali. She stomped over to Kara, pushed her to the ground, and began forcefully tearing off clothes over high-pitched screeching. Minutes later, the quite shy and completely unharmed drow woman had her hands wrapped around her chest and her knees crossed in a poor attempt to hide her gray-brown skin.

"There! You look absolutely STUNNING!" Athela cooed, planting a long, drunk kiss on Kara's cheek before sweeping the drow off her feet. "NOW SWIM!"

The stunned and once again shrieking drow was flung through the air and into the nearby alcove with a splash. Spluttering and coming up to the surface to wipe away the white hair plastered to her face with blood, she gasped and began swimming back to the edge, where the others were laughing good-naturedly.

When she reached the edge of the sandy shore and saw them all clapping or smiling, she couldn't help but take in the mood and pointed a challenging finger in Athela's direction. "I'll get you back for that!"

"Oh, will you?!" Athela replied slyly with a confident folding of her arms. "And just how do you intend to do that? You're far too weak to throw ME!"

"I'll get my teammate AZMOTH to help me throw you in! Right, Azmoth?!" Kara called out, and Azmoth quickly spun on his heel from where he'd been cooking alongside Genua.

The hellscape brutalisk gave off a savage, predatory grin. "YESSSSS!!!"

"WAIT!" Athela shrieked, sprinting away from the larger demon and hiding behind the drow. "WAIT WAIT WAIT! How about a deal?!"

"What deal?!" Kara replied skeptically, enjoying the laughter of the others as Azmoth continued to stalk around her with claws and wings extended.

Athela paused, put both hands on Kara's shoulders from behind, and leaned forward to speak into her ear. "We can make a bet! If Fay and I win at beer pong against you and Azmoth, you don't tell Azmoth to attack me and I get to use you as a chair for the remainder of the descent!"

"A chair?!" Kara exclaimed. "No! Why would I do that?!"

Athela snickered and began to whisper. "Because if you and Azmoth win, I'll do you a solid."

The next whispers were so low that no one but Kara could hear, but her eyes widened and the gray-brown skin of her face went a bright shade of embarrassed red.

She turned around. "Are you being serious, Athela?"

"Absolutely. But you have to win first, and I'm not going to go easy. I've been wanting a good chair for a while now!"

"You're sure?"

"I'm positive! Would I lie?"

"But . . . but what about—"

"I said, I'm sure! And no, the plethora of possible problems you're thinking about won't actually be a problem." Athela winked. "I've already thought long and hard about it."

Kara extended her hand without a moment's hesitation. "Shake on it."

"Ha! So eager!" Athela cackled, took her hand, and the two women vigorously shook. "I look forward to beating your ass, bitch!"

"Not a chance," Kara said, excitedly skipping off over the sand to where

Azmoth was now waiting. Pulling the large demon aside, the dark elf began to make battle plans—and began drying herself off near the fire.

Riven watched the whole thing unfold with more than a mild amount of curiosity, and being buzzed, he had a hard time ripping his gaze away from Kara's rather muscular and very exposed rear end.

"Eyes up here!" Fay yelled, snapping her fingers and then grabbing at her barely covered blue breasts. "I'm the succubus here and I demand attention!"

Riven laughed and blushed slightly at being caught, but he didn't disobey and let his eyes linger awhile. "Sorry. I'm a little drunk."

"No need to apologize! We get it!" Athela retorted, almost tripping over Fay's tail on the way to the table and smacking the succubus on the back before standing at attention and saluting. "Do we have permission to proceed with the game, Master-sir Riven?!"

"Got any last-second questions?" Riven asked the other prince, feeling a rumble of hunger in his stomach.

Prince Rantali quickly dragged his gaze off Fay and nodded with abandon. "I think I have the rules down! And was that your stomach I heard? We'd better get that food going fast! I'd say you can have some blood from my slave, but there's an entire ocean of it right here!"

Riven spat on the ground to his right and got into a throwing position. "Nah, I'm good on the blood. It's a side effect of Gluttony . . . I actually need to eat people once in a while to keep me going."

"Really? Like actually consume them whole? We do that in my kingdom, too, and I'd offer you the man I've taken so you can eat—but I wouldn't have much left for myself."

"Something like that. And don't worry about it, I just get . . . debuffs if I don't feast. I'll figure it out—don't think on it much."

"Debuffs even if you've drunk blood recently? Fascinating! But I can't say I'll be very good at this game. You ladies across the table will have to go easy on me!"

Athela snorted in derision, her eyes scanning Riven's defined body rather hungrily—but unlike Riven, she wasn't hungry for food. "Yeah, yeah, I don't think so, blondie. Fay and I are pros! There ain't NO way we're going to lose this time around!"

Riven grinned, fangs on full display. "We'll see about that!"

Two hours passed.

"WE WON!!! WE WON!!!" Kara slammed into Azmoth like a battering ram and wrapped him in a hug as the winged demon howled to the skies in victory. "THAT WAS SO CLOSE! I WAS ALMOST A CHAIR!"

Athela, for her part, groaned in disappointment, kneeling in the sand with her head between her hands, as Fay sighed loudly and strutted off with a seductive sway to her hips and a smile in Riven's direction. "Find me in the shrubbery after you're done eating, hon! We haven't tangled in a while, but give me a few minutes first! I'll even do that thing you like with my tongue!"

Riven immediately coughed up the drink he was downing and followed the succubus's outline into the red trees beyond the firelight, having a very hard time containing his lower half's excitement. "Did I just hear her right?"

"I believe you did, you lucky bastard," Prince Rantali replied with a grin. "A few minutes, she said? What do you think she's doing back there?"

"Wouldn't you like to know." Riven jammed an elbow into Rantali's side. "That's for staring!"

"Certainly you can't blame me!"

"I don't!"

"So why'd you elbow me?!"

"Because you deserved it."

Despite Riven's claims of trying to stay sober, Gluttony twice over informed him that they were still safe and that he was keeping watch. At the sin's approval, Riven let himself continue to slip further and further into a drunken haze, became much louder, and began to lose himself to the merriment.

It was genuinely a fun time.

They went swimming more than once, played beer pong a few more times, had a game of cards going, and were eating a lot of meat from their storage and the numerous blood squid they'd killed. The aquatic monsters were actually quite tasty, though that might've just been Riven's hunger growing by the second.

Unfortunately, the monster meat wasn't cutting it. He needed to eat mortal meat.

Perhaps he should ask Prince Rantali if he could eat the enslaved man chained up nearby, just like the other prince had offered?

No, he was Rantali's property. He was to be Rantali's thrall. He couldn't just steal the man's food . . . that was Rantali's prey.

Riven's hunger became palpable.

His eyes darted to Kara, who was occasionally shooting him nervous glances now while talking to Athela in hushed whispers, and he felt himself starting to drool as he drunkenly considered eating her instead of the squid currently in his hands. She was very pretty, with long brown legs and defined abdominal muscles—and he wondered if dark elf would taste as good as the human necromancer he'd hunted down, killed, and eaten back on Floor Two. That was the last time he'd eaten someone, and Gluttony's hunger—his own hunger—was rapidly expanding like a flower in full bloom.

Perhaps that muscular rear end of hers would make for a tasty snack after he killed her. He'd do it quickly and painlessly—he did like her after all. Maybe the other vampires would want to share her meat? She was only cattle in their eyes, and right now he agreed. Genua might taste good, too, but she was carrying his kid and draining her blood wouldn't be enough. He'd have to actually kill and eat Genua, and that simply wasn't an option while she was pregnant. Maybe another time?

Saliva began dripping off his fangs, his eyes dilated while staring at the rather attractive, half-naked young woman, and his breathing picked up. He heard his stomach rumble again as he began to have flashbacks to his other kills since bonding with Gluttony, the absolute exotic sensations he got as he murdered and ate his victims while Gluttony sucked in their souls like a soda pop. He began to picture Kara Blackbow in their place, his hands digging into her intestines as he gorged himself on the stunning drow woman.

What would Allie say if she knew?

What would his minions say?

His dark thoughts were forced back as he smacked himself upside the forehead with a strike far more powerful than what was probably necessary. Catching his breath, his pupils contracted and his hungry smile settled down. His fangs stopped releasing venom, and he hurriedly wiped the drool off his face before Kara noticed that he'd been contemplating murdering her.

Immense amounts of guilt washed over him, and he stood up—quickly looking around to the horizon for signs of distant battle. With other teams still present in the vicinity, he quickly found what he was looking for and redirected his hunger toward them. The hunger flared as his Snipe ability homed in on a distant set of orcs—both of which were completely unaware they were even being observed. His eyes dilated again, his fangs sprouted, and his smile stretched to unnatural proportions as he slowly began to wrap himself in Blessing of the Crow.

"Riven, what are you doing?" Athela asked, coming up and groping his pectoral muscles with a coy grin. "God, you are so fucking hot. I don't tell you that enough, but you're a hunk! Aren't you going to join Fay? She's been wanting you for quite some time now, and she's always complaining about how she doesn't get enough!"

"I'll help her out in a little while . . . tell her I'll be just slightly late," Riven whispered, pushing Athela aside as he began to pick up speed. "I'll be right back. Give me ten minutes."

"Huh? You never turn down sex! RIVEN?!" Athela yelled—but her voice was lost to the sound of a sonic boom as Riven's body exploded with power.

In an instant he was gone, flashing forward and creating tidal waves of energy in his wake as he traveled like a missile across the red ocean toward the other team less than a mile off. He was hungry. He was starving. And he absolutely, without a doubt, needed to feed . . .

Lest he hurt Kara or Genua instead.

CHAPTER 6

In the blink of an eye, Aktab's large dark-metal axe came down with a blinding flash of Unholy light—slicing off the head of an insectoid Azag warrior. The headhunters of the Azag hive clusters were truly the superior hunters here in the ocean of blood, and had made quick work of many of the other groups they'd come across—but Aktab's tribe and the other orc tribes of the Green Hand had been at war with the Azag clusters for untold millennia. He knew a thing or two about killing the beasts, and a feral grin spread across his masculine face, his lower fangs protruding when he curled his lips.

His eyes pierced the ocean and into the very soul of another one of the creatures; he then brandished his axe. "Come."

The Azag mantis screeched and used its wings to propel itself through the blood at rocket speed—six legs spiraling and four mantis blades stretched out wide for a pincer strike. The yellow eyes of the other participant widened in rage at seeing its mate killed, but despite the martial art it propelled itself ahead with, the headhunter was no match for the orc barbarian.

Aktab swatted the mantis's strike with his pauldron and armored left forearm, batting it away before exposing his dark-green skin and the rest of his unarmored body as his knee smashed into the Azag's left wing.

There was a crunch and screech, and the mantis blurred left with a blink step, sending out a jet of acid from its mandibles.

Aktab merely laughed and launched himself up through the ocean and into the air, where he could see his other comrades finishing off the rest of the mantises without much problem. He raised his axe high, summoning a pillar of green lightning from the skies to smash into his axe before flinging the blade at the monster who'd followed him into the air.

There was a resounding ***CRACK*** and the smell of charred flesh met his nostrils as he landed on the nearby island with the gory remnants of the beast splattering around him. He stood smiling and proud, bald head catching much of the gore as it fell, and grinned at his wife, who stood with a spear in hand not far off. "Not bad, right?!"

Aktab flexed, expanding his already large muscles, and teasingly wiggled his eyebrows at the huntress, who pretended not to be impressed with a snort and an eye roll. But he could see how she looked at him from the corner of his eye, and Aktab knew that he would be rewarded for his display in front of the others soon enough.

Killing in front of his wife, Citri, was always a way to turn her on. It made him look fierce and brought honor to the clan. Even if he was a bit silly whenever he did it.

One of the two other orc warriors laughed and came to slap Aktab on the back. "It was a good kill, even if Citri won't admit it!"

"Thank you, Brother Fram! I can always count on you to call out a good thing when you see it!" Aktab replied, smugly waltzing over to where the other Azag bodies were. More importantly, where their blood tokens and spatial bags were, as Citri and the final member of their team were now rummaging through the luggage with abandon.

"Heads, heads, and more heads," Citri muttered, her head shaking in dismay as she continued to pull out the collected heads of numerous other descenders that'd fallen prey to the mantis pack. "I'll never understand their obsession with collecting skulls."

"It is a tradition of theirs, for worthy enemies," Aktab said, nudging her playfully with his knee and getting a scowl from the kneeling orc huntress below him. "For others, they use their bodies as egg incubators. You know this—you've been to their recently conquered worlds on the outer rim of the Pajaji."

"Yes . . . truly disgusting creatures," Citri said with dismay. She got up and handed one of the spatial sacks to her husband. "Perhaps you'd like to finish going through it? I don't feel up to the task now that—"

A scream from Brother Fram caught their attention, and the other three orcs quickly whirled around to see him getting dragged through some kind of spatial rift in a snap-second of time. One moment he was there, being pulled into the darkness with thick, sticky nets of Unholy energy, and the next he was just gone.

It'd happened so fast.

Aktab barely had time to blink before a long red spike covered in Black Lightning crashed into the other orc warrior still with them, coming from another direction and impaling the man through the stomach. The protective wards and defensive lifesaving treasures didn't even last a moment, shattering on impact. Critical energy rippled along the other orc's exposed abdomen and ripped an enormous hole through his gut before spreading up into his chest, where his heart burst in a spray of blood. The orc warrior's eyes went wide in wordless shock before his body was flung off its feet in a spinning arc. His smoldering remains were sent skipping like a pebble upon a lake, crashing over the island and ending with a splash in the blood ocean nearly a hundred yards away.

"IT'S A TRAP!" Aktab roared, activating all his boosting skills and turning to the spot where the spike of energy had come from, but then he saw the look of horror on his wife's face as she stared at something behind him. She was reaching

out with one hand, a spell taught to her by one of the dark shamans in their village on her lips as she frantically cast to summon the magic to her fingertips, but
her expression told him that Citri would doubtless be too late.

Aktab needed to act.

With all his power, he swiveled and swung, unleashing everything he had
directly behind him with a crushing, triply enhanced blow from his axe. The
dark steel sang with bloodlust and his body swelled, muscles building, until his
strike blindly slammed into something solid.

There was a crash of power, and the cold sensation of something entering
his chest. He felt his heart stop in that instant, a tugging sensation that screamed
wrongness, and he blinked in horror as he beheld a strange red-eyed man staring
back at him. It was a vampire, as pale as day, with strange black sclera and simmering Unholy tattoos littering his mostly bare body. A vast aura of what Aktab
could only describe as supreme, unrelenting hunger blasted from the man's body,
and Aktab was forced to take a knee as his skin started to freeze and his wife
screamed his name in horrified denial.

As he hit the floor, he came down to the level of the man's hands, which
cupped Aktab's still-beating heart in bloody fingers. Aktab felt his body sway
from side to side as the sound around him faded and his vision turned to black.

"AKTAB!" the orc woman screamed in horrified dismay as Riven took a bite of
the beating heart, savoring the flavor on his tongue as the scent of his fresh kill
radiated through his nostrils.

It tasted so, so good . . . and a thrilling, tingling sensation ran up his spine
when his fangs sank into the meat.

Riven's mind was completely focused on that overwhelming, overpowering
sensation, uncaring of anything and everything else, as he let his knees hit the
sand while gorging himself on the organ with ravenous abandon.

"YOU MONSTER!" The trembling green-skinned woman let out a sob,
and then without delay she flung some kind of plague cloud in his direction,
similar to what Fay often used.

The cloud never hit.

In an instant, Riven was behind the woman. Coating his arms and hands in
gauntleted claws of crimson, he smashed her weak body into the ground.

He felt the crunch of bones and heard her pained scream, but above all he
felt the pulsing, ravenous call of the need to devour. He didn't even register her
as a person, ignoring her sobs as he suppressed her mana and delivered a clean,
quick killing strike to her forehead by smashing in her skull. Because although
he was uncontrollably hungry, he was not intentionally cruel. He did not pro-
long her suffering, and with her wails gone and everyone in the vicinity very
dead, he settled down to eat.

As his hands trembled with delight, a smile spread literally from ear to ear
and his fangs extended. He felt Gluttony's overpowering presence consume his

thoughts. He began digging through her muscles and organs without another thought or care in the world, gorging himself on the dead huntress and rapidly stripping her bones of flesh as he tore off pieces of her and shoved them into his mouth. Often swallowing whole and not even bothering to chew, he only barely acknowledged Athela's presence in the background as she watched.

He only barely acknowledged her sadistic smile, only barely registered the ocean of blood around him that began to stream up into the sky like pillars supporting the heavens, and didn't register the faint words that left her mouth as she tapped a curious finger to her pitch-black lips: "My man is finally growing up . . . That blood farm is going to have to come along sooner rather than later."

A calm, slowly rotating vortex of blood covered the sky for miles around Riven in all directions, soaking up blood from the ocean as it formed tiny, concentrated threads of power that wrapped themselves together and reached for him far below. The tingling sensation he felt as these threads condensed and needled their way into his black tattoos was a euphoria, adding to the content sensation he felt while he continued to devour his victims and as the bloody threads of extremely condensed blood energy intertwined with the ancient language on his skin.

[As a pureblooded vampire, you have finally come to embrace your predatory heritage and have fed on enough prey to expand your bloodline. For further expansions, you will need to continue feeding on mortals and will expedite the process by increasing both the amount of blood you drain and increasing the variety of races you feed on. Please choose one of the following for the trait Bloodline Expansion 1:
- **Increased Regeneration**
- **Improved Vampiric Perception**
- **Blood Golem Creation**
- **Enhanced Thrall Minions]**

The vortex in the sky dissipated as the last lingering remnants of it were drawn into Riven's body. The notification disappeared into his status page and closed as he began to regain his self-awareness.

Riven exited his fugue state in a haze of bliss, blood covering his entire front and meat hanging from his mouth. Two skeletons, stripped of the majority of their flesh, lay on the sand nearby, and Athela, still wearing her bikini, watched him with puzzled amazement only a couple feet away. She had one hand supporting her chin, the other tapping her knee, and gave him a loving smile when he finally acknowledged her presence.

"Hey, babe!" she said sweetly. "Enjoy your meal? I'd been wondering what would happen when a pureblood like you unlocked their first bloodline expansion! Quite impressive stuff! But, you know, Fay isn't going to be very happy with you if you don't hurry up. It's been more than ten minutes."

Riven stared at the demoness, horror slowly creeping in, as he realized that she'd witnessed his actions. He looked down at his messy chest and blood-covered hands before spitting the meat in his mouth off to the side. "Athela . . . how much did you see?"

She gave him a knowing grin, scooted over across the island sand, and put a gentle palm against his stained cheek. "All of it."

He blanched.

What would she think of him?

Was she disgusted?

Did she—

His thoughts were interrupted when she leaned over and pressed her forehead against his. Sighing and stroking the back of his neck, she opened her eyes again and seemed to peer into his soul as she opened the floodgates of emotions in her mind. Through their link, he only felt sympathy, love, and acceptance.

And a good bit of lust, but he ignored that part, because, frankly, he was too overcome with emotions of his own. She didn't care one bit that he was a monster. Did she?

"You're not a monster, Riven," she said, pulling back and giving them just a bit of space, wiping gore from his hair. "You're my monster. And I love you. How long were you going to keep this a secret from us?"

Riven felt a sinking feeling of guilt settle into his stomach, though it was still overwhelmed by the sense of relief that she didn't think any less of him after witnessing what he'd done. "I'm not sure."

"Do you not trust us to love you anyway?" she asked, genuinely curious. "Genua told us about your condition. Fay and me. We've known since the last floor, and Gluttony himself has been hinting that you need to expand your bloodlines by adding more variety and volume to your feeding."

He didn't bother replying, just cast his gaze to the ground.

Athela tsked and drew him into a warm hug. Embracing him with her warm body pressed against his, she just held him there for a long, long time, until he eventually took her in his own arms and gave her a loving hug back. "You don't need to hide anything from me, Riven. Not ever. I'm your princess, remember?"

Riven, who'd kept his composure up until that moment, hugged her tighter and let out a quick sob of laughter. Burying his head into her neck, he continued to let tears stream down his face as they laughed together. "Athela, times like this remind me why I'm so lucky to have you."

"Yes, yes, I am great!" she said with a swish of her hair. "I'm pretty damn awesome, I know, I know! But very seriously, are you done eating now?"

Riven sniffed, then nodded, continuing to smile. "Yes."

She nodded in satisfaction. "Good. Then it's time to tell you a secret of our own."

"You have a secret you haven't been sharing?"

"Definitely! And you can't be mad. It's only been a little while anyways, a few days."

Riven pretended to scowl. "All right. Why haven't you told me yet? Is it something serious?"

She pondered his question for a bit and shook her head. "Nothing that will harm you directly. But we might have . . . bent the rules a little bit. We both wanted to do it—it wasn't just one of us."

"O-oh . . ." His features slowly fell, and a look of worried jealousy settled in. He nervously began to fidget, looking across the ocean to where their own island had been settled and where Fay's illusions kept the majority of it obscured. "You . . . you and Fay didn't . . ."

His voice trailed off, and a sinking feeling of dread and hurt began to rail against his mind. There was no way they'd do something like that. No way . . . right?

Athela raised an eyebrow in confusion and turned his head back to her by gently realigning his chin, meeting his eyes. "We didn't what?"

Riven pursed his lips. He felt stupid for even asking, hypocritical in some ways, but the way she'd phrased it . . . he had to ask. "I hope you're not saying that you two cheated on me."

Before she had registered exactly what he said, he quickly continued to clear the air. "Not that I ever thought you would! And honestly, in many ways, I don't even have room to talk, because I know you've both made large exceptions for me . . . WAIT! Wait, don't say anything yet."

He held up his hands as she opened her mouth to speak. "No, I need to finish talking first before you reply."

Taking in a deep breath, he avoided her gaze, shamefaced. "I know it's completely hypocritical of me to even ask this. I remember how hard it was when you two had it in for one another, and how you settled the differences by sharing, but I had thought it was just us three. If I'm not enough, if this isn't enough, or if one or both of you need something more and want to move on, then let me know."

There was a very, very long lull in the conversation after that.

Slowly composing herself, Athela leveled a steady gaze his way, hands clasped on her lap as she knelt beside him. "You know, you did sleep with Kathrine. You even intend to marry her because of the Blood Moon Requiem's mandates to create more with the gift of Malignant Prophecy."

"I don't have to do that," Riven said adamantly. "Not if you two don't want me to. I can tell my great-grandmother to fuck right off and never see Kathrine again."

Another pause.

"You impregnated Genua."

Riven grimaced. "We weren't even together back then. None of us were. Sure, I slept with Fay that day, too, but—"

"And yet I'm still with you and have to watch you raise another woman's children. Do you realize how that makes me feel?" Athela held up a hand to his lips, irritation obvious on her countenance. "What if I did tell you that we'd cheated on you? What then?"

Riven's face paled, he remained silent for a time, and tears began welling up under his eyes as he looked away. It took an even longer amount of time to compose himself than it had for Athela. "I'd be extremely hurt because you'd have done it behind my back. The trust would have been broken. I'm not sure what I'd do. And so, I'd very much like to know if that's what happened. If that's what you're hinting at, being your secret."

Athela evaluated her boyfriend in silence and finally shook her head. "This conversation has been enlightening, but no. Neither Fay nor I have slept with anyone else other than you and Genua. But you already knew about Genua, and we felt like it was okay to do because you've also slept with her and she's your thrall."

Riven still averted his gaze, but his tense posture visibly relaxed and he let his shoulders slump. He wiped his eyes. "Okay. That's good to know."

"I want you to know, Riven, now that we're on the subject . . . Eh. How do I put this?" She scratched her chin thoughtfully, looking up at the star-laden sky. "It was . . . It was very hard for me, at first, to accept Fay. Harder than it was to realize that Genua has your child inside her. Back when you'd initially chosen me as the one you wanted to be with, I chose to open myself up to having a relationship that included Fay because I knew it would make you happy. But since then, I've discovered that I'm very much into her, too, and it's opened up an entirely new avenue of experiences I'd never explored before. I would never hurt you, Riven, I would never cheat on you, and if I ever wanted to introduce someone else into the relationship, I'd talk to you first. But also know that I'm very aware of how fragile men's egos are."

She gave him a wink. "I would never do anything that I even thought would make you jealous or upset. I am truly in love with you, Riven, and if having Fay around makes you happy, then I'm happy. If you choose to once again explore things with Genua, then I'm fine with it. You'll be taking care of her two kids soon anyways, and she is acceptable. If you choose not to do that because you're content with Fay and me, then all I can say is great and that I'm happy as long as you're happy. Same thing with Kathrine."

Athela held up her hands in a shrug. "I used to be a very jealous person, but I know you care, and I've had a lot of fun with the way things are right now. I would never ruin it. But if it made you feel better, you could always give me a minion's mandate, ordering me to never do something like that."

"I don't ever want to force you to do anything, Athela."

"Then don't. But I wouldn't mind, if it gave you peace of mind. You've never ordered me to do anything against my will except in jest, like when you forced me to keep hitting myself the other day as punishment for stealing Fay's snack."

She grinned, and the two of them laughed together as she nudged him and snuggled up against his chest.

"I suppose that was well deserved, though," she said eventually, as he otherwise sat in silence. "No, the secret that Fay and I had was something else entirely. We were going to surprise you with it on Christmas, but if you want to know—"

"I don't want to know if it's a surprise present. Save it for Christmas," Riven said, holding her close and leaning into her. "I'm sorry. I don't mean to be such a pussy—just the thought of you with another man really sucked. God, I feel like such a hypocrite saying that."

"With another MAN, huh? Oddly specific. Your feelings are your feelings." Athela shrugged, leaning back into him comfortingly and stroking his back. "It's not something I'll ever need. I can't speak for Fay, but that's how I feel about it. And she's obsessed with you—she's literally waiting for you to go pounce on her right now, so you should probably oblige her before she gets huffy!"

Riven rolled his eyes with a wide smile and ran his hand through her hair. "Yeah. She's been rather aggressive lately."

"Indeed. Also, I should probably ask, what do you think of Kara? She's rather nice, isn't she?"

"Of course she's nice. She seemed absolutely crazy at first, but I think she's just had a rough life. Why?"

"Do you think she's pretty?"

Riven scoffed. "Yes, but not as nearly as pretty as you or Fay. You don't have anything to worry about."

"Good answer!" Athela giggled and pulled his face toward her to plant a kiss on his lips. "Which leads me to another question. I realize you said that you're jealous when it comes to other men. But would you, theoretically, be jealous of other women? Say, perhaps, if we got permission from you first, would you be angry if Fay and I experimented with other females outside our relationship?"

"Outside of our relationship? That completely depends on the dynamic of that other relationship," Riven replied. "If that's what you want, I truly would be a hypocrite to deny you that. Honestly, seeing you date other women wouldn't bother me that much as long as you asked first, and as long as that woman, who- ever it was, didn't try to steal you away from me emotionally. I want to be first priority, just like you and Fay are mine."

"Nice!" Athela pumped her fist.

"What do you mean, 'nice'?!" Riven asked with a laugh. "Did you have someone in mind—perhaps Kara, since you brought her up? Aren't Fay and Genua enough for you?"

"Oh, they're more than enough! But as long as you're all right with it as long as it's women, we wouldn't have a problem expanding our horizons!" Athela replied smugly. "I've developed a little bit of a crush on Kara. We were going to bring this up together, but since we're already here talking about it I might as well get it out. We didn't think that you'd be jealous of other women, and it appears we were right, given our relationship dynamic and your earlier reaction when you found out that Fay and I were using Genua. We wouldn't have pursued it if you weren't comfortable with it, but now that we know you are . . . it makes things rather exciting!"

"Is that right?"

"It is! But there's one small problem." Athela held up her fingers and pushed her thumb and pointer finger together. "Kara doesn't want to be a thrall."

Riven blinked. "So? I don't want her to be a thrall, either. Thralls are mind slaves, and I like Kara."

"Yes, but how are Fay and I supposed to seduce Kara if she's not a thrall?"

"The old-fashioned way?"

"But she's not into girls."

Riven snickered at Athela's unamused expression. "Well, that's tough shit for you, then. Find another girl to date. Maybe Kathrine would be into it, if she manages to survive whatever she's going through right now. I hope she's all right, anyways."

"Yeah, me, too," Athela stated with a small frown. "But as you've said many times now, we can't help Kathrine and can only hope. Back to the moment, though! About Kara—she isn't into girls, but she is into you."

Riven raised an eyebrow. "I said she's pretty, but I'm quite comfortable with the status quo. I don't want another girlfriend, Athela."

"Oh, come on!" Athela pleaded, a sly and seductive smile on her lips as she backed up with a fake pout. "Do Fay and me a solid! Be our wingman!"

"You're seriously asking me to wingman for you two so that you can sleep with Kara?"

"Yes!" Athela nodded aggressively. "Using you to fish for straight women is the equivalent of using catnip for cats, or crack for a crackhead! I mean, just look at this handsome jawline! You're fucking beautiful!"

Riven straight-faced her as she pinched both his cheeks and wiggled them around.

"Weren't you just saying that you were hypocritical and acknowledged that Fay and I had made big exceptions for you?!" Athela pressed, an eager light filling her eyes. "And you even said you're not jealous of other women as long as they don't try to take us away from you, right? Come on, Riven! Be our wingman and help your bisexual girlfriend out a bit! Add her to your harem!"

Riven, for his part, pursed his lips, unamused. "I'm not getting another girlfriend, Athela. I can barely juggle you two as it is, and the Kathrine thing is only in name because of the requiem."

"Okay, well what about occasional flings?! It would be fun to spice things up from time to time, wouldn't it?!"

His eyes narrowed. "Well . . . perhaps I can see that. How do you know she's not into girls, though? Have you even tried pursuing her yet if you were going to ask me for permission first?"

"More or less dropped a couple hints and felt out the waters," Athela replied noncommittally. "I didn't actually do anything, though, not without you saying I could. I fell flat on my face with the flirting, too, so to speak, but she ogles you every chance she gets with big puppy-dog eyes. You have to have seen it."

Riven couldn't necessarily disagree, after taking note of things when Allie had pointed them out the first time. "Okay, but how are you going to use me to get to her?"

"Simple! Fay and I already made a bet with her, one that we lost on purpose!"

"The bet you two made when you were whispering at the beer pong table?"

"Mmm-hmm!"

"You're such a degenerate. And what did that bet entail?"

Athela cackled and tugged her knees up to her chest, but didn't deny the accusation. "We told her that we'd get you drunk and rope her into a foursome with us later today if we lost. And of course, we lost intentionally so that we would have the chance to sleep with her, too."

"That's so fucked."

"I'm not fucked yet, but I will be if you agree!"

"Seriously, Athela, do you have no moral compass?"

"You saying that while rolling your eyes and smirking doesn't really drive the message home. But no, I do not have any moral qualms about what we're about to do, as long as you're not jealous or upset about it. She'd be into it if you were there—no harm, no foul!"

Riven snorted and proceeded to get up. "I'm assuming that Fay is waiting for me and you're going to show up shortly afterward with Kara, then?"

Athela beamed a smile and gave two thumbs-up. "You got it! I let them know you'd be late when I saw what you were up to. Just make sure to do a good job for Kara so that she feels satisfied whenever it's my turn. Okay?"

"You're putting a lot of pressure on me here. I'm not sure I can perform."

"Oh, Riven, Riven, Riven . . . I have no doubt in my mind that you'll do fine. More than fine, actually. As I've said, you're quite the catch, and I'm honestly baffled that you'd ever be jealous of any other man, given who you are and what you look like. Now, let's get going so we don't piss Fay off any more than we already have! I'm excited!"

"Mmm-hmm. Oh, and Athela?"

"Yes?"

"Don't tell the others what you saw here. I don't need them knowing specifics."

"Of course, Riven. I would never do something like that without your say-so."

CHAPTER 7

[As a pureblooded vampire, you have finally come to embrace your predatory heritage and have fed on enough prey to expand your bloodline. For further expansions, you will need to continue feeding on mortals and will expedite the process by increasing both the amount of blood you drain and increasing the variety of races you feed on. Please choose one of the following for the trait Bloodline Expansion 1:
- **Increased Regeneration**
- **Improved Vampiric Perception**
- **Blood Golem Creation**
- **Enhanced Thrall Minions]**

Riven wiped the sweat from his face and pondered which one he should choose. There weren't any descriptions beyond the basic titles, so he couldn't really compare well. Maybe Prince Rantali would have some insights, coming from a royal vampiric lineage in one of the other universes?

He should ask when he got back.

"Thanks, baby, you did a really good job!" Fay panted next to him, scratching and massaging his bare back in a way that made his skin crawl. "That was amazing, and I have no doubt that Kara will be coming back for seconds after this—as long as Athela doesn't get too crazy!"

"I'm surprised you went along with this."

"Why?"

"Because you were overtly jealous when it came to Athela less than a year ago."

Fay pursed her lips in thought. "Well, I was less secure in our relationship than I am now, and Athela was an entirely different case. As I've said before, I would have been all right with anyone else at the time, but Athela felt like a threat to my bond with you. I'm glad it worked out the way it did, though!"

Riven nodded, tired from the recent physical exertion, as his attention turned to where Athela was intertwined with the bound dark elf on the island's forest floor. Kara was currently blindfolded and screeching through a gag as Athela had her way with her, so at first glance he would say Fay was wrong. But Kara had been more than happy to reciprocate for all of them after she'd finished, and had insisted on finishing whatever Athela wanted her to do, too, which may have been a bit on the crazier BDSM side, given what Riven was witnessing.

He supposed it fit Athela's personality.

Riven dismissed the notification, lovingly ruffled Fay's hair, and stood up to get dressed. "You should join them. I'm going to head over to the camp and talk to Rantali. I have some questions regarding my vampiric bloodline expansions."

"Are you sure you don't want to stay for another round?" Fay asked, but she stayed seated and leaned back to get a better view. "It'll be fun . . ."

Riven chuckled at her lustful expression. "It was certainly fun, but we've already been here for almost an hour! You two vixens are crazy."

Fay gave him a pouting expression with pooched lips but began to crawl over to the other two women with a backward glance. "Fine, but if you change your mind, you know where to find us!"

Riven gave her a thumbs-up, finished putting on his pants, and headed out of the foliage and shrubbery toward the camp on the island's shoreline.

It didn't take long to get there.

"Aha! The triumphant hero returns!" Prince Rantali remarked upon Riven's entrance onto the beach. "I didn't know you were such a ladies' man, Riven! How was the drow?"

"Her name is Kara." Riven passed him by and reached for a meat skewer being handed to him by Genua. "Thanks, Genua. Your cooking is really something else lately."

The elf thrall beamed with delight while kneeling next to the firepit. "Thank you! That is very kind of you to say!"

Riven took a seat in a chair next to Prince Rantali and across from Retesh, noting that Azmoth was flying across the bloody sea to catch more squid monsters in the distance. "I still can't believe this stuff is all real."

"What stuff?" Rantali asked, taking a smoking pipe from one of his men and inhaling deeply. He blew out a ring of smoke and offered the pipe to Riven.

Riven refused it politely with a shake of his head. "I'm good, thanks. As for what stuff I'm referring to . . . it's all this."

Riven gestured to the pocket realm around them. Then he snapped his fingers, and a wisp of blood magic formed over his palm before disappearing entirely.

"Back on my homeworld, before the integration, I didn't know magic existed."

Prince Rantali took in another deep inhale from his pipe and let the smoke out in a long, slow stream. His red eyes evaluated Riven's curious expression with interest. "No magic? What kind of barbaric world did you hail from? I've heard the rumors of how you, the lost prince, were found on an outer-rim world. But again, my kingdom of Garth is far removed from the politics of the bigger players in the multiverse. I know little beyond mere rumors."

Riven leaned back in his chair and started tearing off pieces of meat from the skewer. "My planet had legends about magic, but nothing solid. Regardless, that is not why I came back early despite the other three remaining behind to have fun."

Riven grinned in amusement. "Anyways, I have questions for you about my expanded bloodline. I was hoping you could help."

Rantali raised both eyebrows and put the pipe down. "So that's what the sky turned red for. Now it makes sense, though usually vampires' first bloodline expansion happens as a very young child. So that is rather odd. I had been wondering . . . but your pureblood lineage is far greater than most, if not all, of what my kingdom can give advice for. I do not mean to say that I cannot offer wisdom and advice on these matters, but would you not wish to ask those of the Blood Moon Requiem? It is usually left to family to discuss such private matters. Surely at the end of this floor, when we reach the final sacrificial altar, Elysium will grant you communication with them. And if not them, then who?"

Riven didn't bother mentioning that he'd only been a vampire for less than two years. Or at least, before that he'd been posing as a human by means unknown to him. Likely his parents' work.

"I have been thinking the same thing," Riven replied. "And if you do not know what it is that you are seeing, then I trust you to be honest enough to tell me. But if you do have knowledge on the matter, then I feel there is no reason to wait."

Prince Rantali nodded gradually. "Then I would be honored to help if I can. Tell me what it is you have been offered."

"Four options: Increased Regeneration, Improved Vampiric Perception, Blood Golem Creation, and Enhanced Thrall Minions. None of them give any descriptions beyond the titles. Any input?"

Prince Rantali thought about it, then whistled. "You have four good options here. Two are obviously better, though. Increased Regeneration will obviously heal you faster, and Improved Vampiric Perception will simply expand your range of dark-sight and hearing heartbeats. But the Blood Golem Creation and Enhanced Thrall Minions expansions are quite rare. And I do feel qualified to speak to you in detail on such matters."

Riven waved at him to go on, and Prince Rantali continued after another period of thought.

"Blood Golem Creation obviously allows you to create blood golems. What the title does not tell you is that you must choose between two paths if you do this: You must choose an internal or external path. Internal is self, where you can create blood golems that inherit some form of your power, though they'll never be as strong as you. The external path is others, where you can create copies of other people if you use their blood, but again, they'll never be as powerful as the original."

"And Enhanced Thralls?"

"Enhanced Thrall Minions will make them far tougher to kill, giving them a hefty endurance boost, while also imbuing them with regeneration properties usually only seen by vampires. You're also able to create them slightly faster than normal. If you have a lot of thralls, or have a thrall you particularly don't want to die, Enhanced Thrall Minions is a very good choice to take. I would recommend—"

Riven didn't think about it any further and selected Enhanced Thrall Minions while looking straight at Genua. She had his kid inside her, and there was no way he'd let her come close to death again like she had when that naga had nearly assassinated her. "You ain't dyin' on me anytime soon, old lady!"

[You have picked Enhanced Thrall Minions. You are now able to create thralls at a 10% increased rate. All thralls under your direct control will gain two hundred base stat points to Endurance and a 65% bonus to base Endurance and regain the Vampiric Regeneration trait.]

Genua's body stiffened as the trait took hold, and she let out a brief, surprised gasp as the bones and organs inside her became more solid. But it only lasted for a moment, and her red eyes narrowed in Riven's direction with a scowl. "I am not OLD! Especially not for an elf. I don't even have any wrinkles."

Riven chuckled. "How old are you, exactly?"

"Forty-two years of age."

"You're ancient."

"Hey! Athela is two centuries old! Isn't she? And SHE says that she's young for a demon!"

"She's an old hag, too."

"Oh, now you're just trying to be rude!" Genua grinned and rolled her eyes, going back to cooking and ignoring Riven's laughter.

Narg, in his nether realm, still felt drunk days later. He was in massive amounts of pain and coming in and out of consciousness every couple of minutes.

[Evolution failed.]
[Evolution failed.]
[Evolution failed.]

Something was wrong. The insights he'd obtained must have been wrong. He didn't understand and frantically tried to stop his body from mutating so that he could begin the cycle anew. But the energy inside him refused to be quelled, and it appeared that Elysium wouldn't accept his attempt to stop the process.

Narg was afraid he was going to die.

[Evolution failed.]
[Evolution failed.]
[Evolution failed.]

His green skin bulged. His orange eyes popped in a gore-filled mess. His bones cracked and his organs ruptured as he continued to reheal all the damage at an ever-increasing and rapid pace. He wanted to scream whenever he was awake enough to realize what was going on, but either his lungs didn't work, he didn't have a properly formed mouth at the time, or he was simply in too much shock due to the pain.

[Evolution failed.]
[Evolution failed.]
[Evolution halted.]
[Malformation detected. Soul damage accrued. No other souls have access to this nether realm. Do you wish to contact your bonded master for assistance?]

Malformation? Soul damage? Narg would have groaned if he could manage it. This wasn't unheard-of, especially in his family's lineage. They were, for lack of better words, genetically dispositioned to this particular problem. But it hadn't happened in a few centuries, especially not at a low E-grade transition state, and he just happened to have it now, given his terrible luck.

He'd already been underperforming as a minion, and had been 100 percent useless on this new floor because he simply hadn't been there. Not that it seemed like they even noticed, or needed his help, which stung that much more. What would Riven say if his master knew that Narg was defective? It may take decades for this kind of defect to go away in order to let him try for an evolution again. And he wouldn't get another shot at entering the Abyssal Descent.

[Soul lattice decay detected. No other souls have access to this nether realm. Do you wish to contact your bonded master for assistance?]

Great. Just great. Even the insights he'd acquired from the last floor were disappearing.

Why had Lillith, of all people, picked him? What had she seen in him that made her decide it was a good idea to put the weight of his entire clan's pride and hopes on his metaphorical shoulders? Gluttony was certain to gobble him right up when the Great Maw saw this. There was no way Narg was coming out of this alive. Even if he did, it would be in extreme shame, not only to himself, but for his family.

He was, just as he'd always been, a failure.

Regret and depression washed over him. He wanted to be great, he wanted to be useful, he wanted to help. But what could he, a defective, small, runt-of-the-litter beholder demon do for people like Riven? For the three other ARCH-demons in his retinue? He didn't hold a candle to them. Not to a single one.

Perhaps . . . perhaps it was time to give up. To do the right thing, save as much face as he could, and let Gluttony's reincarnation know that a better demon should be selected for this spot.

"What the system calls a malformation was left there intentionally," a deep, thundering voice called out to him from behind.

Unfortunately, Narg was too damaged to move, even here in his own nether realm. Instead he remained sluglike, limp, and, by all appearances, dead. However, that didn't stop the surprise from welling up inside him. How had someone come into this place without his permission? That should be absolutely impossible. And there hadn't been a notification requesting access, so how?

Was Narg actually going insane?

"I am speaking directly into your mind," the voice said once again. This time, the visage of Gluttony flashed through Narg's thoughts, with a deep burst of hunger that left Narg paralyzed. Except he'd already been paralyzed. Now he was doubly so.

The voice laughed at his thoughts. "I apologize for startling you, little one. Please do not think that I would throw you away over a birth defect. But once again, this is not actually a defect. It is not a malformation. It was left there intentionally by your ancestors—intentionally. You just don't see it for what it is."

To this, Narg remained silent and stumped. But his curiosity was piqued, and his shock at being addressed directly by the Great Maw was only dwarfed by his reverence toward the spiritual entity. If he and his bloodline didn't have a malformation, then what was it? Why would Elysium call it that? Why was it left there intentionally?

"I will preserve your soul lattice while you figure it out, but the answer remains inside you, little one," Gluttony said, as Narg felt the insights he'd gained with his soul lattice and soul expansion not only reinforce themselves but double and then triple.

His one good working eye widened in amazement as he felt the original sin's malignant energy running through him in tidal waves that washed away his pain and suffering but did not entirely heal him, either.

"Look inward, deep in your soul, where what Elysium deems to be a malformation is birthed," Gluttony said as his deep voice began to fade away. "There you will find your answer, if you only take the time to unravel what it is. Do not panic, know that I will not cast you aside, and stay the path. We will be seeing you soon."

It was like a great weight had been lifted, and Narg wanted to laugh in delight and cry at the same time. But he was still in slug mode and didn't budge. Instead, he just let himself relax and rejoice in feeling the Great Maw's presence, and in the new knowledge that he was not cursed to shame his family after all.

Regaining his mental fortitude, he did just what Gluttony said and soared into his spiritual world, where he tried to unfurl the mysteries of what his ancestors had apparently left there on purpose. It may take him some time, and he may not get it all right at once, but he would not disappoint the Great Maw. He would come out victorious and finally be of some use after what could only be seen as an embarrassing show so far.

"This will go down in the history books as the easiest floor descent in the history of my kingdom!" Prince Narzkal Rantali guffawed while making his way onto the yacht made of blood ice and dragging along the bald slave he used as a lunch box for fresh blood. "Ridiculous!"

"Truly," one of his knights agreed, walking up the ramp. "This has actually been rather enjoyable. It's a shame we have to part ways after this."

Riven gave the man a polite smile and helped Genua up the ramp to make sure she didn't fall. She gave him a pleased nod of thanks and settled down on one of the seats before Azmoth landed on the deck.

"Narg is having some issues with his insights and evolution, so he won't be back for a bit," Riven said to the rest as they came onboard one by one. Retesh looked rather bored, Athela absolutely giddy, Fay looked satisfied, and Kara wore a deep blush that didn't seem to want to go away.

Though she did intentionally brush by Riven on the way to her seat and was brave enough to hold eye contact for a solid few seconds before sitting down next to Athela at the front. It was obvious she was still nervous and unsure of herself, though after her tango with the rest of them, she certainly wasn't trying to hide in the background like she'd been after Allie's rant.

"Are the bone wyrms good to go?" Riven asked.

Retesh gave the affirmative. "They're in formation."

"Anyone else have anything to say before we get going?" Riven asked the rest.

Surprisingly enough, it was Kara who raised her hand to speak. "Do you mind if I speak to you in private on the way to the last altar?"

Riven cleared his throat and gave her a friendly smile. "Sure. Not a problem at all. But if that's everything, let's get moving. Kara, you can sit in the front with me so we can talk while I steer. We should get there within the hour since we already scouted it out, and as long as there aren't any monster swarms of other teams trying to get in our way, it should be smooth sailing through the rest of this floor."

CHAPTER 8

The ocean rushed past and the yacht created waves as Riven's mana blasted out the back, propelling them at high speed. Meanwhile, Riven's Storm Lances of Blood and Shadow arranged in patterns around his totems. The totems themselves were given control over the magic chained to Riven's soul, and although they could not produce actual Storm Lances themselves yet, they could produce similar magics and had enough of a hold over them to autocast if enemies were inbound.

They sat in the very front of the yacht, farther away from the rest of the group in a semisecluded location. Or at least as secluded as one could be on a ship this size.

"So . . . What did you want to talk to me about?" Riven asked casually while continuing to steer the large boat. This time around no one was partying, as they expected to encounter more serious situations after leaving this floor. "Does it have to do with what . . . uh . . . we did together recently? I hope you didn't feel like Athela or Fay were pressuring you."

Kara furiously shook her head and blushed, but kept her eyes on him and didn't look away with her hands clenched on her lap. "No! No, not at all—it was very enjoyable, Your Excellency!"

She fidgeted with her hands and smiled awkwardly. "I'd, um, do it again if the time comes! But that isn't what I came to talk to you about."

"Oh!" He smiled. "Good to hear. All right, well, go on and tell me, then. And please don't call me 'excellency.'"

She hesitated and tucked her hair behind her ears before adjusting her cloak around her shoulders. "Um . . . What about Majesty? Or would you like me to call you—"

"Just call me Riven, please," he said with a barely stifled sigh. But when he saw how uncertain she was, he gave a firm squeeze to her shoulder and smiled encouragingly. "I prefer Riven from the people I enjoy being around. Just pretend like you don't know I'm Gluttony's reincarnation. Forget everything my sister said when she was in bitch mode. It was certainly uncalled-for, and I'm sorry she said those things to you."

Kara stuttered in her response. "I w-would never consider your sister a bitch! Please don't—"

"Well, she was certainly being a bitch then, regardless of whether or not you want to say it," Riven replied without hesitating. "I'll talk to her about it next time I see her, even if you won't be there to see it. Just know that it's coming, and that I am truly sorry for her putting you on the spot like that. She of all people has little to no room to talk about the things she said."

A Storm Lance smashed into a gigantic squid that tried to leap out of the water as one of his totems activated, and the corpse sprayed viscera all over the yacht. Riven barely had time to deflect the bulk of it with an ice shield, but he heard cursing and screams of disgust in the background, which made him cackle a bit.

Kara stared, wide-eyed and horrified, at the remnants of the titanic squid now plastered against the shield, but Riven flung it away a second later and she regained her composure. "Riven, do you feel completely at ease right now?"

"Yes."

She paused. "How does it feel?"

"How does what feel?"

"Being completely in control of situations like this all the time."

"All the time?! Ha! Definitely not the case, my friend. Definitely not." Riven shook his head. "I am the supreme victim of happenstance through my life, and in many aspects I simply got lucky. I'd say that 50 percent of what I've done is because of me, and 50 percent of what I've done is because of the heritage I have and the people I have come to know."

"That could be said for most if not all people."

Riven thought about it and gave a cheeky smile. "Yeah, I suppose you're right!"

She gave him a momentarily flat look, then burst into laughter at his expression and waved a hand in front of her face. "I should probably get to why I came to talk to you, then."

"Yes. You should. You look like it's been eating you up inside."

Kara grimaced. "More or less. Ever since I found out I had to come here with my father's demands to reach Floor Forty or be disowned, I've had something of a life crisis. I thought I'd die in that room two floors back until you found me and helped me for no reason."

"It wasn't for no reason."

"Riven, please be real with me."

"I am. Everyone has a reason for doing the things they do."

"And what was yours? Boredom?" Kara replied with a sour expression. "Or was I just another pretty face to take advantage of?"

Riven's expression fell, and his words came out with a hint of sadness. "I really hope you don't think that."

Kara, for her part, looked shocked that she'd even said it and quickly hid her face behind her hands. "I didn't mean it. I apologize. If someone like you wanted to take advantage of me, you could do it a million different ways. There's no way I could stop you and no reason for you to hide it behind nice words. There'd be no reason to gift me this bow you'd created, as if you hadn't just made an absolutely amazing weapon many would kill for in the course of a few minutes. You wouldn't have spent three billion coins on me, either, a sum that could bankrupt my entire clan, in order to save my life. I just am not used to people being kind to me, not since my mother died. It's easy to snap, and it wasn't long ago that I'd felt like I'd lost my mind, and I even tried to kill you because I just assumed you were the same vampire who'd stolen my things. I was and still am a complete mess."

Riven stared ahead, focusing on the oncoming ocean that continued to pass them by at high speed. "There's nothing to forgive. I'm not angry."

"Really?"

"Yes, really. If anything, I feel bad for you. Outside of you trying to stab me when we first met, of course!" He winked when she began to laugh, causing her to hide her face again. "But you're beating around the bush, so to speak. What did you really want to talk about?"

Kara let out a long sigh. "My father had sent me here with the demand that I reach Floor Forty or be disowned by the family. It was essentially a death sentence, due to political pressure from Zafima's mother, as we talked about before. It was in that moment that I realized . . . that I realized no one truly cares about me."

Her voice cracked with a stifled sob. "No one. No one left in my family cared. No one in the entire world, the universe, or even the multiverse cared about Kara Blackbow. Not until you, a complete stranger, came along and showed me the smallest bit of kindness, and that was after I tried to stab you."

Her words petered out, and she sniffled while wiping at her eyes. "I just . . . I want you to know that I appreciate what you did. And that if I can ever repay the favor to you, I will. But I don't know how someone as worthless as me could ever help someone like you, a prince of an S-grade faction and the idolized reincarnation of an original sin that demonkind literally worships! I tried thinking of things that I could do to show you what it meant to me, but everything that I thought of seemed absolutely futile and meaningless in the end. I thought about trying to help you to the end of the Abyssal Descent, but I would only be a burden and would essentially be freeloading off your power, because there's no way I could make it by myself. I thought about trying to pay you back—in small amounts, over many decades—so that our clan could save face, but it'd take generations to do so and there's no chance my father would agree for someone as lowly as me. I thought about becoming your thrall, but I can't stomach the idea of my mind not being my own. I thought that if I did turn into a thrall, it would be spitting in your face after you'd gone out of your way to save me, especially after I overheard you say something along those lines on the last floor. That in turn made me even more certain that I wanted to pay you back somehow, and I thought that perhaps showing you how I felt through making love would be an appropriate expression of my feelings . . . but even that is a farce. There's no way I could compete with Athela and Fay, and they seemed to be more interested in me than you were when we—"

"To be fair," Riven cut her off with a raised hand, "I thoroughly enjoyed it. Don't think I didn't. But yes, I'm emotionally invested in those two and barely know you. I think you're playing me up as the hero a bit too much here."

"But you ARE a hero! To me!" Kara said with a wide smile and wet eyes. She clasped her hands in front of her. "What may seem like something small to you is literally life-changing for someone like me. And you're the only person in this entire cosmos that has taken the time and energy to help me."

"You're going to make me blush, woman. Please don't do that."

Kara choked back a laugh but managed to shake her head in exasperation with an eye roll. "By the gods. You are truly something else. What I am trying to say, Riven, oh great reincarnation of Gluttony, is that I have only come up with two means of ever paying you back. And I want you to choose one."

Riven skeptically pooched his lips. "Uh-huh. And what would those two means be? Pitch it to me straight."

Kara blinked away more tears. "I want to be your sacrifice at the last altar like Prince Rantali told you to—"

"Absolutely fucking not." Riven nearly stopped the boat to smack the dumb bitch. "I nearly stopped this boat to smack you, dumb bitch! Do you think that I went through all this just to kill your depressed ass?! No! NO! I already said that you're not getting sacrificed, so don't pitch that stupid bullshit again or I really will stop this motherfucking boat and smack a ho. This is you going back to crazy-mode Kara, like the one where you tried to stab me for looking like another vampire asshat even though I look FAR better than that asshat vampire who stole all your shit!"

Kara blinked at the slew of cursing and insults, but merely giggled instead of getting offended. "Fine. But if you don't do that, then the only other option I see is to let me work for you until my life debt is paid, in whatever way I can."

"Kara, be realistic, there's no way I can get you back to my world from here."

"You're Gluttony's reincarnation and a prince of the Blood Moon Requiem. You already spent three billion to save my life. There are less expensive means of traversing universes, so of course you can."

Riven thought about it.

Was she right? He had no idea how traversing universes worked.

But yeah, she was probably right. With his connections, he could probably get it done. He even had a few items on him that may be able to do it. But why would he?

He stopped to stare at her, as she continued to silently cry with a happy smile, on her knees with her hands clasped pleadingly in front of her. She'd been sent here to die by her own family. In that moment, he realized that she truly had nothing. Nothing but the idea that he gave an inkling of a shit about her, when literally no one else did.

It broke his heart.

Letting out a groan and rubbing the bridge of his nose, he exhaled with a wheeze. "Fine. I'll consider it, but no promises."

"REALLY?!"

"Yes, but I'm only taking you on as a friend. Okay? Don't get any ideas."

Her gaze softened and her hands fell to her lap. "All I was wanting was a friend."

Goddamn it, he needed to harden himself by eating more people so shit like this didn't tug at his heart like she was doing right now. She was just so fucking pitiful!

"There are a few ways I can think of off the top of my head," Riven eventually said after a long bout of silence. "First is we could try to add you to the guild and have you access the guild hall feature to teleport home. Second is my staff can create portals to places I've already portaled through, such as my world, Panu, at Riven's Eye Wormhole. But I'm not convinced either of those options are enough to traverse across universes. Third is I could always hire someone to take you there by ship, but that'd take a long time, I'd have to pull a lot of favors, and it may be unsafe. Yet again, I don't know if any of that will actually work. I'll have to think about this, but I'll try to get it done before we leave the descent."

Her lips quivered and she nodded before lunging forward and throwing her arms around him in a bear hug. "Thanks."

"Yeah, no problem. Now let me go before you make me cry, too. The reincarnation of Gluttony isn't supposed to cry. I'm just supposed to kill and eat things and look badass."

She sputtered a laugh, squeezed him hard one more time, and did as he asked by letting go. "You don't know what this means to me—"

"I said shut up and go away, didn't I?! You're making me get emotional! Less QQ and more pew pew! Go away—Athela probably wants to hit on you and try to bed you again anyways."

Smiling wide, Kara yet again shut up and gave him a firm shoulder squeeze like he'd done to her earlier. Then she stood, brushed against him one last time, and left the front of the boat to go sit next to Athela farther back.

[You have entered the pocket realm of Floor Twenty-Two: Ocean of Wrath. You have been designated team leader of Team DEEZ NUTZ. Your objectives are simple: survive the monster attacks for at least twenty-four hours while traveling over or through the ocean of blood. Acquire gifts from the sacrificial altars, where opportunities to enhance your gifts will be presented to you should you decide to take them at the last altar, where contact may also be established

with outside entities to help to further your goals at a price. You must touch all three altars from Floor Twenty-Two in order to proceed to Floor Twenty-Three. The majority of identification information will continue to be unavailable until Floor Forty.]

[You have touched two of three sacrificial altars, accepting two Blood Tokens to be used at the very last sacrificial altar without having taken the opportunity to sacrifice any of your party members. You have stolen eighteen Blood Tokens from a rival team. You have three mandatory hours left to spend on this floor.]

The third and final sacrificial altar was straight ahead, looming over them like a spire from hell that flowed up into the sky, where a flat platform was waiting for them, just like the others. It, too, was covered in a shield that prevented people from flying to the top, meaning that a straight walk was the only way to get up there. At the very least, the spiral staircase was huge and big enough for demons even Azmoth's size in his larger form to traverse, so it wasn't cramped.

"Everyone off," Riven called, parking the ice yacht next to the spiral staircase. "And no funny business. Athela, I'm looking at you."

"I'm an angel! Figuratively speaking, of course!" She made a heart symbol with her hands and put on an innocent face.

"That's a gods-damned lie and you know it! Now, move that ass of yours before I have Azmoth carry you!"

Azmoth let out an evil laugh and cracked his knuckles.

Athela grumbled and stuck her tongue out at both of them, but jogged off the yacht along with the others as they all started up the staircase that wound around the altar's tower. Unfortunately, he heard the telltale thuds of heartbeats far overhead and was quick to inform the others that there may be another group waiting in ambush, or just passing through. Either way, given how this entire floor revolved around sacrificing other people for blood tokens to exchange for prizes at the end, it wouldn't surprise Riven at all if they came across campers. They'd already seen it once before.

"Azmoth, to the front, buddy. Possible ambush ahead—take your giant form. Athela, you're in second, and when we get near the top, scout for traps. Retesh, Genua, Fay, and Kara, to the back with me as usual."

"Azmoth likes ambushes!" he replied, shoving ahead of the other vampires and Retesh, who more than happily gave up their spots at the lead in order to let the bigger, far tankier demon take any hits thrown their way. Azmoth then began to morph, his bones and armor cracking and snapping with a rush of flames as he became many times larger, eventually presenting at about fifty feet in height with his wings, appendages, and shields all following suit.

The lich, archer, and two support mages quickly adjusted their own spots in line, letting Athela take second place. Prince Rantali and the other warriors took the middle, just ahead of the casters, while Riven kept guard at their flank, with Kara's bow having locked in the arrows Riven made for her from Blood Lances, and Fay holding her grimoire tight against her chest.

Around and around the spiraling staircase they went, higher and higher as the ocean below became smaller.

It wasn't long before the sound of battle cries and metal on metal ripped through the air, as arrows and spears rained down the staircase near the last third of the way up. The curve didn't allow Riven to see who was attacking his largest archdemon, but sparks of the projectiles continued to skid off Azmoth's huge frame and the shields he'd brought up in front of him. Athela hadn't even had time to get ahead at this point, but she didn't care as she vanished into thin air with a malevolent laugh.

"SHIELD WALL!" Prince Rantali roared as he and the three vampire knights next to him all slammed their shields into the spiral staircase floor and projected four large barriers ahead of them, protecting themselves and the casters behind.

An explosion of green Unholy light rocked the spire, pushing Azmoth back a single step before he roared and rushed ahead with a burst of flame.

"Keep going, we're right behind you," Riven called out to Prince Rantali in his tacky set of golden armor, and the other vampire quickly acknowledged this by passing the order along to his men as they kept the projected barrier shields out in front of them and proceeded up the stairs.

Screams and the echoes of battle filled the stairway, and Athela had no doubt joined in the fray up ahead as screams of "MONSTROUS DRIDER" and "TWO ARCHDEMONS" filled the hallway, alongside the remains of multiple enemies now smashed against the walls, ceiling, and floors.

But there were too many of them to be just one group, and Riven's hearing confirmed it as more and more heartbeats started filling the stairway from above. Now that they were closer, he could tell the individual beats apart, whereas earlier and farther below it'd been hard to do so.

Interesting. They continued to march, and slowly but surely the battle came into view.

It wasn't one group, but dozens or even hundreds. That, or someone in the enemy camp had some kind of minion ability or enslaving power, but identification information didn't work here, so he couldn't be quite sure. Regardless, his two massive archdemons were being piled with attacks on the enormous stairway by dozens of other descenders, who hurled curses, projectiles, lightning strikes, and fireballs in a vain attempt to bring Athela and Azmoth down. The descenders seemed rather weak, though, far weaker than many of the other groups that'd been present. That didn't mean their enemies were weak by normal standards, but by descent standards? Absolutely. Their numbers made up for it, but in a one-to-one match they'd be rather poor in the power category.

Retesh clicked his bony fingers together and raised his staff to start absorbing ambient mana into its gemstone. "Go!"

From behind their group, the dozens of bone wyrms Retesh had created earlier began swarming up the stairs. The lich then proceeded to raise his hands out to either side, and from thin air, siege weapons of familiar make began to take form. They were large, strange, cone-shaped things made from bone that glowed with green and teal energy within the holes at their tops. They looked almost like spiraling seashells with an evil twist, and they were the same creations that Retesh had used to attack Riven back on Floor Two's boss fight, when Riven had had to fight off his entire team to win it. Cannonballs of miasma quickly formed within the cores of each of these siege engines, and within moments there were dozens of the miasmic projectiles flashing overhead and into the enemy lines. From what Riven could gather, each of these siege weapons were actually attacks from the lich himself, as they were drawing on his own mana, given the rippling mana signatures in the air between them. But the attacks were being concentrated and empowered with whatever the creations or skill did, exemplifying their explosive power and range.

"Genua, unleash your aura for passive healing and smite any motherfucker who comes too close. Are you able to concentrate it on Athela and Azmoth?"

"Yes, I'll concentrate the effects on them. The aura will also damage any enemies within its effect and give them bleeding debuff stacks."

"Good. Prince Rantali, if you want to go ahead and fight, you can. I'll be staying back here to make sure the other casters are safe. Otherwise you can keep the barriers up and just watch."

"We're fine watching, thanks!"

Riven chuckled at the man's remark. "Fine. Kara, try to snipe as many of their casters as you can."

"Um . . . Okay! B-but there are so many! How do I know who to target?!" she replied, her arrow literally shaking in her grip as she drew it up and aimed at one of the distant wizards throwing useless lightning bolts at Azmoth's back as he stomped through the enemy crowds, leaving carnage in his wake.

Riven exchanged a look with Fay and then put a hand on Kara's shoulder. "Steady yourself. Take in a few deep breaths and pretend this is just a shooting range. There's no reason to be scared."

She shifted her gray eyes to stare at him wordlessly, but hardened her jaw and tried to stop the shaking. It only worked partly, but it was better than previously. Riven didn't know how she'd made it to level 200 with that kind of mindset, and was curious what her story was. He'd have to ask later, but nerves could be fixed.

"Are you going to help?" she asked sheepishly. "With the fight?"

He smiled. "Only if needed. It's time to pull your weight! Now shoot!"

He watched the arrow fly overhead, and it did end up hitting someone, though it certainly wasn't her target. Instead it was an armored, tanky chaos dwarf with burning black eyes, who let off a howl of pain as the arrow ripped through his shoulder and sent him spiraling down a few steps.

"Good," Riven said, patting her on the back encouragingly and moving on.

Fay, for her part, had already set up a wide swath of curse traps in front of their back line and was setting them off farther ahead into enemy lines. They were far more powerful now that she'd become an archdemon, with the flashing runes lighting up and blowing away multiple people at a time as she lazily pointed to spots she wanted to eradicate. A dreamwalker zone was also in effect, making enemies see them at odd angles or not at all depending on where they stood, as their projectiles fired wide and way off the mark well over half the time.

"Riven, do you mind if I go collect some specimens?" Fay asked casually, keeping her eyes ahead but beginning to transform as her greater succubus traits began to manifest. Her horns changed from small, pointy ones to long, curling goat's horns wrapping around the sides of her head, forcing her to take off her hat. Her tail began to turn from black to blue and grew neon blades down its center with a long, pointed stinger at its end. "May I?"

"Specimens of what?"

"Enemies. It has to do with my new insight and ability."

"You're not going to tell me more?"

"Not unless you force me to! It's a surprise!"

Riven pursed his lips. "Then go right ahead, but be careful! You never know when some asshole is going to bring out one of those swords that almost killed Athela back on Panu, and we surely aren't the only ones that have such a thing. You're not as sturdy as the other two archdemons and I get worried that—"

"You worry about me too much! Ha-ha, but that's why I adore you!" She covered his mouth with a hand, blushing, and gave his forehead a nuzzle with her nose before laughing again and taking off with a quick flap of her wings. "I'll be right back!"

Coating herself in illusory magic, she headed into the fray and disappeared entirely, though there were signs of her progress as people were sliced apart and skewered by something invisible or, in some stranger cases, they disappeared entirely.

Just what exactly was she collecting from them?

And what was this surprise she was talking about?

Riven really hadn't the faintest clue. It would have helped if she told him what her ability was, but he wasn't about to spoil the surprise that Athela and Fay were concocting behind the scenes. In some ways, he was a little bit excited to see whatever it was.

CHAPTER 9

One would have thought that Fay overpowering other level 200s while simultaneously not killing them outright was a hard task without Athela's help. Fay's core skill set was based in illusion and trickery, centered around her curse traps and dreamwalker zone. However, she was also adept in many utility-based skills, two of which were Silvertongue and Charm. They only worked on enemies far weaker than herself, with poor Willpower, but these idiots fit that bill to a tee.

"It would mean so much to me if you dropped your weapons, darling . . ." the succubus said with a wide smile and glowing pink eyes as she infused the charm into her selected target while keeping their area invisible to the rest of the battlefield. Soothing words dripped off her tongue, infusing the command into her target's soul to add on to the prior effect and compound it. "And put these on . . . before taking this potion."

[Charm (Depravity): Infatuate any enemies within range of sight that look upon you when activating this ability, causing them to lose focus. The farther away they are from you, the less effect this ability will have. The more Willpower the enemy has, the less effect this ability will have. Channeling ability that costs increasing amounts of mana over time.]

[Silvertongue (Unholy Succubus Trait): Soak your words with Unholy mana to briefly capture the minds of lesser beings, allowing only those with a less Willpower than you to be affected and enabling you to persuade them more easily. This spell scales with both Willpower and negative Charisma, as well as the amount of mana you put into it. As a Greater Succubus, this is an inherent trait that works even better on those attracted to females. Moderately high mana cost, low cooldown.]

"Y-yes, Mistress!" the entranced, white-scaled draconic man replied as he took the energy-suppression manacles and helped shackle himself. "Perhaps we will have time alone after this, to speak and—"

"Yes, of course, darling. We'll have all the time in the world!" Fay said sweetly, patting his cheek and leading his hands to the uncapped potion that sparkled with an eerie gray light. "Now, drink, and go lie down with the others there. We can talk later."

The draconic man she'd seduced relaxed the spines across his scaled neck, sighed while staring puppy-dog eyes at her, and drank the potion she'd given him before lumbering over to the two other passed-out bodies on the floor.

Taking care to expand her dreamwalker zone farther on as Athela and Azmoth continued to slaughter these unusually weak descenders up the stairwell Fay thoughtfully frowned. There was something odd about the entire situation, but at the same time, it also meant that she had a far easier experience charming and controlling them. Given that she now had three quite rare variants captured, with the last of them drifting off into a dreamless sleep via the potion she'd just given the man, she wasn't going to complain. She'd immediately gone for the species that were far rarer on Panu, ones that they'd not have the opportunity to find and capture there, given that Riven would need a wide spread of blood types for his furthered bloodline expansions. They also needed to be mortal. This excluded demons, angels, and undead, but left most of the other races open for grabs.

The draconic warrior with white scales was the last she'd take. Sleeping next to him was a witch of a rare merhuman variant Fay hadn't ever seen before, with deep-yellow skin, purple eyes and hair, webs between her fingers, and gills along her neck. The witch had been the easiest to subdue. The first target she'd acquired was a half-ogre barbarian of some kind, though he was so mutilated that Fay wouldn't be surprised if he died before Riven got a chance to taste his blood.

Despite this, she opened the portal after making sure all their shackles were fastened and shoved them inside with her hands and tail, closing the prison realm of Fay's Dreamscape Dungeon with a pop.

"All in a day's work!" she said while slapping her hands together to brush off the muck from strenuously pushing the half ogre inside. "Now, where did that smexy Riven get off to?!"

He was still in the back line and hadn't used any of his own spells or aura control at all yet. He still wanted to see what his Shadow-Blood storm aura's empowering effects had on his minions, but that could wait for a fight that didn't make him want to yawn.

Riven was both thoroughly impressed with his own team and thoroughly disgusted with the lack of fighting prowess this other side had. Were they intentionally throwing bodies at him to wear his mana down? Did they even know it was him? Because he had an unlimited amount of ambient blood mana at his disposal on this floor. How was a team like this supposed to surpass this or any of the lower descent floors?

Watching Athela and Azmoth slaughter everything in their path with Fay and Genua supporting them was like watching kids ruthlessly stomp through an ant pile. The rampaging archdemons were even making it a contest, seeing who could kill in the most extreme displays of gore and violence. Their enemies fought back furiously but did little to no damage, often missing their targets thanks to Fay's illusions, and what damage did manage to hit them was quickly healed by woven threads of blood mists that circled their side of the battlefield thanks to Genua's new passive aura. Riven literally didn't need to do a damn thing, and it was also good practice for Kara. Because despite these opponents not being on par with him or his archdemons, or even his thrall, they were on par with the drow archer.

He leaned on his staff and glanced over at the still-shaky dark elf, who'd grown slightly more confident while firing arrows now that she realized she probably wasn't in any danger. She was still traumatized from the time she'd nearly been eaten by that monster two floors ago, right before Riven had saved her, and it showed. Perhaps she'd be better working at the guild as a bartender or maid rather than a warrior. She didn't have the heart for it, unless things changed. That, or maybe she'd just need babysitting for a while and could join Hakim's team for lower-level and less dangerous missions should the guild take any on in the future. He certainly didn't see himself remaining king of the necropolis long-term, or perhaps only in name. Allie would be the one running it. The more he thought about the potentials of guild life, with adventuring and small jobs and perhaps some off-world excursions together like this, the more he liked it.

Jackal's flaming eye sockets in its horned skull suddenly flared with intense brightness for no apparent reason, getting Riven's attention with a surprised raise of the eyebrows. "Everything okay, buddy?"

The staff quivered in his hands again and then remained still once more.

"Well, that's odd." Riven scratched his head. That certainly wasn't normal, but not being able to talk to the staff was something of a hassle. Even in its demonic canine form, it wasn't much of a conversationalist. It had a baseline consciousness and intelligence, but smarts weren't really in its repertoire. Even Messenger, the armor covering Riven from the bridge of his nose down to his toes, was more responsive when it came to questions, where the gluttonous maw across his chest would open up and occasionally point to things with its tendrils. Basic things that it wanted to eat, like bodies or cheese or pie.

Usually it was bodies that were too far off for it to grab without Riven flying over.

"Doing a great job, guys!" Riven called over the screams, explosions, and clashing of metal as he pulled out a pipe and casually watched the slaughterfest on the enormous spiral staircase. "Lookin' good!"

"You lazy asshole!" Genua laughed with a side-eye underneath her blood priestess hood and head ornament. She was becoming more and more obviously pregnant as the days went on and kept her hands underneath her belly while cycling divinity into her aura that leaked into the clouds above. Those same aura clouds powered by her faith stat both healed his tanks and peeled the skin off her enemies.

Riven smirked underneath Messenger's facemask, picked up Jackal and twirled it about in one hand while checking the rear for any potential interlopers coming up behind them. "This is a good experience for you, Genua! I don't know what you mean by 'lazy asshole,' and it's considered rather rude for a vampire's thralls to call them out like that!"

He pointed Jackal's skull top in the direction of her aura's clouds. "By the way, those are pretty damn potent! I'm impressed!"

"It is all thanks to you, Master. And the Blood God, of course." Genua bowed her head in respect. "I am glad that our children have such a good father figure!"

Our children?

Was she talking about Len alongside the unborn child?

Riven immediately felt a bit queasy and slightly uncomfortable. He knew that Genua had been wanting him to adopt Len, and he certainly would if that's what she wanted. He owed it to them, especially to Len, for having killed her real father and her big sister. But that was only if Len would accept him in that role, a role that Genua apparently already mentally placed him in despite the few talks they'd had about needing to sit down with Len about it first.

It'd been hard enough having that initial talk back in the woods near Hakim's cabin, when Riven had first admitted to Len that he'd been the one to kill them. It didn't help his case very much that it'd been somewhat in self-defense—Len had thought him strong enough to choose between different options of what he could have done instead. She was also right. If Riven had wanted to, he probably could have done it a different way and let Ethel live despite Ethel's attempt to kill him. Maybe. Probably. He didn't know for sure, but it was definitely a possibility he'd ruled out at the time in favor of Azmoth's suicide bomb in order to make sure that bastard Prophet had died.

"Genua . . ." Riven said, coming to stand next to her as he lowered his voice for a more private conversation, given the line of vampires and the drow archer still next to them. "I'm still not sure Len is going to accept me as her dad. We should probably hold off on assuming that she will until we have that talk with her."

Genua looked very confused and turned ninety degrees to look at him with rapidly blinking red eyes. "Hmm? I don't understand what you mean by that. You're her father!"

Riven's polite smile dropped into a more stoic frown. "Genua, seriously. I told you that I'd adopt her, but—"

"Adopt her?" Genua asked again, even more confused as she furrowed her brows, and then began to laugh with a singsong chime to her voice. She lifted one of her hands off her belly and tugged at his left cheek lovingly, which was very strange behavior coming from the high elf thrall. "Riven! Stop joking around! You're her biological father, just like the child I carry now. Stop being so silly!"

"Eh . . . What?" Messenger's face mask withdrew to reveal his entire face, and he aggressively scratched his chin with narrowed eyes. "Genua, is this some kind of prank?"

"What do you mean, dear?" she said, completely straight-faced with a flush to her cheeks. "You're asking really weird questions. I should be asking the same of you! What are you going on about, with adopting Len? Oh, those memories of the day I gave birth still ring clear to me. Don't you remember it, too?! Can you believe it's been so long and how much she's grown up since then?! I vividly remember the day that Len was born—how could I forget! You were with me in Greenstalk Village nearly seven years ago now, before our planet merged into Panu. You held my hand and told me that the birthing women would be late to help as they were at another delivery, and so you had to talk me through it for half the time I was in labor!"

Riven's eyes went from narrowed to wide with shock, and he felt a lump starting to form in his throat. "Oh . . . Eh, er, hmm. Genua? Are you sure that memory was with me?"

Genua frowned, and then shoved one of his shoulders a bit irritatedly after realizing he was serious. "Riven, it actually kind of makes me angry that you don't remember that day. That's a core memory for me, for us. Do you seriously not remember Len's birth? I hope for your sake that you don't ever tell her that. It'd break her heart."

His skin began to feel clammy and cold and he began to try formulating what the next question would be. The question that he dreaded to ask, but he had to do it. "Genua . . . that memory was probably with the man named Farrod. Your ex-husband, the man that I—"

"I was NEVER married to anyone else!" Genua hissed violently, eyes widening in a menacing fashion as divinity sputtered along her body. It was a reaction so fierce and so abrupt that she almost reached out as if to strike him, but she regained her composure less than two seconds later, returning to the free-spirited version of herself that she'd presented over the last couple of days. "Don't be silly! You've always been my husband!"

The battle continued to rage around them, and she returned to looking ahead, concentrating on healing after Riven remained speechless for the next ten seconds.

His voice came out as a whisper when he did decide to speak, and his hand gripped Jackal's shaft to the point that his knuckles were turning white underneath the ivory plating and bloodsilk threads of the armor he wore. "Do you remember Ethel? Do you remember your other daughter, Ethel?"

Genua once again furrowed her brows in confusion, then stared at him long and hard. "I've never had another daughter. WE have never had another daughter, Riven. It's only been Len, and the child I'm now pregnant with. I'm beginning to tire of these asinine questions, Riven. Please, don't make jokes like this again. It's beginning to bother me."

Riven was shocked. Dumbfounded. A mixture of emotions swirled up inside him and he couldn't put into words just what that mixture all meant to him. He wanted to cry, to sink down into a hole and never come out again. All the talks he'd ever had about thralls and how they were mind slaves were one thing on paper, and he'd even seen the results firsthand as Genua had gone from hate, to acceptance, to liking him, and eventually, to lusting after him—and even seeing him as her husband now.

It was not only fucking weird, but it was fucking sad. And he was to blame, even if she had been the one to ask for this. Perhaps this was what she had wanted, to forget the family members he'd murdered. But to him, it was a new weight put on his shoulders, knowledge that Ethel in particular would be forever forgotten by the mother who'd once loved her, due to a vampiric virus that raged in Genua's body and through her mind.

Worse yet was that Len was not a thrall and would forever remember her big sister and father. What would Len have to say when she realized that her mom didn't recognize the names of Ethel and Farrod anymore?

What the fuck?

What the actual fuck?

Just what the fuck had he done? When had the transition gone from persuasive to an absolute override of memories? When had that happened? He hadn't even known that it WOULD happen!

Nodding stoically, he turned to leave, but was stopped when Genua reached out to grab his wrist.

"Dearest, don't look so sad! We're doing so well!" she said happily, drawing him in and giving him a peck on the cheek. "We'll get Lillith back in no time, and then we'll be able to go home and see Len again as a family! I'm sure she misses you! Maybe we can have a family baking night like we used to do back in the village, or we can all go fishing together! Don't you think?"

"Uh—um, yeah. That'd be . . . That'd be great." He tried to give an affectionate peck back but needed to pull away quickly after while wiping at his eyes. "I'm not sad, I just—I just have something in my eyes. Sorry."

Genua didn't look convinced, but let go of his wrist with another knowing side-eye. "Fine. Let me know if you wish to talk about it. I'm here for you, Master!"

Master?

Hadn't she just called him her husband? Hadn't she called him "dearest" just now?

Did she even know what she was saying anymore? Or did she think that he was both husband and master now?

Jesus Christ.

"Absolutely, Genua. Keep up the good work. You're doing great, and know that I appreciate the effort."

Five minutes later, Fay returned. They'd gained ground, but these enemies hadn't given up yet despite massive losses. Riven was convinced that there was some kind of portal up above producing them, given the constant stream of opponents, and he was even more convinced that these were not normal descent contestants given their lacking power, which raised the question of where they were coming from and who they were.

More than that, though, was the knowledge that he'd been very thoroughly mistaken about what thralls actually were and what vampiric venom containing his mind-altering virus could do. He had underestimated just how vampirism affected a thrall's mind, and what it meant to truly be a mind slave.

"Genua's really performing out there! Just look at how fast Azmoth's gash healed a moment ago!" Fay exclaimed, whooping and cheering on her comrades in the front lines. "GET THEM, GUYS! YES, TEAR OFF THEIR LIMBS, JUST LIKE THAT! MAKE THEM SQUEAL! STOMP THEM INTO THE GROUND AND TURN THEM INTO PASTE!"

The succubus nudged Riven eagerly. "Damn, Azmoth is really having fun with this! But back to Genua. Do you think that perhaps we could get you to make an entire squad of thralls? She's far superior to most thralls I've seen, and I'm pretty sure it's because you're a pureblood. That, or Gluttony has something to do with it. My lord Gluttony? Would you happen to know?"

Gluttony's maw erupted in space next to them. "No, my child. This is my first-ever reincarnation, and though vampires do contain many of the traits I desire, such as the need to feed and a high affinity for blood, I am afraid I don't know much about this particular subject."

"Hmm . . ." Fay said, tapping her blue lips as Gluttony disappeared again and bobbing her horned head from side to side. "Well, either way, the quality of your thralls is on another level. You should seriously put together an elite squad for your own personal guard! I know you have the willpower to do it."

Riven half-heartedly smiled back at her, still leaning hard on Jackal's shaft while his mind went into overdrive at the implications of what Genua's conversation now meant to him, and what it meant should he ever decide to acquire more thralls in the future. He let out a shallow breath. "Yeah. They'd be pretty powerful."

"Right?!" Fay exclaimed happily while bobbing up and down on her toes, tail slapping against the floor. "OOOOooooh, it'd be so cool! Just imagining going back to Panu with an entire set of ten or however many thralls you can get before leaving here, all of them at level 200 or above, all of them with a taste of your own powerful bloodline and just absolutely CRUSHING the other top-ten rankers on the power board! You'd be unstoppable. That's it! That's the answer."

She harrumphed, making her large breasts protrude and arching her back with a sage nod. "It'll be a plan for the ages! What do you think about starting now? . . . Riven? Riven? Hello?"

Fay waved her grimoire in front of his face a few times to get his attention. "Planet Fay to Riven?! Are you there?!"

"Yeah. I'm here. I'm just deep in thought, sorry, babe. I apologize." He pulled her into a firm side hug, beginning to scratch the back of her head and around her horns just like she liked.

She shuddered in ecstasy and melted into his embrace with a drawn-out, happy sigh. "Yes, this is the stuff. You need to do this more often."

"Anything you want, Fay. I'd be more than happy to give you some of those full-body massages again."

"Those full-body massages always turn into—"

"Yeah, and you like it when it does!"

"Fair point." She elbowed him in the side as the two of them started to laugh. "There we go! There's my happy Riven again! So what do you think about the thrall squad idea?!"

Riven considered it for a while and clicked his tongue. "I've very recently had some unexpected insights concerning thralls. Yes, Genua is a great asset to the team now . . . but I would never want to turn people who didn't deserve it. Not after what . . . Eh, for another time maybe. But yes, I'm fine with the idea, as long as they're terrible people."

"Terrible people?" Fay repeated, hands on her hips while squinting her eyes. "What does that mean? By what definition is someone terrible?"

"People that have done horrible and cruel things needlessly. Use your imagination." He held up a finger. "Or people that have outright attacked us that we'd kill anyways. Such as these guys."

He gestured to the crowd of oncoming enemies that continued to die like flies.

She clapped her hands excitedly in front of her and began to hop up and down again. "Great! Great, that's awesome to hear! Did you want me to capture one now for you?"

Riven shook his head and dismissed the notion with only a single glance upward, stepping over some mangled bodies on the way and picking up one of the spatial sacks the vampires and Kara had missed while looting. "Nah. We have no way to take them with us to the next floor, do we? Unless we drag them along as captives and use them to fill our own party, but then we'd have to look after them on the descent down and that'd be tiring."

Fay gave him a sheepish grin. "Right! Of course, of course . . . If only we had some way of transporting fifty or so prisoners in an alternate dimension or something. Wouldn't that be nice?!"

Riven chuckled and smacked her hand away as she tried to grope his ass. "It'd be great. Maybe one day we can find an item like that. It'd be nice to hold prisoners there for me to eat and feed on, or for changing them into thralls over the long term. I wonder if something like that is on the Elysium markets? If so it's gotta be expensive, but I haven't even heard of anything like that around."

Fay became pink in the cheeks again and let out a long whistle. "Yeah . . . it'd certainly be nice. Oh, look! There's the top of the stairway! Maybe we can finally get off this damnable floor and on to the next one. I'm a little bit interested to see just how many people are still up there after having killed so many on the way up the stairs!"

CHAPTER 10

The top platform beyond the stairway was finally in sight, and Riven had been correct. There was a portal of some kind spitting out enemies on the opposite side of where the main sacrificial altar was, but watching it was very odd.

The portal wasn't like any he'd ever seen before. It was more like a flat pool of blood about thirty feet around, perfectly circular, that continuously took the shapes of these people and their belongings. The process took more than thirty seconds for each person to form, and even after his team had killed them down to the last man, they would not talk unless he or Fay used their Silvertongue abilities on the targets. Even then, they seemed to have no recollection of who they were, why they were attacking him, or how they'd gotten here. But every time they released their hold on the enemy in question, that enemy would go into a rage and try attacking them again without any self-preservation in mind.

"This is troubling," Prince Rantali said as yet another of the people formed from the blood pool was wasted by one of Retesh's stave blasts. "There is no mention of such a thing in the documents provided for me by my kingdom. I think that this would have been of particular note because of how this floor has remained the same over the course of many ages."

"Do you think it leads somewhere else? Or is it a new addition to the floor?" one of the vampiric knights asked thoughtfully. "We could—HEY!"

The shackled, bald prisoner in rags that Prince Rantali had been dragging along to feed on quickly dashed toward the blood pool with a scream of defiance. "I WILL NOT BECOME ONE OF YOUR THRALLS!"

With a splash, the man landed in the pool and began to sink. Riven wasn't sure if he'd expected to go through to the other side after the knight's comment, or if the possibility of a two-way portal had given light to the prisoner's escape attempt, but it didn't matter because it didn't work. Within mere seconds, they heard thrashing and screaming from the pool of blood as the man tried to get back out, his face peeking over the top just twice as everyone else just watched, before a large brown leech rose up out of the liquid and chomped down on the man's skull. The beast sucked the poor guy back down into the depths and quickly disappeared as a new enemy began to slowly form out of the blood once more.

"I know what this is," Genua said, surprising the others as they focused their attention on the blood priestess. "Or what it once was."

She knelt beside the pool and dipped her hand into the liquid without fear, though Riven took a step forward and placed himself next to her to make sure she wasn't dragged down like the other guy.

Reaching in farther, all the way up to her shoulder, whispering to the pool like a mother would a child, she eventually withdrew her arm. On her palm, the enormous leech that'd eaten the prior man had perched its head, and it let her pet it as the enormous monster purred like a cat receiving an ear scratch.

"This was a pool of atonement, stolen from the Blood God's realm, but it is now corrupted in a way that I cannot quite understand and carries the scent of blasphemy. It was once a powerful artifact meant to collect and keep damned souls, nurturing them into servants for the Blood God. And it should not be here . . ." she said, letting the leech sink back to the depths after another whispered word, watching the creature slip back into the inky red. She cocked her head to one side as if worried and then glanced back at Riven next to her. "My connection to the Blood God was . . . It was just cut off."

"What do you mean, it was cut off?!" Prince Rantali asked, suddenly frantic and panicked. "A priestess of the Blood God cannot simply have their connection cut without the intervention of another god, or a being equal to—"

Prince Rantali's words were muted as a massive geyser of blood erupted from the pool to swallow Riven whole. It pushed away his allies and overpowered him entirely, suppressing Riven's aura like one would snuff out the life of a fly by smashing it between one's fingers. Riven writhed and kicked but was quickly pulled away into the swirling red pool before anyone could do anything about it.

In an instant, his reality shifted.

Riven was staring back out at his friends, none of whom could enter the pool now. He could only see them as they frantically attempted to break through, but it was an absolute and impenetrable barrier. His hands touched the silky-smooth exterior, once again trying to press forward and infusing his mana into the effort, but nothing came. Even Athela's mind link that they used for speech once in a while wasn't working.

"This indeed appears to be a warped S-grade artifact that is somehow linked to the Abyssal Descent's Floor Twenty-Two," Gluttony said from within Riven's soul. "I don't think that we are meant to break out by brute force. But I also don't believe this was put here by Elysium accidentally—it has likely been part of this floor for eons and was made to appear only if certain criteria were met. There will be a way out; the laws of balance concerning Elysium's trials demand it. We merely need to find out what that way out is and why we were separated from the others and cast into this item."

His eyes widened. What was an S-grade artifact doing here of all places, in an F-grade soul lattice–building event? Entire D-, C-, B-, and A-grade nations far more powerful than the Thane Necropolis would commit genocide to get their hands on something like this. Riven gave a once-over to his surroundings to make sure nothing was coming for him. There were a few leeches the size of his arm or bigger swimming around, and one as big as a passenger airplane, but they all ignored him entirely. One even brushed up against his arm but did not attack. There were also speckled lights farther in the depths that he couldn't make out from here in detail, and the relatively small barrier between the artifact's insides and the Abyssal Descent on the opposite side, but that was it.

"Curious," Riven muttered, speaking through the blood without issue. To others it may have been toxic, or would have drowned them, but he could breathe this stuff as if it was air infused with energy. "I really need to make a bath like this back home."

Gluttony laughed, and Riven began to draw out a message in shadow along the interior of the barrier. "I am going to explore. I'll be back."

Then, grinning, he added, "Team Deez Nutz ain't scurd."

The attempt at humor landed poorly, despite Athela being the one to come up with the original team name.

Athela and Fay both appeared to be frantically yelling and trying to break through, while Prince Rantali and the others looked nervous. Everyone except Genua, that was, who remained calm and nodded to let him know the message was received.

And honestly he couldn't blame her. If anything, the others were overreacting, he was literally surrounded by the type of mana that he had a 100 percent affinity for, and he was nearly unkillable in this kind of environment as long as nothing beyond the E-grade was waiting for him here. Or perhaps that was overconfidence speaking?

Though the thought that this was supposed to be an S-grade artifact was not encouraging. Riven had acquired all this power, enough to destroy entire cities, in the F-grade. C-grades could theoretically wipe out populations of entire planets when on a rampage, and S-grades could obliterate the planet entirely if it wasn't reinforced somehow. He didn't let his minions know what he was dealing with, though, because Athela looked like she was already having a panic attack on the other side.

Waving and turning around, Riven began to swim farther into the depths.

That was when he got the notification that made him rather curious about what he'd find here. It seemed that Elysium, or whoever had placed this here, didn't want the gods peeking.

[An extra formation against outside spying has been added to the ones already in place during the Abyssal Descent. Twelve SSS-grade layer formations of antisight, magical penetration rebuff, antidivination, karma-cutting, and antiseeding have been added to this artifact's interior. You have been cleansed of all potential tracers, child of Blood.]

"How . . . strangely familiar . . ." Riven said, touching down on a sandy bottom indicating the ocean's floor. Whether this ocean was part of the artifact, part of Floor Twenty-Two, or part of both, Riven couldn't be certain, but that wasn't the part that he recognized.

In front of him was a gigantic cylindrical hole, carved from the bedrock, that led down into the earth. In and along the cylinder were the swirling lights of souls, millions of them, in glowing spiritual clouds so thick that despite the giant chasm leading downward, he couldn't see what was at the far end. Were these the souls that'd been leaking out of the blood pool into the other side?

Riven thought yes. It was the only explanation that made sense, and he was able to read the basic outline of what the enchantments around these souls could do. Each of them was ready to be taken out and molded into a true shape, enslaved beings ready to be given form. The enchantments layering each of these bright souls like painted orbs were similar to the vampiric thrall markings along Genua's own soul core realm, but they had a stark difference. When Genua had become a blood priestess, some of those markings had manifested on her skin, expressing themselves as sigils of power that bound her more tightly to the Blood subpillar. But these . . .

These markings were familiar in a way that reminded Riven of the runic language seen during Allie's descent into the underdark, when she'd found the vampiric precursors. She'd only discussed it once, but had copied out many of the runic markings to see if he perhaps had a better understanding of what they meant, given he was linked more closely to the Blood subpillar than she was, and sometimes the pillars spoke to their users. Riven hadn't had such a moment then, but now, as he looked at the swirling mass of souls, he was beginning to have that experience here.

The sea of blood around him contracted, forcing itself into his body little by little, and visions began to appear one by one.

The images that came and went in the blink of an eye rapidly cycled through his thoughts as the Blood subpillar itself reached out and touched him. Images that he didn't quite comprehend at times. Riven saw the Blood subpillar split into five pieces, with four of them being hidden in different corners of a dark expanse as the fifth fragment came up into the light. He saw raging wars as entire civilizations were eradicated, fighting over the different pieces as eons passed by. He even saw Gluttony being born from Blood, and, eons later, watched Gluttony claim one of the fragments for himself, dragging it into his abyssal maw to swallow it whole. Then, the last image of significance was the rise of the Blood God, resting on a throne carved from the flesh of other gods that'd competed for his mantle. Riven couldn't quite make out what the Blood God looked like, but the instinctual knowledge that this was the new supremacy over the Blood subpillar was as clear as day.

Other images were less impactful and less meaningful. It was all genocides, wars, and slaughter. Fuel for the fire as the Blood subpillar took a new shape from whence it'd been sundered.

He snapped out of the trance and immediately called out to Gluttony. "Did you see that?"

The sin's reply was quick. "Yes."

"What do they mean? You were a part of one of the visions, and . . ." Riven's voice trailed off expectantly.

"It is unfortunate, but that aspect of my knowledge has been carved from me," Gluttony said sourly. "Part of the pact with Elysium was that I lose not only power, but knowledge regarding many of my past exploits. I only vaguely remember finding that shard in a previous lifetime, but what I did with it or how it came to be, I do not know. However, I will send a message to my priests in the enclaves after we leave the Abyssal Descent, and will ask them if they know anything about the Blood subpillar's sundering, or the five pieces it had split into. It feels . . . important. As if a piece of not only the pillar, but me, is missing after having looked upon the vision. I hadn't even recalled it at all up until now . . ."

Riven growled a curse at Elysium under his breath. "All right. Time to swim through the clouds of souls?"

"It appears to be the way forward, so yes. Unless you'd rather sit here and, as you say, 'twiddle your thumbs.' I don't know what twiddling is and I don't think you do, either, but I'm beginning to like Earth-human sayings."

Riven chuckled, not confirming or denying the accusation of lacking such knowledge, and without delay he leaped into the chasm to begin diving again.

The blood flowed around him, embracing him as he sped past the entangled souls at a steady pace. As time went on, the cylindrical chasm began to turn from sand to stone, with the same odd runic language that held aspects of Blood affinity, yet they were different from the type of Blood he was used to. Regardless of this, his subpillar still sang to him every time he saw such a marking, with the pillar itself expressing to him that these were part of a whole he hadn't known existed.

Was this why Genua had said this place had the taint of blasphemy? Why would the current Blood God want to keep knowledge like this hidden, if that was the case? Why would Elysium put this here, a hidden part of an otherwise constant floor in the Abyssal Descent? Why had it appeared only for him, with no mention of it in Prince Rantali's records?

"Gluttony . . . I have a question about my thrall. I was hoping you could help," Riven said as he flowed through the undercurrents with the ease and grace of a fish.

Gluttony already knew what he was about to ask. "You were hoping you could restore Genua's memories."

"That's exactly right."

"Possible, but it would be a hard thing to do. The vampiric virus you injected her with is meant to override any thoughts, impulses, or obligations that counteract being your loyal servant. It creates the perfect, obedient, adoring slave to your will, only leaving behind the remnants of the original person that do not conflict with your own desires or interests. As I have previously stated, I have not had much experience with vampires before. Your kind were created by a pantheon of gods long lost to time, the same ones who created the precursors your sister talked about. I have also lost much of my previous knowledge after being released from my abyssal prison, so even if I did once know more, I have no knowledge of it now. But my theory is that it could be reversible if you found a way to reprogram the viruses. That, in turn, would require a significant knowledge set on not only the Blood subpillar, but how vampires were created in the first place and how the virus works."

Gluttony paused. "But why would you want to reverse it? This is what Genua wanted. She was in turmoil, and now she is happy. Would you really deprive her of that, just to make your guilt less of a burden? As I see it, you have done her a favor. Ignorance, in this case, is bliss. So unless you can somehow find Ethel's likely hibernating soul in the black beyond of existence, somewhere in the immeasurable void that spans realities, and return her soul back to this realm, it would be in Genua's best interest to keep her this way. Not even I at the very peak of my power would have found that an easy task to perform, even if I'd been given a trillion years to do it. Not after the souls have been mixed into infinity and scattered to the winds, and it becomes dangerous when you begin to dive into the deeper realms of existence where even the darkness of the void is gone and only madness thrives."

That . . . didn't sound creepy at all. Nope, not one bit.

"It just feels wrong, and I feel terrible about it. Especially for her daughter Len."

"Until there is an opportunity to fix it, which is questionable at best, you should not dwell on such things. It may be impossible to fix, but if you wish to do so, only worry about it when the opportunity to repair what is broken presents itself. And right now, I believe we have bigger problems than whether or not your pet thrall remembers her dead daughter."

Riven was about to ask what Gluttony meant when the clouds of souls in front of him parted.

It was . . . a tomb?

Riven had come to an end of the cylindrical drop, but before him was an open cavern that spanned miles, its entire outer perimeter lined with hundreds of thousands of coffins. They each had their own platform jutting out of the walls, with the same strange sigils expressing Blood affinity that didn't match what he had come to know of his own Blood subpillar. Yet his pillar continued to scream at him, wanting him to touch these markings and devour their essence, to repair what had once been lost. There was also a gargantuan crystal statue at the far end of an enormous blue-shelled clam with a small but vibrant red orb shimmering in its half-open mouth.

The orb . . . now that caught his attention. Even given its relatively tiny size at such a long distance away, the purity it contained was godlike and burned in his mana sense like a sun amid an otherwise desolate tundra.

Energy resonated out of it that was spectacular, pure, refined to a point that he could barely stop himself from salivating. It whispered to him across the currents, wanting to be taken, and promised power should he do so.

"What is that?" Riven asked, his fangs extended in excitement as his eyes went wide. "That orb about a mile from here . . . I want it."

He pushed forward, making straight for the open mouth of the clam. But the second Riven floated a couple feet into the vast chasm before him, the runic sigils on all the coffins turned from red to a deep blue. A strange aura began to permeate the area as the ground began to tremble in an earthquake. The entrance into the chasm was abruptly sealed shut with a thick white light reminiscent of the times he'd had the dungeon boss battle with the satyr warlord in Negrada, or when he'd faced off against the giant rat monster and the invaders near Hakim's hometown, and a notification displayed itself.

```
===========================================================
```

WARNING
WARNING
WARNING
HIDDEN TRIAL BOSS FIGHT: BLUEBLOOD PRECURSOR CLAM HAS BEEN INITIATED.
ELYSIUM HAS SEALED OFF YOUR POINT OF EXIT UNTIL THE BATTLE IS COMPLETE.

SPECIAL EVENT: THE CLAM'S PEARL IS A CONDENSED AND FILTERED BLOOD MAGIC RELIC PROCESSED OVER THE COURSE OF TWENTY-THREE TRILLION YEARS, WITH THREE OF FIVE PATHS FOR THE SUBPILLAR OF BLOOD STILL LINGERING INSIDE THE PEARL'S CORE. IF YOU OBTAIN THIS TREASURE WITHOUT DAMAGING IT, THE BOONS IT WILL PROVIDE YOU INTO THE TRUE NATURE OF THE BLOOD SUBPILLAR ARE NEARLY UNPARALLELED. WARNING: THE CLAM'S PEARL IS CONSIDERED A TABOO, HERETICAL ARTIFACT BY THE CURRENT BLOOD GOD.

BEGINNING BATTLE IN
5 . . .
4 . . .
3 . . .
2 . . .
1 . . .

```
===========================================================
```

The blue crystal statue of the clam snapped shut to create a sonic boom that scattered sand and stone, and the runes along the coffins on the walls all exploded simultaneously with ripping torrents of power shooting out toward the clam at high speed and increasing velocity. The clam grew in size, rapidly becoming larger than a football stadium, its shell warping and the ruby light from the orb it held beginning to blind Riven with its brightness. Cracks along the tomb's bottom ripped into fissures, and blue ribbons of power began seeping from the fissures and formed along the edges of the clam's mouth.

But the aura was just oppressive, and it crashed into Riven like a tidal wave. He was thrown back in a rush, slamming into the white barrier Elysium had sealed him in with, and he struggled to stay conscious as his mind was assaulted by an alien presence. It was unlike any other he had encountered to date, completely enraged and on an entirely different level from any opponent he'd ever fought before.

He was caught completely by surprise given just how powerful this monster was, and fear began to settle into the back of his mind. Bones in his face and ribs started to crack under the immense pressure, and his lungs were being squished. Was this creature even F-grade? It had to be at the very least at peak E-grade, or possibly even early D-grade. But he had few comparisons when it came to the D-grade and couldn't be certain. Despite all the blood mana around Riven fueling his body in an endless torrent of extra power, he simply couldn't detach himself from the wall due to the pressure as he fought back with his own aura, spiraling tendrils of dark storm twisting into crimson folds of ice as his eyes flashed bright red. Jackal came up in front of him of its own accord and he flooded mana into the staff, increasing its potency while he used it as a shield of sorts against the blue ribbons of power continuing to crush him like a frog under a boot. His totems immediately began to crack and dissolve when he brought them out, so he quickly deposited them back into his spatial sack when he saw they'd be of no use, but that goddamned aura the clam produced was just unfathomably powerful. It was also as in tune with the Blood subpillar as Riven, and was perhaps even more complete in its synergy, given his recent understanding that he was truly lacking insights into what the Blood subpillar had been in previous eras.

With a scream of determination and as red cracks started glowing and spiderwebbing out from his eyes, Riven roared in defiance and lifted Jackal up high through their mental connection.

The storm answered.

Thunderclouds of red and black erupted from his position, spitting out Black Lightning and needlelike projectiles in all directions as whirlwinds of shadow caressed the area around him. The stone walls shattered and groaned. The ocean between himself and the clam began to freeze sporadically in chunks, and Elysium's barrier that he'd been pressed up against rapidly began to frost.

"I will not die here!" Riven hissed through bared fangs, and with herculean effort, he managed to peel himself off the wall bit by bit and limb by limb.

Fighting with everything he had, he pushed harder than he ever had before as his own aura slammed into the opponent's blue tide. The passives of both combatants crackled and roared, tearing at each other like beasts coming to reincarnate themselves amid the sea of blood that was tossed about with rabid ferociousness.

A voice echoed out from the clam, a booming laugh that didn't sound human at all. Nor did it sound demonic. Rather, it sounded simply foreign, alien, like the ancient sea creature's very will itself.

"I have waited for untold amounts of time, lingering in the hidden depths of the Abyssal Descent in hopes that one of the multiverse's best young talents would trigger Elysium's promise. Long has it been since a promising child of Blood has made it to my lair, and longer still since one withstood the test of my aura. But today, I feel something different in you. Now, finally, I may be put to rest . . . Come, vampire, and show me that you are worthy of my secrets! That you are worthy of pursuing the path of recreating that which has been broken, and unchaining your race from the shackles of the traitorous throne!"

CHAPTER 11

He pushed himself to his absolute limit just to stay upright under the massive amounts of pressure the clam's aura was exerting. The mere action of lifting his head against a force that could crush mountains was strenuous, but his own aura was maintaining its hold.

Profane Blessing of the Crow exploded around Riven's body to enhance his speed and stamina with wisps of red and black trailing off his skin, shimmering amid the storm as he raised his staff toward the beast. Dozens of Critical Storm Lances bloomed around him, drawing back on tightening Wretched Snares that prepared them for launch. Thousands of Gluttonous Storm Razors erupted in a swirling vortex, spinning their blades at extreme speeds while rotating around his position. Black Lightning strikes snapped out at random amid a booming roar produced by his aura's storm, and pillars of crystallized red ice began growing up through the chasm all around him.

Finally at an equilibrium with the aggressive foreign energy trying to crush him, Riven breathed normally. His mind sank into a state of Zen, becoming one with the blood around him, as he fed upon the ambient energy in big swaths of intake that flooded his soul pillar like a tidal wave.

"This is a peak E-grade monster," Gluttony said in Riven's mind. "Almost at the cusp of evolving more. Be wary, it will not be an easy fight, and I don't want to lose my prized new host to an early death."

Riven was thinking the same thing. His life was truly on the line this time, and despite his greed at wanting that blasphemous pearl in the clam's mouth, he decided to take the risk of summoning his Legionaries from the Blood God's realm anyways.

The pearl wasn't good to him if he was dead. And the wards here might very well block the Blood God from seeing inside even if he did summon the Legionaries.

Riven grunted his acknowledgment to Gluttony's information, let go of Jackal so it hovered in front of him, then smashed both his hands together. As he tore them apart with strings of blood and death mana ripping through space between his fingers, eight flashes of light appeared, four to either side of where he floated.

[Legionaries of the Blood God (Death/Blood) (Tier 2): This is a temporary summoning spell that does not require minion slots. You may summon up to eight Elite-class Bloodstricken Undead from the Blood God's realm, equal in combat level to your own, and may designate whether or not you wish to summon Blood Knights, Blood Sorcerers, Blood Assassins, or a combination of the three when you do so. Undead are nonsentient and last for five minutes before disappearing. One-day cooldown time. Very high mana cost.]

[Summoned Blood Sorcerer, Bloodstricken Undead, Level 200 ELITE]
[Summoned Blood Sorcerer, Bloodstricken Undead, Level 200 ELITE]
[Summoned Blood Sorcerer, Bloodstricken Undead, Level 200 ELITE]
[Summoned Blood Sorcerer, Bloodstricken Undead, Level 200 ELITE]
[Summoned Blood Sorcerer, Bloodstricken Undead, Level 200 ELITE]
[Summoned Blood Sorcerer, Bloodstricken Undead, Level 200 ELITE]
[Summoned Blood Sorcerer, Bloodstricken Undead, Level 200 ELITE]
[Summoned Blood Sorcerer, Bloodstricken Undead, Level 200 ELITE]

Eight hooded skulls, their foreheads etched with Unholy crimson runes, stared with crimson orbs for eyes in their sockets. All eight sorcerers wore crimson robes with shifting black runic sigils and held staves with ruby orbs that flickered with blood mana. He only ever used this spell when he was in truly dire need, and now was as good a time as any to get them onboard.

Yet the clam before him seemed content just to watch and wait, up until this point only having unleashed its aura that continued to pound into his own with continued furiosity.

"I have not seen bloodstricken in quite some time," the clam mused, rumbling from its position on the floor in the miles-wide chasm. "But they are not enough."

Then the clam moved.

The stadium-sized beast launched itself off the stone floor, rocketing toward Riven as its mouth closed down tight. Blue ribbons trailed out behind it to propel it forward as its shell gained a solid layer of protective power.

"SHIT!"

Riven unleashed his own attack to stall the monster's advance. Arcs of Black Lightning rumbled throughout the storm clouds and veered toward his opponent with thunderous booms. Enormous pillars of ice surged up and forward to crash into the oncoming clam like a train, exploding with crystallized shrapnel and clouds of frost when they buckled under the pressure. The needlelike rain oriented itself to hail down on the clam as it pushed forward. Gluttonous Storm Razors smashed and cracked through the top layers of the clam's barrier defenses, adding corrosive Sin afflictions with each strike that continued to stack by the thousands.

But still the clam continued to fly through the ocean unhindered, despite large chunks of its barrier tearing off and burning away under the assault.

Riven tore a black hole through space behind himself and each of his sorcerer summons just before the clam made impact, teleporting them and their mass of gathering lances all via riftwalk as a crash resounded on the opposite side of the room. Debris and rubble began raining down from the ceiling and walls where Riven had just been, where the clam had created an enormous crater along the back, and underneath it all, an exposed additional layer of Elysium's seal could be seen under the rock layers. This entire chasm likely had the seal underneath the outer rim.

If Riven had stayed where he was, he would have been utterly crushed.

Raising his free hand, Riven clenched his fist and detonated all the razors still embedded in the clam's remnant barrier.

[Gluttonous Storm Razors (Blood/Shadow/Sin): All your Storm Razors will acquire stacking gluttonous afflictions upon impact. This affliction slowly eats away and corrodes your enemy over time as Sin damage unless dispelled, and the affliction can stack. Should you decide to detonate a selected razor, that detonation will burn through the nearby afflictions as fuel for an additional burst of Sin damage.]

The monster's defenses were torn asunder in a flash of purple light, launching pieces of solidified mana in all directions as Riven grinned. "Fire!"

His sorcerers all followed his command, each shooting off somewhere between ten and twenty Blood Lances each that raced across the chasm at high speed with piercing tips. Riven's own Critical Storm Lances were far faster given the imbuement of Snipe and the propulsion of the slingshot snares attached at their backs, and the crackling black arcs of lightning and blood trailing behind them started to attack the residual mana of the clam's aura in explosive strikes.

CRASH

Dozens of Riven's lances blurred forward and made impact, piercing through the rebuilding barriers the clam was constructing on the fly and tearing through into the clam's shell. The monster made a rumbling noise and continued its turn toward him, though seemingly unbothered by the attack as it completely ignored the other, lesser Blood Lances that his summons were firing. Some of the normal Blood Lances flung by his summoned sorcerers didn't even pierce the barrier at all as it rebuilt itself, and others that did manage to break through the barrier didn't manage to proceed farther into the shell, shattering when they made contact. He silently thanked his lucky stars that his own lances had a serious piercing upgrade with his latest evolution, and realized that his sorcerers would be somewhat useless against this opponent outside of simply draining its mana barrier by knocking chunks off.

[<u>Critical Storm Lance (Blood/Shadow)</u>**: Your third evolution of
Blood Lances are now wreathed in double the amount of Black
Lightning as they previously were, have twice the flight speed, travel
50% farther when imbued with Snipe, and leave trails of lingering
Black and Red storm energy in their flight paths that can strike out
at enemies for a short time should they get too close. Chance for
armor-piercing strikes and critical strike damage are both drastically
increased with this evolution.]**

"This thing is an absolute tank!"
CRACK-SNAP-WHOOSH
Three sorcerers on his left collapsed in on themselves amid the loud snapping
of reinforced bones when a swirling orb of blue blood tore a hole in the ocean
like a gravity well. They didn't last more than a second, putting up minimal
resistance before they were snuffed out like flies.

If it wasn't for Riven's enhanced reflexes under Blessing of the Crow, he
would have likely met a similar fate when another one of those blue gravity wells
appeared right in front of him, too, sucking all the blood in the area into a concentrated pit of devouring magic.

He flashed backward, using Messenger's flight to further reinforce the power
he was putting into manipulating the environment around him for faster movement. A series of barriers from his sorcerers engulfed two more of the gravity
wells that popped up in adjacent areas he was soaring through, delaying and
containing the clam's mana long enough for Riven and the other casters to get
out of the way.

He dodged, riftwalked, and spun around to return fire when his eyes went
wide and his jaw dropped.

From the shell of the creature a mile from his position, large bumps the
size of hills were forming. Those bumps were opening up with charged energy
underneath the hard outer layer with a power spike that was rapidly increasing
to surpass even his own maximum output.
WHOOMPH
KABOOM
In the blink of an eye, the clam discharged, and it was like watching a
futuristic battleship unleash an entire payload all at once. An intake of ambient
blood mana caused the clam's shell to expand and then contract, releasing tens
of thousands of short, pointed missiles that blew apart the area surrounding the
clam in their expansion. Riven watched in horror as tens of thousands turned into
hundreds of thousands, and his gut sank more when all those missiles that'd been
expanding out in all directions simultaneously turned to home in on his location.

They were locked on.

"Holy shit . . ."

"MOVE!" Gluttony screamed as the missiles began to pick up velocity, each breaking the sound barrier with individual sonic booms that shattered space in between the clam and Riven with a maelstrom of ear-shattering sound.

Riven immediately opened another rift, only for the clam to let out a pulse from its shell, creating the visage of a blue moon behind the clam like a sunrise peeking over the horizon. Riven's rift shut down instantly, and his horror mounted as a system notification appeared.

[You have been afflicted with the debuff <u>Blood Curse of the Blue Moon's Exchange</u>. This debuff can only be active on a single target and a single ability, at the cost of 10% of the caster's maximum Health. Blueblood Precursor Clam has paid the blood price and has selected Riftwalk as its chosen ability to lock down during this curse's duration of thirty minutes. This curse cannot be dispelled by any means below the caster's own grade, the maximum health lost by the caster cannot be healed for thirty minutes, nor can the caster reuse this curse for sixty minutes.]

"WHAT KIND OF BULLSHITTERY IS THAT?! THE BASTARD JUST GIMPED ME!"

The enemy's barrage was beyond Riven's maximum output. Gravity wells were appearing around his position to trap him inside the area. And thirty minutes of not using Riftwalk was a nail in the coffin he was about to be buried in after he was ripped apart by the mountain of missiles headed right at him.

His sorcerers attempted to stall the oncoming barrage in a valiant sacrifice to save him, but they were wiped out like flies before a tsunami. Riven cycled the vast majority of his mana into one singular ability sigil on his pillars, eradicating all his forming missiles in a quick gambit for speed. Profane Blessing of the Crow exploded with energy as the soul sigil was fed to maximum capacity, causing Riven's muscles to bulge and tear before rapidly repairing themselves as he turned to flee.

Innumerable missiles bore down on his location, his body radiated with energy as his aura continued to battle the ever-oppressive clam's will, and it was suddenly game time.

Riven rocketed backward with an earth-shattering explosion of mana that eradicated all the closest missiles in a shock wave of energy as he rushed headlong into the forming storm clouds of his aura.

The missiles followed.

He ducked and wove, using Jackal's passively stored energy reserves to blast more of the enemy missiles as icy pillars rose up from the ground to intercept the wave of carnage homing in on his body. Black Lightning strikes with enormous twisters of shadow and red ice crackled and boomed, tearing apart hundreds of the speeding torpedoes that actively tried to swerve around these obstacles while trailing his flight.

Riven considered his options.

His summons were gone, and he couldn't call on any of his other minions, either—he'd just tried again, to no avail. Blood Nova was something he was keeping in reserve given its cooldown, and if he was given the opportunity, it could possibly even be a finishing move due to the empowering effect the ambient blood mana would have on his explosive projectile spell. Blaze of Profane Glory would have been a good option if he wasn't literally swimming through an ocean of blood right now. He guessed that the flames would do SOMETHING but might be snuffed out rather fast given the potent, wet environment of almost purely foreign mana when regarding the Infernal subpillar.

He banked left when he came up against the wall, still thinking fast as he felt an impending series of missiles at the forefront come within range.

CRACK-SNAP-CRASH

Messenger's left spiked gauntlet whipped out to literally punch the speeding projectiles before contact, and Riven's right hand used Jackal to bat them away with explosions of hellfire on contact with each strike. Watching the ambient blood mana snuff out Jackal's passive fiery blasts with each smack, he was doubly sure that Blaze of Profane Glory would be a no-go.

CRACK-CRACK-CRACK-CRACK-CRACK-CRACK-CRACK

Stone exploded behind him as if the wall had been hit by a Gatling gun, with shrapnel blasting out in a wave that followed his trail by mere meters despite traveling faster than the speed of sound. Dozens and then hundreds of missiles smashed into the stone wall he was speeding along, pressed up to it and flying by with only inches between himself and the outer perimeter as the storm of black and red raged overhead, a limitless hail of blue roaring through it. The storm filtered a good number of the missiles, but it wasn't as much as he'd like, considering his own aura storm was being suppressed by the clam's aura.

But the sieve effect wasn't insignificant. Passing through that storm with all the lightning strikes and twisters ravaging the barrage across black thunderclouds and deadly red hail, it reduced the number of threats by about a fourth.

What else could he do to get rid of these things? Surely the clam had used some kind of trump card—there was no way it could cast that ability twice. Even if it was peak E-grade.

Right?

If that wasn't the case, if Riven was wrong, he was rather fucked. But he had to think positive here and banked on the idea that the barrage the clam had sent was a onetime deal for the remainder of this fight. Attacks on that scale generally were single use with long cooldowns.

He needed to lead the projectiles repeatedly through his storm, through swaths of Wretched Snares, into swarms of his ravenous beetles, and across the paths of Critical Storm Lances with lingering energy trails until the bombardment was dealt with. Anything to whittle away the number of homing missiles hot on his ass. The key to this plan was making sure he didn't die before he'd exhausted the enemy's barrage, and giving that homing effect and that hundreds of thousands of missiles were currently locked onto him, it was going to be a rough patch.

Riven began to—

SMASH

His left arm was nearly ripped off in a spray of blood and tendon when a missile smashed through it and detonated. He was sent spinning, skipping like a stone on a lake until he came to a skidding halt half embedded in the rock wall. He also felt a cold sensation spreading up from the wound of his shoulder where Messenger had been mangled, and the flesh began to freeze as the blue discoloration wrapped itself along his blood vessels.

[You have been poisoned by Oathseeker Missile. Three stacks of Freeze Venom have been applied.]

That was only a single missile that'd landed, potent enough to tear through Sin-affiliated armor that was easily some of the best—if not the very best—that Panu had to offer. If any more of those missiles managed to hit him, Riven was very likely a goner.

Gluttony's soul projection intercepted the next oncoming swarm as his maw ripped through space and opened wide, black tendrils spilling out with a demonic roar. Riven was dazed but not completely out of it, and despite Gluttony taking out tens of thousands of the missiles by smashing them aside or swallowing them whole, Riven and Gluttony were still too weak at this stage to compete against the monster head-on.

Gluttony's visage evaporated with a shriek of rage when the barrage became too much, as his soul clone projection was banished back to Riven's inner realm.

But it'd given Riven time to get his bearings back.

"FfffffFFFFFFFFAAAAAAAAAAAAAA!!!!!"

His good hand gripped the mangled shoulder, fingers digging deep into the exposed wound. Withdrawing Messenger's extension at a mental command to his armor, he formed claws along his fingertips and ripped off his own left arm to stop the freezing poison from spreading farther.

The pain was extreme.

Panting and sealing the wound closed, he tossed aside his limb and blurred to the right, avoiding another series of impacts as the stone wall once again shattered like exploding glass in a trail behind him.

"I'M NOT DONE YET!" Riven yelled, laughing like a madman as the adrenaline spiked. He wove around another incoming formation of the barrage, twisting through five of them and smashing aside the rest with another explosive blow of Jackal while maintaining his extreme speed via Profane Blessing of the Crow.

His body was basically a nuclear reactor at this point, pumping out so much energy that his very skin was starting to peel off, and if not for his vampiric regeneration he'd probably be dead numerous times over. His eyes darted about, catching movement in his peripherals that he constantly dodged or blasted away. It was only when he had a moment to think clearly that he enacted his previously constructed plan and opened his mouth to unleash a swarm of ravenous beetles.

The insects erupted out of him like he was belching one of the plagues of Egypt. The Sin spell cast them out, projectile vomiting thousands of the tiny creatures that intercepted the missiles one by one in massive detonations and explosions as Riven continued to peel off and zigzag through the storm, with the lightning strikes, hail, and twisters continuing to batter the following blue torpedoes.

Numerous massive nets of Wretched Snares were cast out in clumps, expanding with sharpened, prickly black ropes that entangled entire clusters of the missiles to bring them down.

Critical Storm Lances were cast out at the clam's distant shell whenever he got a chance to peek at it through the absolute shitshow around him, leaving trailing ribbons of raw storm energy behind the supersonic projectiles of Blood and Shadow that struck out and lashed at the barrage, too.

Explosions and shrapnel went everywhere. It was all-encompassing, the part of the storm he found himself in, and it was absolutely maddening the kinds of maneuvers he was using to zip around giant pillars of crimson ice rising off the walls and floor. Those same pillars continued to shatter just as fast as they appeared, while the outer stone wall continued to detonate all around him in a massive roar of sound and fury.

This Floor Twenty-Two had been something of a joke up until now. Unfortunately, the way things were currently going, he'd be lucky to get out alive.

CHAPTER 12

Ten minutes of fighting passed him by, but those ten minutes felt like an eternity as death's door was hanging wide-open for him to drop in at any moment.

[Malignant Prophecy has activ—]
[Malignant Prophecy has been blocked.]
[Malignant Prophecy has been blocked.]
[Malignant Prophecy has been blocked.]
[Malignant Prophecy has been blocked.]

BLOCKED?!

Riven had known it was bad, but with Malignant Prophecy trying to intervene on his behalf AND being blocked? It was less than encouraging, so now he was truly pulling out all the stops as he tried different combinations and attack methods in a game of cat and mouse, where he now found himself in the position of a mouse. New gravity wells tried to catch him off guard and the clam would occasionally try to crush him with battering-ram style attacks whenever he seemed tied down by the missile barrage. The entire place looked like a madhouse of flashing lights and violent energies that constantly shook the underground chasm. With his left arm missing and regenerating at a far slower pace than what was normal, even for a grievous wound such as that, and with over half of the enemy's bombardment still trailing him through the storms and swarms and ribbons and snares, he couldn't wait any longer to take the fight to the enemy.

He had to go on the offensive, not just take potshots at it whenever an opening occurred. Thankfully his Gluttonous Storm Razors seemed to do some damage to the peak E-grade entity by stacking Sin afflictions that ate away at the giant clam's shell, and his Critical Storm Lances hit even harder with piercing effects, but they took longer to manifest than the swarms of razors he could summon with a snap of his fingers.

What really sucked was that Voodoo Doll, Hell's Armor, Blaze of Profane Glory, Black Lightning, and Legionaries of the Blood God all had either failed him in one way or the other, or simply didn't penetrate the clam's outer defenses. Riftwalk was sealed. Soul clone projections were down after Gluttony's main projection had been banished back into Riven's soul. His storm was great at taking out some of the incoming homing missiles but did only small amounts of damage to the clam's main body with the passive aura effect. Furious Storm's passive buildups from his staff worked to an extent, but only in moderate amounts and only at close range. Ravenous Beetle Swarm was very effective when the projected summons got close, but occasional pulses of blue energy would wipe them out whenever the swarm eating away at the clam's exterior became too prevalent. Unlike the razors, which left behind Sin afflictions even if they shattered, the beetles did more damage but were themselves needed to maintain a steady stream of said damage. The beetles were also slower than the razors and had a harder time catching the clam whenever it changed positions, because despite how large the thing was, the monster was certainly not slow.

There were the options of Gluttony's Aspect of Demonic Heritage, his Tier-3 Sin skill, as well as his Tier-3 Blood Nova for a hard hitter at range. The problem with these was that he had only a single shot at using either one of them for this battle given their significant cooldown times, and he wanted to wear the clam down if at all possible in order to make those skills count.

Funnily enough, though, despite the real danger to his life, Riven was beginning to have fun in a way that only extreme joyrides had given him in the past. He'd felt this way from time to time since the system had intervened in Earth's destiny, and he rarely got to go all out like he was now.

"COM'ERE, BIG BOY!"

He spun, smashing through homing missiles with storm energy that surged out from his kicking leg as he flung another Storm Lance in a trailing arc straight into the oncoming clam. Dodging another projectile and creating a nova of flame with his staff when it connected with the shell, Riven skidded along the gigantic creature's top layer and backflipped off it before reattaching himself to the clam with a Wretched Snare from where his arm stump was.

The immense speed of the clam's charge had sent the creature ripping through the ocean beneath him, and Riven was violently tugged along for the ride when his snare went tight. He crashed back down onto the scarred shell, pockmarked with abundant fissures and cracks.

One of those areas in particular was deeper and more riddled with damage than all the others.

In front of where Riven stood and exactly where he'd shot his last Storm Lance, there was a large crater in the clam that smoldered and crackled with remnant Sin and storm energy. A stark contrast to the deep-blue shell, the pit Riven was digging crackled with red and black and was a solid twenty yards deep and about twice that in diameter. It was the largest of a few areas he'd been working on during the battle, and if he could just get through the shell into the softer underside . . . That was when things would get real.

CRUNCH

The clam smashed into another wall of the cavern, sending stone chip debris flying everywhere in a cloud of hail.

He was flung forward, but the snare attaching him to the clam's back kept him tethered like a seat belt despite the tremendous force, and after he regained his footing, he turned with a wild look in his eyes to point his staff down into the nearby pit.

"I'LL BE TAKING THAT PEARL!"

[Furious Storm: This staff can passively build up charges of Furious Storm, which utilizes a supercharged dose of any single energy from the pillars of Sin, Unholy, Shadow, Death, Blood, and Infernal. You may only unleash one type of energy at a time. Power of Furious Storm depends on the amount of charge emitted.]

Riven's staff erupted with built-up energy at close range for the twelfth time, sending a healthy dose of Sin energy into the large crater with a beam of condensed purple light. The beam connected with the pit's bottom, a laser twice the size of his arm eating away at the clam's defenses and reinvigorating nearby gluttonous afflictions to further their corrosive effects.

"You are quite the pest . . ." the clam's alien voice muttered as its body began to pulse. "I can see why you were allowed to access this hidden trial. Elysium chose well, but your test is still not over—you must kill me first. A task I am afraid you still might not be up to."

The clam exploded with raw power, sending that strange, foreign blue blood mana crashing into its surroundings in all directions and hurling Riven's body toward the ceiling.

However, Riven had already encased himself in an orb of crystallized red ice. His storm roared around him, twisters and cyclones ripping apart the oncoming missiles and gravity wells as an enormous, charged Critical Storm Lance began to form along Riven's outstretched arm.

Black Lightning crackled along his limb with a red hiss as the lance began to form, and with a gesture and a flare of energy along his skin the lance grew to extreme proportions. It erupted off his body and condensed at high speed with a snap of energy, rocketing toward the largest of the craters with a resounding ***CRACK***.

A large piece of the shell shattered.

"HA-HAAAAAA!" Riven spun the staff in his remaining hand and smacked away another two missiles and dodged another three with a blur to the left, instantly creating a dome of ice around himself before layering it to withstand the impact of yet another two. "GOTCHA, BITCH!"

Snares tore through the air in swaths, lightning danced around him, and streams of energy swirled in the air behind trails of lances as he continued to snipe the clam while beginning to build up another swarm of Gluttonous Storm Razors. Pushing off the stone wall and landing on a platform of ice, he raced around a series of crimson pillars that sprang up from the walls and ground, maintaining a flight path on the side opposite the oncoming missiles tracking him. Pieces of the pillars ripped apart and sprayed in various directions with subsequent booms, and shifting his body weight while launching himself toward the turning clam's body, he shot the swarm of razors out toward the shell's crater again.

The crackling, spinning razors flashed forward, tinted with purple light while shredding through another barrier the clam tried to pull up.

Riven didn't have time to see how many of them had landed properly before he needed to speed away again as more of the nearby walls were evaporated in sprays of stone, and he raced into a nearby storm cloud to emerge out the other side.

Only to meet a long, fleshy tendril that slithered out from the clam's mouth and slapped him into the next century.

"UMPH!"

CRACK

BOOM

Like a speeding bullet he was sent smashing through two of his own crystallized pillars, through a chunk of detached wall, and cratering into the floor far below in a dramatic, earth-shattering crash.

"How does it feel to be hit with my appendage, vampire?" The clam laughed in a booming voice. "It has been too long since I've used it! Ah, the thrill of this battle is quite stimulating!"

Riven, still in the crater, sent out an enormous discharge of Black Lightning and sped away from the crater while circling back around. He cocked an eyebrow. "Appendage? The way you talk about it makes things sound quite iffy."

"If I am to believe this monster . . ." Gluttony said warily, "I believe he just smacked you with his penis."

"He did NOT! Clams don't even have those."

"He even used the word *stimulating.*"

"THAT WAS NOT A PENIS! It was just a strange, fleshy tendril or something!"

The clam let out another laugh. "What if I were to say that it WAS?!"

"THEN I'D SAY IT'S RATHER SMALL FOR A CLAM OF YOUR SIZE!" Riven's staff smashed through a gravity well right when it appeared beside him and he shot ahead through the storm, narrowly avoiding a sharp blade-shaped pulse of energy released from the clam's mouth when it opened wide.

Bubbles blasted out through the blood ocean, popping and sending Riven into a concussive nightmare that he only barely penetrated by condensing the mana around him into a sharpened cone. Ripping out the other side and seeing the wide-open mouth of the enormous clam in front of him, he was about to take a chance and send a Blood Nova inside when Gluttony intervened.

"UP!"

Gluttony tugged on Riven's body, forcing him to veer off course and only barely avoiding the snapping jaws of the clam when it lunged forward. The impact sent a shock wave of energy through Riven's body, but he rotated with his change of direction and blasted energy into his feet, causing him to rocket over the clam's dorsal shell again and straight toward the large crater he'd been working on all this time.

The fleshy tendril followed.

"Penis incoming," Gluttony commented, starting to feel a bit more confident about their chances now that the tide had very recently turned. Confident enough to make stupid jokes, anyway.

Riven was not amused as he crashed directly along the crater's perimeter and anchored himself again with another Wretched Snare, the sticky black ropes tying him down like an anchor. "That snakelike thing is not a fucking penis, dipshit!"

"That's not a very kind thing to say to your buddy, Riven."

"You're supposed to be the epitome of evil, but instead you're here making dick jokes!"

"I've just never had a reincarnation get slapped by a penis before—"

"YOU'VE NEVER BEEN REINCARNATED BEFORE, EITHER!" Riven ignored the laughter and sent yet another empowered lance directly into the deepened crater. The shell's bottom actually cracked all the way through this time with a small spray of flesh, and Riven threw up a pillar of Crimson Ice to skewer the large fleshy tendril racing toward him from the front of the clam's mouth, eliciting a pained roar from the monster he was currently latched to. "If ANYTHING, that is a tongue! Nefajia crecus Blood Nova!"

His hand released the staff and underwent the proper motions as he spoke the words, finally seeing an opportunity to dig all the way into the clam from the outside. The area around him shattered, trembled, and split. A huge shock wave smashed through the ocean and tore asunder all the nearby projectiles heading his way, followed by an enormous, condensed globe of swirling blood mana that vaporized the entire interior of the crater with tremendous force.

KABOOM

Riven's Wretched Snare tether snapped as he was thrown off by the impact of his own spell, but he took far less damage than the clam did. The fissure that'd been at the bottom of that crater was ripped open entirely, with fragments of shell and a purplish flesh underneath spraying out of the beast in dozens of house-sized chunks.

The clam let out a feral scream of rage and pain, whirling and spinning rapidly before crashing into the nearby wall again and then flopping onto the floor with yet another crash.

It was now or never.

[Gluttony's Aspect of Demonic Heritage (Sin) (Tier 3): A martial art that enhances you through the power of your fully formed Mark of the Sinner. Your body merges with your soul clone for one minute, allowing you to take on an ultimate demonic form as an aspect of the great maw. Very long cooldown, which can be reduced by killing and eating others.]

His body exploded as the tattoos along his skin all lit up from black to violet and Messenger ripped off his skin to fly into his spatial sack, making room for the change and taking Riven's cloak with it.

His arm grew back instantly. Muscles tore apart and rebuilt themselves. A long black tail sprouted from his backside; his bare chest split open to reveal a vertical gluttonous maw with razor-sharp teeth. Huge demonic horns sprouted from his head, and his hair receded to reveal pitch-black skin with glowing violet sigils emblazoned upon his skin, and his hands and feet exploded with claws. Legs snapped backward and grew larger, inverting like a T. rex, and spikes tore open across his spine while he grew to five times his normal height. Bone gaffs tore out of his kneecaps and elbows, and his teeth grew like knives.

Flapping four black and violet demonic wings many times his own height to gain momentum, his demonic body surged forward with a scream of feral rage. Thirty feet tall and well over a few thousand pounds, he extended his claws and torpedoed toward the open, gaping wound in the clam's shell.

It was time to finish this, and the glint in his eyes was a testament to the violence Riven was about to unleash on this absurdly tanky creature, even if it was the last thing he'd do.

The clam's voice echoed within the chasm as it opened its mouth to expose the pearl. "I . . . surrender."

==

CONGRATULATIONS
CONGRATULATIONS
CONGRATULATIONS
YOU HAVE DEFEATED THE HIDDEN TRIAL BOSS: BLUEBLOOD PRECURSOR CLAM. ELYSIUM HAS UNSEALED YOUR POINT OF EXIT. YOU NOW HAVE TWO CHOICES: FINISH THE BATTLE AND ATTEMPT TO KILL THE CLAM FULLY, GAINING FAVOR WITH THE BLOOD GOD, OR ACCEPT THE CLAM'S SURRENDER.

YOU MAY CLAIM THE CLAM'S PEARL NOW IF YOU WISH TO LET THE CLAM LIVE. SHOULD YOU CHOOSE TO GAIN FAVOR WITH THE BLOOD GOD FOR MORE HIDDEN PRIZES, PLEASE ACKNOWLEDGE YOUR WILLINGNESS TO

CONTINUE THE FIGHT NOW.

==

The missiles around him all exploded without preamble. The gravity wells disappeared, too, and the clam kept its mouth open with the shining pearl on its . . . tongue . . . in full view for Riven to take should he accept the surrender.

Riven paused midflight, veering left and flaring his wings to come to an abrupt—and quite surprised—stop. "Surrender in a boss fight? Is that even a thing?"

"Apparently for this trial, it is," Gluttony said. "That is an identifiable system message. Elysium does not lie about things like this. If it considers the battle complete, then it is complete, should you want to take this out."

Silence.

And then more silence.

Riven already knew what he was going to choose. Despite being royally pissed off at this monster that'd nearly crushed or eaten or blown him up a billion times, and even after having finally dealt some serious damage to the beast, he wasn't stupid enough to try and continue a fight that he had a very real chance of dying in, despite enjoying having gone all out for the first time in quite a while. Even if the odds were now in his favor, the clam wasn't something he'd want to tango with again anytime soon, and a way out was something Riven would be more than happy to take.

"You'll answer my questions if I agree?" Riven asked as the seconds on his transformation ticked by.

"Yes," the clam eventually said. "I will answer whatever it is you wish to ask, and you may have the pearl as promised. My surrender is absolute, and I find you a worthy contender for the task at hand. I wish to converse with you about what I'm tasked to do here and hope that we can come to terms before one of us is slain in prolonged battle. Please, accept my pearl and allow me to talk so that you may understand what treasure you truly hold in your grasp."

CHAPTER 13

[You have chosen to end the boss fight. The Blood God has not been made aware of what transpired here, per the agreement with the deceased gods of the previous Blood Pantheon. You have obtained the following rewards:]

[Prize 1]
[Trishard Blood Pearl (C-Grade Blasphemous Blood Artifact): This relic has condensed the affinities from three of five paths the subpillar of Blood may take, and has been impermanently bound to you, Riven Thane, as its new wielder. This item is shielded from the Blood God's farsight, detection, and scrying abilities, and will be viewed as a normal Blood artifact by all but the most powerful of his Blood clergy, Blood precursors, and the bearer of this item. This item holds long-lost and buried secrets of the Blood subpillar and is marked as an extremely taboo artifact by the current Blood God. Study and meditate on this item for further insights into powers now lost to all but the dead. +200% bonus to Dao insights regarding the Blood subpillar while meditating with this item in hand. Large amounts of blood mana of any type may be stored inside this Trishard Blood Pearl, and it creates ambient blood mana at a steady rate to either be used as stored mana or to be used to change environments. This item may be stored within your soul space at will. Must naturally be of 99% Blood affinity or more to properly wield this item.

- Supercharged Blood: Take an additional thirty seconds of channeling a Blood skill through this item to create a supercharged variant. This skill is incredibly potent, and overuse may damage your mana channels.

Within this item, secrets concerning the Supreme Path of Red and Black Domination, the Supreme Path of Blazing Azure Creation (Taboo), and the Supreme Path of Gold and Silver Stairways (Taboo) are present but hidden. Unlocking these secrets to their

fullest will add additional splitting pillar growths from your baseline
Blood subpillar within your soul realm.]

[Prize 2]
[**Blasphemous Enriched Blood Lake (Unique Guild Hall Add-On)**:
A large portion of the Blueblood Precursor Clam's realm has been
cut off from the Abyssal Descent and has been molded into a
hyperdense, energy-rich cultivation resource for you to use. This
lake will appear as a normal blood lake to any clergy of the Blood
God and may also provide an ample environment for growing
exotic Blood-affinity plants and Dao treasures. While the wielder
of this item meditates within or near the lake, the current Blood
God will be blind to any taboo experimentations and objects, and
abundant amounts of Blood energies will be available to your call.
The Blueblood Precursor Clam, along with the leech swarms of the
Abyssal Descent's Floor Twenty-Two, will reside within this lake and
are disguised from being blasphemous creatures while they remain
within or near the lake, and they will protect your guild hall with
their lives should it come under attack.
- **This add-on feature will be available to you at all times through
  any guild hall you own until used.]**

Riven held out his hand as Messenger wrapped around his body again, and he
shakily took the extended pearl from the clam's appendage with a gentle touch.
The pearl was only slightly larger than a baseball and was incredibly heavy to
the touch when he first grasped it given the extreme density of the mana within.
It was like holding a thousand nuclear bombs between his fingertips, and the
purity of the mana was like a supernova to his mana senses. Cycling blood mana
through it caused the item to float, though, and it hovered an inch off his open
palm.

He rolled it around in his hands for a time, admiring the absolute godlike
aura this item gave off. A C-grade artifact when he was only in the F-grade was
akin to giving a Stone Age tribe a military-grade bazooka to bring along to their
next scuffle, and though he could likely get better items from the Blood Moon
Requiem or the Church of Gluttony, would they be able to provide said items
that he could actually use right now?

Ninety-nine-point-nine-nine-nine percent of items like this one had
strict use requirements that prevented relatively weak people—like him in the
F-grade—from using immensely powerful artifacts. He knew not only because
of his own limited experiences, or due to the shopping at various conclaves, but
also because he'd discussed these ideas with Lillith. Before she'd been kidnapped
by the system, he'd very specifically asked Lillith for an SSS-grade weapon from
the church to use with Gluttony's upcoming second class, but she'd said that it'd

be impossible and was more likely to kill Riven upon trying to use it due to the severe gap in power, similar to how the ring had burned Riven back in Negrada's hellscape dungeon when he'd first tried it on so early in Chalgathi's trials. Be it level, stat, faction, pillar, or race requirements, or a combination of those things, most higher-grade items would have him out of the loop. But this C-grade one only had a 99 percent Blood affinity requirement, which for most people would be a far harder obstacle to overcome. But not for him. And on top of that, the real treasure here was the knowledge it could pass on to him should he learn about the three paths purified somewhere within the depths of this swirling orb.

Even now, he could see occasional flickers of blue in the deeper core of the pearl whenever the blood circulated certain ways, though he didn't see any signs of gold and silver. Not yet, anyway. Perhaps that would come later, or perhaps not. Perhaps it didn't have anything to do with those colors and was merely a play on words. He was looking forward to finding out, though, and was particularly curious about the single path that was not labeled as taboo by the Blood God: the Supreme Path of Red and Black Domination. Had he already started down this path with his more basic and likely far weaker Path of Red and Black? He was guessing yes, though a mental prod to Gluttony revealed no answers. Gluttony merely gave a mental shrug and reminded Riven that his memories had been strip-mined by Elysium as part of the pact to get out of his abyssal prison.

"It's like a small piece of heaven . . ." Riven muttered, holding the pearl up against his chest.

The clam laughed and lowered its appendage back into its shell before snapping its mouth shut, but it still projected its words through the bloody ocean without a problem. "Heaven, you say? I never would have thought to see the day a reincarnation of Gluttony himself would claim such a thing. Hail, scion of the Great Maw, and welcome to the Abyssal Descent. You performed admirably, and it is an honor to have one such as you claim the pearl. With our partnership, it is my hope that you can one day truly aspire to recreate the lost fragments of the Blood subpillar."

"It is a figure of speech from my old world. Forgive me, Gluttony." Riven's body shuddered as the whispers of the pearl embraced him in body and soul, and it took a lot of effort to keep his eyes open with the lines of power drawing into him like fonts of bliss. Even now, his soul lattice was expanding rapidly and the long-standing cracks of his once-shattered soul realm that'd been patched back together by Gluttony were now not only disappearing entirely, but were being reinforced.

"Tell me . . ." Riven whispered. "Specifically about the enriched lake . . . Why now? Why this?"

The clam rumbled, and the cavern shook. "Do you not wish to have it?"

"It is not that I do not wish it to be mine. Having your support at my beck and call near the place I call home would be suitable, certainly. The same could be said for the leeches. But it is strange . . . that a guild hall add-on would be what you chose to give, rather than something else."

Riven's eyes lifted, and he shakily put the pearl into his soul space, exhaling sharply when it entered his chest. He almost wanted to dig it out again right then and there, but the power it was radiating was just too distracting for him to think clearly while touching it. "Lillith was gathering rare plants for a garden at the guild hall, back on the second floor of the descent. It was as if she was expecting to not have access to them ever again."

"Lillith of the Black Skies?" the clam asked.

"The one and only. She spoke in a way that hinted at an upcoming calamity." Riven raised an eyebrow, but the clam did not reply. "Gluttony will not answer me in great detail, either, as he says he is not entirely sure of the situation at large and does not want to feed me false pretenses. I feel like he's lying."

At this, Gluttony's laugh echoed throughout the room, but otherwise the great sin did not say anything to nullify Riven's thoughts.

When the clam did not reply, Riven continued with a frustrated edge tugging at the corners of his lips. "Jarntus Bemule, a human earl of the Idorac Federation in Universe 10 and of a planet bordering my own ancestral home of House Wraithtide, came to me in one of the trading communes earlier in the descent as well. He spoke of how his leaders are pooling all their military might into one solar system in preparation for . . . something. Of what he is not sure. And my mother . . ."

Riven trailed off upon remembering his mother's visionary message back on the first floor. "She, too, has hinted of something big to come. Guild halls have the ability to transition between locations, between worlds, even, and I can't help but feel like this gift of yours also correlates with all of these. A preparation for things to come. Am I wrong?"

There was a long pause.

"I believe Gluttony would be a better candidate to speak on such things, as I am but a mere guardian," the clam eventually said. "But I can tell you what I have observed while being banished here in the Abyssal Descent for so long."

Another pause, and Riven gestured for the clam to continue.

"Cracks . . . are forming along the outer perimeters of Elysium's borders—" The clam began again. "Cracks in the very membrane of what Elysium is. It is just a guess, but I believe that the multiverse is breaking down. Why or how, I cannot say, but what will follow is likely anyone's guess. The scope and outcome are vague, but such things do not happen without reason or without consequence, and binding a piece of this realm to your guild hall in the form of a lake is just a means to keep an eye on you while you fulfill the wishes of a pantheon long dead. A pantheon that I made a promise to before being put here so long ago."

"I see. It is unfortunate you do not know more, but I appreciate the insight nonetheless." Riven gave a small bow of respect, noting the clam's shell was already rapidly repairing itself. "I have many questions about the Blood God, the fractured pieces of the Blood subpillar, and what this pearl actually is. What it all means, why it all happened the way it did, and why me. You said you would explain, and I wish you to keep that promise. I intend to pursue this taboo path down the road of Blood, as it feels right . . . and it is what Gluttony wants. I require your insights."

The clam let out another laugh. "I intend to answer all of that, vampire descendant. Though that will take time—likely many weeks, if not months, to go over the full history of how and why such as you ask. For now, let us discuss the basics . . . We will have much more time later when you return to your guild hall and apply the lake to it. And if I am correct, after overhearing your words in your stay on Floor Twenty-Two, I do believe it is in your best interest to proceed at a faster pace through the descent to make it back to your homeworld. The world quests of integrating planets always grow harder to subvert should you sit on them, and it would not be wise to let your enemies grow in strength while you dawdle here listening to an old clam and his stories for too long."

[You have reentered the pocket realm of <u>Floor Twenty-Two: Ocean of Wrath</u>. You are designated team leader of Team DEEZ NUTZ. Your objectives are simple: Survive the monster attacks for at least twenty-four hours while traveling over or through the ocean of blood. Acquire gifts from the sacrificial altars, where opportunities to enhance your gifts will be presented to you should you decide to take them at the last altar, where contact may also be established with outside entities to help to further your goals at a price. You must touch all three altars from Floor <u>Twenty-Two</u> in order to proceed to Floor <u>Twenty-Three</u>. The majority of identification information will continue to be unavailable until Floor Forty.]

[You have touched two of three sacrificial altars, accepting two Blood Tokens to be used at the very last sacrificial altar without having taken the opportunity to sacrifice any of your party members. You have two mandatory hours left to spend on this floor.]

Riven emerged from the bloody pool as a thunderous roar of souls ripped out of the artifact and flooded toward the sky. They had been trapped there in the blood ocean, in what Genua had called a Pool of Atonement. He was a bit agitated that he couldn't take the S-grade artifact with him, but at the end of the day he probably wouldn't qualify to use it anyways and didn't really have a use for it, either. So he'd requested the clam let the souls go, and he watched as the tiny lights spiraled out toward the dark skies above before vanishing into the nothingness of the abyss.

Free at last.

"UMPH!" He nearly lost his breath when Athela's body smashed into him with a bear hug, as the demoness violently sobbed and fell to her knees with tears rolling down her face.

"Riven!" She hiccuped and cried, burying her forehead against the abdominal armor of Messenger as he felt his ribs about to pop. "R-Riven, I was s-so worried!"

She coughed and trembled, and Riven knelt down to scoop her up in his arms while holding her tight.

"I'm fine," Riven said with a smile, brushing his fingers through her hair to massage her scalp comfortingly as she clung to him like glue. "Everything's fine. I'm sorry I scared you."

Fay was almost equally upset, biting her nails and trembling on the sidelines, but her tears were those of relief, and she gave Athela a moment to hug him before coming over herself.

"You definitely scared us," Fay said, leaning in and shakily embracing him. "But I had faith in you. When the notification for the boss battle came up, the letters were somewhat scrambled and we all freaked out. It said something about a clam? Like I said, the notification was blurred due to antiscrying wards. We tried breaking in numerous times but couldn't do it."

"I was not worried," Genua promptly stated.

Kara looked slightly shocked, pale eyes wide while staring at him. Despite everything she'd seen and now knew, she was still adapting to the idea of what and who Riven was. "You . . . soloed a hidden event boss monster by yourself? In the Abyssal Descent?"

Azmoth gave a grunt and nodded aggressively, flaming wings flaring out to either side while he crossed his arms. "Not worried. Riven too overpowered. Agree with Genua."

Prince Rantali let out an amused huff when he side-eyed Azmoth and pushed a golden-gauntleted hand through his bloodied blond hair. "Just what happened inside that thing?! And why are there souls flying out? Did you get any prizes for defeating the boss monster in there?"

Riven hesitated. He knew that the description of the pearl said it would hide the fact it was a taboo, blasphemous item from most other people, but nothing in the multiverse was infallible. For now, at least until they passed this floor after contacting what would probably be the Blood Moon Requiem at the last sacrificial altar, he would keep the pearl hidden. He didn't need any S-grade monsters like his great-grandmother looking at it up close with some kind of item-detection ability that'd pierce the veil. If he did talk about the pearl, he'd make sure he didn't tell Rantali—another vampire and child of the Blood God—that the item was indeed blasphemous. For the same reason he didn't want to reveal anything about the information that the clam had given him regarding the Supreme Path of Blazing Azure Creation, which was the strain the clam was most affiliated with. The descriptions had been temporarily vague, but the gist of it was that if he managed to explore those paths down the Blood subpillar, he'd be able to unlock different aspects of what blood could do. Not much to go off, but Riven would have a lot of time to talk things out when meditating on the pearl and when the clam was acting as a guard dog to his guild hall.

"That's a bit complicated. How about we finish this floor first?" Riven replied.

Prince Rantali nodded and gave Riven a small bow. "That is fine if you don't want to say, but unfortunately I am not sure that we can proceed together past this point. It depends on the floor, but if we can, then certainly I will accompany you! It would be an honor."

Deferring to Riven, Prince Rantali stepped aside and gestured toward the obsidian sacrificial altar at the other end of the platform they stood on.

Riven ruffled Athela's hair, slapped Fay's backside, fist-bumped Azmoth, and gave Genua a warm smile while beginning to walk forward. None of the others said much, including Retesh and Kara, but rather they, too, inclined their heads with respect as Riven used Jackal like a walking stick to cross the bloodied stone.

The staff clicked along the floor as the rest fell into line, and wordlessly Riven used his open left palm to produce the blood tokens they'd gathered from the orcs he'd eaten and the Azag hive warriors the orcs had killed just before that. The crimson coins shimmered in the air in front of him.

The altar itself was just like all the others: a large slab of obsidian stone covered in dried blood, although this one had the naked dead body of another participant pinned to the stone with a large spear jutting from the man's chest. Bones of the dead were scattered all around its base, and Riven's feet crunched over the piles until he came to the altar's front. Ripping the spear out of the dead man on top and unceremoniously pushing the body off the altar's flat surface with the head of his staff, he flung the spear aside and slapped the blood tokens down.

[Thirty-one Blood Tokens received by the last sacrificial altar. The Abyssal Descent will pay fifty-seven Blood Tokens for Prince Rantali's sacrifice, forty-nine Blood Tokens for Kara's sacrifice—]

Riven swiped the notification away. "I decline to sacrifice anyone. And no, no one else will be coming forward to speak for the party."

[Each Blood Token is a valuable bargaining chip. Before making your decision on whether or not to sacrifice anyone, review the list of—]

"I said no. There will be no sacrifices."

Riven swiped it away a second time. He saw all his party members also decline their own messages when Elysium tried to bribe them, too, and he could almost hear Kara's sigh of nervous relief when she saw that he'd maintained his stance on not killing her. Despite the dark elf's previous offer to sacrifice herself, he knew she still wanted to live. More than anything, he suspected that she'd given him the self-proclaimed ultimatum of sacrificing her to make up her debt—or choosing to have her on for a life debt where she'd work to repay it indefinitely—as a way to have an in and stay with him after this event dive. He chuckled at the idea, because it was a poorly disguised ticket to a better life for her in more ways than one, but he wasn't about to tell her that he'd seen through the obvious ruse, because at the end of the day it was harmless to him and his team. If anything, Athela would enjoy it.

He still seriously doubted she'd be a good asset in terms of fighting power, but he wouldn't mind hiring her on as a guild manager or something like that. She didn't seem to enjoy the pursuit of power or fighting at all, so he had a heavy guess that she'd latch onto the idea like a moth to flame, but that was all a discussion for another day.

[The Abyssal Descent acknowledges your choice. No further Blood Tokens will be dispensed. You have touched three of three sacrificial altars. You have two mandatory hours left to spend on this floor.]

[No prior gifts have been given at other altars due to lack of sacrifices. Do you wish to apply these new gifts and upgrades to yourself or spread the benefits over your entire team?]

[Entire team has been selected. Thirty-one Blood Tokens have been absorbed by the sacrificial altar. Converting Blood Tokens now for gifts and enhancements.]

Without warning, Riven's spatial sack flashed, and the jade halberd he'd bought on Floor Two was brought out by the system. He'd barely looked at the thing since getting it, but Gluttony had wanted it for whenever the second class was created, so that was that. All around him, other members of the group had items of their own start to flash out of spatial bags, or they were simply torn off the bodies of the wearers for inspection by Elysium. Athela's black tiara, Azmoth's Shengari Shields, Prince Rantali's breastplate, Kara's quiver, and Retesh's tattered old cloak joined the halberd. Each of the items began to glisten and shimmer as the obsidian altar reached out with crimson threads from its base to touch the items simultaneously. Small and large alterations along the various items took place in their own distinct ways, and a few new items appeared in front of the vampiric knights Prince Rantali had brought along. Fay and Genua had new items built from thin air as particles condensed to take shape in front of them.

It took a few minutes, but at the end of it, Riven was pleased with the results. Each of them had bonuses that weren't anything to scoff at.

Fay had received a simple but effective bone wand with a single Unholy rune at the base that amplified curse magic and nullified the cost such magics took on her in the form of pain or HP. The green affliction fireballs the succubus Lavini had taught Fay to use on Floor One were often disregarded due to the significant pain these flames caused Fay, but using the wand to cast them would help solve this problem.

[**<u>Bone Wand of Curse Reduction</u>: Channel curse magics through this wand to amplify their effectiveness and power by 10%. Pain, debuffs, and other curse costs caused are reduced by 66%. Cast time while using this wand is also reduced by 18%. This weapon requires a combat level of 200 and an Unholy affinity of 46% to use.**]

Fay was outwardly excited, and turned to repeatedly slap Riven's shoulder like a dog itching a scratch. "Wow! Riven, this is just what I've been wanting! Items that can reduce curse costs are like, super rare!"

WHACK-WHACK-WHACK-WHACK-WHACK

"Okay! Okay, just stop hitting me!" Riven laughed, shoving her off him and pushing the new item into her hands.

Genua received prayer beads, of all things. They were colored red and black, just like her ornamental headdress and formfitting priestess outfit, and they hung in a loop from her fingers as she studied the sigils carved into each one.

[**<u>Prayer Beads of the Red Dawn's Chant</u>: While holding these prayer beads, you may repeatedly chant the mantra engraved on them in order to increase the efficacy of any miracle you intend to cast. The longer you chant, the more potent your miracle becomes, up to a 50% increase in power and efficacy. +180 Faith. This charm requires a combat level of 200 and a Blood affinity of 59% to use.**]

It was nice to see some good new items for the team, but the upgraded items were only now finishing their transitions.

CHAPTER 14

[You will be required to visit all four Chalgathi altar sites and activate each of the shrines, as well as acquire ten thousand event points before being allowed to leave this event. Doing so will also give you knowledge of the location of Chalgathi's Temple, where Chalgathi's incubation chamber has been hidden.
There are twenty-one registered cultists.
- **Seven Chalgathi cultists, six Chubin cultists, and eight Nekra cultists**

There are nine registered noncultists entering this event.
- **Three Chalgathi noncultists, four Chubin noncultists, and two Nekra noncultists]**

The old notification was dismissed from her vision.

With Riven's temporary absence from Chalgathi's games, the cultists had used their numbers to far outstrip the noncultists meant to save Panu from unleashing the apocalypse beasts. Interrogation methods had revealed to her that the cultists were mostly around the five thousand to sixty-eight-hundred-point mark, while most of the noncultists were trailing behind that and on average sitting around thirty-five to forty-five hundred. Far beyond what Riven had at the moment.

But those odds had drastically changed once Nora had arrived, new and improved—and with a vendetta. It was also now known to her that point accumulation got harder the more people acquired. Point accumulation on the side of the cultists had thus abruptly stagnated, and although the other noncultists weren't necessarily on Nora's team, they wouldn't be able to make up the difference in points to matter enough by the time Riven got back. She would leave the other noncultists alone . . . for now.

"Twinkle, twinkle, little star!"

Blood splattered along the castle's far wall as Nora's singsong voice echoed throughout the corridors with the laughter of her Others.

"How I wonder what you are!"

CRUNCH
SPLAT
RIP

Her target squealed in pained anguish. "HELP ME, YOU COWARD BASTARDS!"

But the others were running for their lives. She moved, ripping off a cultist's arm and beating him to death with it in three quick strokes before dropping the bloodied limb with a splat.

"Up above the world so high . . ."

The abyssal giant's spirit she'd captured rumbled under the twinkling night sky, a shadowy remnant of the creature she'd killed in the labyrinth, its giant foot crushing fleeing peasants that'd decided to support the cultist cause. It reached down, a sickly smile on its face, its eyes a pale white, as magma dripped out of its maw. It grabbed a fleeing man as the peasant tried to scream, but crushed him in its grasp before bringing the corpse to its mouth and chomping down with a gory gnashing of teeth.

Nora stopped her singing, watching the procession of dying people scrambling like ants to flee not only the fortress, but the city itself. All around her, shifting two-dimensional vantablack figures, crazed with gleeful laughter, tore their claws through the spines and innards of their victims. She was the butcher, and everyone else here were lambs for the slaughter.

Bringing a finger up to her black lips, the sickly smile that nearly never left her face was stretched from ear to ear underneath the Chalgathi cowl event item she was forced to wear in this place. It designated her as a noncultist, so these people all knew just why they had to die. They were paying for their sins. Paying for who they'd helped. "Now, now, now . . . Where did that other cultist run off to . . . I swear I smelled her earlier . . . and we can't have them get to ten thousand points without Riven being here, of course!"

A flash of light to the left caused Nora's eyes to dart that way, and she let out a giggling exclamation when she finally found the target she'd been searching for. "Oh, goodie! TIME TO KILL!"

Nora's blades stretched and warped, her limbs elongated to gangly, unnatural things that propelled her forward, and in an instant she was gone. Off to murder another one.

[Blood Token prizes are now finished. You and your minions have been analyzed based on need and want. Narg has not participated in this floor and will not receive any prize. Fay's lack of her entire ability set has been noted due to high cost of pain and self-injury when casting Cursed Affliction Fireball, and so a wand has been made for her to reduce the pain. Genua's desire to make her healing more potent to keep others safe has been noted, so prayer beads that increase the efficacy of her miracles have been granted. Athela's desire

to be a real princess has been noted, so her tiara has been modified to hold influence over her own weaker arachnid counterparts while maintaining the assassin traits of the original tiara. Azmoth's lacking confidence to effectively use his race's traditional Shengari Shields and a desire to use his old Hell-forged Maul has been noted, so the shields have been melted down and remade into a maul fitting of such an arch-demon, while maintaining the size-shifting properties of the shields so the maul will match his own stature. The Unholy halberd Gluttony chose as a temporary weapon has been reevaluated to make it a better long-term weapon, adding Sin aspects to the weapon while maintaining the dissolving acidic effects. Your halberd has been enclosed in an egg and will emerge from its egg to match your secondary class based on how Gluttony forges the class.]

[Fay has received Bone Wand of Curse Reduction]
[Genua has received Prayer Beads of the Red Dawn's Chant]
[Athela's Tiara of Silent Killing has become Tiara of the Spider Princess]
[Azmoth's Shengari Shields have become Infernal Shengari Maul]
[Your awakened weapon Giant's Jade Halberd of Dissolving has become Egg of Halberd's Hatching]

Athela's tiara had grown in size and added intricacy, with the protrusion at the front of the tiara now sticking up just slightly beyond the front of her hood. Carvings of arachnid demons lined the black metal, with the image of her own drider form lifting up the central ruby, and a few more elegant protrusions with their own rubies were now present out to the sides of the tallest central stone on her forehead. She was absolutely ecstatic, more or less because of the tiara's name rather than anything else, and Riven had a hard time not laughing at her excitement. Instead he merely encouraged her and talked about how pretty the tiara was, which made the demoness all the happier.

Azmoth's maul was, for a lack of better words, exactly identical to his old maul except that instead of stone, it was made from the metal of the Shengari Shields that'd been melted away. There were lines of magma and infernal power running up and down the huge weapon, but honestly this one rather confused Riven. He'd had no idea that Azmoth didn't like his new weapons and wondered why the hellscape brutalisk had even used them in the first place if that'd been the case.

"Elder brutalisks say they best," Azmoth said with a shrug. "So I trust, but never like shields much."

Riven had a hard time not facepalming.

Fay's bone wand and Genua's prayer beads had been the first items to come out, and they were rather content with their own gifts.

As for Riven . . .

He scratched his head, looking down at an enormous purple egg that'd engulfed his entire halberd on the ground in front of him. "Not sure what to make of this."

Gluttony had no comment.

When he reached out to touch the egg, it disappeared into Riven's spatial sack and that was that. "Hope everyone got something good! Hold on just a moment—from what Prince Rantali's told me, we should very soon be getting another notification about contacting the outside multiverse before heading into the next phase."

Kara stared at her own notification, gripping her bow tightly in her right hand and her quiver in the other. The quiver had turned into a treasure that people in her homeworld would kill for. That people all over the empire of Purturis would kill for. Even her father, the Ashen Sage, would surely think this quiver an absolute masterpiece.

The quiver now produced the same kinds of Critical Storm Lances that Riven, reincarnation of Gluttony, used in battle, only she had them in arrow form. How much was even one of these arrows worth? The quiver actually spawned them over time and was a perfect match to her bow, with a sphere of red mana on the bottom that produced the projectiles and a black outer casing with red runes running all along the sides, inside and out.

It was just . . . it was just too much. Even if Elysium had been the one to grant it to her, it had come because of her connection to the vampire prince. How was she supposed to repay Riven after all this was said and done? On one hand, when she'd offered to work in his service indefinitely until the debt was paid, she'd not thought she'd have been able to do it in the first place. Three billion Elysium coins and intervention on her behalf to save her life was something not even ten of her could manage over the course of many lifetimes. But she had set her mind to trying.

But with the system taking a passage of Riven's skill set and planting it inside another of her items on his behalf, due to her class? It was yet another reminder at how futile her attempts really would be.

A groan left her lips and she rubbed at her temple while shaking her head upon thinking of the class change she'd obtained when meditating in front of the Shadow sun on the last floor. It was beyond embarrassing, and she'd refused to let anyone except Athela know what it was. It might very well forever stay that way at this rate. She'd rather stick a dagger in her own eye than die of the embarrassment should Riven ever find out.

She'd completely zoned out and didn't even realize they were entering the last part of this floor when Elysium gave her a nudge in the form of a text box.

[Floor Twenty-Two is near completion. Your team has touched three

of three altars with less than two mandatory hours to spend on this floor. As this is the last altar and your Blood Tokens have been spent, you and your teammates are individually given opportunities to select outside influences in the multiverse to converse with. They in turn will have the opportunity to buy or trade with Elysium in order to sway fate in your favor. Notifications to potential related parties have been sent.

You, Kara Blackbow, have one interested outside party willing to pay the 250,000-Elysium-coin fee of establishing communication with you. The interested party requesting an audience is listed below:
- **The Court of Emperor Adali, Ruler of Purturis**

You are able to accept or decline any and all parties at your discretion.]

Kara immediately felt the blood drain away from her face, and her pale eyes widened in shock. The emperor's court wanted to speak to her? Why? Her father was on that court as the Ashen Sage, but he would never have wanted to spend that kind of money just to establish communication with his worthless seventh daughter. She was—

Kara stopped that train of thought. No, things had likely changed after her nemesis Zafima and her ilk delivered news of Riven and the letter he'd signed in his own blood. Whether the emperor's court even believed what had happened was one thing, but if they did believe the story and that their young scions hadn't been tricked, then how would they respond to an imagined slight against Gluttony's reincarnation? Even with the letter he'd signed, perhaps that'd not been enough to calm their nerves.

"Huh. That's more than I'd thought I'd get," Riven muttered ahead of her while scratching his chin in thought. The vampire removed his hood and ran a hand through his hair with a perplexed expression as Fay came over to see what it was about.

"You look worried," Retesh calmly stated from the side, but he wasn't talking to Riven. He was talking to Kara and was leaning on his bone-white staff with neon-teal light shining out of his eyes. "Do you wish to converse with me about your troubles, child?"

Having an ancient lich like this ask Kara about her feelings was rather amusing to her, but appreciated.

She hesitated and eventually equipped the quiver by slinging it over one shoulder. "It's nothing I shouldn't have seen coming. I'm just still adjusting to . . ."

She waved her hands around in the air, at a loss for words while giving a sheepish smile. "Eh, adjusting to this situation I'm in?"

"You and me both, girl," Retesh said with a bone-rattling chuckle. He bent down and let one of his smaller bone wyrms slither up his outstretched arm to wrap around his chest with a hiss. "I am not used to it, either. Integration into this multiverse has certainly made me reevaluate my own worth. Did you know I have a designated world quest back on Panu?"

Kara scrunched her brows in confusion. "Um, no? What do you mean by that?"

"You are familiar with integrating planets and their world quests, yes?"

"Yes, I am."

"Good. What I meant is that I am considered a threat to Panu's residents, enough so that a world quest about my presence was sent out to the rest of the planet. About how they should destroy me so that I do not consume the world's living in my ambition to create a place habitable for undead. And yet . . . I find myself outclassed, overpowered, and overshadowed by both the Thane siblings."

Retesh waved a bone hand in Riven's direction as he talked to his summoned minions. "I have an affinity for Death that reaches all the way up to 91 percent. I have lived for centuries. I have spent my life trying to unravel the mysteries of immortality and reach the ultimate goal of unlocking the subpillar of True Death. So you can only imagine what it was like to hear that Allie Thane, a vampire less than thirty years of age, was able to unlock True Death in such a short time, and was then awarded the body of an Angel of Death. That the Scythe himself granted her a way to convert the living of an entire continent on Panu into undead, akin to what my own goals were of killing and raising entire civilizations by using modified blight plagues, but doing it instantly just as a measure of good will from the death god. Then, if that weren't enough, she inherited the original sin of Wrath and became an undead so perfect that the very void itself reaches out to her as the souls hibernating there feel her presence. Now she has gone back to Panu, and it makes me feel both excited and jealous. Excited that I am able to know one such as her and hopefully learn from her own ascensions, but jealous because of how little work she had to put into it when I have struggled my entire life to claw and bite at whatever gains I have made. Even my affinity for Death started out far lower than it is now, and it boggles the mind at how slow my own ascension into becoming an elder lich from a mortal human man was, when compared to the path Allie Thane has taken in two short years. That world quest labeling me as a threat? Laughable in the face of what Allie Thane is, which is why I will try to join her court as a subordinate. I suspect that you are feeling some of the same toward Riven?"

Kara was rather interested in the old lich's story, especially the part where he'd wanted to tear down civilizations with blight plague and turn them all into undead, but it didn't assuage her nagging feeling about what was about to come. "Somewhat . . . though I would not say that I am jealous of Riven. Perhaps I am jealous of Athela and Fay, but that is because of his affections toward them, not because I am wanting their power. I barely scraped by to level 200 and doubt I'll ever reach the D-grade. I am weak, I hate fighting, and it was nothing less than a miracle that I got to where I am. I would have died without Riven's interference a few floors back, and probably should have died numerous times over before then as well. More than anything, I am just adjusting to the idea that I may actually accompany Riven back to your world, Panu, and am wondering what life there will be like if I manage to make it."

"He said you could accompany him back?" Retesh asked. "Interesting. I do not mean to be rude, but why? As you have said yourself, you don't bring much to our group. And I'm not even sure how he'd manage it to begin with. Crossing universes is no easy feat."

Kara winced, but she'd said it herself and couldn't argue otherwise. "I believe it was a combination of pity, circumstance, and empathy on his part. I will likely remain in his service forever, given the life debt I owe him, but I will attempt to repay the kindness in one way or another."

"Odd to think that an original sin's reincarnation would find it in their heart to have empathy toward you."

Kara laughed. "I agree! But I won't take it for granted."

Riven's voice cut across their conversation when he turned around and finished talking to his three demonic minions and Genua. "Has everyone chosen to accept their requested audiences? Am I all right to proceed?"

Prince Rantali gave a thumbs-up. "My parents will be attending the audience! I should like to introduce you!"

Riven smiled with a nod. "That is fine. Retesh? Kara?"

Retesh summoned a chair of bones from the piles around the altar and leaned back. "I have none. My followers were given instructions to follow the laws of the Thane Necropolis after migrating, so I can't think of a reason why they'd need to speak with me right now, given Allie's return."

Kara's eyes met Riven's, and she felt herself stiffen under his gaze.

"No need to be shy, hon!" Athela teased, jabbing her in the side to produce a yelp. "I thought we'd gotten over this in our little bonding experiment!"

The vampire knights following Prince Rantali laughed.

Blushing profusely, Kara huffed and swatted away Athela's elbow and ignored the way Athela hungrily looked her up and down. "I—I just am nervous, is all."

"Why?" Riven asked simply, shifting his weight to lean on Azmoth's arm.

"Because my audience . . . Um, my father is going to be there. Probably." Kara winced as Riven's face hardened. She knew Riven wasn't a fan of what her father had done to her, but she didn't want this interaction going poorly even if she did end up finding a way to Panu. There was also the chance that she'd have to go back home and wait for the means to do so, and she really didn't want to be in bad graces with her father, Zafima, and especially the leader of her empire. "Eh . . . possibly the emperor, too. Probably. Do I have to accept?"

"Ahh! She's so cute!" Athela laughed, patting Kara on the shoulder. "Of course you don't have to accept!"

"If you don't want to accept, then don't." Riven shrugged indifferently. "Not any of our business."

Kara bit her lip. "Um . . . and if I do accept? Will you all be there with me?"

Fay rolled her eyes as Athela began to laugh louder.

"Quite *unconfident* in ourselves, aren't we?" Riven said with a smirk. "What, do you want us to stand next to you as you speak to them?"

"I, uh—that'd be great!" Kara said, beaming at the idea while looking at the floor and kicking at the ground with one of her leather boots. "It would help a lot . . . actually . . ."

Riven gave her a flat look, then snorted a laugh. "Sure. We can all stand right beside one another and get chummy."

"I'll even hold your hand!" Athela giggled, pressing up against Kara's body and wrapping her obsidian fingers around Kara's own.

Kara stammered something unintelligible, but nodded and accepted her fate. Then she selected the option to accept the audience with her homeland.

"Looks like we're ready, then," Riven said as he made some selections with the system administrator. "Not sure what to expect, but here goes."

[Floor Twenty-Two is near completion. Your team has accepted the following audiences:
- **High Queen Nephridi of the Blood Moon Requiem, Universe 10**
- **The Unholy Archbishop Prek An-Gash of the Church of Gluttony, the Ninth Circle of Hell**
- **The Court of Emperor Adali, Ruler of Purturis, Universe 70**
- **King and Queen Rantali of the Vampiric Kingdom of Garth, Universe 70**

You will have a short time to speak with them one at a time before Elysium offers these outside influences beyond the Abyssal Descent a list of options they may purchase with Elysium coins. The first up is the Vampiric Kingdom of Garth, Universe 70.]

CHAPTER 15

A flat mirror began to rise out of the sacrificial altar. By the time it reached the height of a dozen feet tall and half as wide, the mirror began to glow. Soon the reflection disappeared, and in place of Riven's team staring back at themselves were two individuals that Prince Narzkal Rantali immediately recognized.

"Hello, Mother! Father!" The gold-clad vampire prince waved proudly, puffing out his chest and smiling wide at the two people who were obviously related to him.

They were both blond, just like their son, wearing white and gold formal clothes and tall golden crowns trimmed in marble. They had very pale red eyes, and smooth, attractive features just like most vampires. Both smiled proudly with brilliant white fangs at the forefront of said smiles, and they both waved back to reciprocate their son's enthusiasm.

"Narzkal, my son!" King Rantali said to his son with a boisterous laugh. "I can't believe you've made it so far! Floor Twenty-Two! We're so proud of you, my boy!"

His mother clapped excitedly next to the king. "Narzy, my little baby boy! You look ADORABLE in that golden armor we bought you! I hope you stood out amid all those other scions from around the multiverse—it was the flashiest we could find!"

Prince Narzkal Rantali went a bright shade of red in embarrassment and shot Riven a quick glance. He then cleared his throat as the vampire knights behind him tried to stifle their laughter. "Mother . . . I told you not to call me that in front of my friends!"

"What?! Narzy?! But that's always what I call you!" Queen Rantali frowned. "Are you embarrassed of your nickname? Perhaps I should just call you nagle-tooth like I used to—"

"Mother!" Prince Rantali hissed, nearly turning purple under the growing amounts of suppressed laughter from most of the group now. "Stop it! You're doing this on purpose!"

The queen's frown broke into a sly grin. "I would never!"

"Don't belittle your mother, boy!" King Rantali exclaimed with a frown of his own, though it was obvious he was in on the joke by the way the corners of his lips were twitching. "Show respect to the woman who raised you like a good nagle-tooth!"

Riven snorted rather loudly, pulling his hood down slightly and looking away to hide his amusement, if only a little bit.

Prince Rantali, however, looked mortified. "I'm about to hang up this call!"

"You wouldn't dare!" the queen said with a raised nose. "I'd take away all your toys. Now, dearest Narzy, have you made any good connections with the other scions of promising factions out there? The Abyssal Descent is an opportunity that should not be squandered. I hope you've made some political ties! Who have you teamed up with here for the twenty-second floor? And was there anyone else in the upper floors that you managed to speak to that we'd like to know about?"

Prince Rantali took in a deep breath and slowly released it while a vein pulsed in his forehead. "Yes . . . Mother. As requested, I've reached out to promising people in good faith."

"Aside from that man who supplied you with the black phoenix stone for your fiancée? The one you talked about in your letter?" the queen asked with both eyebrows raised now.

Prince Rantali winced. "I . . . have attempted to establish connections with others aside from that man. Unfortunately most of the scions here believe themselves to be . . . better than us. Too good to associate with a small kingdom from the seventieth universe when most are from earlier universes with far more powerful ancestors."

His father, the king, let his smile fade to a more stern, tight-lipped expression, and the older man let out a long sigh. "To be fair, that isn't entirely unexpected. It may be discouraging, but my great-grandfather went through a similar experience when he, the first of us that profited from the opportunity Elysium presented to our sector of the universe, traveled into the descent. Your mother and I went together and the same thing occurred. That's all right, as long as you try your best."

"He has really great parents . . ." Riven muttered under his breath to Athela, who nodded in agreement. "Damn. I'm a little bit jealous."

"But tell us more about the man in your letter! You said he was another vampire, is that right?! Always good to stick together with our brothers and sisters in blood!" the queen exclaimed, trying to cheer her husband and son up with another excited clap of her hands. "And what about these fine people?! You managed to group together with another team in the descent in order to make it here, as is obvious by the people standing next to you! Who are they?!"

Prince Narzkal Rantali seemed to brighten up, and he even straightened a little bit. "Yes, well, as I described in brief: This man bought the black phoenix stone after he learned my fiancée has blood rot. I couldn't even get inside the trading compound until he showed up to help. I know I didn't give many details because I wasn't sure about how it'd turn out, but I can say that I truly have made a friend."

Prince Rantali smiled Riven's way and motioned for him to walk forward. "It happens to be this man, and I can't speak highly enough of his character. He also lives a rather exciting life! Riven? Do you want to introduce yourself?"

Flushing slightly, it was Riven's turn to be embarrassed. Nevertheless, he took a few steps forward to be in line with Prince Rantali and bowed low at the waist. "Riven Thane. It is a pleasure to meet you both."

King Rantali leaned forward slightly in his chair. "I was wondering whether it was you! You're running around with one of the esteemed priestesses of the Blood God, so it was only fair to assume."

"Are you a pureblood?" the queen asked curiously, tilting her head to the side. "Your eyes are telling, young man. They glow rather brightly."

Riven smiled politely. "I am."

"Ah. Your kind is rare. What an honor! And you were able to pull the strings to save our son's lover?"

"I did."

"If you don't mind me asking, where is it you come from?"

Riven paused, wondering how he should answer that. Then, grinning at Prince Rantali, he got a rather devious idea. In this place they weren't able to identify him anyways, and it would be rather fun to fuck around. "I'm currently hailing from an integrating planet and only joined the multiverse two years ago. I am no one noteworthy; I'm rather poor and merely got lucky enough to find an opportunity to come here through Elysium's integration trials."

The king and queen both looked surprised and a little bit disappointed by this proclamation. They'd already said they hoped their son had made some political connections in the descent, and it was obvious that they'd been expecting Riven to be someone of importance. Being from an integrating world meant he had no political connections at all.

"Oh . . . I see," the king replied, leaning back with a sigh, but he was quick to bring on a warm smile after that and nod enthusiastically. "Well, it makes sense that you two would find each other, then! Some of the older powers in the multiverse can be rather snobbish, but I'm surprised to see a pureblood such as yourself coming from an integration world."

Prince Rantali, for his part, gawked openly at Riven's blatant attempt to swing things in the wrong direction.

"Still, it is a fine thing what you did for our son!" the queen exclaimed, though a bit of her excitement was obviously diminished. "How did you manage to get him into the trading guild if you didn't have connections?"

Riven shrugged and then let out a dramatic groan while kicking away the bones around his feet as if in a place of despair. "I . . . I may have seduced one of the workers there on your son's behalf. It was a terrible experience, truly. But I did it out of the goodness of my heart for a friend in need! It was an ogre woman, about three times my size and with a little beard. She wanted to sleep with Narzkal Rantali here, but . . . then he threw me to the wolves. The poor ogre didn't even buy me dinner first."

"You don't say?" The queen looked shocked. "Did you at least get something for your troubles other than helping our son?"

The rest of the party was dead silent as he replied. They were either shocked, confused, or, in Athela's case, stifling laughter with tremendous effort.

Riven let out another exaggerated sigh. "I'm afraid not. I wasn't even compensated for my efforts by your son, and after the ogre was done having her way with me—"

"HE'S A LIAR AND A BASTARD!" Prince Narzkal Rantali half laughed, half yelled, pointing an accusatory finger in Riven's direction. "He's a prince of the Blood Moon Requiem and is the reincarnation of Gluttony! Mother, Father, I swear to you that I did NO such thing as throw him to the mercy of some brutish ogre woman! I would never!"

Dead.

Silence.

Hung in the air.

Prince Narzkal Rantali seemed to have realized what he had called Riven and paled. "I . . . I may have misspoken there."

"A liar and a bastard? Misspoken? That's quite the tall tale you've made up on the spot, Narzy." His mother gave him a scathing look with arms crossed underneath the bosom of her gold dress. "I truly hope for your sake that you didn't actually make this blood brother of ours sleep with a troll to seduce your way inside. What did you promise him in return? Did you do it, and if you did, did you really give him nothing at all for his troubles?"

"Not a troll, an ogre," Riven corrected solemnly, feigning a shudder. "Her thighs were like warty green tree trunks. She nearly snapped my back."

"I TAKE THAT BACK, HE'S STILL A LIAR AND A BASTARD!" Prince Narzkal Rantali roared, yet again pointing a finger in Riven's direction. "He did not seduce any OGRE!"

"Troll," Riven corrected.

"You just said—"

"I'm not the one that makes the rules here." Riven shrugged.

"Well, WHATEVER it was you didn't sleep with, you're still a prince of the Blood Moon Requiem and you're Gluttony's reincarnation!"

The king and queen weren't buying it one bit and shot each other wary glances. Perhaps they thought their son may be going crazy.

Riven shot a sad glance at the unamused vampire royals in the mirror. "King and Queen Rantali, I hate to be the bearer of bad news . . . but I do believe your son is starting to lose his mind as a side effect of the last floor. When we encountered the suns to help our soul lattices grow—"

"I am not losing my mind!" Prince Rantali exclaimed. "He's just joking! I promise you that's who he actually is!"

"Would the reincarnation of an original sin joke like that?" Riven asked casually, giving him a knowing look. "Come now, Narzy, we've had this discussion five times already. You're a friend, that's why I slept with that troll for you. But you need medical help and a Dao expert to help regain your mind."

"HE'S THE REINCARNATION—"

Riven cut him off with a raised hand and once again turned to the mirror. Both of Prince Rantali's parents wore very concerned looks and were whispering to each other while staring at their son. "I am not the reincarnation of Gluttony. What would the chances of that even be? One in many trillions, or worse? He is merely confused, severely so, and as I said, he is losing his mind due to whatever happened with the last floor. King and Queen Rantali, it is my belief that your son needs to withdraw from this place before he truly dives further into madness and loses himself entirely."

Prince Rantali's jaw dropped, and he threw out his hands to either side before spinning around on the rest of the group. "Hey! All of you! Tell them the truth!"

The vampire knights stared dumbly at the prince, then at Riven, then at the prince, and then at the mirror with their king and queen displayed ahead of them.

One of the vampire knights stepped forward. "I believe . . . that your son is going mad."

"BRUTUS, YOU LITTLE BASTARD! THIS ISN'T FUNNY!"

Riven could see the twinkle in the knight's red eye as he cleared his throat and shook his head sadly. "It is as our new friend Riven here says. We all believe that the young prince here has taken the brunt of a Dao insight too strong for his mind to make sense of, and his mind is breaking. It would be wise to demand he come home so that he can proceed with treatment, as already suggested."

Prince Rantali spun on his heel, looking utterly betrayed at all the others who maintained straight faces. "Kara! Stop this nonsense here and now! I helped you out earlier when you confided in me, right? Kara, tell them!"

Kara looked away in shame, turning completely around.

"He has ARCHDEMONS as minions!" Prince Rantali exclaimed, pointing at Athela, Fay, and Azmoth one by one. "They literally worship him! You should have seen the way they treated him inside the compound where I got the black phoenix stone! Even Lillith of the Black Skies was there!"

Dead.

Silence.

Once again.

"And where is Lillith now?" Riven asked calmly. "Surely you could point her out for us."

Prince Rantali stomped his foot. "She's trapped on Floor Fifty because Elysium put her there!"

Riven slowly turned to the mirror, frowning with a shake of his head. "I am a warlock, yes, but I am certainly not worshipped. My demons regularly insult and threaten me, and it is only through my sheer Willpower that I am able to maintain control over their puny, pea-sized minds."

"Okay, that's just going too far, you little shithead twerp!" Athela said, jabbing Riven in the side as he yelped.

Fay smacked him in the back of the head with a humph.

Even Azmoth swatted at him with one of his wings, making Riven dodge out of the way to avoid being burned.

"Be still, foul creatures!" Riven exclaimed, but this time simultaneously putting their contracts to use for the first time . . . ever?

Yeah, ever.

All three demons immediately froze, unable to break the bindings of their contracts as Riven wiped his hands off from falling on Athela's face. He inwardly cackled at the wide-eyed glare she gave him and the muffled cursing, and flicked her on the forehead before turning around to bow once again.

"As you can see, they hold little to no respect for me. That certainly isn't how Gluttony's reincarnation would be treated by demonkind, and the imaginary Lillith is nowhere to be seen. Your son is going mad, and I feel like it is my solemn duty to let you know as his friend so that you can try to convince him to go home before it is too late."

Prince Rantali's parents continued silently whispering to one another for a short while before Queen Rantali rubbed the bridge of her nose and let out a groan.

"Narzy . . . perhaps it would be best to have you come home, just in case they're right."

"They're conspiring against me! This is just a joke!" Prince Rantali insisted. "They're just being ridiculous!"

"No, son. It is you who are being ridiculous," the queen stated, putting on a loving smile. "Come home and we will get you a Dao healer. I'm glad you've made such good friends, dear, because it truly does look like your mind has been broken. That's all right, though! You did very well getting to the twenty-second floor, and we are very proud of you and your accomplishments!"

"B-but . . . But I . . ." Prince Narzkal Rantali was truly at a loss for words.

Riven nodded in agreement like an old sage would, hands clasped behind his back. "Yes, Narzy. Indeed, indeed. Although, perhaps we—"

A moment later, a very large pop-up notification appeared for the entire group to see, cutting Riven off midsentence.

[Floor Twenty-Two is near completion. Your team has accepted the following audiences:
- **High Queen Nephridi of the Blood Moon Requiem, Universe 10**
- **The Unholy Archbishop Prek An-Gash of the Church of Gluttony, the Ninth Circle of Hell**
- **The Court of Emperor Adali, Ruler of Purturis, Universe 70**
- **King and Queen Rantali of the Vampiric Kingdom of Garth, Universe 70**

You will have a short time to speak with them one at a time before Elysium offers these outside influences beyond the Abyssal Descent a list of options they may purchase with Elysium coins.

Warning: The Vampiric Kingdom of Garth, Universe 70, only has eight minutes remaining to speak. Please hasten and have your audience select from their listed options to buy, provided courtesy of Elysium.]

The thing was, this notification was large enough for everyone there to read it at a distance. Including King and Queen Rantali, who began to slowly lose their composure as their eyes widened and their jaws became slack.

"Gig's up, boys," Riven said in defeat, as the area around him erupted with laughter, the loudest of which came from Prince Rantali's own personal guard.

"Fuckin' bastards," Prince Rantali spat, glaring at Riven with arms folded over his chest. "Not funny. Not funny at all! Do you realize how disappointed my parents were going to be with me if I didn't acquire at least ONE noteworthy acquaintance outside my kingdom?! I'd be ruined! Ruined, I say! They were even questioning my character, thinking that I made a fellow vampire go and sleep with a troll just to get inside a trading guild!"

"Would you have done it, though?"

"Probably."

"Always figured you were the type of man to like trolls."

"I MEANT that I'd make a fellow vampire do it for—"

"Yeah, yeah. Just don't tell your fiancée. I don't know how she'd take it, knowing that you were into her and also into trolls. Kinda gross, but you do you, homeboy. You . . . do . . . you . . ."

Queen Rantali gleefully laughed alongside her husband on the other end. "It was a genuine pleasure meeting you, Riven Thane! But are you sure you don't prefer some kind of title?"

"Riven's fine, thanks," he replied with a wave of his hand. "I don't need any self-aggrandizing stuff like that. Sorry about the joke, though, I just couldn't help it. Call it a personality flaw."

"I hope to see more of that personality flaw in future years," King Rantali said with a chortle. "Please feel free to come visit if you're ever in the area. Enjoy the gift! And try not to pick on my son so much—he's a bit fragile."

"Thanks for the vote of confidence . . ." Prince Rantali muttered.

Both of his parents waved and called out to their boy with love and affection, and in the next instant they were gone.

"Nice people," Riven said with a fond smile at seeing the two older vampires leave. "I like them. Tell them I said that when you get back."

"Oh, I'm sure they'll be head over heels about it." Prince Rantali grunted in irritation. "It would have been nice if we could just buy these bonuses ourselves instead of relying on our elders. That way I wouldn't be so thoroughly embarrassed right now!"

Riven was about to think of something witty to say, but a new notification appeared for the billionth time that day and gave him pause.

[Your time with King and Queen Rantali of the Vampiric Kingdom of Garth, Universe 70, is now over.

King and Queen Rantali have bought your group the following:
- **Abyssal Spirit Guide (three million Elysium coins): A spirit guide that has walked the halls of the descent for a long, long time. The spirit will remain with you while descending and can guide you to the fastest possible routes to further levels. Faster, however, does not mean safer.**

Proceeding to the next audience: The Court of Emperor Adali, Ruler of Purturis, Universe 70]

"Oh . . . Kara?" Riven said, motioning her over. "I think yours is up next . . ."

Kara was already nervously biting her nails and stiffened at his words, just before a new mirror ripped out of the sacrificial altar like the first had done. Only this time, instead of two happy-go-lucky vampire royals, they saw a bunch of very stern, very angry-looking dark elves in a boxy room at a circular table. They all wore elegant cultivator clothes, had either lavender, blue, or pale-gray eyes, and different shades of silver or white hair. Hot tea was simmering on a few plates in front of different occupants of the room, with different assortments of meats and pastries alongside fruit trays. It was rather bright, with large windows in the painted wood of wherever it was they sat, and despite the room mostly being full of men, it was a woman who stood up to speak first.

She was stunningly pretty, of middle age and wore a very tight blue dress that hugged the curves of her body. With her hair pinned up and long ribbons drooping down past her hands from where they'd been tied at her wrists, she pointed a slender finger in Kara's direction with a snarl. "What did you do with my daughter, you wretched bitch?! Where is Zafima?! Why is she not home yet?! And how are you still alive?!"

CHAPTER 16

Kara looked like a deer caught in the headlights, stunned and confused while standing there awkwardly and not knowing what to say.

As for Riven? Hot anger flared inside his chest, but he kept his composure and merely remained at his new friend's side just like she'd asked them to do. These were her people, not his.

"Sit DOWN, woman! And do it NOW! You are but a mere concubine and you will only speak when spoken to. Know your place," a dark elf man in the very center of the room snapped with a venomous glare. He wore a basic blue-jade circlet around his head and sat in lotus position, with a long and neatly trimmed white beard, though he didn't look all that old.

Other members of the court of Emperor Adali, ruler of Purturis, gave the woman scathing glares of their own or shook their heads in obvious disgust.

The self-proclaimed mother of Zafima stiffened, but she gave the central man a respectful bow within seconds. "Yes, Emperor. Forgive me; my emotions got the best of me."

"It wouldn't be the first time." Emperor Adali snorted. "The next time you speak out of turn, you will be flogged."

The room turned utterly silent, and the concubine bowed her head in shame while maintaining clenched fists.

Then the emperor cleared his throat, stroked his beard, and turned his blue eyes to Kara and her team. His gaze lingered on Riven and Prince Rantali the longest, before turning his attention to Kara, who offered him a hasty bow before halfway prostrating herself.

"F-forgive me if I have done anything wrong, Your Majesty!" Kara began on bent knees.

But the man's hand cut through the air to dismiss her words. "Please, Miss Blackbow. I have a few questions for you before we begin."

Kara's eyes flicked to another hooded man in black robes off to the left, who Riven noted looked quite similar to Kara but in male form, and she nodded hesitantly. "Very well, Emperor Adali. I will do my best to answer any questions you may have."

Silence again ensued.

The emperor tapped his steepled fingers together in contemplation, continuing to look the party members over one by one. "The Abyssal Descent . . . is a gateway to help the young of our nation ascend to greater heights by building on the foundations of their soul lattices. The insights the Abyssal Descent provides are far beyond our own means here in Purturis, and by Elysium's grace we have been given many generations' worth of tickets through the actions of our own empire, and by our vampiric allies in the kingdom of Garth."

The emperor gave a respectful nod of acknowledgment to the vampiric prince to Riven's left. "It is a pleasant surprise to see you, Prince Narzkal Rantali. Please forgive my intrusion, but these questions must be asked."

"No need to apologize, Emperor Adali," Prince Rantali replied with perfect posture and a practiced smile. "Please, act like I'm not here."

The emperor nodded again and sighed when his eyes fell back on Kara. "These tickets are treasures in their own rights, and it has come to my attention that not only was a ticket squandered on a person with as little talent as you in order to settle a dispute between two rather childish members of my very own court, but that you were also sabotaged by your own team and others of our empire when you arrived. This is rather . . . troubling to me. I hope you do not take offense as to what I said, but usually these tickets are only given to our best and brightest. To allow our offspring to intermingle with the scions of the greater powers in this multiverse is not something we take lightly. We need our best face forward when the actions of our youth can reflect on our empire as a whole."

Kara remained pale-faced and kneeling, averting her gaze as long as the man would permit it.

Emperor Adali made eye contact with Riven for only a split second before peeling away with a grimace. "Even more troubling are rumors of what has happened in the Abyssal Descent after you were sabotaged. In fact, I would even say it is more than just rumor, given there were multiple eyewitnesses to what happened on Floor Twenty-One. Multiple witnesses that immediately left the Abyssal Descent, dismissing their own opportunities for gains in order to inform me as quickly as possible of what had occurred for the betterment of our empire. So that I could attempt to try and perform . . . damage control. Do you deny any of this?"

Kara nervously twitched. "I . . . um . . . I don't deny it. I will not comment on the reasons why I was sent here—those reasons are better asked of my father, the Ashen Sage. I am a mere seventh daughter and was bound to his request. I will admit, however, that I was sabotaged, and without help I likely would have died down here."

Zafima's mother took in a sharp breath of air and made to stand, but the emperor shot a scathing glare at her again and she rapidly sat back down.

The emperor remained furiously glaring at the middle-aged dark elf woman for well over ten seconds of silence before speaking to Kara again. "Over a dozen eyewitness accounts, to be exact. Tell me, Kara Blackbow, do Zafima Chinwa and Numin Thorn yet live?"

Kara took a moment, furrowing her brows and fidgeting with the hem of her shirt. "I'm afraid I don't understand, Your Majesty. Zafima and Numin did stay behind to try and make amends, but . . ."

She shot Riven a furtive glance. "But they went through the portal to go home. They should be in Purturis now. Are you saying that you don't know where they are?"

"THE BITCH HAD THEM KILLED! SHE MUST HAVE BRIBED THE OTHERS INTO TELLING THESE LIES!" Zafima's mother screamed, launching to her feet and pointing a trembling finger in Kara's direction. Spit flew out of her mouth and tears ran down her cheeks as she snarled and snapped her words out the way any mother would if they'd lost their child. "IT IS IMPOSSIBLE THAT A LOWLY BLACKBOW BEFRIENDED A REINCARNATION IN SUCH A WAY! I SEE NOTHING BUT IMPOSTORS, AND I DEMAND JUSTICE! MY LITTLE GIRL WAS MURDERED BY THAT USELESS—"

SHUNK

The woman abruptly gasped, coughing up blood as a blade ripped through her back and out the front side of her left breast. Eyes wide and horrified, the drow woman tried to scream, but it was muffled by a hand over her mouth as a drow guard twisted the blade and wrenched it out.

Kara's father grinned wolfishly on the sidelines.

"I thought I told you to speak only when spoken to, Alris," Emperor Adali said with a seething look of rage as the woman's body dropped to the ground and she began to convulse. "With matters of such importance, if true, it is not only your daughter that put our empire in jeopardy, but it is you and your plans as well. I was going to forgive it, but not anymore. Not if you can't keep silent when ordered to do so and make yourself out to be a fool in front of one of the inheritors of the very hells themselves, you foolish concubine."

Ignoring the gasping woman as her lungs filled with blood and her pierced heart spasmed in the final moments of her life, Emperor Adali rested his gaze on Riven. "It is likely, based on what Kara is telling me, that Zafima and Numin knew what awaited them when they came back. We will find them, and when we do, they will be executed. I had people gifted in reading minds go over the accounts of our young warriors when they got back and had Dao specialists extract the lingering affinities left on their bodies soon after leaving the Abyssal Descent. Yours, reincarnation of Gluttony, is the most pure form of gluttonous sin I have ever seen. I had heard that Zafima personally threatened you with the name of our empire, oh Great Maw. Please . . . allow me to offer our official apology if what my concubine's daughter did managed to offend you."

The emperor bowed his head low, touching the floor in tandem with all the others, who did the same. "If there is anything that we can do to make amends, name it. I would gladly send tribute to your church for a thousand years if it pleases you. I will also send you the head of the sorceress Zafima and the warrior Numin once we find them, after I send the head of Zafima's mother to your nearest conclave as a starting gift, and I only ask your forgiveness for this offense."

Riven was slightly confused that Zafima and Numin hadn't made it back home, given that he'd supplied a writ of forgiveness. It appeared they'd not thought it to be enough. Looking at Zafima's dead mother, whose pupils were now dilating in death, Riven had a hard time not feeling bad for her. She'd been abandoned by her daughter, but had also been an absolute bitch who'd put Kara's life in jeopardy. He had to remember that.

His more primal thoughts surged to the forefront.

Honestly . . . He was a cold-blooded killer who ate people now. He wasn't the good guy anymore. Why should he even care at all?

She even looked rather good to eat—looking at her corpse made him hungry and he was starting to regret that she wasn't here to sample. Zafima's mother was just cattle at the end of the day.

Just like those orcs he'd recently eaten.

Right?

Gluttony sent a pulse of hunger through him and acknowledged his thoughts in the affirmative, causing Riven to grin. Yes . . . these dark elves were just meat. Things to be drained and eaten, like cows, pigs, or sheep. And if he kept Kara around as a pet, then that was his prerogative. He was pureblooded vampire royalty, the reincarnation of Gluttony, and taking care of lesser species like Kara would be no different from the people of Earth when they had pet dogs. Hell, some farmers even kept pet cows before butchering them for food. Not that he planned on eating Kara, even if she looked like she'd taste rather good, but the idea was the same.

Where did that put him when it came to his Sarak slaves from House Wraithtide's homeworld of Luteski? He still wanted to treat them well . . . didn't he?

But . . . in the end, they were lesser creatures, too.

Just like the other vampires had told him. He was only lately beginning to understand that there was a significant difference between vampires and the cattle they fed on.

The prey they hunted.

Mortals . . . were beneath him.

"Forgiveness is already granted . . ." Riven said nonchalantly. "There will be no retribution from the factions that I represent. Though I will be taking Kara with me. She has decided to offer me a life debt after I intervened on her behalf, a life debt that I have accepted. I will attempt to bring her back directly from the descent, but if I cannot, then I expect you to treat her well until I send someone to fetch her. That is all that I expect from you, nothing more."

For effect and confirmation of who he was, Gluttony's maw flashed in the background behind where Riven stood, causing many of the dark elves on the other side of the communication line to go pale just when they'd started showing signs of relief.

"You have my word that she will be taken care of to the utmost of our ability while she waits for departure, should the need arise," Emperor Adali of Purturis said with a stiff smile, getting up from his prostration to stand. "Thank you for your generosity and understanding, reincarnation of Gluttony. Our humble empire is in your debt. With that in mind, please accept the gift we have chosen to buy for your team as an expression of our sincerity of gratitude."

Kara was in a state of shock for the very small amount of time spent conversing with her homeland afterward, and refused to speak to her father at all. So without further ado, the connection was cut and she resigned herself to sitting on a bone chair that Retesh constructed for her in the background. She looked a little lost but was far happier and less nervous than she'd been going into that conversation.

[Your time with the Court of Emperor Adali, Ruler of Purturis, Universe 70, is now over.

The Court of Emperor Adali has bought your group the following:
- **One thousand tickets to the Abyssal Descent (these tickets have been removed from Emperor Adali's spatial bag and transferred to you, cost averted): These tickets allow entry into the Abyssal Descent, one ticket per person.**

King and Queen Rantali have bought your group the following:
- **Abyssal Spirit Guide (three million Elysium coins): A spirit guide that has walked the halls of the descent for a long, long time. The spirit will remain with you while descending and can guide you to the fastest possible routes to further levels. Faster, however, does not mean safer.**

Proceeding to the next audience: the Unholy Archbishop Prek An-Gash of the Church of Gluttony, the Ninth Circle of Hell]

"Nice of them to grant us a portion of their tickets like that," Riven said thoughtfully. "This will be great for the best and brightest of the Thane Necropolis to use. Prince Rantali, remind me to get a copy of those manuscripts about the descent. I think it'll be helpful to have."

"I will simply give you mine before we part ways," Prince Rantali said with arms wide. "I don't intend to stay here much longer anyways. At most we'll be able to travel with you for another floor, but the deeper areas won't allow such things, and I have no doubt that I am not qualified to go it alone."

"And what are we?!" one of the vampiric knights he'd brought along asked.

Prince Rantali snickered. "Bumbling idiots, that's what."

"Now, that's just not fair."

"It was you three traitors that took Riven's side when he was trying to fool my parents! Don't you give me those disparaging looks!"

Riven ignored the squabbling vampires and watched yet another mirror slide silently out the top of the sacrificial altar. Just like the last two mirrors, this one rapidly changed its visage into a two-way communication line.

And on the other side of that mirror was a large humanoid figure in a dark room wrapped in mummy-like bandaging, with gray skin and deep-green eyes. He was a dozen feet tall even in a sitting position, held a gray stone staff the size of a small tree with Gluttony's maw depicted on three distinct sides of the staff's head, and he wore a black cloak with red metal trimming along the edges.

The most notable thing about him, though, was that he resembled Cthulhu to the letter. Prek An-Gash, Unholy archbishop of the Church of Gluttony and a resident of the Ninth Circle of Hell, was the exact same race that Cthulhu had been. Whatever that race was.

Perhaps Riven would ask.

Would that be rude?

Riven shrugged. Might as well get it out that he was an uneducated country bumpkin from a mortal world so that he didn't embarrass himself in front of one of the leaders of Gluttony's church.

"My race . . . is called Cthalia, Lord Reincarnation," the gray-skinned humanoid said aloud in a deep voice that somehow made the very mirror shake even on this side of the exchange, with the tentacles coming off his face fluttering amid the words. "And yes, I, Archbishop Prek An-Gash, can read your thoughts. Gluttony, it makes my heart tremble with glee to see that you have finally returned to us . . . This humble keeper of your sacred texts welcomes thee back into the realms!"

With a mental nudge from Gluttony, Riven took a back seat to the original sin and let the Great Maw have control over his body. The third eye in his forehead opened up with a flare of deep-purple light, and his aura changed from one of blood and cold to one of supreme hunger in an instant.

The others of his party were staggered by the abrupt change in the atmosphere around them, and Gluttony extended a hand to the mirror with a look of collected calmness. A strand of mana created from the purest sin rushed out to the mirror, and on the other side, Prek An-Gash did the same.

The two cords of Sin energy touched, and Riven felt his mind link with the archbishop for only a moment before his body was overwhelmed with raw power. This being was far beyond him, and he knew without doubt that even being across realms, the connection they shared now would enable the demon on the other end to crush Riven to paste if he'd wanted to. But there was only joy and excitement coming at him through the mind link, and right before Riven passed out due to the stress of this unimaginably powerful being in the hells sharing his aura and thoughts, Riven heard Gluttony speak.

"Prek, my old friend . . ." Gluttony said happily while the darkness closed around Riven's mind. "It has been far, far too long . . ."

CHAPTER 17

A brief stop by Brightsville had informed Allie of all she needed to know about what'd happened concerning Mara, Kathrine, and Crendir No-Name. Tre'Zix of the Purple Claw of the Klinac'Tal Clan had even verified it with his own eyes before making reports, with significant casualties on the other side but failing to retrieve the captured duo.

She was anything but pleased with his efforts, even if Crendir had used dozens of escape and warding treasures to get away. Unfortunately, no one seemed able to answer any questions about the whereabouts of Nin and Vin, either, but she was sure there was a good reason for that. She'd figure it out after she saved Mara.

Gliding through endless dark tunnels, across the deserted vampiric city, and finally into the silent halls of the underground precursor labyrinth, Allie's obsidian wings cast death on every hostile she came across without so much as a twitch. She'd been powerful before, but now she was on another level—the plants and wildlife in the underdark simply withered and died whenever she extended her aura, the very rock around her would blacken and crack with wisps of gray and teal lights that would stream up off the floor, and that wasn't even with her primary fighting form active. Anything less than level 120 instantly keeled over, the breath leaving their bodies as her presence settled like a silencing wave of cold energy.

During the days of searching and travel, she'd had to phase out of her Angel of Wrath form into her Angel of Death form in order to make sure the rage didn't continue to build. She currently looked like she had before the transition into the reincarnation of Wrath, but the sin inside her was simmering and just waiting to be unleashed if she would only allow it to leave.

"Are you angry with me for causing you to strike out at your brother?" Wrath whispered in her head. "Embrace the feeling . . . you'll need to harness that power for the rest of your life!"

Allie staunchly ignored the ancient entity, continuing to glide through the underdark as her pale, bare skin let off ghostly trails like a phantom. Her state of calm and calculated killing intent was razor-sharp, focused on her singular objective: rescue Mara. She was down here somewhere, and Allie could literally feel life—or the absence of it—at incredible distances now. She just needed to find her friend and everything would be fine.

Wrath let out a low, demonic laugh that echoed through her skull as the whispers and shadows of her new followers surged through the underdark with her like a violent promise. The creatures from an age lost to time moved at her command, and they were the most peculiar mix of demons, angels, and undead she'd ever seen. She wasn't even sure what some of the hybrids were, rather, they may just be extremely advanced undead, but some of their biology and soul signatures were both strange and yet also familiar to her. Perhaps they were just like she was now. Perhaps they were even like Fimrindle in some ways, given he, too, was a part demon and part undead entity.

Was that a coincidence?

A communication orb in her right hand pulsed, and the voice of Tre'Zix cut through the silence. "This humble servant of Gluttony wishes to inform the newly anointed reincarnation of Wrath that the whereabouts of your prey have been found again."

Allie's fist clenched, and she stopped midflight with a flare of her four wings. "Is it as we suspected?"

The archdemon on the other side hissed his response. "Yes . . . the vampire and his remaining comrades are attempting to make it to the precursor temple where you found the coffin of the deceased elder god. My clan and I are currently watching him fight precursor sentries at the temple's base in the jungle. Mara and Kathrine are still alive."

Allie's fist relaxed, and she let out a long sigh of delight. The tension in her forehead diminished, and she closed her eyes while taking in a deep breath. "Good . . . We will be there within the hour."

"Do you wish us to capture him for you? My clan will not fail again, now that we are aware of the kinds of treasures he holds."

"No, not unless Mara and Kathrine's lives are in jeopardy. I do not doubt your capabilities, but if what you said about these escape treasures is true, I don't want to chance losing them yet again. He is already in the E-grade, and Elysium's reset of your level and Dao has made suppressing his energy to prevent pillar activation unlikely. You may be able to kill him in a fight, but not before he uses another one of those damnable trinkets. Right now it is likely that only I could completely suppress his soul quickly enough to prevent infusing energy into an escape talisman, so watch and wait, make sure you don't lose him, and keep me updated."

"That may be so, but if Crendir gets ahold of the Elder God's power—"

Allie cut Tre'Zix off with a harsh rebuke as her voice rose. "Mara's life comes before the world quest. I will not risk losing her over some dead god's essence. Keep her in your sights, and only move if her life is in danger or if you are absolutely sure you can secure her first. Securing Mara is the priority, and only after you do so are you able to strike. Otherwise you will wait for me. That is final."

There was a pause on the other side of the communication line. It was obvious he didn't agree with her decision, but it wasn't his call to make. "As you wish. I look forward to the intermingled success of both Gluttony and Wrath in this new age. May Sin guide you."

His small party of survivors reached the outer temple.

Crendir sent out a slashing arc at more of the blue precursor monsters, splattering another dozen of the odd creatures like a cleaver chopping through watermelon. He and his two remaining soldiers were covered in gore, as were the two chained prisoners they had to drag along. He was irritated that they had to keep the ghoul for this long, as she'd intentionally slowed them down over recent days, but she seemed to know more specifics about where they needed to go, while Kathrine seemed somewhat vague in her own knowledge. But he was also unwilling to kill Kathrine outright as he wanted her for himself—her lineage was strong and their children might even receive the gift of Malignant Prophecy if he got lucky, and at worst he could always sell her back to her family for an astronomical amount of money before running if the plan didn't go as expected.

Crendir wondered if his fiancée would even accept him back after all was said and done. But then again, the deeper he went down this rabbit hole, the more he understood the implications this would have for the vampire race as a whole. The markings along the labyrinth grounds and here on the temple walls told a tale as old as the tenth universe, perhaps even older, but revised from the teachings of the current Blood God. A history lost to time and hidden by deceit.

This was all far bigger than him. He understood why Elder Thune was so adamant about getting it done. Crendir needed to see this through.

"Shut the door and get inside!" Crendir shouted, stabbing a hulking, mutated ape creature with toothy suckers like a lamprey in place of a face. Bile and gore splattered all over his dented armor, but he shoulder-checked the next one and blurred forward, killing seven more of the monsters in the blink of an eye. "I SAID, SHUT THE DOOR!"

Faras, the soldier not currently tasked with keeping the prisoners on a tight leash, slammed his broadsword into a chain keeping the temple's stone slab up. The reinforced chain sparked, and as Crendir continued to mow down the enraged, swarming precursors, Faras continued to chop away.

"It's giving! Just hold a moment!" Faras yelled, raising his blade one more time as he infused it with his Dao. The blade shimmered, but he let out a scream when a piercing blue projectile flashed through his left shoulder.

Faras was spun off his feet, flattening to the floor with a grunt. Another projectile bounced off his helmet, smashing his face back into the floor, and Crendir snarled his rage.

"Incompetent FOOL!" Crendir rushed back, abandoning the choke point for only a few moments as he began smashing his own sword into the damaged chain.

The chain then snapped, and the enchanted stone slab crashed down on a dozen precursors as the fanged humanoids crumpled like paper.

A flash of Crendir's aura saw the remaining precursors who'd made it into the passage wither and rot, and the vampire leaned on his sword with a heaving breath while glaring down at the soldier, who was picking himself up. "Those wounds should regenerate soon enough. Get up."

Crendir kicked the man, causing Faras to wince, and turned back to Kathrine and Mara, who were being held in place by thick chains and suppression collars.

"Which . . . way . . ." Crendir asked, sneering with his fangs on full display. "And do not make the mistake of attempting to trick me again, or by the Blood God, I will just kill you both and find the way myself now that we're so close."

Kathrine was too weak from blood loss and beatings to reply, her head flopping to the side with her eyes only partway open as her fingers twitched.

Mara was not in great shape, either, but she was at least able to glare at him and maintain a more normal composure. Spitting black blood onto the ground in front of him, she arched her neck and head-bobbed down one of the three hallways leading farther into the temple. She rasped, "That way."

Crendir remained skeptical, eyeing the other two passages, but they all took sharp turns that prevented him from seeing more than twenty yards out. "Fine. But you're going first. If there are any more traps, you'll be the one triggering them."

Shoving the bound ghoul woman down the corridor and causing her to stumble, he kicked her when she didn't get up. "MOVE!"

Wincing and taking in a ragged breath, Mara grudgingly got to her feet and started down the corridor with a sullen expression. Deep cuts riddled her body, some of the wounds still leaked the black blood indicative of her race, and her hair was matted to the right side of her head, but she continued on anyway.

The trek through the temple was long and slow, and there were a few precursors still lingering inside that had to be dealt with, but the traps had all been triggered long ago, with their shattered remains or scorched runes showing signs of use.

Crendir began to smile as he saw evidence of previous passage, and his heartbeat quickened in excitement. The ghoul bitch wasn't lying after all, and he could almost feel the victory within his grasp. The only things slowing them down were Kathrine and Mara, and both of them were solidly beaten to keep them going whenever they stumbled or fell.

"I . . . I think I can feel it!" Faras gasped in excitement as they entered a large room filled with the bodies of a battle that had to be months old. Other dead vampires, likely locals, were scattered amid the corpses of precursors, with a few heads mounted on spikes and an altar to some unknown god along the far wall.

Crendir could feel it, too. A permeating aura of blood leaked out into the surroundings the farther in they went, it latched on to his Blood subpillar like a leech, but the feeling was invigorating. It wasn't the type of blood energy he was used to, but it felt like a long-lost piece to a puzzle was settling inside him as the soothing aura electrified his very soul.

A small, indiscriminate movement caught Crendir's attention at the periphery of his vision, and he whipped around to stare down the hallway they'd come through.

Nothing.

Absolutely nothing.

Was he seeing things?

Crendir sent out a pulse of his aura, causing the old bodies to rot faster as their coagulated blood was ripped from their insides. But there was no scream, no response, no roar of anger or pain that he'd been expecting.

He listened for heartbeats.

Still nothing.

Frowning, he felt his wrist twitch as the man holding the prisoners' chains asked, "See something, Commander?"

Damn it. Crendir couldn't even remember the man's name. He shook his head and turned around to begin walking once more. "It must be nothing. Carry on, we need to hurry. We're probably still being tracked."

Heading farther into the temple, what Crendir and his comrades didn't see was the chameleon flicker of insectoid chitin as multiple pairs of yellow eyes flashed brightly in the darkness.

Crendir stood in awe, a feeling of reverence coming over him while he beheld the inner sanctum.

The room was very large, a dome in the center of the pyramid, with large spikes sticking out along the walls. Only half of the spikes had any bodies on them, and the corpses looked withered and dry, while the other half of the spikes looked like they'd once been in use but had been torn halfway off, cut off, or obliterated by something. These particular remnants of spikes on the ground were still covered in dried black blood but radiated sinister energies of sacrifice.

Signs of battle also marred the area, with long gashes along the stone. Pentagrams and runes etched into the circumference of the dome flickered or were completely dead. Bending down and touching one of the gashes in the stone, Crendir winced and yanked his hand back when a violently potent remnant of Shadow energy lashed out at him.

His eyebrows raised in surprise. Whatever or whoever had caused these markings had had a fundamentally different view of how Shadow worked, and it made him jealous to think that a Dao insight so potent was even able to be achieved. Especially on a backwater world like this one.

Truly, Panu was an oddity when it came to integrating planets.

More than anything else, though, what caught Crendir's attention was the large coffin in the center of the room. It was laid out on a large and slightly raised platform, and the stone of the coffin was carved intricately in patterns that radiated and pulsed the energy that now permeated most of the temple. This was the source, and it was both ancient and powerful.

Just looking at the coffin gave Crendir a sense of foreboding and dread, and he felt his own soul energies being slowly sucked out of him to feed the coffin with every staggered breath he took.

"By Elysium . . ." Crendir muttered, red eyes wide and taking a step forward. He reached a hand out and ever so slowly touched the coffin. "This is it! This is actually it!"

A pulse of that same energy that'd invigorated him earlier swept through his soul with a thousand times more potency, and Crendir let out a gasp of excited envy as he coveted the secrets of what this coffin held. But he knew he couldn't try to absorb them just yet; he didn't even open the coffin, as he still had to take the vial supplied to him by Elder Thune. Crendir was not a true pureblood, and the mixture in the vial would help him absorb the fallen god's essence long enough for his body to stabilize.

Withdrawing the small crystal vial from his spatial sack, Crendir lifted the vial to his lips and quickly downed the substance as the others watched behind him.

[You have drunk Voluminous Bloodline Inheritance Factor, temporarily upgrading the quality of your vampiric bloodlines to pureblood quality. It is possible to make this a permanent change, should you meet the necessary Dao requirements.]

He turned around, grin wide, as he sneered at the two bloodied prisoners on their knees at the room's edge. "All that trouble to try and keep me off the scent, all that time wasted . . . If only you'd done as you were told the first time, I may have let you live!"

His two soldiers laughed, and Mara nervously bit her cracked lip while Kathrine barely supported herself with obvious head trauma after the last beating.

"You said you wouldn't take our lives if—" Mara began with a quivering voice, only for Crendir to lash out with a pulse of his aura again.

The aura collided with Mara's body like a violent slap to the face, and she reeled back as pockets of black blood were leeched out of her body and her skin began to shrivel. The ghoul woman screamed, writhing on the floor as the vampire soldiers laughed louder at her obvious agony.

"Yes . . . Scream for me and die like a dog, and perhaps—" Crendir's eyes saw a flash of purple blades and a yellow gaze as a tearing motion split space itself in front of him.

Crendir stopped monologuing, dropped the used vial, and created a barrier of blood, intercepting the attack that caused the entire gigantic dome room to shudder with the force as his two guards were annihilated in sprays of gore.

Like chameleons, the spiked chitin and skin of six mantis-like archdemons began converting from the colors of their surroundings to that of a deep-burgundy red. Scythe-like purple blades along their arms, demonic horns sprouting from their heads, pincers clicking, and yellow eyes boring into him, the mantis creatures flared their wings toward him with hissing and the sound of strange laughter.

One of the mantises picked Mara up and administered some kind of liquid into the ghoul's mouth through a long, fleshy, tubelike tongue, and the decay effects of Crendir's aura were quickly subdued and even reversed as Mara began to gasp. They did the same to Kathrine next, though she remained in a semi-comatose state despite her wounds visibly healing to the naked eye.

"Ah yes . . . We've been hunting you for some time now, little vampire!" the one Crendir had come to know as Tre'Zix crowed, laughing as his huge forelegs smashed into the stone with a hiss of delight. "You've been quite the slippery one! To think that you'd have gotten this far with meager trinkets is somewhat befuddling, even if your level is technically higher than ours is right now . . . It brings me great shame to have let you go, and even greater pleasure to see you die before me now!"

Crendir was too shocked to react.

Before he even knew what was happening, five of the six mantis demons sprang. Two went left, two went right, and Tre'Zix launched himself overhead with a flare of his wings as purple scythes infused with Sin erupted in explosions of raw energy. The pack hunters were coordinated and hit him in a dozen different places at once, puncturing Crendir's vampiric armor, cleaving off his arms and legs, and skewering him all over. Gore and blood erupted out of his body like a volcano as his jaw was ripped off, his neck sliced open, his intestines ripped from his insides.

But his lifesaving trinkets all simultaneously activated at once in response. With over fifty of the incredibly expensive amulets and rings flaring to activate at the abrupt change in his life force, they exploded in a shower of light that knocked the archdemons back with angry screeches. Tre'Zix and his comrades all hit the floor and walls on their own feet, though, twisting in the air to land like cats and shielding themselves with barriers of their own as the rebuffing white light sought to kill them while simultaneously healing Crendir.

His limbs stitched back together. His jaw reattached itself. His intestines reentered his torso and the wound zipped shut like it'd never been there before.

WHUMPH

A thick wall of green Unholy power suddenly separated Crendir from the archdemons, and he blinked in shock while wiping the sweat from his eyes. None of his protective trinkets did something like this, nor did they have the ability to produce a barrier of this quality. So just what was creating it?

He saw Tre'Zix scream in rage on the other side of the barrier, wings flaring again as he smashed a purple blade against the thick green wall to create sparks of malignant energies and shock waves across the room. The words and attacks were muffled in volume, though. "GREED WORMS! I'LL GUT YOU FOR THIS! I'LL GUT YOU ALL!"

He'd never seen the archdemon so thoroughly enraged before in the few short times he'd had the misfortune of meeting Tre'Zix.

The sound of a wooden staff tapping on the stone gave Crendir pause, and he hesitantly turned his attention to the right, where a human figure had walked through a shifting portal just behind the coffin.

It was a tall, red-skinned tiefling, toned but not large, and likely blind due to the black bandage wrapped around his eyes and the back of his head. He wore no shirt, and had baggy pants coming down to scale boots that glinted in the light of the magics on display. In his right hand he held a staff with the severed heads of various species hanging from strings off the top, and behind him were similarly dressed tieflings with luminous purple eyes, who were only slightly smaller in stature and wielded various curved blades instead of staves.

"Tut, tut, you didn't think Elysium would allow you to come to this integrating world without competition, did you? You look so surprised! Come now, Tre'Zix, there is no reason to be so angry! Your efforts will prove futile unless you want to whack at it for at least a minute! By then it'll be too late." The tiefling man chuckled, coming to the Unholy barrier and tapping it with one of his knuckles. He seemed completely uncaring of the attacks now raining down on the barrier with whirlwind speeds and cocked his head with a mocking frown. "You and I both know that you assassin types don't gain shield-penetrating abilities of any worth until the D-grade. You'll have a rather hard time breaking through that spell weave now that we've all been reset!"

Some of the other tieflings laughed along with him, and the blindfolded man turned around to stare at Crendir, still on the floor. His frown grew deeper, this time being more genuine. "What in Greed's name are you still doing on the floor, boy?! We don't have time to be dawdling around like this! You have an important part to play and we can't have you stupidly staring up at your would-be murderers with that dumb look on your face. My word, I hope the Gambler knows what he's doing aligning our forces with that incompetent Elder Thune and his goons."

The entire temple rumbled, and the tiefling abruptly looked up as the ground began shaking underneath him. Surprise and then anger crossed the caster's visage as the stone of the ceiling began turning black and cracks began to spread with illuminating neon-teal and gray lights as a vast aura permeated the room.

"Oh my," the tiefling muttered, watching his barrier begin to show cracks of its own, spreading from the ceiling, as a feminine scream of utter rage crashed down on their location. "This is not good. You four, get the coffin. You and you, grab that vampire brat. It appears the reincarnation of Wrath has come a little bit sooner than we'd expected."

Six shirtless tiefling soldiers with grim expressions rushed to secure Crendir and the fallen elder god's coffin, and the four with the coffin let off pained grunts as the magics started eating away at their flesh and sucking in their essence at the touch. But they kept at it and rushed headlong into the portal the tiefling caster had made.

Crendir was still utterly dumbstruck at all that was going on around him and let out a scream as a huge, clawed hand made from bone and ghost plasma smashed through the ceiling.

Ripping off the temple's roof, a huge horned devil made entirely from bones and encased in the body of a phantom glared down with neon-teal flames for eyes. It was absolutely monstrous, and the aura it produced reeked of death and violence. Above the devil were well over two dozen angels of death with glares that could kill, all of which were floating around a singular six-armed, four-winged woman whose black skeleton could be seen through her own phantasmal body. She was beautiful, yet menacing, and just looking at her made Crendir vomit blood as he gasped and hit the ground.

"Oh, hello there, big boy!" The tiefling laughed sheepishly, stepping backward as Crendir was dragged along the floor and the barrier began to shatter. "It's been a few eons! Barktarus, was it?! And, of course, the reincarnation of Wrath herself! Who could forget? It's been a pleasure, but I do believe that it's time for me to leave. Goodbye for now!"

Tre'Zix slammed an empowered blade into the barrier as Allie's aura continued to leave cracks all around it, and the Unholy energy exploded into fragments of green and black light.

The tiefling caster shrieked and jumped through the portal the same moment Crendir was dragged through, and in an instant they were gone from the underdark.

Crendir had somehow made it out alive.

CHAPTER 18

Sunlight filtered through a crack in the curtains, and cold rags lay on her cheek to cool her off.

Mara's head was killing her and her left arm still trembled from time to time from the lingering pain of Crendir's aura attack. It'd been soul-deep, from an E-grade, and the decay had left lingering marks on her inner pillar constructs as well as her outer body, but she was recovering nonetheless. Sweating from fatigue with shallow breaths, her eyes fluttered open when the door to her room in the Brightsville guild hall swung open.

In stepped Allie, in an elegant, formfitting black dress. Pale-white skin, silver eyes, and long, silky brown hair trailing past her left shoulder over her breast made her one of the most beautiful women Mara had ever seen. A slender platinum crown adorned her head—it was plain but pristine and had a series of curved spikes along the outer edge.

"You truly look like a queen now," Mara said weakly, smiling and trying to sit up with a pained wince. "Was it my imagination, or did you look a lot scarier before I passed out and ended up here?"

Allie confidently strode over to her bedside, sat on the mattress, and kissed Mara's forehead before pushing the ghoul woman back down. "That is unimportant. What is important is that you are alive."

Allie stroked Mara's face like a mother would a child and gave her a sad smile. "I have been told that man, Crendir, killed Nin and Vin. It took me questioning over a dozen people before Tre'Zix finally told me . . . I think most people are scared of what and who I am."

"For good reason—" Mara replied, coughing at the end. Spitting black blood into a bucket on the side, she let out a groan. That turned into a frown, and tears began to collect in the corners of her eyes. "Yes . . . I was there. I saw them tortured and killed from only a few feet away. They went cursing him to the end . . . and did not give in to his demands."

Allie's fingers tightened slightly on the bedside, but otherwise there was no change in her expression. "They were . . . good friends. I wish I had known them better."

"They were, and me, too."

Silence ensued.

It took a while for Allie to collect her thoughts, and when she did, she had to sniffle and wipe at her face before clearing her throat. "I will avenge them. Their remains will be buried in the backyard, next to Jose's tombstone. If I'd been back here on Panu, I might have been able to reattach their souls and—"

"Stop," Mara said adamantly, glaring up at Allie with a shake of her head. "You cannot rewrite history, and there was no way for us to know that Crendir would do what he did. You can only look forward, but putting yourself in the past and blaming yourself for not being there is a mistake any of us could have made."

Allie opened her mouth to reply, but no words came out, and she slowly lay down next to her friend to give her a hug.

"Your crown is poking me in the eye," Mara said with a little laugh.

Allie buried her face farther into Mara's armpit and stifled a sob, gripping her best friend harder before violently throwing the crown to the side of the room. "I'm sorry you went through what you did, Mara. I'm so glad you're okay."

Now it was Mara's turn to hug Allie back, and despite her hacking coughs, Allie didn't want to let go.

"Have you talked to Lahn yet?" Mara eventually asked, voice still weak from fatigue.

She could feel Allie twitch, but there was no response.

"It's been half a year since he last saw you," Mara said slowly, peeling Allie's wet face away. "You should see him. A lot has changed since you left to explore the underdark."

Allie's face scrunched up, and she bit her lip, avoiding Mara's eyes. "I know. He's dating someone else now. I was told by Wrath."

"'Dating someone else' is . . . a bit of a stretch," Mara said hesitantly, trying to find the right words. "More like . . . he thinks you forgot about him and abandoned him, so he's trying to move on. He's not in a relationship, Allie. But he does consider himself single and has been on dates."

"Why would he—"

Mara interrupted sharply. "Why would he not? You haven't reached out to him even once."

"I was away!" Allie protested with a squeak.

Mara gave her a dubious look. "Was he supposed to know that? You didn't even say goodbye. You're a terrible girlfriend. The royal ball you were supposed to go to with him as your date . . . he went alone, and he was made fun of. I should know—I was there briefly."

Allie's face fell.

"That was, until other young women started pursuing him anyways," Mara said, sighing. "His brother and sister aren't making as much fun of him now, though they still do despise him. I only kept in light touch with him from time to time before being captured, but the little information he shared with me didn't paint a pretty picture. He's not handled your perceived rejection well. He may even resent you."

Allie's face fell even more.

They stayed like that for a while, just hugging each other, and it seemed that Allie needed more comforting than Mara despite Mara having had the more strenuous ordeal.

Mara didn't mind, though. "How's Kathrine, by the way? Is she all right?"

Allie shrugged. "Depends on your definition of all right. She's traumatized, that's for sure . . . she won't leave Riven's room."

"You gave her Riven's room?"

"Of course. Why wouldn't I, considering their dynamic? She doesn't trust her own soldiers from the Blood Moon Requiem, either, not after what happened."

Mara considered this. "I guess that makes sense. Does you being the reincarnation of Wrath change anything between us?"

"No."

"Good."

"You can't get rid of me that easily, Mara."

The ghoul woman chuckled, then hacked another coughing fit. "Thanks for saving me, Allie. I knew you'd come."

Allie snorted. "Yeah, I really fucked that one up. I should have . . . I should have done things differently in a lot of ways. I'm not always as impenetrable or as competent as I think I might be. But it's as you said—I shouldn't live in the past and should look forward instead. I'll just try to do better, now that I recognize I have a lot of learning to do, in more ways than one."

Mara hesitated. "Are you going to hunt Crendir down?"

"Of course. I already have people working on it . . . but the Greed operatives that whisked him away did a good job at covering their tracks. Tre'Zix is . . . frustrated with me. I can see it in the way he looks at me."

"Why?"

Allie shook her head. "Nothing for you to worry about, Mara. Do you mind if I stay here for a while and sleep next to you? I've had a long day and . . . and I think I need a breather before dealing with all that's happened."

Mara smiled and nodded. "Of course, Allie. But if you want to make it to the next big event in Mandon, where Lahn is going to be attending another social gathering for young noble singles . . . you have to have a plan. At least if the information my spies collected is correct. I received a report this morning . . ."

Mara trailed off with a teasing smile. "You're going to have to clean up your act and think of a good way to apologize. Otherwise you're going to really lose him. That's assuming that you still want to be with him."

Allie rapidly blinked. "You have spies monitoring Lahn? When is it?"

"A few days from now. And of course?! What else are they good for?"

"How pretty are the other girls he's talking to?"

Mara grinned wider. "They're not as pretty as you, I'm sure."

Allie let out a breath. "Do you think he'll forgive me for being so stupid about all this if I explain why I was gone?"

Mara raised an eyebrow. "Forgiveness? That's up to him to decide. It's certainly not a guarantee, but you're quite the catch, and you were the one to bring him up when everyone else was putting him down. I have a feeling that at the very least, he will listen to what you have to say."

[Your time with the Unholy Archbishop Prek An-Gash of the Church of Gluttony, the Ninth Circle of Hell, is now over.

The Unholy Archbishop Prek An-Gash has bought your group the following:
- **E-grade Abyssal Cultivation Array (12.7 million Elysium coins): An array that draws on the powers of Sin, the Abyss, and all the branches of the Unholy foundational pillar to help expedite your cultivation. Drastically improves your foundations when creating your soul lattice to move into the E-grade. This device will shatter once your ascension has completed.**

The Court of Emperor Adali has bought your group the following:
- **One thousand tickets to the Abyssal Descent (these tickets have been directly removed from Emperor Adali's spatial bag and have been transferred to you, cost averted): These tickets allow entry into the Abyssal Descent, one ticket per person.**

King and Queen Rantali have bought your group the following:
- **Abyssal Spirit Guide (three million Elysium coins): A spirit guide that has walked the halls of the descent for a long, long time. The spirit will remain with you while descending and can guide you to the fastest possible routes to further levels. Faster, however, does not mean safer.**

Proceeding to the next audience: High Queen Nephridi of the Blood Moon Requiem, Universe 10]

Riven did not recall anything from the conversation between Prek An-Gash and Gluttony. He'd completely blacked out, but he was finally aware of his surroundings now that the connection was cut. All his allies were passed out, too. Athela, Fay, Prince Rantali, Retesh, Azmoth, Kara, and all the vampire knights with them were splayed out on the ground in various positions and breathing shallowly.

"I apologize for Prek's presence overwhelming them so," Gluttony said casually as the next mirror began to rise out of the sacrificial altar. "Once one goes beyond the S-grade and into the SS-grade, the very multiverse warps around them. Prek is one such entity . . . He wished to let you know that he is happy you were chosen and wishes to speak with you at length when you grow strong enough to stand before him.

Riven was still orienting himself and felt rather dizzy, wobbling from side to side and leaning on his staff to make sure he didn't fall over. Riven just couldn't quite comprehend the immense amount of power behind the Cthalia demon. But he could vividly remember how the presence had felt—it hadn't even been hostile, and Riven's mind had been crushed like a bug under an asteroid.

His state of shock did not last long, as a familiar feminine voice reached out to him through the Abyssal Descent's connection.

"Riven! It's so nice to finally see you again!"

His head whipped up, coming face-to-face with his great-grandmother. The woman still looked rather young, considering she was thousands of years old at the very least, and she wore a brilliant white smile with fangs protruding. Wearing a slender one-piece white dress, she sat on a couch with a goblet of blood in her hand, with no one else but a single thrall servant behind the furniture to await her orders.

"I see you've made it quite far in the Abyssal Descent. Congratulations," she said with a nod, raising her goblet and not giving a single shit about the people passed out behind him on the ground. "Though I expect you will probably go much farther. I must admit, I'm not quite sure how to address you now that you have Gluttony living inside your soul . . . Do you mind if we keep up our relations as it was? Or would Gluttony find that disrespectful?"

"That's fine, Grandmother," Riven said with a very slight bow. Not one that showed utter subservience, but one that showed respect. "I appreciate you coming to talk to me. I've had quite a few questions that I thought you could answer."

"Of course!" High Queen Nephridi said with a wink. "I'd be delighted to help. You know, Elysium's rules on viewership are quite strict concerning your journey as of late. We don't get to see much of what you do anymore because of how intertwined your path has become with the fate of Panu. If by showing us it can cause irreparable damage to you, Elysium either staggers the footage or doesn't show us at all . . . and that just isn't as fun."

Amused, Riven folded his arms. "Well, I'm sorry I can't be as exciting as I once was."

"Oh dear, I didn't say that!" Nephridi said with a grin. "You're just too exciting for your own good. Now, before your questions, I do have some good news!"

"And what's that?"

"Kathrine is alive—your heretic sister, Allie, has saved her!" Nephridi chuckled under her breath and took a sip of her wine. "I didn't see Wrath coming into the picture, but with you two, I probably shouldn't be all that surprised anymore. Regardless, Kathrine was saved and your future wife is now resting in your room back at the guild hall in Brightsville. We in the Blood Moon Requiem are all very interested in how your children will turn out, considering Gluttony now runs through your blood. You're certain to have some of the most powerful offspring a vampire has ever conceived! It's quite exciting!"

Riven gave a half-hearted smile. He was certainly happy that Kathrine was all right—he liked her as a person—but being reminded that he was expected to marry the girl as part of his family's duty to an empire he wasn't even sure he liked didn't sit well with him. Just what had the Blood Moon Requiem done for him, anyways?

They'd supplied an army for Panu, sure, but Crendir had betrayed them. Elder Thune had been a huge pain in Riven's ass from day one. Jalel had tried killing him. Lord Justo Barimont had tried to force himself on Riven's sister. Riven and Allie had almost been assassinated by jealous nobles the very first day of contact with the Blood Moon Requiem, and Kathrine would have died then, too, if not for Riven's Malignant Prophecy activating. Other than Kathrine and General Viku, who else did he even like from his ancestral homeland? Honestly, if not for the fact that the Blood Moon Requiem was an S-grade faction that had a reputation for committing genocides against other galactic factions, one that would pose a danger to him even as Gluttony's reincarnation if push came to shove, he wasn't sure he'd waste his time on them. What was to stop them from assassinating him to save their bloodline from getting into the wrong hands?

Which brought up his first question.

"Allie isn't in any danger, is she?" Riven asked flatly, staring up at the ancient monster disguised as a young woman. His red eyes narrowed. "And where does she stand in the requiem now?"

His grandmother's face fell slightly, and she straightened her posture to sit more erect. "Inquisitors from the church have been talking to me about this very subject over the past day. We are . . . in a tough spot."

Riven's lips thinned in response to that. "I hope you're not going to tell me what I think you're going to tell me."

Nephridi held up her hands placatingly. "Calm down, boy. Let me finish first. Allie is no longer a pureblooded vampire, so she cannot retain her title as princess, but she has been allowed to retain her spot as a noble of House Wraithtide—as long as you don't do anything heretical, too. The Blood God is upset that she chose the path of death and Wrath over his own gifts, but is willing to overlook it as long as the reincarnation of Gluttony remains true to the ways of the vampire."

She gave him a pointed look.

Riven winced internally. He'd already become a heretic with the Blueblood Precursor Clam's gifts, but he wasn't about to say that, either.

Taking his silence as her cue to continue, Nephridi cleared her throat and waved her hand. "Having one of our kind as a bastion for the demons is no doubt a profitable tie for all involved. I'm sure Gluttony would probably agree, but there are only gains to be made when the children of Blood and the children of Sin can find common ground with you, a pureblooded vampire, a child of the Blood God, and Gluttony's reincarnation. So as long as Allie does not do anything to directly oppose the Blood Moon Requiem or the Blood God, and as long as you play your own part in this, the church and the empire are willing to embrace you both."

Riven's eyebrow twitched.

"That still includes marrying Kathrine and bearing children with the gift," his grandmother reminded him while eyeing Athela, Genua, and Fay on the ground. She gestured to them dismissively with her right hand. "Even if you do have these playthings on the side. Not to be rude, of course, I endorse your time with them, but it is very important that Kathrine is the one to bear your heirs. The more with the gift we can create, the stronger our empire becomes. It is why we have become so strong in the past, and I have no doubt, as I said before, that your children will likely be the strongest our empire has ever seen."

Riven's eyebrow twitched again. He was not a thing to be owned, and being told what to do in this situation was fucking infuriating. It didn't necessarily hurt him to obey, but it was a point of pride.

Gluttony whispered in his head, "Once we become strong enough, these demands will be meaningless. For now, play along—it can only help us, and my forces are not what they once were. The Blood Moon Requiem is a powerful faction that we can use as leverage until we gain the former glory of what I used to be and then surpass it. At that time, no one will ever be able to tell you what to do ever again."

Silence ensued.

Riven gritted his teeth, but eventually gave a curt nod. "Yes, Grandmother. I will do as you ask."

"Good! Very good. I'm sure the priests and inquisitors will be more than happy to hear that you're still in line with our plans!" she replied, beaming. "With that reminder out in the open, we believe that Kathrine should stay in your guild hall on Panu where it is safe for the foreseeable future. There are traitors in our ranks . . . Most specifically, that bastard Elder Thune, and he obviously has agents on your planet, given Crendir's situation."

Her features immediately became violently gleeful, and the bloody goblet cracked in her grasp. "I'm sure you've heard by now that he has been . . . involved . . . with things happening on Panu."

"Oh, definitely," Riven said, somewhat surprised that Thune been outright labeled a traitor. "What did he do specifically to get caught, though? To get marked like that?"

She let out what was nearly a growl, shaking her head and trying to calm herself. "The old bastard was found out to have a hand in Kathrine's disappearance—how and why are complicated, but he has links to a taboo cult of traitorous vampires trying to resurrect some ancient pantheon of elder blood gods. Ones that existed before the current order was set in place. When we found out, I immediately set out with inquisitors and my personal guard to kill him, but he'd already vanished by the time we got to his quarters in the capital, and he'd somehow relocated all the planets he owns elsewhere. They're not even located in the Blood Moon Requiem's borders anymore—the star systems they belonged to were simply gone when our fleets arrived to cleanse them. How he even did it without Elysium's intervention is a mystery to all of us, but we have scientists and priests exploring different possibilities, and a bounty for his whereabouts has been posted across all of Universe 10. If he is still here, which is far likelier than hopping entire universes with star systems of those sizes, then it will only be a matter of time before we find him again."

Riven was still hung up on the fact that Elder Thune was part of a cult that likely had a lot of the answers Riven himself was looking for. "The world quest on Panu . . . that elder god is one of the ones Elder Thune is looking for? One of the lost pantheon?"

"Highly likely, yes," Nephridi said with a scowl. "Which is why it cannot remain. The fallen god's essence must be destroyed, not absorbed, and it must be done at any cost. The Blood God even dispensed a religious quest to your sister in hopes that she takes these matters very seriously, and we stress that should you have contact with her, you also take these matters just as seriously. It would mean the difference between making a bonding relationship between vampire-kind and the demon kin of the hells versus an all-out blood feud between the races of demons and vampires should you and your sister not comply."

She gave Riven another stern look. "This is not a threat, Riven. It's a warning over concerns for your own well-being. I'm just telling you how the Blood God will react. He will call down a religious crusade across the cosmos upon both you and your sister, regardless of Wrath and Gluttony being involved, if the ancient bloodlines lost to time are once again brought to light. Doubtless the followers of Wrath and Gluttony will try to intervene on your behalf, leading to needless genocides on both sides. Trillions will die if either you or Allie attempt to take the elder god's power for yourselves, and there isn't a single thing that I could do to stop it."

Ah . . . fuck.

Gluttony internally chuckled but refrained from commenting.

Riven, however, felt cold sweat dripping down his back as he realized just how big a deal being a heretic actually was. "I . . . I see. I will keep that in mind as I go forward. Thank you for the warning. Do you happen to know what Allie's quests say? I'd like to see them for myself if you have access to that information."

His grandmother threw the cracked goblet backward at her thrall servant, muttering something about a new glass, and nodded. "Of course! Of course I do. They've come out on Elysium's cortex for the entire empire to read, and it's been a rather exciting topic of discussion! Take a look, and then we can get on to the supreme prize I've bought for you in hopes that you make it to the very bottom of the descent! Just remember, Riven, I'm on your side. I'm on Allie's side, too. Never forget that! And if she manages to purge Crendir and the elder god's essence from Panu entirely, if she manages to kill him and destroy the ancient heritage, she will be a hero for all of vampire-kind. Let us both pray that she manages to do so."

Cute words from someone who'd tried to whore Allie off to the highest bidder, or, at the very least, was letting other people in the empire do it without intervening. But Riven didn't say that out loud.

Drawing up a system notification on her end, she magnified it for him to read, and soon he was going over Allie's quest information in detail as his grandmother waited patiently for him to finish.

[New system quest UPDATE: Save Mara and Kathrine and secure the Fallen Vampiric God's Essence.

Congratulations! You have completed half of this quest by saving Mara and Kathrine from death. You will not receive system prizes until the other half is completed as described below:

Crendir No-Name, a traitorous E-grade commander from the Blood Moon Requiem, has decided to take matters into his own hands concerning World Quest 4: Blood of the Fallen God. He is attempting to rob you and your planet of the fallen god's essence and opportunity. He is not a pureblooded vampire, but he has been given a means of temporarily disguising himself as a pureblood—becoming one of only a few on your planet who can benefit from drinking the ancient god's blood—and will be able to absorb it without issue.

He has already begun the absorbing process, which will take approximately sixty-two days from now to complete. Crendir No-Name has been given a quest of his own that will reward him with extremely valuable prizes should he succeed—including a portal off Panu to anywhere in the multiverse if he successfully fulfills all his own requirements, INCLUDING AN ENTIRELY NEW ALTERNATIVE BRANCH OF THE BLOOD SUBPILLAR THAT WILL BE RESTORED BY ELYSIUM'S WILL SHOULD HE ABSORB THE BLOOD PROPERLY.

Stop him before he obtains this taboo power and leaves the planet, and secure the ancient one's blood for Riven, or destroy it entirely if this cannot be done. Perhaps your brother, as a pureblooded vampire himself, will benefit if you manage to secure the ancient Blood subpillar alternative? Let the race commence.]

[New religious quest dispensed: Destroy the Fallen God's Bloodline—

You have previously been denounced as an apostate by the Blood God and have angered nearly all vampiric factions across the multiverse in doing so. You are hated by many and loved by few; the Blood God extends to you a new olive branch in light of recent events: Kill Crendir No-Name and purge the Fallen God's blood from the face of Panu entirely. Destroy all remnant artifacts of the ancient, alternate Blood subpillar, and you will be forgiven of your sins. Despite your ascension into Wrath's reincarnation, the Blood God will not tolerate allowing the ancient Blood subpillar alternative to revive itself by way of Elysium's laws. Destroying the ancient Fallen God's blood entirely will result with a gift of one planet to add to your budding empire, one of your choosing within the Blood God's domain, all additional slaves residing on that planet to rule over, devotion from any clergy of the Blood God residing on that planet, and all associated resources on said planet. You will also be labeled a Hero of Blood, and be given a short-range E-grade stargate setup for traversing between planets in adjacent solar systems should you choose to accept. Meanwhile, a crusade will be declared upon your faction and upon Wrath's church should you succeed in killing Crendir yet choose to allow this subpillar to exist. Pick and choose wisely.]

CHAPTER 19

When Riven had asked his great-grandmother about a means to bring Kara back to Panu from the Abyssal Descent, the old vampire had raised a skeptical eyebrow but answered all his questions concerning possible outcomes.

His staff would not work regardless of its Portal Master trait because it could not cross universes.

"It would need to be within the A-grade at least, and your staff is still an F-grade item," she'd said with a shake of her head. "You could try it, but I guarantee the portals will fail."

He'd then asked about the potential of hiring Kara on to the guild hall. To this, his grandmother gave a half shrug. "It is possible. As long as you're willing to keep her confined to your guild hall's borders, then I'm sure Elysium would allow it, just like you contracted Fay's brother, but you'd need to pay the system fee as well as the regular pay to the hired servant."

"Any chance I could have an escorting ship pick her up?"

Nephridi snickered. "We could certainly do that, but not for someone like her. Our ships that are able to transcend galaxies alone are more valuable than her life ten thousand times over, and you're speaking of sending a higher-class vessel, risking it and the crew against the dangers of the outer dark, and blowing through blockades of fighting religious factions that've quarantined your world to drop her off? No, I think not."

Riven had completely forgotten about the blockades. He'd been told once a while ago that battles frequently occurred around Elysium's barrier surrounding Panu, usually between entire armadas of various factions that both supported and opposed Gluttony's return. He could only imagine that it'd gotten worse—or would get worse, considering Allie's timely ascendancy. But he was also somewhat removed from the entire thing in many aspects as—should he and Allie succeed in Panu's conquest—they'd likely be moving the planet anyways, per Elysium's prize.

The armadas would only be a concern if Riven and Allie failed in their attempt. He knew without a doubt that the Blood Moon Requiem would intervene alongside the Church of Gluttony and the Church of Wrath in full force should that happen and an escape attempt be made off Panu, but that was still years away.

How long did it take the best ships available to cross universes, anyways? He honestly didn't know.

The talks continued on for a time, and he came to the conclusion that the guild hall method of bringing Kara over would probably be best, though the distance fee would no doubt be astronomical. Even he might have to raise some cash if the distance was too great, his grandmother told him, but it was otherwise possible. She did, however, say that he'd been rather stupid for putting up three billion for an F-grade mortal, and chided him thoroughly for it before buying him an item to help him descend and then disappearing as the communication lines were cut. It was unfortunate that Elysium limited their buys to only one item and didn't allow Riven his own access to buy anything else from the external options. But by the time she left, the rest of his team was up and about, having recovered from the archbishop's potent presence.

[Your time with High Queen Nephridi of the Blood Moon Requiem, Universe 10, is now over.

High Queen Nephridi has bought your group the following:
- **Map Layout of All Shortcuts Down to Floor Forty-Five (5.2 million Elysium coins): An addition to the Abyssal Spirit Guide you've already been gifted: This three-dimensional map shows all paths to shortcuts downward into the floors below. This map will burn up and destroy itself after you finish Floor Forty-Five.**

The Unholy Archbishop Prek An-Gash has bought your group the following:
- **E-grade Abyssal Cultivation Array (12.7 million Elysium coins): An array that draws on the powers of Sin, the Abyss, and all the branches of the Unholy foundational pillar to help expedite your cultivation. Drastically improves your foundations when creating your soul lattice to move into the E-grade. This device will shatter once your ascension has completed.**

The Court of Emperor Adali has bought your group the following:
- **One thousand tickets to the Abyssal Descent (these tickets have been directly removed from Emperor Adali's spatial bag and have been transferred to you, cost averted): These tickets allow entry into the Abyssal Descent, one ticket per person.**

King and Queen Rantali have bought your group the following:
- **Abyssal Spirit Guide (three million Elysium coins): A spirit guide that has walked the halls of the descent for a long, long time. The spirit will remain with you while descending and can guide you**

to the fastest possible routes to further levels. Faster, however, does not mean safer.

You've completed Floor Twenty-Two: Ocean of Wrath. Proceeding to Floor Twenty-Three: The Silent Chamber.]

Before Riven knew what hit him, he and his friends were all standing in the next floor. A totem shrine twice his height, glowing with Unholy green light, was the only thing penetrating the surrounding darkness, and a circular stone carving in an otherwise perfectly smooth stone floor was projecting a barrier around the shrine with flickering wisps of gray. Outside the circle and beyond the barrier, mutilated bodies numbering in the many dozens lay in various positions, some very old and some very new.

But his eyes, even with vampiric sight, could not penetrate the depths of their surroundings. The land appeared to just fade away—there was no sky, and soon enough a system notification hailed the start of the next event.

[Floor Twenty-Three, the Silent Chamber, is now open to you. On this floor, the cursed enemies you encounter will be unkillable. They will not know where you are unless you make noise, as they are completely blind. Your goal, along with each member of the team that is not a minion, will be to find soul lattice enhancement pills hidden in the outer darkness. Each of your members will need to collect their own set of three before moving on; you cannot give pills to one another. The only safe zone is within the barrier surrounding this altar. Good luck.]

The notification snapped closed, and he turned around to view the rest of his party.

The abyssal spirit floating off to his left held a cube that projected rotating three-dimensional images. It appeared to be a wraith of some kind, but was made out of black abyssal energy instead of the normal kind of plasma seen with most undead.

"It appears you're still with us, Prince Rantali," Riven said with a smirk as the other prince looked around dubiously. "You look like you just came out of a bad nap."

"Don't think you're funny!" Athela remarked, snapping her own notifications closed with a scowl and putting her hands on her hips. "You were the only one that managed to stay awake through the last two encounters, weren't you?! That's so unfair!"

Riven shook his head. "I was knocked out by Prek as well, but I did recover far faster than anyone else and spoke to High Queen Nephridi. Elder Thune has been labeled a heretic and a traitor, so there's that, and Allie saved Kathrine."

"Oh good! Yay! I'm glad Kathrine's all right!"

Prince Rantali grunted and interrupted Athela's cheers. "I wish I'd been able to speak with your grandmother—she's a legend both figuratively and literally. Damn it all . . ."

Some of the nearby vampire knights nodded in agreement with mutters of their own.

Riven ignored them. "The question becomes just what we can learn from this wraith and his map, and then how we're going to proceed with this level. I want to speed up our progress to reach Lillith—I need to get back to Chalgathi's trials soon and want to be done with this descent within two weeks at most."

He turned to the wraith with the cube. "So, spirit guide . . . Is it possible to reach Floor Fifty within two weeks?"

The abyssal wraith slowly nodded while wisps of its ethereal black body moved in and out of the physical plane. It rotated the cube, ripped it in half, and a flood of neon-teal energy laid out a three-dimensional map that sprawled for many meters in all directions.

When the abyssal spirit guide spoke, his voice was raspy, like he'd smoked too many cigarettes. "The Abyssal Descent is always changing, with a few noteworthy exceptions, but even so, the floors that do change always hold some kind of relative similarities. They also hold means to expediting your way down, if you know what to look for, so I would say yes. It is very possible to make it to the fiftieth floor within fourteen days . . . but you must be willing to take big risks to do so."

The wraith held his hands out to the side. "And my name is Barbos."

Dark clouds hung over Brightsville, but that was the norm now. Only rarely did the sun ever peek out over the Death-attuned lands.

Allie's inner circle had now expanded, and they filled the stadium alongside Tre'Zix who was here acting as a representative of Riven's gluttonous forces. The concentration of Sin and Death here was so potent that she wasn't sure a normal mortal person would be able to survive for more than a few seconds.

Once again wearing the sleek platinum crown of spikes, she sat on Tyranus's head next to Mara and scratched her undead drake's scales, eliciting pleasurable moans from the giant beast. It was funny how much like a dog he was, aside from the vastly improved intelligence and power. The draconic beast had also leveled up quite a bit, reaching level 197 in large part due to her own power leaking through to him as he continued his fights for the Thane Necropolis in her absence. He'd become something of a symbol for the press to focus on, with numerous scars now marring his bones and singed areas marking his flesh. Nor was he the only undead drake in their army, either, not after Retesh's forces had fled the northlands across the sea to come here, and there were even a few of the larger dragon variants, too. Tyranus was now most often seen flying over the seas in the north, skirmishing against the merpeople and naga or against Judith's forces that pursued the fleeing undead peoples as they tried to escape genocide.

To say that Allie was proud of Tyranus's accomplishments during her time away was an understatement.

Fimrindle was there, too, sitting as still as usual in lotus position next to the drake's head.

Barktarus the Wrathful, the giant bone-wraith devil, was there with neon flames rippling out of his skull face while he hunched over the slaughtered body of an ox that'd been delivered at his request. Barktarus was one of three commanders that followed Wrath's banishment into the abyss, and according to Wrath, he was the most violent and slaughter-hungry of them all. The devil had a wraith's outline wrapped around his spiked bone body, much like Allie's own body whenever she chose to transform into the Angel of Wrath, as opposed to the Angel of Death form she wore now.

Jebil of the Horror-Crux was Wrath's second commander. An ancient tiefling lich, his body's skin had long lost its red color and turned a stark black, with lines of gray light filtering out of cracks where the skin had been sewn back together with magical threads, very reminiscent of her friend Mara's ghoul body. Jebil also lacked any lips, which made his yellowed teeth look like they were constantly, grotesquely smiling, and he'd chosen to gouge out his own eyes in favor of using mana sight, which left craters in his head where the eyes should have been. Wielding dual bone wands, he was renowned for his ability in magical duels and was far faster than most other casters in both agility and his movement skill sets.

Then there was Amelia Deathfeather, an archangel of death who commanded all other angels of death now sitting, standing, or floating within the stadium. She never removed her metal mask, which was a plain white porcelain without any holes for the eyes or nose. The mask wrapped around her face and clung there without issue, allowing long strands of black hair to fall about her shoulders and down her back. According to Wrath, angels grew more wings the longer they lived if they didn't get direct evolutions for the additional limbs, and Amelia's six absolutely massive black wings indicated that she was prehistoric. Green eyeballs were growing out of the feathers of some of her wings, looking around rather creepily, but her figure was tall and muscular in a very feminine way. Instead of robes or armor like some of the other angels sported, she wore tight wraps like a mummy that covered about two-thirds of her body.

Other demons and undead of both hybrid and nonhybrid varieties were present on the outskirts and waiting patiently to hear what Allie and Wrath had to say, but it was Amelia Deathfeather who spoke first.

"We answer the lion's call," the masked six-winged angel said in a whisper, bowing her head as all the other angels did the same. "Reincarnation, we thank you for hosting our parent sin in your soul aperture."

Allie gave a slight nod of acknowledgment but felt Wrath himself coming to the forefront in the coming seconds.

Just like Riven's soul clone that produced the Great Maw, Allie's own version of soul clone produced the Wrathful Lion. Taken form, it was the size of a horse but lacked fur. Colored dark purple, it was all solid muscle, devoid of fat, with a rigid and sharp look to it. Instead of a fur mane, it had flexible purple spikes that moved as it turned its head. Razor-sharp claws were out at all times, with a long, whiplike tail that ended in a stinger, and its teeth were that of a saber-tooth with huge canines.

"My old friends . . ." Wrath said as he took on physical form and jumped up beside Allie to brush against her before sitting. "It's been a very long time since we had such a thorough get-together."

Chuckles echoed around the stadium, but they were short-lived.

"You have all seen the signs of a dawning new age . . . and we are finally here," Wrath continued after silence claimed the arena once again. "I have found a satisfactory vessel to grow in, we have achieved freedom from Elysium's prison with a second chance at life, and we do so with our friends in Gluttony's entourage close by for mutual support."

Wrath gave Tre'Zix a nod of acknowledgment. "But we are weak in our current state, and this is only the beginning. As you all know, our levels and Dao accomplishments have been reset. We retain some of what we once had but only a mere morsel compared to our previous power. Many of you are still at level 1 in the F-grade, and although I don't doubt that you could probably still win against those far above what you are, you will still need to work hard to reach E-grade as soon as possible. Within the next few months, Jebil of the Horror-Crux will dispense assignments to each of you in the wars that Allie Thane's armies are dealing with now. Panu is an integrating world and we have only a relatively short amount of time to take this planet for ourselves in order to gain Elysium's gift of relocating this planet and hiding it from the greater multiverse to grow. Our worst enemies will doubtless try to come for us when the integration phase is over, and though many of our older followers remain, the faith that our church once had is lacking. We have been gone far too long, as have all the sins and commandments, and we represent a threat to the newer powers that rose up to fill the void of power we left behind."

Jebil the tiefling lich nodded in satisfaction, smiling from underneath his hood.

"The items many of you had have also degraded in power from once-almighty treasures to shadows of their former selves—" Wrath began again. "But per Elysium's agreement, they will ascend at the same rate all of you do. They should not remain worthless F-grade items for long. It is at my command that all of you join the war efforts near Chicago, at the sea borders north of Umbra, and within the hellscape dungeon of Negrada to level yourselves by bathing in slaughter and blood. Gluttony's forces are already on all three fronts and will assist us with any knowledge we may require."

Barktarus cracked his neck and rose to his full height, which was similar to Azmoth's in his giant form. "Master, which of us will you send with Tre'Zix to find Greed's men and the vampire traitor?"

The lion's head turned to the six-winged angel in tight wrappings, staring down the numerous eyes focusing on him from among black feathers. "Amelia Deathfeather is best suited to finding that which is lost. Barkarus, you will be at the forefront of our forces with Jebil. Amelia, bring your angels with you to join the clan of Tre'Zix. We must find the vampire whelp before he absorbs the fallen Blood God's essence, if not for Gluttony's reincarnation, then as a bargaining chip to play with the new Blood God."

"Do you not require one of us to be at your side, my liege?" Amelia queried in a motherly tone from underneath her porcelain mask. "Sometimes you get a bit out of control, and I'd hate to have to resurrect your vessel so early after just having arrived."

Wrath bared his teeth, and the spines on his mane flared outward. "I am not a weak cub, Amelia. Do not coddle me. My vessel is one of only a handful of E-grades on this entire planet."

Some of the others in the stadium laughed at the exchange, but Amelia shook her head in dismay and flicked her wrist. "Fine. Allie, do not let yourself die. Knowing him, I would hate to have to wait another five thousand years to find a vessel that Wrath deems acceptable."

More laughter and murmurs of agreement.

"And what will you be doing, Master?" the deep, booming voice of Barktarus the bone-wraith devil asked while spreading his wings with neon-teal membranes stretched between bones. "What are your plans as Jebil and I take to the fields of battle and Amelia leaves with Gluttony's envoy?"

The Wrathful Lion turned to stare at Allie, who'd remained quiet next to Mara this entire exchange. "Allie and I have some personal matters to attend to before anything else."

The city of Mandon was still in need of repair after Rippenvire's invasion over half a year ago, but it'd come a long way. The multilayered city still reached into the skies to inspire those who looked on it, and the top layer in particular where the previous king, Arthur Brix, lived had been especially tended to. The man was no longer king, but labeled the very first duke under Allie's banner in the new status quo of the Thane Necropolis, while all other nobles had been reduced to barons and counts. Realistically the entire power structure of the Thane Necropolis was still in the making, but knowing that they retained some form of nobility made many of the old, rich families of the region of Dawn less upset about being integrated into the greater power.

"Are you feeling all right?" Lady Shovi Lucio asked her youngest son, coming to stand next to Lahn on the balcony overlooking the sprawling flower gardens that'd been planted only two months before, after the catastrophe and ruin had been cleaned up.

Lahn let out a long sigh, eyes sad as he stared out across the fields of brilliantly colored flowers with teal eyes and pale skin. Adjusting his well-made suit, he tapped one of his boots against the stone railing and leaned over to stare down the fifty-foot drop. "The flowers are a rather nice reminder of how things used to be. I'm amazed the alchemists could come up with a way to retain the greenery by adjusting the genomes of Death-attuned plants—it's almost like the attack on Mandon never happened."

Shovi raised an eyebrow and tussled his now-brown hair. "Did you not like the silver coloring?"

"I like my original brown better. Bought the dye from a vendor in Angor's Midtown two stories below."

She smiled, but brought her own silver locks in front of her to stare at them. "I like mine. Fits the red dress I have on rather nicely! Or so your father tells me."

Lahn tried not to grimace at the mention of his father. Glancing over his shoulder, he saw his asshole of a dad and his two siblings, Parius and Linela, mingling with the crowds of people. They were almost all deathtouched enlightened here, meaning they didn't look all that different from when they'd been alive aside from the color changes, cold flesh, limited pain, and Death attunements they now possessed. Most of the mortal humanoid races had gone this route, including their old enemies, the Tereen elves in the conquered neighboring province, though the humans of Dawn had adapted better to their new reality than the undead elves had.

In fact, many of Dawn's people were outright optimistic about their futures.

"With the Thanes protecting us, why even have an army in Dawn?" he heard one noble say while laughing and drinking from crystal goblets farther into the open-air ballroom.

"It's only a matter of time before this war is over," another man in tight-fitting Victorian garb said in agreement.

"Panu will be ours, and we'll be at the top of the food chain as early adopters." A woman in a ball gown enthusiastically nodded in agreement.

Lahn turned away with a grimace, catching his mother's stare on the way back to look at the flowering fields. "I'm truly all right, Mother. Just down."

"Is this about Allie abandoning you again?" Shovi asked hesitantly, already knowing the answer. "You've been on five dates just in the past month, Lahn. I did like Allie, and I'm disappointed, too, but you'll find someone else who is just as good."

Lahn tried not to scoff, and his hands gripped the railing hard. "She showed me love even while I was ill, Mother. I just thought . . . I just thought that she was different. That's all. Even after her return from wherever she went, she still hasn't come back to see me days later. She's forgotten about me. And I was fool enough to think that maybe, just maybe, she'd want to at least give me closure."

Shovi's eyes fell, but she reached out a hand to grasp her son's and squeezed. "She may have left . . . but I'll always love you, Lahn. Always and forever. You're still my baby boy."

Warmth spread in his chest, and he gave her a gentle smile that replaced his now ever-present scowl. "Thanks, Mom. I know you will, and I'll never forget it. You're the best parent I could ever ask for."

The sound of a bell ringing caused everyone to turn around and the laughter to subside.

Duke Arthur Brix wore a wide, brilliantly white smile and stroked his neatly trimmed brown beard, casting glances over the crowd from where he stood atop a raised platform in the back of the ballroom as the orchestra was setting up string instruments. "Hello, everyone, and welcome to my humble house! I hope you're all enjoying the party, but I wanted to let you know that we'll be clearing out the dance floor soon so that our younger members of the nobility can get to know one another better. At the end of the night, married couples will also be allowed to dance and I hope to see you there, as I will take to the dance floor, too!"

His eyes cast to Lahn with a twinkle. "My daughters are looking for suitors and I can't have them childless forever! They may not be princesses anymore, but who cares when they have the faces of angels!"

"DAD!" one of the young women nearby exclaimed before punching him and hiding her face in embarrassment.

Laughter erupted from the crowd before he waved his hands for silence again.

"Now, now, before I get murdered by my own family!" He laughed while raising a crystal glass. "A toast to the recovery of our dominion! May Dawn flourish under the Thane Necropolis's rule. Long live Riven and Allie Thane!"

Lahn's jaw clenched, but he lifted his glass anyway. "Long live Riven and Allie Thane."

There was a loud cheer, and soon the floor was cleared as music began to play.

A very pretty young woman, the daughter of the duke, started making her way through the crowds in a green dress that hugged her hips. She only had eyes for Lahn as other young men tried to stop and talk to her, but she brushed by them with a growing smile.

"Here she comes!" Shovi whispered excitedly, prodding her son forward. "This'll be the third time she's approached you, Lahn! She's strikingly beautiful—go talk to her and maybe you'll get another date! The last one was fun, yes?"

Lahn's heart lifted slightly at seeing Aurora approach, and his eyes softened. The cold steel cage wrapped around his heart began to loosen, and a smile played at his lips as he remembered the first kiss he'd shared with her. "Yes . . . the last date was rather fun indeed."

Chugging his glass of wine, he shoved it into his mother's hand and winked. "Wish me luck!"

"Oh, you don't need it, but good luck anyways!" Shovi giggled as he made his way through the bustling crowds to leave her behind. "Good luck, Lahn. You're a genuinely kind person and deserving of happiness. I truly hope you find it."

CHAPTER 20

The abyssal spirit guide was doing wonders for their progression, and they'd made good time given the shortcuts it'd provided. Frankly, Riven was having a grand time at it, too.

[**Floor Twenty-Three: the Silent Chamber, has been completed. You have acquired three soul lattice enhancement pills.**]

[**Floor Twenty-Four: Abyssal Shores, has been completed. You have defeated Floor Boss: Rancid Keeper of Blight. All undead in your party, including you, gain 1% increase to your Death subpillar affinity.**]

[**Floor Twenty-Five: Garden of Hunger, has been completed. You've chosen the prize of Guild Hall Add On: Unholy Garden Apparatus to take with you.**]

[**Athela and Fay are both ready to ascend into the E-grade and will automatically do so upon your own ascension.**]

[**Floor Twenty-Six: Wings of Chaos, has been completed. You have freed seven other teams here in the Abyssal Descent from certain death, and Prince Rantali's team has decided to leave the Abyssal Descent at this time. You have been awarded with an Abyssal Speaker Stone Guild Hall Add-On that allows you to communicate with up to seven different souls across the multiverse at will should they accept their end of this gift. Prince Rantali, High Queen Nephridi, Archbishop Prek An-Gash, and General Viku have all accepted their communication link and may be contacted whenever you are within the guild hall's area of effect.**]

[**Floor Twenty-Seven: the Black Mountain, has been completed.**

The swarm of obsidian lava scorpions has been decimated without a single loss on your end. Infernal Dao Pill has been taken as a prize.]

[Azmoth has taken the Infernal Dao Pill, expanding his soul core and soul lattice. Azmoth is ready to ascend into the E-grade and will automatically do so upon your own ascension.]

[Narg is nearly ready for an evolutionary race change. Please stand by as your bonded Beholder Demon finishes his final adjustments over the coming days.]

[Floor Twenty-Eight: the Shadow Bridge, is now open to you. Cross a bridge spanning the depths of the shadow realms, where not even the brightest light can penetrate. Walk the straight line to the end under an aura of permeating darkness that tears at the soul, and you may pass on to the next floor with a boon for your soul lattice.]

Shadow realms was an understatement. Even his vampiric sight didn't work here. He was completely blind, but fuck sight! It was overrated anyways. Riven didn't need it—he could do this all fucking day!

CRUNCH

SQUEAL

"Die for me!!!" Riven cackled as his crystallized gauntlet of blood magic carved through the shadow beast in a swath of blood. He whipped around and shot a blast of inferno down the front of the bridge, eradicating over a hundred of the little arachnid bastards in an instant. Even with the blast of flame, he couldn't actually see, but he did hear the spiders dying via the cries they made as their corpses shriveled into burned, charred husks.

Pulsing mana waves rippled out from his body on repeat every half second, creating a sonar of sorts just like Lillith had taught him to do when finding assassins. He was having a field day. Athela was the same and easily carved through the enemies at their rear with her arachnid blade limbs and the twin katanas that she spun around like batons while flashing here and there with dance-like movements.

Not so much for the rest of his party, though. Azmoth was second to last, using his wings to shield the others while crawling as he was able to take a real beating without much worry. Narg was still absent, undergoing some kind of evolutionary change—and a birth defect? Riven wasn't entirely sure what that was about, but he'd had a few notifications now about the process. Thankfully, Prince Rantali had left and there were fewer people to protect now, but Fay, Genua, Retesh, and Kara were in the middle of the pack and panicking due to their inability to accurately pinpoint the enemies coming for them. Retesh and Fay could do so to a limited extent but not what was needed for this floor, while

Kara was downright useless and frequently screamed over the sounds of battle to make sure she wasn't alone and that she was going in the right direction.

"Riven, WE CAN'T SEE!" she screamed, eyes closed and on all fours while bumping repeatedly into Retesh right in front of her.

"Yes, you've said that about nine times now! Just follow the bridge and keep crawling!" Riven laughed over the storm of his own energies that crackled around them, smashing Jackal down onto another dog-sized spider in a blast of Unholy energy and spinning the staff around, creating a blade of blood on the top end and slicing through another four spiders in quick succession. "Huh. I kind of miss having you as a spear-sword. Your mana recovery has gone way up and your magical blasts are way better, but smashing and cutting things with you really just scratches an itch, ya know?"

Jackal gave an inward confirmation, agreeing with Riven's assessment as Riven skewered yet another spider with the crystallized blood blade protruding from Jackal's skull. Smashing Jackal downward yet again in a fiery explosion of Infernal energy, Riven lifted a hand and went full Sith lord on the bastards while electrifying another three hundred of them with outstretched fingers. "Huzzah!"

"Is this really the time to be playing around?!" Genua called out over the blasts of magic, thunderclaps of Riven's aura storm, and splattering carnage. "I'm leaning toward Kara's assessment that this isn't very safe! Especially for our baby!"

"Oh, quiet you old wench and keep crawling!"

"I'm going to divorce you if you call me an old wench again!"

Riven was about to retort that they'd never been married in the first place, but Genua had lost her goddamn mind. She now believed the remembered experiences with her late husband, the one Riven had murdered, were actually experiences she'd shared with Riven, and it was likely his fault in more ways than one. Even worse, he felt guilty about it despite their attempt to murder him and felt like he had an obligation to take care of the insane elf along with her daughter Len whenever he got back. So he just grunted, played along for her sake, and continued blasting. Muttering to himself, he thought back to that Pixar movie he couldn't quite remember with the orange and blue fish.

Finding Nemo, was it?

"Just keep swimming, just keep swimming . . . Dun-dun-dun, I can't remember the other words!" He saw another swarm of much larger spiders appear on the bridge ahead of them. His eyes narrowed and his hands began to rotate with the staff as a ball of condensed blood energy gathered in front of him. A shock wave radiated out from his body and shattered the oncoming front line of spiders right before his hands thrust forward to unleash the magic. "Nefajia crecus Blood Nova."

The bridge before him shook under the monumental energy unleashed, and an ear-shattering boom sent the growing orb of blood forward like a gigantic cannonball. It rolled through the enemies like they were bowling pins and splattered dark guts everywhere, and watching it through his echolocation mana sense made it all the more fun.

"Gotcha, bitch!" He turned around and shouted over the screaming wussies in the middle. "ONWARD, PLEBIANS! Thou art too slow, and I am growing tired of your shrill feminine screams! Especially you, Azmoth!"

Azmoth grunted from the back, wings spread and still on all fours just like the others so that he didn't accidentally smash them. "Riven asking for pummeling after this, I think."

Athela cackled from beyond the brutalisk with an enthusiastic "OH, HE DESERVES IT, ALL RIGHT!"

"Fucking ungrateful peasant minions," Riven muttered, but loud enough for all the others to hear.

Retesh chuckled and shook his head, his bone fingers scraping at the long bridge. "May the Scythe strike me dead so that I don't have to listen to these rambling fools any longer. But if fate holds, it'll be them that get me killed first."

Allie cleaned off a piece of gore she'd missed after torturing one of the captured vampire traitors, using a dainty hand to wipe her cheek with a handkerchief and triple-checking the mirror to make sure she looked presentable. Truthfully, she could have mutilated and killed those assholes later, but she'd been putting off going to this event because of her nerves.

Hatefully and brutally murdering people made things better and gave her a sense of calm, while simultaneously appeasing Wrath in the back of her mind.

A knock at the door came.

"Enter," Allie called, smoothing out the formfitting black dress that left her shoulders and back bare in order to let her wings out and adjusting her sleek, spiked platinum crown as Mara and two servant girls entered. The servants had come with the manor she'd bought only yesterday, and they gasped and dropped to their knees when they saw who it was.

"C-Chancellor Mara!" one of the maids squeaked while keeping her head low. "You did not say that we were to help dress the queen!"

"Your Majesty!" the other said meekly while repeatedly bowing, obviously a nervous wreck. "We thought we were to help another lady in attendance of Duke Arthur Brix's party! We are not qualified to help one as esteemed and gorgeous as yourself!"

Mara let out a huff of annoyance at the brownnosing. "It appears our queen has already dressed herself, but you may help me with my own dress. Please, fetch the red one from the closet and style my hair until the queen is ready to leave."

"Yes, Chancellor!"

The servant girls nodded rapidly, got to their feet, and hurried to the closet to obtain the desired garment.

Mara slipped out of her work attire, letting the clothes fall to the floor around her as the ghoul woman stared with milky eyes at her best friend.

"You look like you're about to have a panic attack," Mara commented, holding out her arms and stepping into the dress as one of the servants began to pull it up and zip the back. The other servant had a comb ready and was brushing Mara's long black hair out while applying gel to straighten it.

Allie shot Mara a withering look, flaring her wings and almost knocking one of the poor servant girls over in the process. "All is fair in love and war. Do you know that quote?"

"I have heard it." Mara nodded. "I believe it is a saying from your world?"

"It is. It will very much apply in tonight's events, I think," Allie confirmed, turning back to the mirror and then stepping into a pair of high-heeled black boots that came up to her knees. "I fucking hate these shoes. I can barely walk in them, but they look too good not to put on."

"Since when is Queen Allie Thane, the Butcher of Carnis, Angel of Death, reincarnation of Wrath, concerned with how good her shoes look?" Mara giggled with a wink. "You're unbelievably nervous for someone usually so confident."

Allie shot her another glare. "Don't start."

"Just saying . . ." Mara whistled while perfumes were applied by the servants.

"I don't need any perfume. I've already applied some of the best money can buy," Allie remarked when the deathtouched enlightened women shot her questioning glances. "Mara, who else is going to be there aside from Lahn?"

Mara shrugged. "Some of the other nobles of Dawn. Your appointed duke is obviously hosting, so he'll be there, and Lahn's family will probably be there, too. But this event is focused on mingling the young of the noble houses in order to find wives and husbands . . . Dawn needs to repopulate after Rippenvire's attack and the recent war against Tereen, so you can expect a strong presence of younger people like yourself."

Allie tsked in annoyance, her pale face turning into a grimace. "I should just murder them all and be done with it."

The two servants froze in place, horrified but neither brave enough to address it.

"She's joking," Mara said placatingly to the servant girls. "Allie, you should really be careful about the things you say in the presence of others in case they take it literally."

"Eat a bag of dicks, Mara. I do what I want."

"Eat a bag of what?!"

"You heard me, bitch!"

Allie let out a laugh and grinned for the first time all day and swatted Mara's face with a wing. "That's what you get for telling me how to live my life."

Mara rubbed the bridge of her nose where she'd been whacked and glared back. "You're starting to sound like Riven and Athela. Isn't that something they often say?"

"It is."

"Are you nervous they aren't back yet?"

Allie scoffed. "Absolutely not. He'll be back and soon enough likely overtake me for the number-one spot on Panu's power boards again if things keep going the way they have been, and then I'll be forced to one-up him again to show him who's boss."

"Mmm. I see. Well, are you ready to go?" Mara asked, thanking the two servants and stepping away to put a hand on Allie's bare shoulder, staring at their dresses in the long mirror and appreciating the style of the craftsmanship. "We look great."

"Mara, are you even dating anyone nowadays?"

"Allie, my private life is off-limits."

"That's not fair! You know everything about mine!"

"Tough tits, bitch." Mara gave Allie a jab to the ribs and smirked when Allie recoiled. "Now, put on your big-girl panties and look the part. We're about to make a splash, and you MUST maintain your composure while there. Remember what you promised me—no tantrums, no killing, and no matter what, no giving in to Wrath's impulses if you see Lahn dancing with another girl. Got it?"

Allie grumbled in a whisper. "Yes, Mom."

"What was that?!"

"I said yes! So shut up and come along, I don't want to have to go all by myself and lord knows your stubby ghoul legs are going to slow me down since you can't fly!"

"I think I'm offended."

"Good. Nin and Vin would have wanted it that way."

Mara snickered, then her face fell slightly with a hint of sadness. "Yes . . . yes, I suppose they would have."

Arthur Brix's home, rebuilt on the top layer of the city, was quite elaborate. Mages had cleared the clouds, and starlight from nebulas far above created a beautiful tapestry in the night sky as the sound of music and dancing from within the palace could be heard even from the front gate.

Even now, hours late to the event, there was still a moderate line of people waiting to get in as they presented themselves to the palace guards with invitations at the ready. They were all dressed in their fanciest clothes and loudly bragged to one another about the estates, businesses, and wealth they owned while trying to attract those of the opposite sex nearby. It was a mating ritual of the wealthy, with snobby parents trying to play matchmaker in hushed whispers as their young adult children flirted casually.

Pulling up in a nondescript carriage with tinted windows, the horses came to a stop, and Allie studied the line with a worried frown. "I don't see Lahn or his family."

"That's because they're probably already inside, idiot." Mara smacked Allie upside the forehead with an open palm and laughed at the expression she made. "That's what you get for hitting me with your wing!"

"Humph."

Allie lifted her nose, took in a deep breath, and closed her eyes. Folding one hand on top of the other, she proceeded to breathe in and out to calm herself, nervously tapping one foot, and eventually gained the courage to get out. "Here goes nothing. Let's hope that he'll at least see me, so that I can try to explain why I haven't talked to him in so long."

"All you can do is your best," Mara happily agreed and pulled the latch to swing the door open. "After you, majesty dearest."

"Oh, shut it."

Steeling herself after another brief eye roll, Allie stepped out of the carriage. People were already watching to see who the unmarked carriage had brought, and the click of her heels on cobblestone was met with resounding gasps and hushed whispers as she stretched her wings after being in that cramped space for so long.

Dead silence ensued, and slowly but surely many of the noble families knelt and bowed their heads in submission as she stared out at them. The palace guards gawked but quickly followed suit, and the only sound was now coming from inside the palace itself, where people were still blissfully unaware of Allie's presence.

"You may rise," Allie said to the crowd, and they all quickly stood as one of the more prominent families she'd met in Mandon came to greet her.

Though she couldn't remember their names.

"Your Majesty!" a man with a cane and a pointy, short beard said excitedly, flashing his wife in a pink ball gown a wide grin before coming to stop in front of the pair of women. "And Chancellor Mara! What an absolutely exquisite surprise! No one had informed us that you'd both be attending the duke's ball tonight. Was this a spontaneous decision or a surprise he has yet to tell us about?!"

"You both look utterly stunning, might I add!" the wife in pink exclaimed with a wave of a fan. "Absolutely beautiful! Are either of you looking for a husband? This is a mingling event for the young nobles to meet after all—may I introduce you two lovely women to a few of the young men our family knows?"

Mara shook her head with a polite smile. "No, thank you. I believe the queen already has her sights set on someone very particular."

"Oh really?!" the wife exclaimed jubilantly. "My, my! Is he here, then?!"

Allie gave the woman a half-hearted smile. "He is . . . though whether or not he'll receive my presence well is to be determined."

"What fool would not receive your presence with anything but joy?!" the husband said in very real shock. "You're a hero to our people and beyond stunning, if I may be as bold as my wife here! You will have no problem in your endeavors, whoever it may be. I am sure of it."

"Agreed!" the wife chipped in.

Allie laughed. "If only I had your confidence in myself."

They probably would have kept on talking, but Allie cut the conversation short with a curt nod and another forced smile before simply walking away. Moving with Mara beside her and bypassing the entire line, Allie came to the gates, where the palace guards promptly stood aside with another low bow.

"Your Majesty!" the lead guard in shiny armor said, saluting as he stood straight again. "Chancellor! I apologize! We were not made aware of your coming! Otherwise we'd have had an announcer call it to the crowds!"

Allie pursed her lips, thought about it, and then said, "How about you escort us in and do the honors for us?"

"Y-you wish me to announce your presence to the ballroom?" the guard asked curiously. "I would be honored, Your Majesty! Please, follow me! There are refreshments in the guest hall beyond the ballroom if you need any, and there are private lounges with balcony views overlooking the flowering fields on the second floor if you wish to have a more scenic view."

"One question, before we go," Allie pressed, holding up a finger before the man could turn to lead them in. "Wings? Or no wings? I want a man's opinion on the subject."

In another second, her wings had retracted back into her skin, leaving only her bare back where they'd once been protruding. She then extended them as the black feathers pressed outward and retracted them once more.

"Well?" she asked curiously, eyebrow raised. "What do you think?"

The soldier looked helplessly to Mara, who gave no indication of what she thought, and then he glanced at his compatriots, who all shook their heads.

"I . . ." He hesitated, weighing his options in case he said something wrong. "I believe you'd probably navigate the passages and crowds better without wings, Your Majesty. You look stunning either way."

Allie chuckled at the remark, holding a hand to her lips as her wings slowly disappeared into her back. "Quite the diplomatic response. Very well, no wings it is. Please, take us inside and introduce us. I am curious to see what Duke Arthur Brix has done with his new palace. He's quite the bragging type, so I can only hope it lives up to expectations."

The palace guard nodded, quickly turned, and began leading both women past a series of well-kept gardens and inside.

The music became louder as they walked, and Allie didn't say anything else as she felt her heart beating rapidly in her chest despite her efforts to keep herself composed. She couldn't believe how undeniably stupid she'd been in not contacting Lahn for so long, but honestly, she'd taken him for granted. In her mind, she'd felt like he'd never leave her and she had nothing to worry about. Not that he hadn't deserved an explanation, but she'd thought he didn't need one since he'd basically worshipped her prior to her leaving.

That had been a mistake, a foolish and arrogant mistake, and now she realized that it'd also been selfish. She'd not done it on purpose, but he'd been put on the back burner in her mind as more pressing issues arose. She'd not considered how he'd feel if she just left to attend to these things without actually trying to initiate contact to keep him in the loop. From Mara's point of view, if it was accurate, he'd felt abandoned.

That was entirely, 100 percent, her own fault. Allie had already acknowledged that.

So no matter what she saw here, no matter what his reaction to her was, she would take it in stride and try to do better next time. If there was a next time, and if he hadn't already been stolen by some rabid bitch in the—

She felt her nails biting deep into the flesh of her palms and realized she was gritting her teeth as an electric trickle of Sin snapped out and killed a nearby potted plant. Already there were murmurs and more gasps as they continued to follow the palace guard through the entrance hall and past groups of noble families playing politics with one another, so she quickly reined in her building rage at something that she hadn't even verified yet and healed her hand before anyone noticed the wound. This required a delicate hand, not a violent one, even if she needed to win her man back from the clutches of some undeserving hag.

"Easy, tiger . . ." Mara whispered out the side of her mouth, leaning in. "Remember what you promised."

Allie grunted her affirmation, and within a few short seconds they were under the arch of the entryway leading into the ballroom.

And boy oh boy, the duke had not lied about his estate in the bragging letters he'd sent her when inviting her over for tea.

Crystal chandeliers hung from an arched ceiling painted with scenes of battles, some of which were even depicting her. Large stained glass windows illuminated by glowstones rose up from the floor to the ceiling, with Roman-style pillars holding up the roof on the perimeter where tables and alcoholic beverages were set. The archway they stood in actually had a wide staircase leading down into a hollowed-out bottom spanning dozens of yards across to accommodate where the landscape had dipped on the hill that this palace was built on, allowing Allie a bird's-eye view of the rest of the party dancing below as the orchestra played music over jovial laughter.

But that all stopped as people began looking up to the archway where she stood, and it went dead silent when the palace guard cleared his throat and jammed the butt of his spear three times on the floor to get their attention.

"Esteemed ladies and gentlemen, nobles and aristocrats!" the palace guard shouted at the top of his lungs, and he turned to grandly gesture with a flourishing bow toward the two women at his right. "May I present Chancellor Mara, and the very legend of our fine necropolis, Queen Allie Thane, who has chosen to grace us with her presence tonight! Please, welcome them both with me as they descend to the dance floor!"

CHAPTER 21

A thundering round of applause met Lahn's ears as he stared wide-eyed up at the stunning visage of his ex-girlfriend, who just happened to be queen of this entire continent. Everything about her was perfect, from the way the tight black dress hugged her body to the way her silver eyes glowed lightly in the warm light of the ballroom.

Though he could tell even from here that the smile she gave the crowd was a forced one. Usually whenever she was genuinely happy, the corners of her eyes would scrunch up in amusement, so he had to guess that she was now just being polite. Perhaps she was here on official business to talk to the duke, but he could tell that she'd not wanted to come just by the way she held herself stiff and erect.

Where had she been all this time?

"Wow, the queen really is pretty. And so young!" Aurora exclaimed over the excited clapping and chitchat around the room. "It's amazing to think she's the most powerful person on this planet! Can you believe it?"

The young woman glanced up at the man she was holding by the arm, her fingers entangled in his. Her green ball gown glittered with diamonds as she moved, and her brows furrowed under blond locks of hair while she tilted her head to the side with a concerned expression. "Lahn? Is everything okay? You look sick."

Indeed, he felt sick. His entire world was crashing down around him, and it only got worse as Allie made her way down the stairs from the entrance arch. Young and old men alike stared at her like hungry vultures, many of them even approaching Allie as they took their chances to try and introduce themselves. They were the best of Dawn, falling over like little boys in a candy shop, and Allie was the candy jar.

A candy jar that Lahn used to call his own.

The music started up again, though the dances were still paused temporarily due to the queen's entrance, and people began to talk in audible conversations about why she might be here. He watched her as she politely engaged in conversation with over two dozen men, one after another, and when she let out a laugh at a witty joke told by a particularly handsome knight of the realm, Lahn literally felt like he was going to puke.

"Lahn?" Aurora asked once again.

He blinked rapidly, snapping out of his staring trance. "Um, yes, Aurora. Sorry, I just don't feel very good. I may be coming down with sickness of some sort. I apologize."

She put a hand to his forehead and came away with sweat. "Oh my god, you're burning up! Here, let me go get you some cold water!"

Getting up to stand, the former princess bent over and kissed him on the forehead before trailing a hand across his shoulder seductively. "I'll be right back!"

Allie's heart slammed in her chest as she watched a pretty young woman kiss Lahn on the forehead and run off with a giggle. She'd seen the way they were holding hands—she'd spotted them immediately upon entering this blasted place and had started making her way over to the pair—but she was allowing all these over-reaching buffoons to slow her down so she had the opportunity to collect herself.

Mara was gone, having told Allie this was her battle to fight, but she was on the sidelines and talking to some merchant acquaintances that ran one of the larger guilds of their empire and was ready to be there for emotional support if Allie needed it.

"You could just violently kill the girl . . ." Wrath whispered, laughing into her head. "Stuff her body in a box and sink it in the ocean. Killing the competition has always worked for me . . ."

She firmly pushed the sin back into a box in the back of her mind, but not before a pulse of rage crashed into her mind like a battering ram. It was all she could do to keep herself upright, and she felt her bones literally creaking with pent-up energy as she tried not to lash out or cry.

That dirty bitch had kissed Lahn, right in front of her, and despite all of Allie's power, she felt helpless to do anything about it.

The rumors were right. He really had moved on.

Perhaps coming here had been a mistake.

"You are truly a rose with no equal!" one of the more handsome young men said from her right, loud enough to snap her out of her own wallowing misery. Gelled-back black hair and a large build with a tight-fitting vest was the name of the game for this guy.

She let her eyes lift, meeting his chiseled jawline and letting her gaze wander over his large biceps. He was cute. Perhaps . . .

She shifted her gaze to Lahn, who was intentionally avoiding looking at her now. At least, it was probably intentional. He'd heard the announcement about her arrival, right?

Perhaps she'd try to make Lahn jealous. Lahn had always been very insecure about her past lovers after all. Especially the thralls she'd since disposed of, but even when it came to her ex-boyfriends back on Earth. It was a petty thing, but would certainly make her feel better after seeing that whore kiss Lahn in the very same room Allie occupied.

He was flaunting that whore in front of Allie on purpose, wasn't he?

Or maybe not. Maybe that was just Wrath making her unnaturally angry again for no reason. But this felt justified—she was fucking pissed that the bitch had dared to do such a thing in her presence.

But she couldn't be violent here—she'd promised Mara. This was a different kind of battle than the ones she was used to. Why did other women have to find Lahn attractive? Why now?

Allie would make a move and would see if he cared, and then she'd try to figure out whether or not she should approach. If Lahn did seem to care, she'd go. If not, she honestly didn't know what she'd do. She hadn't thought that far ahead.

"A rose with no equal? Is that so?" Allie said, taking a real interest in the conversation for the first time since arriving. She put on a fake but wide smile and turned her full attention on the handsome young man. "I am flattered. What's your name?"

She lifted her hand, and the nobleman seemed immediately shocked to be singled out among the crowd, but also incredibly eager as he bent to kiss the top of her extended hand.

"Adam Zrinski, Your Majesty! My family owns one of the largest mines in the necropolis. We supply the army with power stones and mithril. Perhaps you've heard of the Zrinskis?" he said, standing erect and absolutely delighted amid the irritated scowls and side-eyes his peers were giving him. "Are you here for the dance? Or something more political?"

She smiled seductively, doing an obvious once-over of the man's tall figure with her eyes before replying, "A little bit of both."

He grinned wickedly, catching the hint. "Well, would I be too forward in asking you for your first dance when the floor opens again? It would make my day if you'd grace me with such an opportunity!"

Shooting a quick glance left to see if Lahn had noticed, she realized that he wasn't even there anymore. Where he'd gone she had no idea, but her heart fell when she saw the woman in the green ball gown trailing after a shadow onto a balcony.

He'd left.

Lahn had just gotten up . . . and left. Without saying a word to her, despite the announcement of her arrival.

This Adam Zrinski brat was immediately forgotten. Biting her lip and fingers curling, she didn't realize that she was staring the way Lahn had exited before a familiar voice called out to her and the nearby crowd parted.

"Allie! So glad you made it!" Duke Arthur Brix came in with a boisterous laugh, wearing a three-piece outfit in various shades of blue. "I never thought I'd get to see you here with how busy you've become! Did my letters finally convince you to see the light? What do you think of the new palace?!"

He gestured around while spinning, arms raised.

Allie had to clear her throat twice and had a hard time keeping herself together, but managed a laugh and a nod. "Y-yes, Arthur. If anything, the letters certainly made it easier to decide on attending."

She chuckled with a shake of her head. "Though, honestly, I came for someone very important and dear to me. Do you mind if we talk in private? Perhaps on one of the balconies?"

Allie could see the hesitation creep across the duke's face, but he hid the expression under a mask of a smile and waved for her to follow. "Of course! This way. I'll grab us a drink."

The Adam Zrinski fellow looked rather crestfallen as Allie left, and she gave him a small wave as her high-heeled boots clicked along the floor behind the duke without another thought about the matter.

The duke acquired two champagne glasses from a server and handed the sparkling beverage to Allie as they made their way out to the opposite end from where she'd seen the blonde woman in green exit. If Allie was right, the balconies were dead ends and Lahn would be out there.

But before they even got halfway to the balcony, through the crowds of admiring people, Arthur Brix turned a curious eye on Allie and gave a small frown. "Are you here for Lahn, perhaps?"

Allie waved to Mara as they passed. "Is it that obvious?"

"No, it wasn't obvious. At least not at first." Arthur faced front again, stroking his short, well-trimmed beard. He took a sip of the champagne and savored it before swallowing. "Everyone was under the impression that you and Lahn weren't courting anymore. Those few that'd known in the first place, that is."

Allie's gaze fell, and her shoulders slumped. "So I am told."

"Is that not the case, then? Lahn has been dating other people, you know."

"People as in multiple?"

Arthur shrugged. "That's what his parents keep telling me. Though the one he seems most intertwined with lately happens to be my daughter Aurora . . . so I do have an inside informant on his life as of late. They haven't been dating long, though, just a few times going out, and it isn't anything exclusive yet."

Allie nearly tripped, silver eyes going wide and a painful aching beginning to grip her heart. "Oh . . . Oh, I see. Lahn and I never truly broke up, but I . . . I did get rather busy."

"Busy enough to disappear for half a year without warning is what I heard," he stated. Turning slowly to face her right before the last balcony's archway, his face scrunched up into something akin to worry. "Is this going to be a problem for her? For Aurora? She's a good daughter with an even better heart. I don't want anything happening to her, so if I need to pull her back—"

Allie held up a hand to cut him off, and she grudgingly shook her head. "I know I have quite a sinister reputation, Arthur. But be assured that no harm will come to your daughter, at least not from me. I will be the first to admit that I have made mistakes . . . but that doesn't mean I won't try to win Lahn back."

Arthur visibly relaxed, letting out a sigh and smiling, but he did cast a quick glance over Allie's shoulder as the crowds mulled about. He squinted in recognition at someone, but returned his focus to Allie not even a moment later. "Very good, then. Well, why come to me? If you want to win Lahn back, then talk to him directly and see where his feelings are."

Adjusting her platinum crown and huffing, Allie avoided his gaze and kicked at the ground absentmindedly. "I'm just nervous. I was wanting a man's advice on how to proceed, and my brother is still stuck in a pocket realm and won't be back for a long time. I was also quite rude to him the last we talked, so I don't know if he's still angry at me, either."

Arthur raised an eyebrow and took another sip of his beverage. "I'd been wondering about that. Is that where you were this entire time? A pocket realm?"

"Yes. I didn't realize it'd take so long to get out, and before that I'd been exploring the underdark with regard to one of the world quests." She lifted her head and sniffled, wiping a tear from her eye. "I was stupid, taking Lahn for granted. I didn't tell him anything of what I was doing because I didn't want to worry him, but Mara said I'd only done the opposite by not explaining things. And then when weeks became months I got caught up in everything, and now I just feel like a stupid little girl still stuck in high school because I'm too scared to go over and say hi to a boy."

"You didn't seem to have a hard time talking to those other young men who swarmed you earlier," Arthur said with a small smile.

Allie huffed and glared at the old bastard. "That was only to make Lahn jealous. It didn't work."

The duke snorted a laugh and nearly choked on his drink. Spluttering slightly, he wiped the liquid from his face and shook his head. "Allie dear, that is not the way to go about these things. If anything, you'll only make it worse by doing that. Mind games and manipulation are not a way into a man's heart."

"There's a saying on my world that goes 'All is fair in love and war.'"

"That . . . isn't necessarily wrong, but you're already in the doghouse, so to speak. That is a saying from your world, too, yes? Communication skills are very important in any relationship, and actions speak louder than words. You flirting with other young men in front of him is in no way going to win his hand back, even if it does make him jealous."

Allie gritted her teeth and avoided eye contact, grinding the heel of her right boot into the floor. "I saw another girl kiss him, and she was even holding his hand."

"Yes, that'd be my daughter Aurora."

"Well, I couldn't just stand by and feel so shitty about myself after watching that! I . . . I don't know. I know this is all my fault, but I got insanely jealous and . . . and my heart hurt seeing it. I just . . ." Allie's lips began to tremble and her cheeks began to flush. She wiped away a tear that'd begun running down her face, then wiped away another, and another. "I just want Lahn back and am afraid I messed things up to where he'll never hold me again. I miss him so fucking much. I don't think I'll ever be able to find someone as pure of heart as that bastard kid ever again unless he decides . . . to give me a second chance. I messed up big-time."

The duke's eyes softened, and he took Allie's drink from her, as she hadn't touched it. Setting both glasses down on a tray after waving over a servant, he put his hands on her shoulders. "As much as I am sad that this may impact my daughter if things go your way, she will recover and doubtless find someone else. However, I am still of the mindset that you should tell these things directly to Lahn instead of trying to make him jealous or confiding in me."

Allie let out a stifled sob, now actively crying while wiping away long streaks of black eyeliner that came with the tears. "I don't know how to tell him that I'm sorry. He's already moved on. I know we weren't dating all that long, but he's special. He's incredibly kind. Not many people are, you know? I'm certainly not, but I crave it from him and he makes me a better person. I just feel like such a moron. I took him for granted."

The music changed to a more upbeat and happier note as the orchestra began another song. A call for the dance floor to open back up again was announced, and the sound of people filing around to make way for the dancers was heard.

Arthur let out another sigh and shook his head. "I believe that you may be surprised. And as for not knowing how to tell him, well, I think he's already heard enough."

Turning her around by the shoulders, Arthur brought Allie face-to-face with a trio of familiar faces.

The duke's daughter Aurora stood in her green ball gown next to Lady Shovi Lucio. Lahn's mother looked quite different with the silver hair coloring, but she looked genuinely happy to see Allie when their eyes met. Aurora not so much. She looked sad and resigned, possibly even disappointed, but still managed to give Allie a polite smile and a nod before turning around and walking away toward the tables holding copious amounts of alcohol.

But the third person was the one that drew Allie's attention the most, and her breath caught in her chest when she saw it was Lahn. He looked better up close, especially after the change into a deathtouched enlightened. Lahn was a bit paler but more muscular now and had even become slightly taller, with neon-teal eyes and the same brown hair she used to run her fingers through on dates. The three-piece suit he wore also looked rather nice.

He was silently crying just like she was, but made no move to wipe the tears away. He was close enough to have heard the entire conversation Allie had just had with Arthur, though she'd been so caught up in her own emotional turmoil that she'd not paid attention to her surroundings and didn't know how long Lahn had been standing there.

Allie had been the centerpiece of attention since arriving, and with the duke that had increased even more so. Now that she was openly crying and staring at someone else who was doing the same, the crowd of people nearby weren't even trying to hide their stares as they whispered to one another in curious undertones.

"Would . . ." Lahn had to stop so his shuddering voice was brought back under control, but his eyes never left hers. "Would you want to join my mother and me for dinner tonight? At . . . um . . . at our table, in the back? I . . ."

He paused, trying to figure out how to say it. "I . . . I've missed you, too. And I think . . . I think you have some explaining to do. But you were there for me when no one else but my mother was, so I forgive you, Allie. I'm just glad you're back."

Allie's eyes scrunched up, and her hands came over her chest to wring her fingers with a nervous tic as the waterworks flowed out. Standing like a deer caught in the headlights, she couldn't think of anything to do except stare at him. She felt very, very small in that moment, and was saved from further embarrassment when Lahn took three long steps forward to wrap her in the warmest hug she'd ever had.

He was saying something, words of some kind, but her mind lingered on the press of his body against hers. Pushing her hands up to wrap around his neck, she pulled his head down and kissed him in front of the entire crowd of onlookers, holding her lips to his for a long, long time as the crowd erupted in gasps and surprised applause.

She finally felt like she was home, and she wouldn't be taking him for granted ever again.

Pulling away, she pulled her crown off her head and buried her face in his chest. "I'd love to come have dinner with you. I'm sorry, Lahn. I'm so, so sorry . . . for making you feel like I'd abandoned you. Thank you for giving me the chance to explain."

Kissing her again on the forehead, he used his sleeves to wipe the mascara off her face and put a hand on her cheek. "Come on. You can tell me all about it over some drinks and good food. These events are . . . if anything, a good source of nutrition."

He gave her a playful wink, took her hand in his, and began walking to collect his mother as the three headed off for the opposite side of the large room where dinner tables had been set up for attendees and their families.

CHAPTER 22

Amelia Deathfeather's blank porcelain mask stared upward as she worked. A three-dimensional tapestry was being woven, rewoven, and undone at a rapid pace, with flickers of various dark arts she was analyzing as all six stretched-out wings with all their eyeballs watched the symphony of complex magics unfold.

Green, red, and then black light shimmered and twisted in the air, with runic sigils flashing and shattering over and over again, and slowly but surely a small hole in space began to form.

The angels of death serving Wrath drew weapons, and Tre'Zix, along with his clan, got ready to enter, taking a front-line position.

"You are . . . quite talented," Tre'Zix told Amelia with a click of his mandibles, purple scythes glinting in the magical light show. "Hacking remnant mana particles over a week old, especially when Greed's goons put curse restrictions on the portal's wormhole . . . I'm very impressed."

"Not all things are handled with outright power," Amelia stated quietly, slowly stitching together the old magics and spreading open the rift through space that'd been there once before. "Some things require . . . a finer touch."

Her fingers flared, and the portal tore completely open. On the other side was a dark cave, and out of that cave a snowstorm was billowing not even fifty feet from their location.

Tre'Zix entered first, his clan following. Amelia Deathfeather followed behind with her own armored entourage, and soon the portal snapped closed behind them.

The hunt for Crendir and Greed's forces on Panu was back in business.

Adam Zrinski, the good-looking musclehead she'd used to make Lahn jealous, was now heading their way as Allie caught up with Shovi. Lahn had gone to get them all more drinks and some food from the banquet tables that were set up much like a buffet, and apparently this Adam character had thought it his opportune moment to swoop in for another chance to talk with the queen.

Allie was having none of it, but she supposed that this was her fault as well.

Getting his hopes up like she'd done was probably something she should avoid in the future, and it made her realize she had a lot of growing up to do.

"Queen Thane!" Adam said, shooting Lady Shovi a dismissive look before beaming back at Allie's sitting figure below his standing shadow. "I was hoping to have a moment of your time for a dance! As you suggested earlier—"

"I suggested nothing." Allie cut him off with a shake of her head. "I'm afraid I'm in a private conversation, and if you haven't noticed, I've already selected a dance partner. You're a good-looking man, Adam. I'm sure you'll find someone else here to dance with."

The young man's face fell, and he tried but failed to suppress a significant degree of frustration, judging by the way his eyebrows twitched, his jawline hardened, and his lips turned at the edges. "Do you speak of the Lucio boy? Lahn, was it? If I may be so bold, why him?"

Shovi's fingernails dug into the tablecloth, and her gaze darkened, but she let Allie do the talking for them both.

"Why is it any of your business who I choose?" Allie asked curiously, tilting her head to the side and putting on a small smile. "I'm the most powerful person on this planet, according to Elysium's rankings, and I can do whatever I want. Who are you to question me?"

The young man was nothing if not persistent, and furrowed his brows while trying to think of how he wanted to phrase his next sentence. "I just believe you could do much better, and for someone of your caliber, I believe that I could—"

"Is everything all right, Allie?" Lahn asked, coming back and setting down a few drinks, followed by two servants carrying three trays of food. "You look agitated. Is he bothering you?"

Sipping on the remnants of her third glass of wine and pushing it to the side, Allie gave Lahn a buzzed grin and shook her head. "Nothing I can't handle, Lahn."

"Yes, Lahn. Your betters are talking," Adam sneered. He was obviously enraged about being cheated out of a dance and perhaps more with Allie after Lahn's untimely intervention, and the way he spat the words made Allie realize there was alcohol on his breath.

Perhaps that's why he was being so blatantly aggressive about this entire situation.

Otherwise he may have had the mind to know better.

"My betters?" Lahn repeated, eyebrows raising in surprise as the dance in the background continued on. The laughter and drinking and flirting was going on in abundance all around them, though there were certainly a few people watching the scene unfold as Lahn got up in Adam's face with a scowl. "What gives you the right to harass my girlfriend like this? She's the ruler of this entire continent, you dimwit! Take your drunken stupidity somewhere else before you do something you regret."

"And are you going to make me regret it?" Adam said, taking out a handkerchief from his pocket and reaching out before slapping Lahn across the face with it. "I would challenge you to a duel of men, to see which of us is better suited for someone as esteemed and beautiful as the queen herself! I'll have you know that she was going to be my date tonight until you, who was nothing but a cripple, showed up and spilled your honeyed words!"

Allie was drunkenly gazing at Lahn during the exchange. She very much could have handled the entire thing herself, but she was enjoying the fact that Lahn was standing up for her instead of backing down like he would have done once upon a time. It made him look rather sexy. He was growing as a person, but she also couldn't have him enter some ridiculous duel, either.

Lahn's face was a bright red now, enraged, and his fists shook. "How dare you! I accept your duel—"

"No, you won't," Allie said, getting up and swaying slightly before forcefully drawing him down into a seat. "Fimrindle, be a dear and take this drunken man away. I do not like being harassed, and doubly so for Lahn."

The scarecrow reaper materialized out of thin air, bowed quickly, and smashed the blunt end of his scythe into Adam's gut.

The young nobleman projectile puked onto the floor with a gasp before he was forcefully dragged out of the ballroom and onto one of the balconies. He began flailing and screaming something Allie couldn't make out before he was promptly thrown off the balcony and down the slope of the hill the palace was built on. Some of the others on the balcony visibly winced when the man let out a scream of pain upon landing, but given Allie's reputation, no one made to go help him, either.

"He'll be fine," Allie said, using her hand to rub the spot where Lahn had been slapped. "Maybe. I don't really care either way. I've killed people for far less, and his actions were nothing if not stupidity incarnate."

Shovi looked a little bit surprised at the quick turn of events, but she nodded her approval and leaned back in her chair, despite the horrified looks of some of the patrons who'd witnessed the attack. "There's a saying where I grew up: A good man is only three drinks away from ruining the rest of his life. Though I don't think that Zrinski brat is going to die with that kind of fall. He'll be fine, and it was a good toss. Thank Fimrindle for me."

"Indubitably," Allie agreed, nodding sagely and hiccuping before pushing her chair up next to Lahn's and giving him a blissful smile of perfect white teeth. "What's that look for? Did I upset you somehow?"

Lahn was grimacing and staring the way Fimrindle had dragged Adam out. "No, not you. I just feel . . ."

He held out his hands, clenching and unclenching them repeatedly. "Like less of a man, when I'm not even able to dissuade jerks like that guy from harassing you. I wish I was stronger, and more respected. People sometimes still see me as the crippled boy, and they look down on me for it."

"They never looked down on you for being crippled, Lahn!" Shovi exclaimed.

"Not most people anyways. Those that did were terrible to begin with and not those who you'd want to associate with."

"Like my siblings and father?" Lahn retorted with a dubious glance.

Shovi's jaw snapped shut, and her gaze hit the table. "I . . . I guess I can't blame you for saying that. You know I'm on your side, Lahn, but I'm also trying to keep this family together."

"Why bother?" Lahn asked, leaning forward and taking some cheese and meat off one of the nearby trays. "I'm not interested in rekindling anything with my siblings after they involved themselves in that attack that nearly killed me at the academy campus. Father is almost as bad."

This . . . was obviously a conversation Lahn and his mother had often. The mood was also growing sour with it, so Allie was rather thankful to be saved when Mara emerged from the dance floor with another young man latched around her arm.

"I see you and Lahn worked things out, then," Mara said with a wink, bringing her dance partner, a tall and lanky fellow with a very symmetrical face, over to stand nervously beside her. "I had my suspicions that budding relationship of yours wouldn't kick the bucket. You're just too cute together."

"We are, aren't we?" Allie said, amused, while wrapping her arms around Lahn's waist. Her eyes flicked to the lanky young man with white hair. "Who did you manage to trick into dancing with you?"

"I did not TRICK anyone!" Mara shot back, smirking and coming around the table to sit at one of the empty seats. "Allie, Lahn, Shovi, this is Bernus Lackoy. Bernus, sit down, sweetie, you're making the queen nervous. She may throw you over the balcony, too, if you keep standing there like a dolt!"

Bernus swallowed audibly, avoiding Allie's gaze, and shakily sat down beside Mara before reaching for a flask in his left pocket. Chugging a large quantity of the contents in one go, he let out a gasp and snapped it back closed with a nervous smile. "H-hello! Bernus Lackoy of House Lackoy, at Your Majesty's service. I hope I'm not intruding—"

"Oh no! Not at all!" Allie said with a wave of her hand. "I've been wondering whether Mara was into girls, so it seems that I now have my answer. You know, I was just harassing her about who she's been seeing, if anyone at all. Have you two been dating for a while? Or did she just pick you up here at the party?"

"H-here at the party, Your Majesty," the young man said with a curt nod, eyes staring at the tablecloth ahead of him. "I'm sorry if I sound a bit stiff. I think I've had too much to drink."

Mara rolled her eyes, and let her long black hair swish out to the right when she tilted her head to look at him. "Bernus has an enchanted flask with extrapotent alcohol in it, and it holds a lot more than you'd think. It's any alcoholic's dream."

"I am no alcoholic!" Bernus protested as the others at the table laughed, but he handed the flask to Lahn without being asked. "I merely enjoy the harder stuff! And knowing King, er, Duke Arthur Brix, he prefers the juicy flavors that taste nice rather than the stuff that'll rock you hard with a single swig."

"That's hellfire brandy, isn't it?" Lahn asked, eyes going wide. "Bernus, this is illegal!"

"WAS illegal. And don't try to pin that on me in front of the queen!" Bernus corrected with a bright smile, chuckling under his breath and tapping his fingers together. "It was only illegal back before Panu was created. The duke retracted all previous illegalities concerning ways to create alcohol after the third month of integration, so we've been selling gallons of this stuff weekly. You should try it!"

"Do you two know each other?" Allie asked curiously, seeing the smirks cast between the two young men. "You seem awfully friendly."

Lahn chuckled and nodded, but refrained from taking a swig of the brandy, much to Bernus's disapproval. "We were friends growing up, but Bernus moved away because of problems with his father's company. Is that right?"

Allie was enjoying the banter, sipping on her drink and rubbing a hand along Lahn's thigh under the table, when she noticed an old man approaching. He was in the getup of a servant but held himself in an odd way that she couldn't quite place. His features —the object being hidden underneath a tablecloth—while he avoided eye contact.

A pulse of mana from her body revealed something with an enchanted and potent signature underneath that cloth, and given the shifty appearance of the old man, her eyes began to narrow in suspicion. Slowly, lines of power began to build around her, and though she only had a few seconds to prepare, it was more than enough.

Only a moment later, she realized that the man wasn't even really undead, but rather dressed to look that way with makeup and a false soul overlapping his soul aperture.

Not five feet away from where she sat, the man dropped the tablecloth to reveal some kind of celestial bomb clenched between his fingers. His eyes were wide with madness, and a toothy grin lit up his face as white and gold light roared to life within his grip.

"FOR THE EMPIRE OF DYING SUNS, YOU WILL DIE HERE TODAY!" the man screamed, and then he flung the bomb at the ground at Allie's feet. "LONG LIVE THE QUEEN!"

The flash of Fimrindle's scythe streaked through the air. In the next moment, the entire room was engulfed with bright white flames. A cracking boom accompanied by a palace-shaking explosion caused the night sky outside to light up, and then there was only silence.

The assassin's attempt on her life . . . had failed.

CHAPTER 23

Over five hundred souls were killed in the explosion, and over five hundred souls were put back into bodies soon thereafter. The assassin's attack had been rather powerful, and had Allie not been present, it might not have worked. The entire palace ballroom was eradicated in a single explosion, and the man sent to kill her had sacrificed himself in the effort.

But in the end, without killing Allie herself, it was a moot point. In fact, all the angels of death had as a racial gift the ability to bring back souls of the dead, planting them back into their bodies within very strict limitations. It wasn't a normal resurrection and played by different rules, but was more of a time- and vicinity-based passive they all had. It was also why undead factions valued their angels so much, if they had any at all given how rare the species was. Perhaps the Empire of Dying Suns hadn't thought about it, or perhaps they didn't know. Perhaps they'd thought the bomb, filled with celestial-grade magics that were especially effective against undead, would be enough to do the job by wiping her out and preventing her from using the passive trait. If so, they'd been wrong, and it'd only taken a couple days of cleanup to retrieve all the souls from the immediate vicinity of the void due to how recent their deaths had been. Most of that time had actually been used to repair or even re-create the bodies of the fallen, rather than actually finding the souls in the first place.

If only Allie had been there in time to save Nin and Vin in the same way.

[Angel's Phantom Touch: Allows you to completely resurrect allies by physically dragging their souls back into the world with your phantasmal body aspect. Does not require activation of an ability. This is contingent on being able to find their souls before they're swallowed and lost to the afterlife, or finding them again once they've already been lost.]

So after making sure all the thankful guests were accounted for, Allie now found herself in the middle of a dark, dank room with the would-be assassin. His half-cooked body was strapped to a large stone table, naked, spread-eagle, and face up, still showing wounds and stitching where his body had been repaired.

His soul, however, danced in between her fingers as a small wisp of light. Somehow the Empire of Dying Suns had modified it—there were unnatural etchings of unfamiliar heavenly power that traced the core in her hands, but she wouldn't figure out why that was unless she went on ahead with the process. The soul pulsed, ready to be eradicated at her whim, but instead of destroying it, she gave off a sinister smile while pushing it back into the man's body.

"I grow tired of these rats harassing me . . ." Allie muttered as she moved. "First Judith, then Crendir, and now this."

Shadowy figures shifted uneasily in the darkness nearby.

"The organs are repaired, Mistress . . . but the bones have carvings that stop us from using his material to bring about one of our own," one of the three hooded necromancers behind her stated, watching curiously as the body began to flinch and jolt, a reaction to the soul that'd been reinfused. "If you wouldn't mind, we would like to keep his body for experimentation purposes after you are done. For the sake of science."

Allie didn't look back, but held up a hand of acknowledgment. "Yes. You may have the assassin after I am done interrogating him. Please, leave me."

The skresh gave a cold, bony smile, causing his jaw to literally unhinge. "Very good, my dark lady. We will leave you to your work, then."

The three necromancers bowed and left out the door between two dozen sets of mindless skeleton warriors keeping watch. With a loud bang, the reinforced steel doors leading out of this place closed, and runes of protection burning black and neon teal began to etch themselves into the hard metal.

"Wakey, wakey . . ." Allie whispered, touching the prisoner's face with the tips of her fingers. "Don't keep me waiting . . ."

Wrath, taking the form of a demonic lion beside her in a swirl of purple light, glared at the man's supine form with predatory malice. "The farther along this road we travel . . . the less likely you will be to find the souls of your lost brothers and sisters. We are lucky this is only the beginning of cultivation, most of the F- and E-grade warriors here don't have the power or know-how to destroy or banish souls."

The lion hesitated when Allie glanced his way and flexed his claws, which gouged into the stone floor. "We should have seen him coming. Those markings on his soul were the work of someone not of this planet, and someone far above the C-grade, meant to hide the celestial presence from my sight in this weakened form."

"Probably one of many Holy factions being imported through the guild mercenary systems?" Allie asked.

"Perhaps. Though it would be a desperate move for the invaders to side with Judith Marcina's forces at this stage in the integration. I am more inclined to think that Elysium has lent the invaders opportunities of their own to adjust for the local populations acquiring strength."

"Why would Elysium do that? It thrives on conflict, but I would think it wouldn't be so eager to balance scales like it does. The strong survive—that is the way of things."

Wrath snorted in dissatisfaction. "I'm sure it has its reasons. But to correct you, it isn't just conflict that Elysium grows on. It is the product of conflict, the ascension into new heights of power and insight. Every time someone or something within Elysium perfects their Dao, evolves into a new grade, gains levels, or achieves enlightenment, Elysium takes a portion of that boon for itself. This fringe world is already turning out to be a volatile playground filled with high-profile players, and the stakes are high. No matter who wins, Elysium will gain by the ascent of the victors—sowing more conflict and escalating how hard overcoming obstacles is will only lead to gains and set foundations for future gains. But even for Elysium, there comes a point at which the laws of balance in the integration worlds are put to a stop and Elysium steps back from the picture to let the way of the world unfold. We are almost at that point now, where no further intervention will be taken and the scales are set."

A deep gasp from the dead man, or what had once been a dead man, paused their conversation.

Allie's pale eyes flitted back to the assassin, who was coughing and sputtering, hyperventilating as he regained consciousness and his life once more. His eyes were wild, and he began to focus in on Allie and Wrath in soul-clone form on either side of his table. He immediately tried to shake off the bindings, but they held firm, and a sneer began to spread across the man's face.

"Unholy abominations! You have robbed me of martyrdom!" The assassin spat onto Allie's flowing robes in disgust. "It saddens me to see the bomb did not work! You belong in the pits of hell, beyond the abyss! Not in our world and in the light! May the heavens smite you! May the angels erase your tainted evils from the land!"

Ah.

A religious fanatic.

They were her favorite people to kill, and had been ever since she'd butchered Prophet's people back in Brightsville. They'd thought themselves so self-righteous, only to die at her hand like dogs.

Allie's grin widened, revealing perfect white teeth, and she drew a long, wicked dagger dripping with acid from her belt. "I believe you have some questions to answer, but first, let's play a little game of how long you can scream, how many times you can die, before you give us the location of your compatriots and tell us how you infiltrated our country in the first place."

"I WILL NEVER TALK, YOU MONSTER!" The assassin spat again. "Do your WORST!"

Allie snickered, shrugged, and drove the acid-covered blade into the man's heart.

The man screamed, writhed, and wailed as his flesh sizzled and magic rippled through his insides. Organs burst and his very soul began to fry under the power she was pouring into him.

"AHHHHHHHHHHHH!!!" His wails became a high-pitched screech. "YOU BITCH! YOU WRETCHED BITCH!"

"You asked for it, you enthusiastic little man." Allie flared her wings as Wrath curled up to watch. "Delight in the knowledge that your comrades will suffer the same fate and that this altar will keep you alive for prolonged torture before I bring you back again. No one attacks my Lahn and gets away with it . . . and know that I derive great pleasure from your pain."

Twisting the blade, she wrenched it out of his chest in a spray of blood, part of his heart meat still on the wicked blade while the man convulsed and began to foam at the mouth. Unholy runes carved into the stone underneath him burned with green and red light when the man's blood filtered into each one.

Setting down the dagger and picking up a pair of nearby pliers, Allie didn't ask a single question as she began to tear off fingers one by one and the screams intensified in the secluded stone room.

It was far too early to ask questions yet. The interrogation would only come after she made her victim squeal.

Floor Thirty-Seven, the Cathedral of the Damned, was one of the creepiest places Riven had ever been to. When he'd arrived on the floor, there'd been no description other than the entrance message with the name of the floor. Souls were kept here by the millions, tormented for eternity in this subsection of hell that'd been quarantined by Elysium for the trial's purposes. They screamed silently, writhing on the perimeters where a swirling vortex of fire flickered and lurched. The burning souls inside the inferno were crazed and out of touch with reality and didn't respond to any attempt at communication.

They simply existed to suffer.

They only knew pain, and it was so prevalent, so all-encompassing, that their minute, indistinct auras overlapped with one another to emit a pervasive ocean of ill intent. Of hunger and sorrow, of agony and horror. This place was the very embodiment of damnation itself, and it very seriously made Riven question the Unholy foundational pillar and its origins. It made him question what Pride's intent was when creating the hells in the first place, because despite being a monster himself, despite as of late killing and eating others that in many regards were innocent, Riven couldn't ever commit to torturing someone literally for all eternity.

It was just plain wrong.

The Cathedral of the Damned was made of bronze-colored stone, placed at the very peak of a volcano that belched lava down its slopes. There was only one guardian at the very beginning of the floor, and they'd killed the creature—a giant fire elemental in the shape of a salamander—easily enough by having Azmoth do all the fighting, since he was immune to the flames. Otherwise the place was eerily silent. Even with the inferno's vortex whirling around the mountain in a dome of hellish light, the flames were oddly muffled, and Riven's footfalls seemed to kick up ash with every step he took toward the cathedral.

Spires climbed hundreds of feet in the air, while gargoyles, devils, and succubi along with other species of winged demons were carved out of the bronze stone in intricate depictions of battles and worship. A large set of double doors big enough for giants to walk through was wide-open, leading into a dark interior, and hundreds of corpses with skin flayed from flesh dangled on large hooked chains.

"I can feel the Blood God's presence inside," Genua said as they stood in front of the archway, hands clasped in prayer before muttering quickly under her breath. "But there are more than just him. There are many altars here . . ."

"Even one designated to me," Riven muttered, his eyes fixating on a large stone depiction of Gluttony's maw near the back left of the room on an elevated platform. "How truly curious."

Inside the cathedral were dozens of altars, just as Genua had noted. They were each intricately detailed, unlabeled, and oozed individual auras that matched their chosen patron. Most were gods, but there were also altars for the seven sins, as well as a few that'd lost their auras of power and now lay in desecration, completely destroyed.

There was the base floor, the second floor where Gluttony's altar was located, and then a third floor farther back, all sharing an open-air space in the middle with railings on the second and third floors that allowed them to look down onto the first. Burning, spiked lamps hung from the ceiling, illuminating tapestries depicting in great detail the battles between the heavens and hells. Thousands of candles illuminated the altars and each of the three floors, and it appeared there was already another party of three cloaked individuals located near the very end of the first floor straight ahead. They seemed to be in a state of prayer, completely ignoring Riven's own party, and kept themselves prostrated before the altar of a large two-headed dragon.

Riven could have heard a pin drop, and his boots caused a faint echo for every step he took after passing through the archway and into the interior. His staff also clicked along the floor, kicking up layers of fine ashen dust that'd doubtless settled in from the volcanic scenery outside.

He did a once-over again, sending out pulses of mana sense to make sure there weren't any others hiding in the crevices and cracks around the cathedral's interior, and turned around to look at the others with a shrug. "I'm not entirely sure what to do here . . . I'm assuming we just approach the altars, yeah?"

Athela exchanged a glance with Fay and both shook their heads. Kara remained a silent observer and as usual was rather submissive to the whims of whatever the others chose to do.

"I can't think of a reason not to approach the altars," Retesh replied, walking in the direction of an altar to the Scythe, depicted by a skeletal cloaked statue with, of course, a scythe in its hands. "Though I believe someone wishes to speak to you, Riven."

Retesh pointed a bony finger at the trio ahead before moving on to the

Scythe's statue. The three cloaked figures had risen from their positions at the two-headed dragon shrine, their shadows cast by burning candles as they stood to their full height of seven or eight feet apiece. Now that they'd turned around, it was apparent that each of them were male dragonkin, wearing little more than basic cloth, but their bodies were covered in protective red and white scales. Yellow eyes bored down on Riven's company with curious interest, and the shortest of them had begun approaching them with slow, measured steps.

Azmoth grunted while maintaining his smaller eight-foot form, lifted his stone maul over one shoulder, and trudged forward to meet the approaching newcomer with wings spread. They came to a stop in the middle, only ten paces away from one another, before the dragonkin's yellow reptilian eyes snapped onto Riven's position to single him out.

"I would have words . . . warlock," the dragonkin said while folding its arms behind its back and puffing out its bare, scaled chest. Flames briefly puffed out of its nose when it gave a snort at a growl Azmoth produced. "Please ask your minion to stand aside so that I am not forced to talk through him."

Riven's lips quirked up with amusement, and he gestured for Azmoth to step to the side. "Sure, but stay where you are. What is it you want?"

Azmoth stomped to the left but kept a close eye on the dragonkin as flames surged around his body in preparation of an attack.

The dragonkin cocked his head sideways at seeing Riven's gluttonous armor, and nodded twice to himself as if debating something. His reptilian lips curled back to display draconic teeth in a smile that could have been taken as threatening if Riven hadn't already had exposure to the dragonkin race while on the first and second floors of the descent. "First and foremost, I am a representative of Hatchmire, 137th son of Overlord Felwing of the First Draconic Fist, conqueror of Universe 9. If you wish for proof of our claim, we can provide it. My name is irrelevant, but if you wish, you may call me Zalzar."

Zalzar gave a low bow. "It is an honor to meet another reincarnation of original sin. Should I refer to you as Gluttony? The last one we met had us call them by the name of the sin they'd reincarnated."

That . . . that caught Riven's interest. How had Zalzar known who he was? And what was this talk about another sin's reincarnation? Riven shifted uneasily, red eyes boring into the two people still standing far in the back of the cathedral's first floor at their chosen altar. "Your backing must be rather impressive . . . to conquer an entire universe. My name is Riven. Which of the other sins has come through this place? I was unaware any of them were here."

Zalzar gave a polite smile and shook his head. "I am unable to say; they wanted their presence to remain anonymous. When dealing with the greater powers of our multiverse, it is prudent to keep the secrets of others, lest you make enemies, and the same privilege will be given to you once we part ways. But I must ask, have you come to broker diplomacy with us as well?"

Mentally, Athela prodded him with a message. "The First Draconic Fist is known to me, Riven. They're incredibly dangerous, a powerful draconic faction that committed genocide against all other races that they don't use for sporting events or food, and they worship a dragon god of some sort. Likely the two-headed altar in the back is a representation, and if I had to guess, one of the two figures in the back is the scion Hatchmire. They also look down on all other races as inferior, but otherwise I don't know much more. The fact that I know about them at all, though, that is a testament to how strong they likely are. Fay's family may know more as they're information brokers, but unfortunately we cannot contact them here."

Riven's eyebrows raised. Addressing Zalzar's question, he shook his head no. "You must forgive me, Zalzar, but I am very new to the multiverse. I had no idea you were even here. I was born on an integrating planet less than thirty years ago and have never heard of the First Draconic Fist. I am probably what you could call . . . uneducated."

Zalzar's expression of surprise was matched by loud chuckling in the back, where the other two dragonkin were baring their teeth in amusement. "You don't say? Thirty years is but the blink of an eye. That is rather surprising, considering who you are and the fact that you're a pureblooded vampire. Not many of your species exist on the frontiers. But if you haven't come for diplomacy's sake, have you come to convene with the gods?"

"Other than trying to find a way down so I can finish my soul lattice properly? Other than that I'm not sure what I'm doing here. I'm going in blind—I'm just here in this cathedral to explore."

Zalzar didn't seem to know what to make of that and turned around to shoot a confused look at the two who were obviously higher rank than him. A series of hand signs was exchanged, and Zalzar cleared his throat with another polite smile. "You're quite a curious one. Well then, my master, Hatchmire of the First Draconic Fist, is wanting to eat a meal in your honor and hopes to discuss more of your origins. He is rather curious about your situation and extends a hand of friendship, as *equals*. Would you like to accept or decline his invitation?"

The word *equals* was emphasized here, Riven was quick to take note. For someone else in Riven's position, this may be taken as a slight. Or as an offense. But for Riven? He didn't give two shits about power plays like that.

"Ooooh! Does he have golden dragonspire wine?!" Fay asked, hopping up and down on the sideline while grabbing Riven's arm.

Zalzar's face scrunched up, and his claws clicked against his scaled chest while holding them at heart level. "How do you know about golden dragonspire wine? I do believe they have better than that . . . but—"

"Then we accept!" Fay enthusiastically exclaimed and began dragging Riven along with a wide smile. "Ooooooh, you're going to enjoy this one, Riven! I can't wait to show you how good that stuff is, and if they have better, then it's going to be a real show!!!"

Riven hadn't known Fay was a wine connoisseur. Still . . . he hesitated. He then shot Athela another query through their mind link after a skeptical glance around him. "Something feels off. Athela, find anything?"

"No assassins or traps to my knowledge," she shot back with a mental shrug, still invisible to his eyes. Though he could generally tell where she was through the minion link. "I'll keep an eye out. The First Draconic Fist is likely far more powerful than even the Blood Moon Requiem, and refusing their invitation would be considered rude. Even for you, I would tread carefully and try not to insult anyone. The sin churches are not as powerful as they once were."

As if reading Riven's mind, Zalzar raised a clawed hand and turned with a swish of a long tail out the back of his robe. "I assure you, Riven, there are no assassins or attempts of subterfuge here. We do not need such underhanded things; we are above them. Our honor as warriors would not permit it."

Riven mentally acknowledged Athela, hesitantly nodded to Zalzar, and glanced Retesh's way. "Anything out of the ordinary over there?"

Retesh the lich was kneeling in front of the Scythe's altar, in a hunched position with his staff over his legs. "Nothing sinister. These are exactly what they appear to be, conduits to the gods you wish to pray to. Whether they respond is up to them."

Frowning, but seeing no obvious reason to decline, Riven gave in to Zalzar's request. "Very well, Zalzar, I accept. Please lead the way. It appears my succubus partner here has swayed me."

The dragonkin seemed quite happy with his response by the way their smiles grew wider. Laughing in good humor, Zalzar motioned for them to follow. "Very good. We have much to discuss, though most of it is trivial. It is always good to set relationships early in the path of cultivation. You never know when someone you meet in the F-grade will turn into a powerful ally in millennia to come."

CHAPTER 24

Having a picnic in an Unholy temple decorated with hanging bodies in the middle of hell was a first for Riven.

Unless his time in Negrada counted. There were a few cathedrals he'd had the pleasure of choking down food in back then while hiding and exploring the place soon after getting Azmoth as his second minion, and corpses had been left to rot there, too.

Maybe it was just a hell thing?

Who knew.

Regardless, introductions were made between the two groups, not including Retesh, who continued to meditate by himself at the altar of the Scythe. Hatchmire, 137th son of Overlord Felwing of the First Draconic Fist, was the largest of the three dragonkin and was built like an absolute tank. Just like his compatriots, he was shirtless and covered in red and white scales. The tattered robe he wore had some kind of energy-dampening effect that Riven couldn't quite pinpoint, but it was certainly more than met the eye. Instead of normal weapons, Hatchmire had engraved incredibly intricate enchantments into his own claws and spines and admitted to being a variation of Unholy monk and pugilist. The others, including Zalzar and the last dragonkin, a man named Albshire with more prominent dorsal spines than the others, were of the same make and fighting style.

"Thank you for humoring our request," Zalzar said, pulling out a large bottle of rainbow liquid that glittered with unnatural light. "As promised, we have better than golden dragonspire wine—we have *diamond* dragonspire wine."

Fay squealed with delight and reached for the bottle, lips parted in an excited smile.

"Your master and I drink first," Hatchmire added while stopping Fay's advance and holding out a jewel-studded chalice for Riven. "It is custom for the nest fathers to drink before all others in my hives. I know that vampires don't often have problems ingesting poison, but I would not be offended if you were to check the drink or the cup."

Fay looked disappointed but didn't object and sat back in her spot on Riven's left.

Zalzar poured the rainbow wine into the chalice a moment later when Hatchmire gave him a nod, and Hatchmire's own cup was filled a moment later. They were both then startled when a small rip in space produced one of Gluttony's tendrils to sample the fluid before confirming to Riven that it was indeed not poisoned.

The rift closed, and so did the tendril, but even that small amount of exposure to the sin was enough to leave the three dragonkin in a state of unease.

Considering the group, Hatchmire turned his gaze upon Kara with a quizzical expression, folding his claws together in thought. "You seem unbothered by the presence of the Great Maw. All others here are higher beings, demons and undead alike, and even the thrall has a hint of greatness. But not you . . . For a lesser race, you handled yourself well. You must be a great warrior."

Kara, who'd been polishing her bow, stiffened at the proclamation and warily glanced up at the dragonkin scion with a shake of her head. "I'm quite the opposite, actually. I'm really quite weak. I've just seen Gluttony more than a couple times now, and Riven's really nice. Without him, I wouldn't be here."

Riven briefly winced at the memory of almost killing and eating Kara in the blood realm a while back, but pushed the images away with a mental nudge. She still hadn't told him what her damn class was, either, but if she wanted privacy, he'd grant it to her. As for the newcomer calling Kara a lesser race? Riven kind of agreed. He'd had a change of heart about mortals since arriving here, for better or worse, and though he didn't necessarily damn them for what they were, he was seeing them more and more as food. As cattle. Much like how humans saw chickens or pigs, only in this case, it was dark elves. Not only was she a dark elf, a mortal, but she was incredibly weak even by her own admission and needed constant protection just to survive here. Honestly, Riven wasn't even sure if he considered Kara more of a person, a pet, or a would-be meal he'd simply spared on a whim before taking a liking to her, and he was having serious internal battles between logic and ethics trying to decide on which.

Hatchmire seemed unconvinced by her proclamation, though he didn't challenge it. His attention instead was focused back on Riven, and he raised the goblet of rainbow liquid to his snout. "A toast to our fortuitous meeting."

"Fortuitous? That is to be determined, but thanks for the food." Riven smirked and lifted his own glass to toast, and downed his drink in a single gulp. His eyes bulged with delight at the sensations dancing along his tongue, and he eyed the bottle with greedy intent before putting the glass in Fay's hand as the bottle was passed around.

His red eyes flicked back to Hatchmire, who was evaluating him in silence as the other two dragonkin began conversing with Riven's party. "You're stronger than you look. The others don't see it, but I do."

Hatchmire's eyes narrowed suspiciously, and he leaned forward to take a piece of monster meat Riven had cooked and stuffed into his spatial sack days past. Chomping down and savoring the flavor, the dragonkin swallowed and asked, "Don't see what?"

"That the dome of flames outside is actually your aura at work," Riven said, tapping his fingers along the staff in his lap in thought. "You've been channeling it this entire time. It's impressive, on par with me, or perhaps even beyond me entirely."

Hatchmire's eyes widened in surprise and delight, and his tail slapped against the floor with a grunt of acknowledgment. "It would surprise me if anyone else had figured it out, but from a reincarnation . . . I should not be surprised. Yes, the flames beyond are under my aura's control. I am using the ambient infernal energies to better cultivate my soul lattice before proceeding to the lower floors. How did you know?"

"Your body's energy signature occasionally gives off fluctuations that match the walls of fire outside. I use a similar method, only my aura favors ice and storm more than heat."

Hatchmire nodded slowly. "I would say I would like to see it, but I become competitive . . . and my hive would be rather upset if I accidentally killed a reincarnation and brought them bad fortune for it."

He showed his predatory teeth in a wide grin.

Riven believed him; it wasn't a bluff. Despite all the power Riven had accumulated, despite his absurd magical control and likely being the exact same level as Hatchmire, the dragonkin's aura control and presence were still beyond him by leaps and bounds. He wouldn't tell any of the others about how much of a difference it really was after his recent revelation when he'd connected the dots, but Riven was absolutely sure that if this scaly bastard wanted them all dead, he could collapse the rotating storm of flames outside on their position and incinerate everything and everyone within seconds.

And there'd probably be very little that even Riven could do to stop him—the area encompassed by the swirling flames outside was just too vast. It made Riven seriously consider just what the upper limits of the multiverse elite were . . . because up until now, he'd considered himself the strongest here in the descent. Foolishly so. Allie's ascension had put that into question, but this wasn't even a question—rather, this dragonkin of the ninth universe was simply godlike when compared to other F-grades.

Then there was also the mention of another sin coming through here to participate in negotiations of diplomacy, despite no system-wide message about another sin being released. Did the original sin who'd passed through have a perk to hide itself from messages like that? If so, why would it even want to? Riven was pretty sure the dragonkin had no reason to bluff, either, so he posed a question:

"Hatchmire . . ." Riven began, stroking his chin with his right hand. "Where would you say you stack up compared to the best of the descent? Do you know?"

"I am likely ninth strongest here, to my knowledge," Hatchmire said flatly.

"You would rank somewhere around seventeenth or eighteenth, if my reports and firsthand evaluations are correct. But the descent only just opened, and there will be more monstrous participants from the elder factions joining us in coming years. I don't think they'd wait more than a decade, given the circumstances regarding Elysium's battle with Galactis, which brings me to my own questions. What do you know about the two multiverses and their conflict? Considering who you are, surely you know something."

Riven's brow furrowed and his hands crossed on his lap. This was not the direction he'd thought the conversation would go in. "I have . . . heard about it. Little more."

"So you do know of it! From who did you hear this?" Hatchmire asked curiously with an undertone of nervousness.

Riven's frown deepened. "Gluttony has hinted at it but won't say exactly what is coming. Lillith of the Black Skies, my mentor, talked to me about it most directly. But I have heard rumors from the Blood Moon Requiem, and also from an earl of the Idorac Federation, an ally and neighbor to the Blood Moon Requiem in Universe 10."

There was a pause as Hatchmire tasted the words one by one.

"And what did they say on the matter? Please, this is of utmost importance to me." Hatchmire scooted forward almost instinctively, and his body had become rigid with anxiety. It was the look of a desperate man, and completely out of place on someone so strong.

Riven tried to think back to exactly what he'd picked up along the way and shook his head. "I can't remember all of it, but what I do remember is this: Lillith told me that it would be in my best interest to keep collecting rare plant and crystal specimens to take back to the guild hall. She said they'll be needed in the future and that the trek through the Abyssal Descent was a good opportunity to collect and buy things for later."

He internally checked with Gluttony, who gave him the mental nod of approval before saying more. ". . . Lillith also hinted that the Church of Gluttony wouldn't be around in the future, but she failed to expand upon it."

Hatchmire's eyes went wide as saucers, and his clawed feet created fissures in the stone floor as they flexed. It was almost . . . horror? Yes, if Riven had to place it, horror or terror would be the most apt description. He let out a slow, shaky breath and stared at the ground. "Not around anymore . . . Does Gluttony confirm this?"

"Gluttony will not say, even to me." Riven shrugged. "Very tight-lipped, that one."

Hatchmire nodded slowly. "As was the other incarnate . . . you've told me far more than they did in just a few sentences. Their bonded sin forbade them entirely from talking on the subject. What did the others in Universe 10 talk about?"

Riven clicked his tongue, remembering Jarntus Bemule, earl of the Idorac

Federation, on a neighboring planet close to the House Wraithtide homeworld, Vartesh. "The earl of the Idorac Federation told me that his king was amassing a central point of power within their core system, ignoring the plights of all other planets and leaving them defenseless in preparation for something unknown. That rumors were spreading of something big coming, and I've been given indistinct reports from my contacts back in the Blood Moon Requiem that they're silently doing the same but to a lesser extent, having multiple pockets of concentrated power instead of just one."

"Can you not ask your high queen about it? About why she is doing this?"

"I probably could, but I'm already caught up in a lot back on the frontier. I haven't had time to focus on that yet. Plus, they have a heretic problem with rogue elders to deal with and only narrowly avoided outright civil war."

Hatchmire looked disappointed but regained his composure moments later as the others ate and drank around them. "Is there any more you have to share on the matter?"

"Unfortunately not. The most I can gather is that this clash between multiverses will cause something to happen, and I'll probably be cut off from support, at least in terms of Gluttony's forces. Given the troop movements in Universe 10, that could just be coincidence, but it seems to match up. I wish I had more—I'm sorry it's so little."

"Lillith's comment about losing access to the Church of Gluttony is more than enough to go on. It is the biggest clue I've received in my time here, so no need to apologize, friend." Hatchmire let out another slow breath to relax himself and let his rigid, hulking muscles ease up. "I was tasked with trying to find clues from other scions before being sent here. I have found little, but that tiny amount of information is more than enough to disturb me. Just rumors and indistinct facts that don't add up, but the draconic fists are completely in the dark about what is to come. Because of our aggression and prowess, we have few allies and even fewer that are willing to part with such delicate information. Whatever is coming is big enough to shift the entire power balance of the cosmos, of the multiverse, of a power hierarchy that has been there for eons . . . Are you sure that Gluttony cannot speak on the matter more?"

Riven mentally checked with Gluttony one more time and raised an eyebrow. "Gluttony says that even the people who know what is coming won't know until it happens, and that this is an unprecedented event. That it will happen within the next few years. That's all he's willing to say, as saying more would apparently lead to disastrous consequences? Not sure why, but that's straight from his big ugly mouth."

A rift opened next to him to produce a gluttonous maw, and a tendril lashed out to slap Riven on the back of the head.

"Ow!" Riven rubbed at the spot right before Gluttony's visage disappeared, and he caught Hatchmire staring at him, bewildered. "What?"

Hatchmire blinked a couple times, laughed, and let out a groan while rubbing at the draconic spines jutting from the center of his forehead. "I don't know whether to laugh or cry. That was funny—your interaction with Gluttony would be considered rather blasphemous to other followers of the Great Maw, but the information Gluttony provided is even worse than I feared. A few years? That is not enough time . . ."

The dragonkin's voice trailed off. "I need to inform my father about this. Thank you, Riven. If we ever meet again, I will remember you to be in good standing with my people."

Riven took another swig from a goblet that Fay pressed to his lips, and he lovingly ruffled her hair before pushing the cup away. "Yes, it's good, but stop, Fay. Adults are talking."

She gave him a pooched-lips pout in response, but humphed and went back to talking with Zalzar and Azmoth about god knows what.

Athela snickered from his right, where she'd been content to avoid eating and just watch everything unfold with a keen eye in case of betrayal from the opposite side. "Adults. Yeah, are you sure you qualify, Riven dearest?"

"Don't make me punish you publicly, princess."

Athela grinned. "I think I'd like that."

Riven stuck out his tongue and winked, then turned his attention back to Hatchmire. "You could always do me a favor, too, and tell me how to get off this floor, since I got no instructions when arriving."

Hatchmire perked up. "Oh, that's no secret. Just kill the guardian beast, which you did, and wait. Eventually a new portal will spawn, which you can choose to close or open at will depending on how far along you are in your soul lattice construction. I've already acquired my own portal down but have been waiting to use it. For some, having altars here so in tune with their gods will be a cultivation boon and the wait can aid your lattice construction. If it isn't so for you, then there is no need to stay here."

Riven snapped his fingers. A flash of movement caused his head to turn, and he saw their wraithlike spirit guide materialize and bend a knee.

"Well?" Riven asked curiously.

The spirit guide nodded. "I cannot find any way out, even with the three-dimensional map Elysium provided, and this floor is a new one. I would assume the dragonkin is telling the truth."

Riven was about to thank the spirit when he heard a familiar voice cry out in pain. He abruptly whirled and got to his feet, only to see Genua sitting at an altar to the Blood God, where a giant stone figure of a man in decorated clergy robes was crying tears of blood. The high elf thrall had at some point in the feast gotten up and headed over but was now lying on her side on the ground and clutching at her swollen stomach.

In a moment he flashed over, kneeling beside Genua with genuine concern, and met her red eyes when she looked up at him. "What happened? Are you okay?"

She winced, and Riven saw her stomach visibly contract.

"The Blood God has declared war on Greed for attempting to revive a lost pillar of Blood. That is what the other bishops and priests tell me," she said through gritted teeth, glancing at the altar, and she let out another cry when her stomach visibly contracted yet again. "I thought you should know."

"Genua, I don't give a shit about that!" Riven said, and his eyes widened even more when he noticed a large puddle of clear fluid at Genua's feet. "Ohhh . . . . Oh no. Ohhhh no, no, no . . . not here."

Reaching out and grabbing his wrist, Genua pulled his attention back to her face. "I don't think we get to choose. Rather, that choice—mmph!—has been made for us!"

Her stomach abruptly tightened and squeezed, and Genua let out a high-pitched scream as her fingers tried to dig into his armored hand.

"Genua, I don't think those kinds of violent contractions are normal! Your entire stomach is smashing your guts!" Riven said, beginning to panic as he tried to figure out how to proceed. "I'm new at this! What should I do?!"

Athela gasped over his shoulder and let out an excited squeal. "RIVEN, SHE'S ABOUT TO GIVE BIRTH, OH MAH GAWD!"

"IS RIVEN ABOUT TO BE A DAD?!" Fay screamed, throwing her goblet of wine up in the air, completely forgotten.

Fay immediately scrambled to her feet and sprinted over, and Azmoth followed suit with big, lumbering steps. Even Retesh and Kara stopped what they were doing to rush over, and what little padding and pillows they had were quickly stuffed under Genua as her contractions came faster and faster.

"Riven, you bastard!" Genua grunted, gripping him like a lifeline now as tears rolled down her face. She was on her back and in obvious torment with her entire body shaking every time her stomach tried to implode. "You did this to me! This is YOUR fault!"

"What do you mean, this is my fault?! You asked to be involved that night!"

"Don't give me excuses! You've already been a poor excuse for a husband and I don't want to hear it now!" Genua snarled and winced. "Just make the pain go away! Please, it really hurts! Please make it stop!"

Riven's heart thudded in his chest. He was completely clueless.

"AaaaaAAAAAAAAAAAHHHHH!!!" Genua let out a scream and began to sob, her body shivering violently underneath him.

All Riven knew to do was wait and watch and accept the torrent of enraged cursing from the thrall as she berated his honor, his tiny manhood, and his lacking ability. This certainly wasn't like any normal pregnancy or any normal birth—the contractions were too widespread and too violent—and he was seriously worried about Genua's health.

And about the health of the baby.

"This is JUST like the last time!" Genua snarled again, lips quivering with intermittent sobs. "Just like w-when Len was b-born! You're so fucking useless!"

Riven blinked. She was obviously getting her memories mixed up again, imprinting them on him when it'd been her first husband who'd really been there. Just like Hatchmire earlier in their conversation, right now Riven didn't know whether to laugh or cry. "I'm sorry! I don't try to be useless!"

"AAAAAAAAAAAAAAAAHHHHHH!!" Her back arched off the ground, and Fay pulled out a healing potion just in case Genua needed it.

He was pushed aside by Kara, of all people, and made to watch only seconds later.

"I've delivered babies before," Kara said, all business while rolling up her sleeves. "Do you have any baltius herb or moore petals? They're found here in the abyss and can help with the process."

He actually did have those plants and quickly began searching his spatial sack for the requested ingredients before handing them over.

Hatchmire cleared his throat behind Riven to momentarily get his attention. "We will stand guard for you at a distance as a sign of thanks for the information you shared."

Riven realized he was trembling, and he nodded absentmindedly. "Thanks."

The large dragonkin looked over Riven's shoulder and grinned, slapping Riven on the back before turning to walk away. "If I heard correctly, congratulations on your first child. I have one hundred and twenty-three kids with seven wives. It never gets any easier to deal with but can be very fulfilling. Welcome to the party, reincarnation of Gluttony. Welcome to fatherhood."

CHAPTER 25

Genua gave birth to a pudgy little girl that day, and with Riven's blessing, she named the little girl Iris. Iris was pretty cute, with only slightly pointed ears, brilliantly pink eyes, tiny, stubby white horns, and a curious, innocent smile. Riven had shakily held her in his arms for a solid five minutes before starting to cry, and he'd handed her back to Genua for the women to fawn over as he tried to regain his composure.

It wasn't sightly for a reincarnation of original sin to sob in front of strangers like this.

Frankly he was embarrassed, but he couldn't help himself. That little girl was the cutest damn thing he'd ever seen, and he'd nearly vomited due to just how cute she was after she'd started gripping his fingers in her tiny hands while giggling.

Unlike most human newborns, Iris was awake and ready to interact with her surroundings from the get-go, and Genua was already stopping her from crawling off as she and the other three girls laughed and played with the child like a doting family. Quite strange how such a small and innocent thing could bring such immense joy not only to him, but to the people in his party as well. Azmoth was especially excited, and watching him interact with the little girl was like watching a flaming rhinoceros trying to play with a bunny, but Iris was equally as excited to yank on Azmoth's gentle claws as she was to crawl up and down Genua's exhausted body while the thrall lay sprawled on her back.

"Auntie Athela is going to make sure you grow up big and strong! Yes she is!" Athela cooed, pressing her nose up next to the giggling baby in Genua's arms and rubbing against Iris's cheeks. "You're so dang cute, yes you are! Oh my goodness, you're so friggin' cute!"

Genua proudly smiled at the baby girl. She could barely sit upright without tipping over due to being exhausted from childbirth, and held her baby out to the demoness. "Do you want to hold her?"

"OOOOOH, CAN I?!" Athela squealed, and eagerly but gently she took Iris up close to her chest and began rocking her back and forth while cross-legged on the ground. "Wow, this is so neat! Thanks, Genua!"

Meanwhile, Fay was pulling out the baby clothes Genua had been making for this very occasion from the spatial bag and began stacking them in a pile. "It's a good thing we made these in different colors, because pink was like our seventh choice! What do you think about these jammies? They match her eyes!"

"I think that'd look wonderful, Fay," Genua said with a warm smile, closing her eyes and letting out a long breath. She was still drop-dead tired from the strenuous effort she'd put in. "Would you mind helping Athela put the clothes on? I just need to lie here for a while. Oh, and Kara?"

The drow elf looked from the baby to the thrall woman while clasping her hands together and on her knees. "Yes, Genua? Can I get you anything else? Are you doing okay?"

Genua chuckled, sighed, and put a hand on Riven's thigh right next to where she lay. "No, Kara, I don't need anything. Yes, I am okay. I just wanted to say thank you for helping. You are appreciated."

Kara's usually nervous attitude shifted to a beaming smile, and she blushed furiously while staring at the floor. "Oh, um, it was nothing! Thank you for thanking me, though! It is nice to hear it."

Azmoth grunted from the side. "Azmoth is no longer baby of group. Iris is baby now."

Riven snorted a boisterous laugh and slapped Azmoth's shoulder. "We've never called you a baby! What are you talking about?"

"Athela call me big flaming baby all the time."

"She does?!"

Athela quirked an eyebrow from where she was rocking Iris to the sound of loud giggles. "Well, that's because he IS a big flaming baby!"

Azmoth turned a flat look on Riven. "See? Athela bullies Azmoth. It make Azmoth sad."

Athela stuck out her tongue. "Well, if you weren't such a baby about being a baby then maybe you wouldn't have your feelings hurt. You're an archdemon, damn it! You're supposed to be scary, not a wuss!"

"Azmoth will crush Athela after she is done holding baby. Then Azmoth will dance on Athela's corpse and wear her tiara as new prince Azmoth is crowned."

"I'D LIKE TO SEE YOU TRY, YOU FLAMING APE! THIS TIARA IS MINE!"

Riven held up a hand to stop the bickering duo. "Stop it, you're going to scare Iris."

Indeed, the yelling had definitely triggered Iris and she was now showing wet lines of water glistening down her puffy cheeks, while her lips trembled and her chubby fingers fidgeted in front of her.

Fay gasped with her hands up to her lips in a horrified expression. "Athela, you whore! You made the baby cry less than an hour after being born! You're a terrible person!"

"That's Azmoth's fault! I had to defend my honor as a bad bitch!"

Genua rolled her eyes, holding up the pajamas Fay had picked out earlier. "Give Iris here, I need to get her clothed."

Reluctantly, Athela handed the baby back to her mother and pouted with folded arms. Without warning Azmoth promptly picked her up and launched her out the front doors of the cathedral like a cannonball. Her shrill scream faded into the distance, but Riven had no doubt she'd be back within a minute or two.

"Azmoth is not baby," the large archdemon said with a huff, and he extended a gentle claw down to Iris again to poke at her and try cheering her up. "Don't worry, Iris, Azmoth protect you from crazy spider wench."

Fay, who was watching Athela sail through the air, shook her head in dismay and closed her eyes. "One day, Riven, when Athela has a child of yours, too, I'll be incredibly interested to see if that kid inherits her ridiculous tendencies or not. It's a scary thought."

Riven grinned wide. "Oh, that'll be on a whole 'nother level."

"Scary indeed," Genua said with a raised eyebrow, fitting the pink infant pajamas over Iris's chubby limbs before holding the silently crying baby to her chest. "There, there, Iris, Mommy has you."

Riven couldn't be help but be a little bit irritated that they'd already scared Iris like that, and he was already thinking about ground rules for whenever they were around his newborn daughter. That would have to come later, though, and for now, he just settled in to lie next to Genua and held out a hand.

Iris latched on again, sniffled, and brought his finger up to her mouth when—

CHOMP

Tiny fangs sank into his finger, and he yelped in startled surprise as Iris closed her eyes and began to drink his blood. He watched, wide-eyed, realizing that what he had assumed to be a toothless little baby wasn't that toothless after all.

"I guess she got the vampire side of you," Genua said, proudly stroking Iris's head and adjusting the fluffy pink clothes while petting the baby girl's head with one hand. "She's gorgeous—just look at those cute pink eyes of hers! I can't wait to introduce her to Len! Len's always wanted a baby sister . . . She'll be so excited."

Staying still and watching Iris fall asleep with his finger in her mouth as the baby drained blood like milk from a bottle, Riven smiled gently and patted her head a few times with his free hand before settling in for the long haul. He almost couldn't believe it, but there she was, lying on Genua's chest right in front of him. Riven was a dad now, and for better or worse, he was now responsible for this little girl's safety and upbringing.

"She's such a cute little chunk, isn't she?" Riven said to Genua, eyes crinkled happily at the corners.

Genua patted the child's back. "Oh, she's a chunk. She'll probably lose the baby fat over the next two years, but she'll remain a chunk until then."

Riven's heart warmed.

Was he ready for this kind of responsibility?

No, not really.

But that didn't mean that he wouldn't try his best, and he was ready to embrace it anyways. He would be the father that he'd never really had, and hopefully one day he could cultivate a genuinely loving relationship with this little girl he'd helped make. Riven was already becoming attached, and he was rather surprisingly excited about the prospect of watching her grow up.

Perhaps he'd even introduce her to anime and *Dragon Ball Z*. Because if a demonic overlord like him was going to have a kid, Iris damn well needed to be a woman of culture.

Riven inspected the altar to Gluttony with a cocked head and hands clasped behind his back. It was an odd sensation, interacting with the altar that led directly to his bonded intertwined sin, and he could tell just by touching it that the altar hadn't been used in millennia despite the signs of wear and tear.

"It shouldn't be much longer until the portal arrives," Fay muttered, stepping up next to him with a flap of her wings. "I'm worried about Iris traveling down here. She's so fragile and . . ."

Fay's voice trailed off. Riven agreed. "Not much we can do about it, though."

"Genua could attempt to go back to the Blood God's realm and—"

"No." Riven shook his head adamantly, turning to look at Fay with a grim expression. "I won't have my child enter that place, ever. And Genua has already tried going back a while ago—she is unable to do it even if she wanted to."

"Are you afraid the Blood God will betray you, then?" Fay asked curiously, a frown painting itself across her lips.

Riven didn't respond. They all knew a priestess had tried to take Riven's child once, and that was before he'd secretly become a heretic. The blood pearl didn't register as heretical outright, but that didn't mean the Blood God couldn't somehow find out. And if he did, Riven was boned.

Taking it out of his spatial bag, he stared at the shifting red orb in his hand. He still had the prize notification information in his system logs from the boss fight, and pulled it up to read. "Yes, it's a very real possibility."

<u>Trishard Blood Pearl (C-Grade Blasphemous Blood Artifact)</u>: This relic has condensed the affinities from three of five paths the sub-pillar of Blood may take and has been impermanently bound to you, Riven Thane, as its new wielder. This item is shielded from the Blood God's farsight, detection, and scrying abilities, and will be viewed as a normal Blood artifact by all but the most powerful of his Blood clergy, Blood precursors, and the bearer of this item. This item holds long lost and buried secrets of the Blood subpillar and is marked as an extremely taboo artifact by the current Blood God. Study and

meditate on this item for further insights into powers now lost to all but the dead. +200% bonus to Dao insights regarding the Blood subpillar while meditating with this item in hand. Large amounts of blood mana of any type may be stored inside this Trishard Blood Pearl, and it creates ambient blood mana at a steady rate to either be used as stored mana or to be used to change environments. This item may be stored within your soul space at will. Must naturally be of 99% Blood affinity or more to properly wield this item.

- <u>Supercharged Blood</u>: Take an additional thirty seconds of channeling a Blood skill through this item to create a supercharged variant. This skill is incredibly potent, and overuse may damage your mana channels.
- Within this item, secrets concerning the <u>Supreme Path of Red and Black Domination, the Supreme Path of Blazing Azure Creation (Taboo)</u>, and the <u>Supreme Path of Gold and Silver Stairways (Taboo)</u> are present but hidden. Unlocking these secrets to their fullest will add additional splitting pillar growths from your baseline Blood subpillar within your soul realm.]

"I don't know why you keep that item—it's such a terrible prize to get for the descent." Fay dubiously looked over the pearl, obviously not seeing what Riven was seeing despite the notification being pulled up right in front of his face. "I'd just throw it away. Or do you like the way it looks?"

Riven smirked slightly. He'd tried this with his minions before and knew they wouldn't see the real message hidden under the altered text, nor could they sense the intensity of the aura leaking off the item, promising secrets to be discovered through experimentation and meditation.

Seeing he wasn't going to answer, Fay let out a huff and turned around to look at the little girl the rest of the party was engaging with. "She's really cute, you know. Your daughter."

"She is, isn't she?"

"Yes. But I still don't think she belongs here, and because of that, I've decided to tell you what my Christmas surprise was going to be."

Riven raised an eyebrow. "Oh? What does that have to do with anything?"

Fay steeled herself and straightened her back. "I think you'll understand when you see it. Athela and I have been working together to get it ready, but now . . . now I think it may be a way to help Iris stay safe as we travel. Not only that, but it may be a way to also take Kara with us, but I can't be sure yet. You still might have to hire her on to the guild as originally planned."

Riven was immediately interested and turned fully to face her. "I'm listening."

Fay's resolve fell slightly, and she smiled sheepishly while fidgeting with her hands. "You know how Athela and I have been doing that thing with our tongues at the end of every session? To your teeth?"

Now Riven was just becoming confused. "Yeah, I think it's weird, but if it turns you on, I don't mind."

Fay sputtered a laugh. "Well, it's not just weird! It has a real purpose. We've been milking you for vampiric venom . . . Ugh. Just come on and find out, let's get this over with."

A portal ripped open in the air beside them, and without another word, Fay dragged Riven inside.

[You have entered Fay's Dreamscape Dungeon, a resting place for damned souls. Current prisoners: five of fifty. Prisoners must be weaker in mind, body, and cultivation than the wielder of this ability to be kept here.]

Stumbling through, disoriented, it took Riven a second to adjust to his surroundings.

Five figures were strung up in the middle of a large stone room, hanging from the ceiling by chains that connected to iron manacles around their ankles and wrists. Candles resting on skulls along the perimeter illuminated the prison with dim light, and tools of torture were laid out on various benches and tables. Anti–energy suppression runes were also carved in the walls, and their effect completely ignored Riven, but he could easily see how it was affecting the five prisoners kept there.

"So THIS is where Numin and Zafima went . . ." Riven muttered, eyeing the drooling, rabid pair of dark elves as they thrashed around in their dangling positions. His eyes lingered upon the shrieking, snarling duo before examining the other three prisoners in detail.

One was a draconic man with white scales, similar to the dragonkin but smaller and of a slightly different species. His claws weren't as dragon-like, either, more akin to the fingers of a human than the dragonkin's, and he lacked the spines the dragonkin had, too. The draconic was rather calm—unusually calm—and curiously stared at the vampire as Riven walked by.

The next was a kind of merwoman Riven had never seen before, with deep-yellow skin, purple eyes, and purple hair, gills along her neck and webs between her fingers and toes. She, too, was unusually calm and stared back without fear, hate, or any kind of obvious negative emotion.

Then, lastly, there was an ogre? Maybe a half ogre, with pale-green skin. Riven didn't even know how the chains held the guy up because he was so big, and damn, was he ugly. Huge, bulky muscles, about eight feet tall, but due to how his body was built, he still looked squat and squarish. He had tusks coming out of his very prominent lower jaw, and his belly was large enough to fit at least two of Riven inside its mass without much issue. Yet again, this ogre didn't seem troubled at all to be here, and even gave Riven a little nod while blinking.

Weird.

"Let's come back to these two first . . ." Riven said, walking over and pointing between the snarling dark elves. "What's going on with their behavior?"

Both drow were drooling and frothing from the corners of their mouths, their eyes were bloodshot, and their veins occasionally pulsed at random. They seemed to not even realize Riven was there until he snapped his fingers in front of Zafima's face, and then she tried to bite him.

She immediately went back to frothing and screeching while nearly giving herself whiplash from the jerking she did while dangling from the ceiling.

Fay seemed surprised. "You don't care that we abducted them? You're not going to ask me about—"

"I don't care as much that you abducted mortals for me to feed on. I very much DO care that you lied to me when I told you to do something and you did something else instead," Riven commented, walking around the two drow and curiously extending a finger to poke at one of the pulsing veins. "I'd told them they could leave, and you and Athela ignored that. Why?"

Fay winced, but she'd known this had been coming. "Um . . . Gluttony said that you needed more variety to feed on in order to unlock other aspects of your vampiric bloodline. Like you did back on the blood-ocean floor, after eating those orcs. You're a bit too nice to do this yourself, so we decided that perhaps we should be the ones that set up a blood farm for you instead . . . by collecting rare and varying species of mortals for you to feed on and eat."

Riven nodded absentmindedly and came back around to stand in front of Numin. "I'm both impressed and disappointed in you two at the same time. We'll all be having a talk about personal boundaries. Trust is pivotal to any relationship, and if I can't have it, then there won't be a relationship. Is that abundantly clear?"

He gave her a sharp look, causing his succubus to recoil.

"Y-yes . . ." Fay said, looking like she was sick to her stomach as her lips began to tremble. "S-sorry, Riven. Please don't—"

"I am not breaking up with you," Riven said sternly, head-bobbing to the two drow dangling ahead of him. "You did this for my benefit. For that, thank you. But keeping me in the dark about these kinds of things is absolutely not okay. I said I'd do something, that I'd let these two go, and you two went behind my back—with Gluttony's encouragement—to do the exact opposite. I'll be having a talk with Gluttony as well, to make it blatantly clear that it will not be acceptable to have him continue down the path of deception regardless of whether it is in my interest. He can find a new fucking vessel if I can't be treated as an equal partner and if he can't find it in himself to not lie to me. After today, the same will go for you and Athela, too. I love you both and I'd die for either of you, but I'll say it again—*I will not be lied to*, or you can both find another warlock to bind with and I'll get new minions. Trust is an absolute must in our relationship dynamic and I will not compromise on it, and that becomes even more important if you and Athela really intend to go dating other girls outside our relationship like you've talked about doing. If I can't trust you two, there's nothing left. Do you understand?"

A tear trickled down Fay's flushed cheek, and she sniffled while wiping it away. Her breathing was becoming hard, frantic, and labored. "Yes, Master. I'm sorry, it won't happen again."

He stared at her long and hard after that to make sure she knew he was deadly serious, then turned his attention back to the flailing drow. "I think they're reacting this way because they're mentally and physically combating the venom you've injected into them. It is making the transition into thralls become much more uncomfortable and difficult. At this point, I don't think it's even reversible—they'd likely die if we stopped the process now. Part of me thinks I should just kill them and get it over with . . . but the other part of me says they deserve this. And yet, I am rather hungry . . . How long have they been force-fed my venom?"

"Since the floor with multiple suns representing the pillars, Master," Fay replied weakly, staring at the ground with red-rimmed eyes.

"That's not very long, but they're already changing rapidly. How much venom have you been forcing down?"

She shrugged. "A lot, I think? Your venom is far more potent than most, Master, and Genua even had her eyes change color. That isn't normal for a thrall, either—Luke Blissfallen didn't have it happen to him when you turned him. It's probably a by-product of your pure bloodline. But that's just Gluttony guessing."

Riven scratched his chin thoughtfully. "I did feed on Genua far more than I did Luke . . . at the time it just felt weird to suck on a guy's neck for blood when Genua was available. You know?"

He gave Fay a small, forced smile, causing her to stifle a laugh as she wiped at her face again. "In fact, whenever I fed off Luke, he usually just drained the blood into a cup for me to drink. I didn't inject much venom into him at all. Where did you get these three?"

"From the blood-ocean floor, where people were coming out of the clam's rift," Fay replied, regaining her composure and calming her breaths.

"Have you been feeding them venom, too?"

"Not yet. We were going to wait for the drow to change first."

Riven raised an eyebrow and placed himself in front of the draconic. "What's your name?"

The draconic blinked, and his voice came out in a deep, masculine tone. "I do not know anymore."

"Anymore? So you knew once?"

"Yes . . . I think so."

Riven nodded. "Do you remember coming out of the blood rift and fighting my team?"

The white-scaled humanoid flitted his tail back and forth and grunted in irritation. "Vaguely, but I was just coming out of my sleep then and the memory is fuzzy."

"Do you remember how you even got into that blood realm?"

"No."

"What is your combat skill set?"

"I am a warrior."

"Specifically through your status page?"

The draconic's pupils dilated for a moment. "It says I am called an Unholy Striker, and I have a handful of physical and distance-clearing abilities. I'm level 200."

"Would you have a problem becoming my thrall now that I've set you free?"

The draconic seemed indifferent. "I wouldn't know any different. I cannot remember my past life. If becoming your thrall gives me the opportunity to experience a new life, then I will gladly take the opportunity."

Riven smiled in satisfaction and went on to the next. "Do you have a name?"

The yellow and purple merwoman shrugged. "Just as the lizard said, I cannot recall. I believe my memories have been wiped, or perhaps I was in there too long to remember my past. Unlike him, I do remember the fight, and I remember glimpses of the ocean the other souls and I resided in. But nothing of significance."

"What is your combat skill set?"

"Level 200 Swamp Witch. I have a variety of curses, debuffs, and stacking afflictions that cause damage over time."

"Ah, you're something like my succubus, then. What is your take on becoming one of my thralls after I set you free?"

The merwoman hesitated and shot the two drow a wary glance. "Will it hurt?"

"It is not likely if you accept what the venom is doing to you. Genua and Luke, my first two thralls, never had much of a problem."

"If I refuse, will you let me go?"

Riven gave her a pleasant smile. "Perhaps at some point. Not anytime soon, though, if what I hear about needing variety to unlock my bloodlines is true. A species such as yourself is going to be very hard to find. I'll be feeding on you for quite some time."

"And if I became your thrall, I'd have my freedom back immediately?"

"Yes, to whatever extent being a thrall allows you to do so."

"That's a fair enough answer," the merwoman replied. Pursing her lips, the witch came to a decision. "I will willingly become your thrall, then, whenever you're ready to start the process."

"Very good." Riven grinned, clapped once, and moved on to the last.

Before Riven could even open his mouth, the ogre began listing off the information he wanted. "Chaos Barbarian, Level 200. Give me freedom and I can become your thrall without question, vampire. My soul has been in a tormented state of boredom for far too long. Give me the opportunity for violence and I will do whatever else you ask."

Riven studied the green-skinned ogre and gave a thumbs-up. "Well, that was rather easy."

"You FOOLS!" Numin, who was still thrashing around in his chains with sweat beading down his bare chest, snarled at the three people Riven's team had taken from the blood-ocean floor. "Do you not know what it means to become a thrall?! You are selling your very minds! Do not give in!"

Blood began to mix with the drool dripping down Numin's chin as the dark elf bit down on his lip, glaring at Riven with a hatred so pure that Riven would be dead a thousand times over if looks could kill.

"Death is better than becoming your thrall!" Numin hissed, spitting at Riven with contempt. "You're a liar and a fraud, vampire!"

Riven let the glob of spit land on his gluttonous chest armor and approached the dark elf while raising one hand. "To be fair, I didn't intend on lying to you. Life just has a funny way of working out sometimes, but I can't say I feel bad about it, either. What you did to Kara was terrible and may have been even worse than what you're experiencing now."

"More lies!" Numin spat, coughing up blood with a gurgling noise as his eyes began to roll into the back of his head while his body convulsed. He managed to gasp out another few words as Zafima began to sob nearby. "Just kill me! Please, kill me!!!"

There was a long pause.

"Is that what you want, too, Zafima?" Riven asked casually. "Your mother was killed by your emperor, and your country will execute the two of you on sight. The transition is already too far gone to fix. It's either this or death."

Zafima was still convulsing, thrashing, and sobbing, but the sobbing became more violent and louder at the news. "I STILL WANT TO LIVE! DON'T KILL ME; I WILL BECOME WHATEVER IT IS YOU WANT! PLEASE, JUST MAKE THE PAIN STOP! MAKE THE PAIN STOPPP!!!"

"I'm pretty sure you can do that yourself, you just have to let it in. Stop fighting the process." Grimacing, Riven snapped his hand forward in a blur. Blood sprayed across the room, and Numin let out a gargling final scream before going limp, his bloodshot eyes becoming lifeless. The very last thing Numin saw in this life was the still-beating heart Riven held in his hand. The one that Riven had pried out of Numin's very own chest.

Placing the heart to his lips, Riven began to eat it like an apple. Considering Zafima for a while, he spoke to Fay. "Despite these drow being lesser beings, cattle for butchering, and a pair of guilty criminals, I find it strange that I still have some remnants of empathy left for them. When my hunger strikes, I find myself washed away without a care in the world—all I need to do is kill and eat. But when my hunger isn't all-encompassing, I find that a part of my humanity has still found a crevice to hide in."

He set the half-eaten heart on the table and began to walk away. "Give Zafima a potion for pain, if we even have any. Make sure she's calmed down or at least sedated before bringing Genua and Iris into this place. Kara, too. I agree with your assessment—having a pocket realm like this one is far safer than allowing them to travel through the Abyssal Descent with the rest of us."

"Yes, Master." Fay subserviently followed behind. Hopeful, she reached out and started to increase her walking speed to catch up. "Is . . . is there anything I can do to make it up to you? For lying?"

She stopped him by grabbing his shoulder and turned him around, then unhitched a latch on her waist and let her skirt fall to the ground around her long bare legs. Standing half naked in front of him, she gave him a flirtatious and hopeful smile while grabbing for his crotch.

Riven looked down, looked back up, gave her a blank stare, and coldly turned away, leaving her rejected in the dim candlelight. "No. I'm sorry, Fay, but this is going to take time to get over. I'm sure I probably will, but I'm going to need some space from physical intimacy for the foreseeable future."

CHAPTER 26

Gluttony's altar didn't react when he'd touched it, at least not in any meaningful way. It truly was just a conduit to try and communicate with the being on the other side, a telephone call they didn't have to answer. But Gluttony was already inside him, so for Riven there was little to no change. Hatchmire had bidden them farewell soon after that, and Riven had taken quite a liking to the guy before they left Floor Thirty-Seven behind. Genua, Kara, and Iris were all tucked safely away in Fay's pocket realm while Riven, Azmoth, Fay, Athela, and Retesh carried on.

The next two floors weren't great. Floor Thirty-Eight was a puzzle room that kept closing in around them and was going to crush them unless they finished it in time, with fifteen puzzles related to different Dao secrets. Each one had a way to channel power through a pillar while under different domains of influence. Riven was quick to figure out that these different domains actually represented different ways the pillars could connect, which was fascinating to him and directly correlated with soul lattice construction. But despite his delight at figuring out various secrets of how to build his soul lattice more effectively, Fay was in a very deep depression and avoided eye contact completely, while Athela was both depressed and angry, occasionally making snarky remarks about how he didn't appreciate the things they tried to do for him.

The talks had obviously not gone over well, and they had many more of these talks across the thirty-seventh and thirty-eighth floors while Retesh and Azmoth tried to pretend it wasn't happening.

It wasn't as though Riven actually wanted Athela and Fay to leave. In fact, it was the opposite—he obviously wanted them to stay and told them that multiple times during their powwows. But he couldn't stay with people who thought so little of him as to completely go behind his back, to assume he couldn't make his own decision with or without their input. He was supposed to be the reincarnation of Gluttony, and if people realized that he wasn't respected by his own lovers and minions, it'd certainly get out. Had he ever lied to them like this? No, he hadn't. So why did they think he'd just roll over and accept what they'd done?

Nor would he use his contractual compulsions to force them to do anything, including forcing them not to lie. What kind of relationship would that be if he did?

So he'd told them in no uncertain terms that they had a decision to make, despite how guilty he felt from the hurt he was obviously inflicting, but he needed them to understand how big of a deal this was to him. The decision was this: Trust was a must, and if they couldn't allow him to have that trust in them through their actions, then they'd need to find somewhere else to be. Or, alternatively, they could keep their contracts and remain as friends, but cut off anything remotely related to a romantic relationship.

In retrospect, after getting to the end of the thirty-eighth floor, he realized he might have gone a bit overboard by telling them that they could find another warlock if they didn't respect him enough to not lie to his face. He might have even been influenced a bit by his anger, and after a one-on-one talk with Gluttony, he felt a bit guilty. The sin had asked them directly to help and had told them Riven would appreciate what they were doing—and to Riven's surprise, Gluttony took all the blame.

Not that he believed the other two were entirely blameless, but when they had a being out of myth that their demonic races worshipped telling them what to do, perhaps he should be a little more forgiving. And the more he thought about it, the more Riven realized how devastated he'd be if the girls actually did call his bluff and leave. Riven had killed hundreds of thousands of innocents to bring Athela back, sacrificing an entire city's worth of men, women, and children. He'd do it again, and he'd do the same for Fay. So why was he putting their relationship in jeopardy over something like this, which was technically a first-time offense?

He shouldn't give ultimatums—it was childish and hurtful and could potentially lead to a disastrous result. He could have just expressed how he'd felt and sat them down like an adult. At this point he couldn't even imagine life without them.

He was still angry with Athela and Fay for what they'd done, but Riven would need to work on how he expressed his feelings from now on.

Floor Thirty-Nine, a test of resolve, came next. The Abyssal Descent forcefully expanded one's mana, stamina, and divinity channels with extremely painful modifications to the soul itself. It made one more powerful, but the pain was so unbearable that Retesh passed out and Fay was left seizing. Riven's vampiric regeneration didn't mean shit in the face of overwhelming soul pressure, and he, too, had collapsed to fade in and out of consciousness. At any moment he could choose to leave, but that wasn't an option for any of them with Lillith on the fiftieth floor, and he was also growing more powerful for each minute he stayed.

Eight hours later the pressure stopped, and Riven was finally able to come back from what felt like the brink of death. He was surrounded by a puddle of his own impurities that'd been purged from his pores and left a stinking muck on his armor and clothes. The others hadn't fared well, either, but Athela and Azmoth had by far fared the best and were only breathing heavily while still remaining upright, though they, too, had the same piles of gunk around them that smelled like rancid piss.

He did get a notification about his mana channels widening by 40 percent, though, which didn't change the total amount of mana his soul produced, but rather changed the amount of that original mana that he could force out in a single instance. His burst damage, in essence, had become more viable, and the same could be said for everyone else there.

"Is everyone okay?" Riven asked, shakily standing and seeing a flare of light in the distance as the next floor's portal opened up.

Athela snorted in derision and shouldered past him, ignoring his hand to help her up. "Yes, Riven. I'm absolutely great, just thinking about all the other warlock men who'd love to have a beautiful archdemon on their team."

The comment certainly stung, and Riven angrily pursed his lips. But he didn't take the bait and let the angry demoness keep walking.

Fay still couldn't look him in the eyes and shakily got up to follow Athela toward the portal.

Riven felt a large clawed hand rest on his shoulder a moment later.

"I know you angry, but they just meant help," Azmoth said, patting Riven's shoulder twice more before being the third in line to start off toward the distant orb of light. "They not mean anything bad when they did what they did. You need have talk before you three stay angry long time."

Retesh, who was hobbling along with his bone staff for support, only shook his head and held up a hand when he caught Riven's eye. "Don't look at me for advice, young man. I haven't had a flesh partner in thousands of years. I don't know my own skull from my pelvis when it comes to what your personal problems entail. But if you wouldn't mind, I could certainly use someone to lean on. My mana channels are in a state of shock, and I can't use my own energy to support my stride."

They'd taken a few hours for a break, just to be topped off in case anyone in the descent tried to assassinate them on the other side. Riven still hadn't seen signs of Greed's forces despite Greed knowing he was down here, and the closer they got to Floor Fifty, the more that worry grew. Narg also wasn't back, still—Riven was completely unable to summon him or even contact him despite numerous attempts. Riven couldn't help but wonder if Narg was even going to make it out of whatever evolutionary trial he was experiencing at all.

The long abyssal stairway was much the same as the others between floors after that. The only difference was that there was a sincere lack of monsters or people, with an ominous silence hanging over the party as they descended the steps. Twice, Riven caught sight of gargantuan void titans beyond Elysium's protective barriers encompassing the staircase, but the creatures were so large and it was so dark that even he couldn't truly figure out what they looked like or what the real scale of the creatures was. Here in the abyss, far from the reach of the mortal realms, the monsters of the deep ruled like gods.

Nothing else of note happened on their trek down, and soon their path out was in sight. But stepping through into Floor Forty was something of a jolting experience, even more so than other floors had been.

**[Identification information has been restored.
<u>Floor Forty: A Dark Delve Through Time and Space, Part 1</u>, is about to begin.]**

WHAM

Riven felt like a truck had just smashed into his face fifty times given the throbbing headache he immediately felt after passing through the rift. He was flat on his stomach, cold stone touching his skin, and was silently cursing the Abyssal Descent and Elysium for throwing him to the ground like that.

"Thank you for accepting our summons, fellow spellcaster," an old man's shrill voice called out to him from somewhere up above and nearby. "Elysium says that you are the one called Riven Thane. Is that correct?"

Disoriented, grimacing, and already having had a bad time with the stress of his girl problems, Riven did not appreciate how high-pitched and irritated the questioner's voice was. He began to push himself up on his hands and knees, shaking his head from the vertigo that was starting to settle down, when the man's voice came yet again:

"Ahem. You are the one called Riven Thane, correct?"

Riven's world stabilized, and he found himself in the middle of an enclosed circular arena devoid of any allies. His entire team was gone, he was alone, but a few hundred robed men and women of various species were sitting on bleachers talking to each other in low tones. Many of them were nonchalantly reading grimoires, looking at crystal balls, casting small spells for entertainment, or looked just plain bored with staves and wands in hand. Many of those spells looked like earth and water manipulation, or even arcane jade and purple variants he wasn't all that familiar with. It looked like an assembly of spellcasters, and most of them certainly weren't even of the Unholy foundational pillar, which Riven thought was quite odd considering he was in the Abyssal Descent. But one look around begged to differ, given he could see blue skies and dotted white clouds through glass windows on the left and right sides of the long hall.

An older man with a long white beard and a janky wizard's hat with stars speckling the blue cloth was glaring down at Riven from over a pair of rimmed glasses, though his eyes went wide when Riven's own lit up a vibrant red to glare back.

"Oh my, a pureblooded vampire. I haven't seen one of your kind for about a thousand years." The old man scribbled something down on a notepad he had up on top of his elevated desk. Then he put the pen down and looked over the spectacles at Riven with raised eyebrows. "But let us carry on so that you can be on your way. As the system notification specified, we have summoned you here today because you have offended one of our members, who claims you unfairly took his minion from him. He hopes to settle this fairly by means of trade and payment but will duel you with the stated prize on offer for his defeat if you wish. This court assumes you have accepted this summons in order to see what kind of recompense he can provide before taking his minion back? Hmm?"

Riven's armor let out a rumbling growl from the vertical maw along his chest when Messenger, and he, sensed multiple people using an identify on him and his items. After his training with Lillith and the Church of Gluttony, though, he could tell that it was all being blocked by the obscuring amulet he'd received from the dark elf Gentry before the man's untimely demise at Greed's hand.

That didn't mean he couldn't identify everyone else here, though.

[Master Arcanist, Human, Level 308]
[Fire Mage, Human, Level 71 ELITE]
[Eyes of the Storm, High Elf, Level 213 ELITE]
[Shaman of the Dread Oak, Ent, Level 49]
[Water Mage Apprentice, Greenscale Naga, Level 8]
[Eclectic Enchantress, Brightbulb Fairy, Level 20]
[Necromancer Adept, Human, Level 105]
[Shaman of Golden Fields, Red Orc, Level 56]

All in all, there were only five people in this entire arena that were a threat to him, and even they were people that Riven could probably take on without too much issue. Feeling out his connections to his minions, they were all intact, every single one of them. They were just, for whatever reason, banished to their nether realms. Retesh was another matter entirely—he had no idea where Retesh had gone and hoped the old lich was okay, but that wasn't nearly as concerning to him. Retesh was more of an acquaintance, and the old bag of bones could likely take care of himself.

Riven relaxed, planted his staff in the ground, and leaned on it. "Yes, my name is Riven Thane, but I'm not entirely sure you know who I am if you're asking me to give up one of my minions. Is this still part of the Abyssal Descent?"

Riven got a few curious glances, but otherwise the people in the stands kept doing whatever it was they were doing to entertain themselves through whatever this was.

The old man's expression grew grim, and he leaned forward even more while keeping the brim of his hat out of his eyes with one hand. "No, young man. This is certainly not the Abyssal Descent. Is that where we summoned you from? If so, there are a lot of people here that'd like to ask you a few questions after the proceedings are done."

Riven continued to look around, finding this entire situation quite odd, when another man about forty years of age walked into the arena's center. He had a cleanly cut black beard with a white streak down the middle, a short crew cut of similar color, vibrant-blue eyes, and an annoyingly handsome face. His long purple robes swept along the stone floor with the click of a black-jeweled wooden staff, and he arrogantly looked Riven up and down before posturing only a few feet away.

[Warlock Slaver, Human, Level 219 ELITE]

"Jarrod Presbell." The man stated his name with a sniff, and yet again looked Riven up and down in slow motion while shaking his head. "Thank you for attending this summons . . . though I did not realize you were of the . . . blood-sucking variety."

He said the last two words with disdain but quickly covered it up with an obviously fake smile. He pulled out a large, jeweled pouch and tossed it to Riven's feet before drawing an enchanted slave collar from his spatial bag while spinning it around one finger. "Because you accepted the summons, I'll assume you are ready to sell her back to me. The pouch should be more than what she is worth on the standard market. Please take a look and let me know if you're satisfied."

The man, Jarrod, seemed rather confident, and Riven didn't have a goddamn clue what this guy was talking about.

"You've lost me," Riven said flatly, kicking the bag of coins back in the other warlock's direction. "I never received any notification about a summoning. Stop fucking around and tell me why I'm here and how to get out of this floor."

Others in the stands began to laugh, and the other warlock looked at Riven like he was stupid. "Excuse me? Did you just kick that pouch in my direction? I have half a mind to teach you some manners, boy! What I'm giving you is a gift, and you haven't even looked at the contents!"

The elderly wizard with the starred hat slammed a large book on his desk to get their attention and coughed loudly a couple of times before intervening. "Rivon, was it?"

"Riven. Not Rivon."

"Bah! Same thing." The old man waved a dismissive hand. "In case you had a hard knock to the head when you landed, and it looked like you did, you've been summoned to the Blue Swan Wizarding Courts."

The old man looked rather proud to say it, but his face fell when Riven didn't show an inkling of recognition.

So the old man continued. "Ahem. As I've already said, this man here, Jarrod, is a member of our society. And as a highly regarded wizarding faction spanning the stars, with the purpose of unlocking our multiverse's mysteries, we take slights against our members rather seriously. Not that you yourself offended him, but the succubus in your possession did. She is Jarrod's property, and Jarrod here has been complaining about the loss of his succubus for nearly a year now. Because we've scried you as being the current owner of that succubus, we sent you a summons, which you must have accepted. If you hadn't accepted, you wouldn't be here right now."

The old man said it as a statement rather than a question, though he did look a little bit confused. Possibly concerned. "You may want to see a healer for head trauma."

"Yes," Jarrod began with arms crossed and foot tapping impatiently. "Come back to your senses so we can get this negotiation over with already. Fay was mine for years, and I want her back. Please—"

The black-haired man bent down and picked up his sack and this time pushed it into Riven's arms. "—take a look at what I'm offering you before you start trying to play hardball. We all know you wouldn't be here if you didn't want to negotiate. You will be treated fairly under the rules of the Blue Swan Wizarding Courts, per the summons."

Riven really didn't know what he was doing here, but now he was in a state of shock on top of the confusion. This man was Fay's last master? What the hell was HE doing here?

Just for curiosity's sake, he opened the coin pouch in his hands and saw perhaps fifty thousand Elysium coins in total.

Riven blinked, almost speechless.

Was Elysium fucking with him since he, Athela, and Fay were having a rough time? Was this Elysium playing some sort of stupid fucking joke? This had to be a joke. No way it wasn't. Why else would Elysium send him here right after he was having a fight with his two minions, right after he'd literally said, "You can find another warlock"?

Was it trying to push him into actually doing so, or was it trying to make a point?

Was there even a correlation? Was this man actually the person he said he was? Hadn't her last master died or something? He honestly couldn't remember, but he DID know she'd been treated like shit by the sole other person who'd held her contract.

Jarrod stroked his finely trimmed beard and gave Riven a perfectly white smile, nodding in satisfaction at Riven's openmouthed expression. "Yes, I thought so. I put in an additional ten thousand coins over standard slave price for an F-grade succubus at her tier. Is she still below level 30? That stupid bitch doesn't have the talent for anything besides sucking my cock! I'll have to put her through some dungeons and force her to fight to catch up, if it's even possible, but I'm sure you see now that I'm paying more than what is fair!"

Riven's hold around Jackal was so tight at this point that he could feel his finger bones starting to snap, and with a very forced smile that displayed his fangs, he looked up from the pouch and let it drop to the floor with the jingle of coins.

He tugged on their connection and summoned her to his location as the pentagram of wings on his chest representing their pact lit up beneath his armor. "Fay."

In an instant she arrived, and she was already kneeling on the floor babbling something ALMOST incoherent while clawing at his legs.

"W-why is HE here?! P-please Riven!" She gasped, sobbing and giving Jarrod a scared, hateful glare between pleading puppy-dog eyes. She wrapped her arms around Riven's leg and buried her face into his thigh. "I d-don't want to leave y-you! Don't force me to w-wear that c-collar and go back to t-that MONSTER! I didn't think y-you were s-serious about m-me finding another warlock! P-please! F-forgive me!"

Jarrod's jaw dropped, and a huge grin spread across his face as he started walking forward. "Fay!!! So nice to see you again . . . No need to say such terrible things about me! We had such great times together!"

He grinned devilishly, but his eyes traced up to Fay's larger curling horns, and a look of surprise overcame him as he staggered to a stop. "Wait, you— You're an archdemon now?! You've evolved?! And you've leveled up so much! How did—"

Riven's fist smashed into Jarrod's chest when he got within range. Ribs audibly cracked, blood flew out of the older man's mouth, and despite the mana shield the other warlock managed to erect a split second before the impact, he was sent flying backward into the stone arena wall, cratering three feet deep with a spray of stone debris and an aftershock of displaced air.

Immediately the entire arena was in an uproar, with defensive and offensive spells flaring from the surprised crowd. Wards along the stone room began to glow bright yellow as well, and the wizard with the starry hat started shouting something and pointing at Riven, only for Riven's aura to descend upon the room like an avalanche.

Immediately, the wards along the stone wall cracked, the windows shattered, the building's supports started to groan, and spells were snuffed out like candles in a gale. People started to gasp for air as they were crushed underneath the immense weight of his presence, and Jarrod, who was the target of Riven's ire, began to scream as bones snapped one by one and blood flew out of his orifices. Even the two level-300-plus people in the room were having a very hard time standing or even breathing, but one of them managed to activate some sort of spell that set alarms blaring.

Pulling Fay up to her feet, Riven gave her a firm hug and brushed a hand through her hair. "I'm sorry I ever said that, and I don't mean it. I didn't back then, either, and I don't want either of you two to go, I was just angry and in the moment. This place—"

Riven gestured around at the dying people as they suffocated and began to frost over as red ice started clinging to their clothes, skin, and surroundings. "This place has nothing to do with trying to get rid of you. It's part of the descent—don't ask me why we're here, because I don't—"

[**Floor Forty: A Dark Delve Through Time and Space, Part 1**, has
begun. Tear out Jarrod's soul, rip it apart, and reclaim the piece of
his soul lattice that he previously used to bind Fay. Then incorporate
that lattice into your own soul before you're hunted down and killed
by the Blue Swan Wizarding Court enforcers. This will be the first
step to incorporate your closest minions into your own soul lattice,
thereby empowering each side of the pact and strengthening your
connections.]

His words cut off, eyebrows arching in surprise, and a sly smile crept across
his face. "Fay, silly, you cry far too often for your own good. The real reason why
I brought you here was to ask if you'd have any problem if I killed this man."

"W-what?" Fay sniffled, and she glared up at him with arms still around his
chest. "You're not going to sell me?"

Riven though he'd die because he rolled his eyes so hard, and bopped her on
the forehead. "I mean this lovingly, but don't be fucking stupid. I didn't come
this far only to sell you off to someone else, and I am so, so sorry I made you
feel like I would."

"Promise?"

"I promise. And you know what? I also promise to make all this up to both
of you after we're finally out."

She sniffed, glared at Jarrod, and then noticed the notification Riven was
trying to show her. She startled in surprise but didn't release her grip. "No, I . . .
I hated him. It was awful, and though I wouldn't have gone out of my way to see
him dead, I wouldn't feel bad if you chose to murder him, either."

Descending E-grades and high-tier F-grades were racing down on their position from a few miles out, Riven could feel it, and that was easily in striking
range for many of that caliber. They likely hadn't blown the building yet because
of all the other people inside.

"Good." Riven gave Fay a kiss on the forehead and squeezed her shoulders,
then turned around and started toward Fay's old master with a sinister grin.
"Because though I hadn't seen this one coming, I can't say I'm going to feel bad
about it, either."

"Riven?"

He paused, and looked back over his shoulder. "Yes, Fay?"

"Are you still mad at me?"

"Fay, I just said that I—"

"No, you said that you wished you hadn't said those things about finding
another warlock." She wiped at her face and this time directed her glare at Riven.
"Tell me you're not mad, and I'll tell you that I won't ever lie to you again like I
did. Unless it's about something silly, like spitting in your food when you're not
looking because I'm irritated with you."

"You've done that?"

"I did it yesterday."

Riven blinked, grinned, and cackled before coming back and sweeping her off her feet. Holding her in the air, he kissed her long and hard before setting her down again as Athela and Azmoth flared into existence through portals of their own. "I forgive both of you. I'm sorry, and I'm not mad."

"Yeah, well, that makes one of us," Athela muttered, not bothering to look at Riven as she made her way over to the man embedded in the wall. Drawing a long red katana, she gutted the man and ripped off his head before tossing the body of Fay's old master in Riven's direction with a splat. She pointed at Riven with accusation in her eyes. "You and me are going to have a talk of our own about how much of an unappreciative jerk you've been. I was watching from the nether realms and I saw everything, but know this—I have well over three thousand viable warlocks gunning to have me as their next minion, and just because you're some big hotshot reincarnation doesn't mean that you'll be able to get away with threatening to leave me like you did!"

Athela's lips quivered, and she stood trembling a ways away from the decapitated body before spitting in Riven's direction. It was probably the most angry she'd ever been, or at least the angriest Riven had ever seen. "You can't just tell me you love me and then make me question everything about our relationship because of one fucking stupid mistake, Riven! I don't think you know how much that hurt. And you know what? I didn't intentionally hurt you. But what you said was intentional, and it very damn well hurt ME!"

CHAPTER 27

Riven wanted to reply to that, and though he felt like he'd overreacted to an extent, he'd certainly been justified in being somewhat angry. However he didn't get time or the opportunity to discuss it, because an incoming lance of silver light vaporized the western wall and came straight for him over the heads of the people he was suppressing.

There was an audible crack of air and a thunderous aftershock as the silver light spiked right into a hastily constructed crimson barrier, and the ice shattered a second later to smash into his armored chest.

He was sent spiraling, flipping head over heels as the peak E-grade attack cut a hole through Messenger and struck adjacent to his heart. A searing pain radiated through his body as he barreled through the opposite wall in a spray of stone debris and came to a crashing halt in a crater outside.

Sirens continued to blare, and he felt more than saw his minions leap into action as they began to engage the incoming cultivators he felt with his mana sense. He felt Athela shift into her enormous drider state, felt Azmoth take on his titanic building-sized stature with flared wings, and felt Fay's dreamwalker zones encompass him to hide him with layers of illusion.

Within a split second, over a dozen E-grades had literally ripped through space overhead with dimensional tears in reality, riding brooms, of all things, with wands and staves at the ready. Azmoth immediately launched himself skyward, causing the building to explode in a shower of tiles and wooden beams as a huge clawed hand snatched a screaming wizard out of the air to crush the man in a splash of crimson that silenced the cry. A huge stone maul of flames tore upward to catch another two closely flying witches who erected barriers in an attempt to thwart the attack, but their mangled, burned bodies were sent spiraling like comets into the ground as the gigantic archdemon ripped skyward after the others with a roar that shook the city.

"Well, that hurts!" Riven grumbled, feeling his flesh knit itself together from the attack and wiping the dust off his armor before looking around. Cackling to himself at the sight of the giant flaming demon in the sky taking on E-grade wizards and witches far beyond what Azmoth should be capable of, Riven had to acknowledge that his minions were truly a step beyond the norm. Fay was joining Azmoth in the sky to take some of the heat off her counterpart; she began creating minefields of invisible curse traps that the enemy combatants had to take time either dispelling, blasting through, or detecting. She also traded attacks, fake copies of herself zipping around the sky in dogfights to dodge elemental strikes, arcane blasts, and gravitational bombs while retaliating with cursed affliction fireballs and lashes of her extending bladed tail.

The resulting spectacle was something of a light show that painted the otherwise blue sky in a myriad of different colors.

"Curious . . ." Riven said aloud, extending his hand to summon Jackal to his open palm. In his opposite hand, the trishard blood pearl, his C-grade blood artifact, appeared. Those he'd been suppressing began to do battle with Athela on the ground and an uproar of sounds met his ears. "Once upon a time, I'd have cared that these people didn't deserve to die. Now, all I see are lesser creatures standing in my way. I don't necessarily want them to die . . . but I don't feel nearly as bad about killing them anymore if it gets the job done. Gluttony . . . does that make me evil?"

The sin internally laughed but gave no other response as Riven's feet began to lift off the ground and into the sky at a slow and steady rate. As Riven rose up above the nearby buildings, the sight of a sprawling magitech metropolis filled with a mixture of medieval fantasy and advanced magical technology met his gaze, and it was truly wonderful to behold. Hover-trains on neon-purple railways, floating castles, and noble estates high up off the ground with elevators and sky ships docked in various places, and the people . . . There were so many of them. Millions, at the very least. The air felt clean, the landscape between city blocks was dotted with parks and greenery, and . . .

And there were tons of screaming people trying to get away from the chaos centered around his position. The entire city was on full alert as more and more spellcasters took to the skies from different points around the metropolis. Mostly they were on brooms, giving the whole thing a Harry Potter kind of feel, but there were a few flying swords, platforms, giant leaves, and bonded flying pets as well. He even saw a few wyverns, but when some of the larger flying ships of war turned their cannons on Azmoth, Riven couldn't just watch any longer.

Lifting his staff in the direction of the two ships in question just as they began to rain cannonballs and magical weaponry onto Azmoth's armored hide as he dived through the clouds, Riven's arm lit up with Black Lightning and a bolt of gut-wrenching power flashed forward a mile out like a scar of void through reality. One of the ships was snapped in half with wooden debris and screaming bodies flying out from the explosion, while the other warship reacted in time to lift magical barriers to deflect the attack. The shields went from 100 percent to flickering and barely there, and the second ship was sent spiraling out in a spinning arc, destabilized and fighting frantically to stay skyborne.

He didn't pull on his aura, not yet. He wasn't a complete monster and there was no need for mass civilian casualties, so Riven decided to keep his strikes as direct and precise as possible to target other combatants. He also started supercharging another Critical Storm Lance with the trishard blood pearl, and felt the skill begin to manifest inside the swirling ball of crimson to immense effect.

> [<u>Supercharged Blood</u>: Take an additional thirty seconds of channeling a Blood skill through this item to create a supercharged variant. This skill is incredibly potent, and overuse may damage your mana channels.]

A man's upper half was sent spiraling from beneath him without warning. "AAAAAAAAAAHHHHHHHHHHHHhhhhhhhhhhhh!!!"

Following the blood trail and flailing arms, Riven looked down on the wrecked hall where Athela was finishing off the last of the people who'd stayed behind to try and fight after they'd murdered Fay's last warlock summoner.

What was his name again?

Jarrod?

Fuck that guy. Riven just wished he had more time to fuck him up before Athela gutted him. The dead warlock's body was still embedded in the stone wall where Riven had launched him with a punch.

"AAAAAAAAHHHHHHHHHHhhhhhhhhhhhhhhhhh!!!"

Riven dodged another screaming severed body just like the first, and glared down at the uppity spider lady throwing dying bodies in his direction. "Athela, you're doing that on purpose. Stop throwing them at me."

"YOU DESERVE IT FOR BEING AN ASSHOLE!" Athela said, smashing another wizard and ripping him apart before throwing both halves at Riven one after the other. "YOU'RE A JERK!"

Riven avoided the bodies easily and flashed down to float in front of her. Smacking the enormous figure of her drider form across the face, Riven unleashed his aura and suppressed his minion entirely through the bond. "Stop trying to attack me. That is an order, since you aren't mature enough to realize this is not the place or time."

She went as rigid as the icy flowers covering parts of her body, still glaring at him with the four red eyes outlined by bright-white skin. "You aren't supposed to use your commands like that, Riven."

"I do what I want, you haughty bitch." Riven grinned and gave her a wink, before bonking his lover on the head with the horned skull of his staff. "That's what you get. Now act serious and stop fucking around—you'll need to buy me time while I absorb Jarrod's piece of soul lattice into my own. Oh, and I love you, too, babe."

He snapped his fingers and administered the command yet again, and with a shrill snarl Athela whipped around and tore into another group of spellcasters rushing through the building's entrance. Riven did not care in the slightest about their screams of pain and their begging to whatever gods they worshipped as he felt his supercharged lance manifest within the pearl of his left hand.

Riven didn't bother using it, seeing no reason to yet and feeling the influx of E-grade signatures coming in hot and fast as the battle in the skies went into overdrive. He'd be unable to beat them all even going full tilt, especially if he wanted to avoid mass bystander casualties, and would probably end up running pretty soon to avoid such a conflict. Using strings of blood to bring up Jarrod's body like a puppet, Riven began to feel around the body for the man's soul and then closed his eyes to focus on the particulars of what he was looking for.

He found the soul within ten seconds. Beyond this realm and in the void on the other side of the veil, thousands of spirits swirled around in inky darkness, but Jarrod's physical body was still acting like an anchor. The soul hadn't had time to completely detach.

Fishing around with tendrils of mana, Riven extracted the soul from the void and drew it into his, where he began to dissect little pieces of the man's spirit as agonizing, unearthly screams wailed from the tiny ball of light. Chuckling malevolently to himself for the pain he was causing the bastard who'd talked about Fay in such a disrespectful manner, Riven peeled back layer by layer to unearth what he was looking for.

The screams became louder and more agonized, but despite how long it seemed, the reality was that only a minute passed before Riven found a part of Jarrod's being resonating with Fay's lingering soul signature. Curiously, Riven picked it out and began cutting the piece of soul lattice off the screeching soul with wisps of Sin and death. For most, destroying a soul was no easy task. Souls naturally resisted destruction like this, but for Riven it was doable. Tedious and it took a lot of effort, but doable. Even now Riven realized that if he was to truly go after complete destruction of the soul in his hands, it would take him a very long time just to get it done, but thankfully this was just a surgical dissection of a tiny piece of the other warlock's soul so that Riven could cannibalize the piece. This was also his first time trying, and it was like Gluttony's teeth were saw blades as he slowly shredded the essence of what the enemy warlock had once been.

He'd have to ask Gluttony if there were any safeguards to this method. Riven was sure there were, but he didn't know the specifics and would need to find out in case anyone tried this kind of thing with him in the future. Otherwise, weapons like the demon-slaying sword that'd been used to kill Athela, the one that Riven had in his spatial bag right now, wouldn't be so valuable, right? The commandments had blessed the blade and made it tear not only through demonic contracts, but through demonic souls, too, making Riven hard-pressed to bring Athela back with only a fragment of her soul leftover via Gluttony's miracle.

Riven again drew Jarrod's weak spirit into his own, closing his eyes and feeling the bastard's soul quiver as Gluttony's presence wrapped around the tiny light, snuffing it out in Riven's inner realm. It would be safer there as he carved the piece he wanted away from the original owner before completely tearing Jarrod apart piece by piece for daring to talk about Fay like he had. Riven then let Jarrod's corpse fall like a rag doll to the ground far below, splatting against the rubble of the building while focusing on the ethereal surgery.

Tilting his head back just an inch, Riven narrowly dodged another piercing lance of silver light that came out of nowhere, but he'd been waiting for the enemy mage to reveal themselves after the initial strike and wasn't caught flat-footed. Eyes blazing red and letting out a madman's laugh, Riven pointed the orb in the direction of the cloaked assailant and unleashed hell in the form of the pearl's supercharged Critical Storm Lance.

The sky was ripped apart, instantly cleaved in two with a wave of crimson and black cutting across the blue expanse out into the horizon with trailing ribbons of storm energy. A massive shock wave followed, then silver robes began to fall to the ground in a cloud of red mist below where his cloaked assailant had been hiding. Simply put, the attack had been too fast to react, and even Riven's senses had a hard time following the magically empowered strike.

CRACK

Riven's eyes widened when another silver bolt of energy just like the first two smashed into his shoulder, cutting clean through armor and musculature with ease. Burning sensations began traveling down his limb, and he grimaced before launching himself to the left in a dizzying display of agility as magical missiles locked onto his position.

He tore through a rift and disappeared, only to reappear dozens of yards away while refocusing on the mage in silver robes he thought he'd killed not long ago with his empowered lance. The enemy combatant was sitting cross-legged on a broom, wearing a witch's hat and long flowing robes, and she looked rather young.

"That hurt," a feminine voice called out from a tear in space that began opening up a half mile out. "And my clones are hard to make. I don't appreciate you vaporizing them. But . . . I've always wanted to kill a vampire."

She laughed while twirling a wand in between her hands, and her peak E-grade aura skyrocketed with suffocating prowess. Smile widening, she stopped spinning the wand and pointed it at him. "One as powerful as you should make a good whetstone! A MYTHIC F-grade warlock? You don't see that ranking often. It's too bad your cultivation will be cut short now that you're facing me! Prepare to die for your transgressions, monster, and for daring to take on the Blue Swan Wizarding Court!"

The sky over their direct location turned black, and a silver moon burned brightly against the dark backdrop as the witch lit up with a flash of light and exploded into ten thousand needles, scattering in all directions.

Just as fast as the witch exploded, her moonlight condensed in an instant beside Riven and her newly formed body reached up to place a hand on Riven's hood. The move was so instantaneous, so fast, that even though Riven registered the movement, he barely had time to react. A piercing lance of silver moonlight ripped through the side of his hood at point-blank range and burned the edge of his skull, but he'd whipped around to retaliate and flash froze the surrounding area to hold the witch in place.

Surprised that her attack had been off by a mere inch, the witch was unable to follow up with another attack and instead dematerialized again with another flash of moonlight, relocating with whatever teleport ability she was using and shivering violently. Peeling off the crimson crystals that were accumulating on her skin and clothes, she glared at Riven as he glared right back. "I should have expected as much from a MYTHIC, even if you are an entire tier below me. This should be interesting."

Riven reached up to touch the back of his head, where a hole still simmered with that strange moonlight the witch was using, and rubbed the coagulated blood between his fingers. Checking internally, the soul lattice dissection was progressing slowly. He could feel more E-grade enforcers homing in on his position and weighed his options. If this woman was indicative of what their best warriors were like, there was no way he could handle more than one or two at a time. Maybe not even one—she was likely around level 350 to 400 to his 200 and was obviously not a slouch, but he couldn't be sure because she wore some kind of talisman that was interfering with his identification attempts. Her speed was slightly better than his own, and he still didn't want to get the local citizens caught up in a fight if he went all out.

Recognizing the soul signatures and general cultivation levels of the people racing toward him versus the ones keeping his demons at bay, he could also tell that the best of them were coming directly for him. Knowing that taking the warlock summoner out would get rid of the demons, they were designating their hard hitters to deal with the source of the problem.

"As much as I would like to stay, I have a date to catch," Riven called out to the witch who was staring him down and probably trying to buy time for reinforcements. He gave a slight bow. "Let's just chalk this up to a misunderstanding. Toodles!"

"Misunderstanding?!" She gawked as he gave her a wave with his fingers. She pointed her shimmering wand in his direction. "You just murdered— WAIT! HEY! WHERE DO YOU THINK YOU'RE GOING?!"

"Ba-buuuuyyyyy!!" Riven laughed, flipping her off and stepping into a rift before she could catch him with her own teleport ability. In an instant he was an entire mile to the south and turned on the thrusters to full throttle while channeling mana into Messenger's flight ability.

He felt the singed material of his decimated shadow rift when the moonlight tore through, forcing the rift shut. But he already had another rift open and was preparing another jump when the witch blurred in his direction with a scream of anger, looking like an enraged firefly as she used her short-ranged teleports and broom to catch up with scathing speed.

"Athela, Fay, Azmoth. Come back." Riven blurred through the skies as enforcers turned to intercept and airships began to unload arsenals in his direction.

His minions heeded the command and were sent back to their nether realms from whatever fights they were engaged in, only for him to reactivate two of the pentagram minion sigils tattooed onto his sternum.

Athela appeared first, utilizing her blood-shifting abilities to turn into a pool of the liquid that wrapped protectively around Riven before extending a tendril of her body into Riven's skin. Burying a piece there, she initiated Body Fusion, which was technically a miracle and used divinity and faith to fuel it. Athela had very little faith to use, so with someone as strong as Riven, she couldn't fully converge like Genua could. It'd only worked on the would-be thralls in Fay's dungeon because they'd been weak. However, Athela could still connect with Riven to a small extent, enough to where she could also grant him another one of her boons:

"Blood Art, Mark of the Hunter," she whispered into his mind.

The world around them abruptly changed to various shades of red, and the demoness marked the targeted witch pursuing them, highlighting their primary pursuer. With each jump they could tell where the insanely powerful witch was going to materialize next, and Riven shifted course accordingly to avoid the enemy caster's teleporting abilities while picking up speed.

Fay appeared next, tearing out of her nether realm at full blast with wings stretched out and flaring bright blue along her tail's spines. She looked over her shoulder, laughing at the entire armada of pursuers in the distance, but her laugh was cut short when the moonlight witch nearly tore a hole through her wing.

Riven was able to pull her to the left through another rift before that happened, though, and he called out over the rush of wind, "Throw out some illusions and hide our main bodies as we cut downward. They'll be unable to follow us as closely or fire off as many attacks if we're among the buildings."

"How much time do you have left with Jarrod's soul?" Fay called back, disguising them from most of their pursuers with an illusory veil as their team dived downward and copies of them continued soaring in a different direction.

Riven checked over his shoulder and cursed when the moonlight witch wasn't fooled by the illusions, but a large chunk of the enemy pursuers continued off toward Fay's decoy as a handful of the broom-flying bastards tore through the skies toward his position. "It's slow going. Maybe another hour?"

Fay winced. "That's not good. Will we be able to hold on for that long?"

Riven began to supercharge another ability within the blood pearl he held and wrapped his arms around Fay to hold her tightly against him. He kept his eyes forward as the cityscape blurred underneath them. "We don't have a choice. I'll need you to keep throwing decoys out, but I think I can travel faster than you can with a trick I'm about to pull. Wrap your legs around me and hold on—we're about to try something really stupid."

The succubus did as told and wrapped her legs and arms around Riven's body with her wings tucked in. Athela's blood body extended to wrap around Fay, too, keeping the succubus tight against Riven's chest while they continued to jump through portals and made it to the upper limit of the city's skyscrapers.

CRASH

A tower's roof next to them was obliterated in a spray of stone when the moonlight witch misfired from hundreds of yards away, and the screams of civilians were lost over the displacement of air.

"Apparently she doesn't care about hitting bystanders after all." Riven raised an eyebrow and continued to push, flickering in and out of the city skyline in multiple locations while portals and illusions continued to spring up around them.

When he felt the Critical Storm Lance manifest inside the pearl, Riven grinned and wrapped a layer of Wretched Snares around the output point. "Hold on tight."

Holding the pearl forward and horizontally over the magitech city below, he unleashed the supercharged spell and felt the roar of power erupt from the item.

Just like the first time, the sky was ripped apart with a wave of crimson and black. Riven's snares latched onto the sniping ability as it took off, and he, along with Fay and Athela, were ripped along right after the lance as it eviscerated space at extreme speed. Before Riven knew it, he was miles away into the horizon with trailing ribbons of storm energy crackling in his wake.

CHAPTER 28

Their pursuers were still coming, but they were far, far behind.

And there was nothing they could do now. He was finally done.

Riven felt the piece of soul lattice snap into place as it was violently ripped out of Fay's previous summoner, and Jarrod's spirit wailed in agony beyond what a physical wound could employ. That alone would have been enough to send the thrilling sensations of glee through Riven's mind, because fuck that guy, but it was also amplified by the enormous surge of energies along his connection to Fay.

Pieces of soul lattice, scaffolding for his future cultivation, snapped together, molding, forming, and merging his soul's tether to Fay's own with layer upon layer. Just like his connection to Athela where they could speak mind to mind, where their connection was rock solid beyond a shadow of a doubt, so, too, had Fay's transformed. The bond was like refined steel, unshakable, and he knew without a doubt that severing their connection like the cultists had many months before would be much harder to accomplish.

Smiling at the warm sensations he got back from the succubus, he let Jarrod's shredded spiritual remnants fall away into the void like trash into a garbage can.

[You have killed Fay's old warlock summoner and have ripped out the piece of his soul lattice that was once holding Fay's contract, absorbing it into your own soul lattice to further solidify your bond. Fay will now experience growth similar to your own and, like Athela, will absorb a piece of Gluttony's power into her own spirit over time.]

[Floor Forty: A Dark Delve Through Time and Space, Part 2, is about to begin.]

WHUMPH

He really couldn't wait to get back to Panu, where portal-hopping wasn't so goddamn prevalent. Just how many pocket realms and related bullshittery did the Abyssal Descent have anyways?

Riven blinked, finding his minions all gone yet again. This time, though, it was different. The bonds through his soul tethers were all there . . . but they were . . . ethereal, almost. It was like he wasn't supposed to be here, like the bonds were not supposed to be there, but a faint whisper, much like how he saw through the ripples of time with Malignant Prophecy on the rare occasions it activated.

But this had nothing to do with Malignant Prophecy actually activating. Rather, the currents of time seemed . . . wrong, and Malignant Prophecy seemed like it wanted to pull him back to wherever he'd been moments ago before he'd arrived in this place.

He was standing alone in a small cave that burned with cinders all along the rock walls. A large lake of lava bubbled and churned to his right, and the skulls and bones of various demons and monsters were piled in one corner. There was also a tunnel leading out and upward, where a large and very dead hellscape brutalisk was impaled by an enormous obsidian spike adjacent to the tunnel's entrance. It was huge, the size of a skyscraper, and the spike piercing it was imparting some kind of acidic poison that was eating away at the monster's spot of fatal injury. This pinned demon was also much bulkier than Azmoth's bigger form was, and it was also female, the very first that Riven had ever seen of this species.

Whatever had killed it must have been quite powerful.

But why was he here?

Based on the Part One of this floor, he assumed that any other parts would also involve incorporating his close minions into his soul lattice. To make them permanent parts of his ascendancy. And if this dead female brutalisk was a hint . . .

He tugged at his tether to Azmoth but was unable to summon the demon or get a response.

Instead . . . he felt an adjacent tugging. One that led over to just below the corpse of the impaled giant in the cave beyond.

Strange.

His shadow-crafted cloak billowed in a hot wind from the mouth of the tunnel, and his warlock's staff clicked audibly across the stones and echoed over the bubbling magma. Red eyes flicked left and right, and he giggled to himself when he thought about how much he looked like a Sith lord.

Though, perhaps . . . just maybe . . . he should lay off the better-than-thou juice. His outlooks on mortals had been evolving rather rapidly, and though he didn't find a flaw in his thinking, that in itself was potentially a problem. Was this really him thinking like this? Was it Gluttony's influence instead? If it was the latter, he'd have to be very careful about not losing himself along the way. His gut told him that he'd just snapped and finally hit the breaking point of not caring anymore after all he'd gone through, but it was better safe than sorry and safeguards may need to be implemented after he did a little bit of introspection.

Cautiously he got up and moved underneath the enormous brutalisk corpse, not seeing any signs of danger upon his approach. Following the pull of his soul tether to Azmoth, he rounded one of the enormous legs. Avoiding the dripping blood of the evolved archdemon's corpse above him, he suddenly stopped when he came to the end of the tether's pull.

There, right in front of him and huddling behind a back claw of the behemoth's foot, was a teeny, tiny baby brutalisk. It was only three feet tall, and its armor plates weren't all grown yet, exposing larger parts of fleshy muscle underneath as it quivered in fear behind the larger claw. It had two of its hands over its face, and two of its hands wrapped around its body while it rocked back and forth, sniffling to itself as it cried. Or cried as much as a brutalisk could considering they had helmetlike metal masks over where their eyes should be, but it was obvious that the small demon was in distress. Next to the baby brutalisk were also fragments of what had once been a thick, ironlike egg.

He tugged on the link between him and his minion, and his eyes widened when he both saw and felt the little baby demon flinch in response. "Azmoth?"

The creature in front of him flinched again, but hesitantly looked up from where it was shivering and stared at him outright. It looked absolutely terrified.

Or rather, Azmoth's younger self looked absolutely terrified. What was even worse was the thick, green poison spreading from a long scratch along Azmoth's right shoulder. Riven could literally see the poison or acid or whatever it was eating holes into the infant, and it was spreading along the veins as the creature's trembling grew more violent.

[**Floor Forty: A Dark Delve Through Time and Space, Part 2**, has begun. One cannot go back in time in their own reality; it is simply impossible. Or . . . can they? Whether or not there is a means to travel through time across all of creation's threads, it is certainly not known among anyone or anything, anywhere, who is currently alive. You have instead been sent to false reality that has a lagging timeline, where Azmoth's false replica will not survive this encounter. His mother has been prematurely killed, and he will die along with her unless the tomb-wyrm's venom is eliminated. Azmoth, in this false reality, is simply destined to become food for the vultures. Or, more accurately, for the tomb-wyrm that killed his mother. Your task, oh gluttonous one, is to save baby Azmoth from the tomb-wyrm's venom. But beware, because the wounds on Azmoth and his mother are still fresh. The tomb-wyrm is still here.]

As a habit ever since Lillith's training on Floor One, Riven regularly pulsed his mana out in waves like echolocation to avoid assassins. Here was no different, and before Riven even finished reading the last line of the notification, he had seen the viper's strike incoming.

The massive creature was perfectly blended into the surroundings, obviously using a cloaking ability, but more than that, much of its body was actually curled up and around into the tunnel's exit. However, the massive circular mouth full of teeth was hard to miss when it moved fast enough to disrupt whatever that stealth ability was, and Riven's pulsing mana finally caught wind of it when the spike launched from deep in the wyrm's throat.

Riven's body shattered space as he ripped through darkness, dragging baby Azmoth along with him as the stone underneath his feet was eradicated in flecks of ejected spine and acid. He was halfway across the cavern lair, charging a Blood Nova within his pearl as his totem swarm flared out in a spinning ring.

Then he got a good look at the beast that'd killed Azmoth's mom as the chameleon effect wore off.

[Level 299 Tomb-Wyrm ELITE]

Large gray scales made from some kind of alloy silently coiled as the creature moved at a dead-silent but semirapid pace toward him. Slithering like a snake across the smoldering stone floor, the beast had no eyes and was two dozen feet in diameter and an unknown length, as most of the body was still up the tunnel into this place. The maw was circular with incurvating teeth lined down the throat in rows, and some kind of muscular mechanism held and propelled obsidian spikes from somewhere deep within the beast's belly. If Riven had to guess, the green acidic poison on those spikes it launched was actually an incredibly potent stomach acid.

The name *tomb-wyrm* was fitting considering how this was probably once the lair of Azmoth's mother and would now become her tomb before she was likely eaten. Before that grim reality took place, though, Riven had to get the fuck out of here, and there was only one way out.

Testing its defenses, Riven launched a flurry of Gluttonous Storm Razors at the creature. Spinning circular blades of extremely sharp blood, infused with Black Lightning and erosive Sin, bloomed around him and rushed like a wave to crash into the monster's scales.

The monster seemed absolutely unhindered and only picked up speed, going from a slow slither to a fast glide. Even the corrosive Sin energies seemed to do little more than simmer and fizzle out, meaning that whatever kind of defenses the wyrm had, they were incredibly good. Riven spat, and plumes of blood began to trickle up his right arm as Azmoth squirmed in his left. Curling his fingers and swinging his staff to point in the direction of the wyrm, Riven let out a Critical Storm Lance that screamed through the air and smashed into the beast's protective scales with a trail of storm energy in its wake.

[You have landed a critical hit. Max damage x 3.]

The projectile caused the wyrm to stagger, and two tiny scales were torn off its side.

But that was it.

Riven stood there, gawking at the giant beast as it let out an ear-piercing scream before launching itself with all its might in his direction.

The spinning totems rotated faster and produced four shields of ice directly in the monster's wake, but the beast crashed through the ice shields like they were paper plates and it did the same to a fifth ice shield that Riven conjured next.

The walls of crimson shattered and sprayed shrapnel in all directions, and the underground cavern shook with the monster's hungry challenge. The friction between silver scales and the stone floor beneath threw up sparks.

Riven took one more glance down at Azmoth, to see that the poison was quickly killing his younger-than-usual friend, and that just wouldn't do. Baby Azmoth had passed out entirely and wasn't even responsive anymore; he was just limp, with large portions of his upper body slowly being eaten away as veins pulsed along the fleshy parts of his body. Riven had to think of something fast. If he was right, this creature hunted through either mana signatures or soul signatures. It certainly didn't use heat, because this entire cavern was volcanic, likely somewhere in the pits of hell, and it didn't have eyes. Riven had the perfect bait and switch for either occasion.

Each of his totems could use mana, and they all had soul fragments inside them. If he couldn't kill the beast fast enough, or at all, then he'd simply draw it away.

[Hive Totems of Bloodforged Rift Sparks (Lesser Artifact, Elite Tier, Level 80 Totem Swarm): These totems come as a set, and new totems can be added to this number at the additional cost of Willpower, with each totem adding exponentially more Willpower to the cost. Cost of Willpower is based upon attitude toward the wielder of this totem set, as well as current combat level. Current requirements: 119 Willpower, Blood subpillar, Shadow subpillar. Bound to Riven Thane.

Adding different types of totems will change the name and description of this totem set.

Current totems in Hive Swarm:

- **Four totems of Bloodforged Rift Sparks**

The Path of Red and Black has been imbued into these totems, along with numerous different sigils, and the creator has used the blood of an ancient avatar of original sin to fuel their growth. These totems have the ability to grow and level up but diminish in level each time one is destroyed. This totem swarm can currently perform the following abilities:

- **Black Lightning**
- **Crimson Ice**
- **Rift]**

He riftwalked right, with his totems, and the beast followed in a mad rush. He did the same again to the left, and the beast was still hot on his heels. Then he poured mana into his four totems, reduced his own mana output—ambient and active—while using one of his totems to riftwalk yet again. This time when he exited the rift, his four totems had gone through four other rifts simultaneously, and the wyrm went from speeding dead set on his location to thrashing in anger. It looked from one location to another, hissing violently and spitting green flecks of acid before choosing one of the totems and barreling toward it.

Riven had been correct.

Commanding his four totems up and out into the tunnels beyond, he began to lead the enormous, tanky bastard of a monster away from the cavern, and he quickly got to work. No doubt the monster would soon return to eat the large corpse on the wall, so this couldn't take long.

Baby Azmoth was in bad, bad shape. Riven didn't know how the stomach acid was spreading but it obviously was by the way the blood vessels were bulging and dissolving, or the black streaks of necrosis along the otherwise red musculature where Azmoth's protective plating hadn't grown in yet. Riven checked his spatial bag first to see if he had any potions that might work, and was relieved when he had a few that might just do the job. Putting down three extremely potent F-grade health potions, a mana potion, a resist-poison potion, and a stamina potion, he drenched Azmoth's wounds and force-fed the baby brutalisk everything. At the same time, he also started using blood manipulation and Voodoo Doll to draw out Azmoth's blood and purify it of toxins, forcefully removing large quantities of green gunk in his mana. At the same time, he also used Voodoo Doll to keep the infant alive.

[Voodoo Doll (Blood) (Tier 2): Scan your target to map out their vessels and infuse your mana into their bloodstream. You then gain the ability to replicate their bloodstream regardless of whether they have extensive wounds, enabling you to keep them alive as long as their brain remains intact. You may also use this ability on hostiles to form painful blood clots. Heart attacks caused by this ability do critical strike damage. Dependent on both Intelligence (90%) and Willpower (10%) stats. Medium cooldown. This is a channeling ability and will not work if interrupted by using other spells.]

He sat there for a solid few minutes just channeling the ability until he was sure that the blood looked more natural, or as natural as demonic blood got. He didn't often see Azmoth's blood, but when he did, it was either burned and black, or a darker burgundy color than mortals'. Worked the same, though, and before he knew it, baby Azmoth was coughing and his wounds were being sealed shut by the potions.

Riven smiled fondly at the whimpering little guy and patted him on the head. Even if this Azmoth wasn't real, it felt right to make sure the projection—or whatever this version of baby Azmoth was—felt safe. "One day, you and me are going to be good friends. You just don't know it yet."

Riven held out a hand to playfully shake the baby demon's clawed fingers, which gripped onto him after a hesitant once-over. Seeing that Riven was the only one in the room, baby Azmoth merely held on to Riven's arm more tightly and began to whine and shake. The kid was likely very traumatized from what'd happened, and it made Riven wonder what'd befallen Azmoth's own mother—being the Azmoth that Riven knew personally and not this baby replica.

Sighing and wondering just what kind of waves he was going to make both here in this existence and the one he came from, Riven put the system shenanigans in the hands of Elysium once again and began to talk to the kid. He didn't know if Azmoth understood the words he was speaking quite yet, but the baby demon certainly did understand images, and as Riven began to slowly explain to the child what was going on and what he wanted, Riven began to feel his connection to his own version of Azmoth resonate.

Their soul connection began to strengthen.

CHAPTER 29

[**Floor Forty: A Dark Delve Through Time and Space, Part 3**, is about to begin. You have had many pivotal moments on your path leading to power, and Elysium has created a series of these moments that you can now replay with the knowledge you have gained. You may truly die during these tests, as your abilities are set back to what you were able to do in the moment, and every single action will provide both a curse and a boon for you or those close to you in reality. Each test has multiple boons for you to choose from, with disguised curses lurking behind each as a price.]

Riven's reality warped, and he suddenly felt weak. The normal heartbeats he'd grown so accustomed to hearing from nearby beings faded away, his dark vision disappeared, and his tattoos faded. His eyes went from a bright, glowing crimson to hazel-green, and he suddenly felt very, very weak. Incredibly so. Weak in both body and his total mana pool.

He was standing on an island, and somehow he'd arrived wearing a thick, hooded, weathered cloak. He was certainly thankful for it, as the night wind was chilly upon his skin. The island was somewhat flat and grass-laden, with a bril-liant moon illuminating the small amount of land in front of him. All around him were dozens of other islands equal to his in height with various slopes or flattened tops—all with their own singular inhabitants that he could barely make out when he looked around. These other islands also drifted among the reflections of the currents below, and just like his own plot of land, they each had a long drop down magnificent cliffs to a calm ocean underneath that shimmered under the stars and cosmos. Seagulls or some kind of other seafaring bird flew overhead, though their features were somewhat indistinguishable due to the dark of night, and little luminescent lights glowed down below where the ocean met the bases of the cliffs. Of particular note, all the islands were shifting—moving in various directions but not making contact with one another as they seemed to swim about the massive body of water while avoiding one another entirely, which made the entire scenario all the more odd.

Wait.
This was familiar.

[Novice Warlock class received.]

Uh, what?

[Starter minions are now available to you through Chalgathi's power. Upon death, minions may be resummoned up to one day later if you pay the blood price in the form of Elysium coins. At higher levels, demonic servants will require mortal soul sacrifices to summon back. Minions may eventually collect evolutions to become stronger at an increased Willpower cost. You may currently only select one:

[Athela the Blood Weaver has been automatically selected for this replay.]

Time leaped forward by five minutes, going past all the mundane decisions he'd made back in the day of Chalgathi's first trial. This place, and these notifications, were exactly what he'd been through before. Looking down he saw his staff, Jackal, was nowhere to be seen, and instead he had that crude, shitty scythe he'd chosen in the first fight against the first cultist he'd killed before getting to Panu.

A sly grin crossed his face. Elysium seemed to think that THIS was a pivotal moment in his growth, and Riven couldn't necessarily disagree. It'd been the first time he'd fought someone else while using magic . . .

Pulling up his status page just to check, he saw that he was registered as a level 1 novice warlock, with only three abilities to his name: Blessing of the Crow, Wretched Snare, and Bloody Razors. He also only had a single level 1 minion, who was obviously Athela.

[One minute until fighting begins.]

His smile grew wider underneath his hood.

"OOOOooohhh!!!" Athela crowed, rapidly tapping all her arachnid legs with excitement as the notification popped up in front of her as well. "LET'S DO THIS!!! FIGHT TO THE DEATH, YEAH!"

He spared the demon a glance, just like he had a year and a half ago. Perhaps two years now—he'd lost track of time. Athela's copy seemed none the wiser about what this was, either. He remembered being so nervous, and needing to steel his nerves before the fight . . .

Not this time, though. Instead, a bloodthirsty smile widened to abnormal proportions as the false reality around him shuddered at his attempt to flex his pillars, but he didn't push it too far against Elysium's restrictions when he felt a sense of foreboding at the attempt.

If he remembered correctly, he'd won, but only barely, and had been seriously injured in the upcoming fight. It would feel good to trash the false memory of the bald fuck just for shits and giggles, but the Floor Forty notification had said his decisions here in this replayed memory would impact his true reality as well. He could also truly die here, which he doubted would happen for numerous reasons, but he supposed it was possible if he didn't take it at least a bit seriously. The main point of focus for him, though, was that there would be a boon and a curse for every decision he made.

That was . . . curious. They related to his soul lattice, yes? What kind of curses would Elysium inflict upon him, and for what reasons?

He wouldn't have long to find out, of that he was sure.

Falling back into his memory's timeline, he went through the motions. It was time, and just to make sure that everything was working right, he gave his spells a try. Raising his free left hand and aiming across the small floating island, he thought, *Bloody Razors*. Instantaneously, two spinning, serrated discs of crimson each about a foot in diameter materialized in the air on either side of his outstretched hand.

They left thin trails of red liquid in the air behind their blurring paths for brief moments until they slammed into the earth twenty yards away, leaving the grass there torn to shreds in little patches around an indentation the magic had cut into the ground before fizzling away into the air. They were so . . . pathetically weak. This was the base form of his spell? This is what it had been?

The sight made him literally laugh out loud. He could summon hundreds of thousands of similar projectiles right now without putting on a sweat. At least, that was the case outside of this memoryscape.

Trying to summon his Black Lightning, Gluttonous Storm Razors, Critical Storm Lance, or Blood Nova all were met with prompts stating that he wasn't able to use those abilities here.

Not that he'd need them, but it was good to know that he was restricted in what he could do despite knowing how to actually cast the spells even without them imprinted on his soul pillars. He'd just have to make do with the two spells on hand.

[Time is up. Your fight to the death is commencing now. If no winner is announced within ten minutes, both participants will die. If you have bonded companions due to your class choice, upon death your minions will be sent to the nether realm to try and find new masters for further exploration in Elysium.]

"BRING IT!" his Blood Weaver screamed when she saw the notification, and waggled a red and black spider foot his way. "I don't want to go back to the nether realms! We'd better win, you hear me?!"

"You're damn right we're going to win." He repeated the line he remembered so vividly and gave her an encouraging nod while adjusting his stance to ready himself.

This time around, he saw the other looming island closing in before the two land masses collided.

The cliff faces made impact with a thunderous clap of noise. Rock slammed into rock with a huge boom, shaking both islands in a spray of debris. The ground shuddered and he waited for the shock waves to pass. When the dust settled, Riven found himself looking at the same bald asshole who'd shoved him and told him to *move it* in the starter trial's pyramid.

Riven needed popcorn for this shit. The only downside to reliving it was knowing this wasn't necessarily real. It certainly felt real, though, and was the closest thing he'd get to handing out a sweet, sweet ass kicking to the man that'd put him through a truly tough fight back in the day.

The larger bald man had chosen a caster's staff . . . but he also had on Chalgathi's amulet. Riven had almost forgotten about how that item and the other pieces would later be forged into Messenger, and instinctively grasped at his chest but found no armor or vertical maw there to greet him as usual.

Aside from that, the other man had chosen a minion that hadn't ever been presented to Riven. It was a huge, skeletal zombie wolf. The creature was large, but not as big as he remembered it being. Perhaps it'd just seemed bigger back then because Riven had been afraid. Patches of rotting flesh and fur with bright-white eyes on glistening bones were the staple. The breath from the creature's decrepit lungs came out as a gaseous cloud of green pouring through sharp fangs, and it was snarling at Riven with a keen hunger. It was two to three times Athela's current size, but Riven only felt amusement now as he stared at the insignificant creature growling at him from across the elevated landscape.

Riven was no longer prey. He was a predator, but the man in this fake reality didn't know that yet.

The cultist spat. "We meet again, *pig.*"

Riven's eyes flashed red for just the barest moment, and he was yet again suppressed by Elysium as he began chuckling to himself, getting a confused look from Athela at his side.

"What are you laughing at?" Athela asked with a cocked head. "And what was that energy you just released? It felt really, really weird!"

But the bald man wasn't done speaking. He stepped forward to point at Riven with an accusatory posturing while warm winds rustled both men's robes. "You probably have no idea what's really going on here, do you? To think that I would be paired with these worthless fools. How was it that any of you got through the labyrinth to begin with? Has Chalgathi become complacent in who he admits into his chosen? Was it not supposed to be us true cultists who received his graces?"

Riven held up a hand to silence the other caster, starting to walk forward to clear the distance. He wanted to get this over with and move on to see what curse and boon he'd get from this particular copied memory. "I believe the time for monologuing is over with, friend. I don't have time for this."

The bald man, who narrowed his eyes at Riven as his zombie wolf began to roar at Riven's approach, slammed his staff into the ground and pointed threateningly Riven's way. "You DARE to interrupt me?! A chosen one of Chalgathi himself?! You will die for your insolence!"

"I'm sure. Now summon your pets and let's get this over with."

The man's brow furrowed in rage. Shadows began erupting from the other caster's staff, and the brief monologue thankfully ended. Condensing and re-forming into one another, the shadows quickly created two skulking, terrier-sized quadrupeds. Their bodies flickered in and out of existence, each with two red eyes glaring at him and claws extending as they hissed his way.

Ah, the Create Shadowling spell. He'd almost chosen that one himself.

[Create Shadowling (Shadow)—create temporary shadow beasts that attack your enemies to do damage. Shadowlings are faster and stronger in dark places.]

"They're quite cute," Riven said, casually stopping at the halfway point to throw his scythe away and holding his hands out to either side. "Like little level 1 puppies."

VHOOM

The air pressure exploded in all directions around him as most of Riven's mana pool was unloaded in a single go. And although Riven couldn't access his true mana reserves or full list of abilities, he was intricately aware of how to manipulate his magic to the fullest now. What was once magical waste was condensed and efficient; what was once a lack of coordination with his spells was now perfect mana handling that could control thousands of projectiles at a single time. The act of spellcasting that'd been so clumsy to him once upon a time was now a second nature to his being, like breathing, and it showed in his display.

Two, ten, and then twenty spinning blades of razor-sharp blood bloomed in the air around his outstretched hands like an embrace of death, and with a thought, they all doubled in size. The look of shock on the cultist's face was all Riven needed to see before he ended it, and with a laugh, Riven flicked his fingers in the man's direction.

They split the air in a flash of crimson, albeit far slower and less powerful than what he was used to. His level 1 enemy counterpart didn't have the ability or foresight to dodge the attack. Ten razors sliced into his body, cutting down his shadow beasts and the zombie wolf that tried to intercept along the way. The cultist briefly let out a high-pitched scream as his limbs and guts were torn off and out of his body in sprays of gore, until his head was decapitated and sent bouncing along the now-wet grass.

Athela just gawked, giving her best impression of a slack-jawed spider while taking in a deep hiss of air. "Whoa . . . YOU'RE AMAZING!!! Damn, I'm good at picking warlocks!"

"You don't know the half of it, babe." He winked at the spider, and Athela's spider form pretended to blush while hiding her arachnid mandibles behind four legs.

"BABE?! We're of different species, Riven! It won't work out between us!"

He winked. "Yeah, yeah. Keep telling yourself that."

"How scandalous! HOW KINKY!" she cried, bouncing up and down on the grass before running over to the scattered guts and forming them into a headdress. "I'll take this as my crown now! Since you did all the work, perhaps you'd like a crown, too?! We can be royal siblings that way!"

Snickering to himself and ignoring the crazy spider, Riven didn't know what else to do. So, coming over to the decapitated head where the cultist's eyes were slowly starting to dilate, he pulled back his foot, stuffed his hands into his pockets, and kicked the head like a soccer ball off the nearby cliff's edge. Peering over and watching it splash into the waves below, he gave a self-satisfied nod.

"As it should be."

The realm copied from his memories froze in an instant.

[Part 3, First Memory's Choice: Cut out the cultist's heart and eat it, OR help Athela create a crown of guts. Choose one and proceed to activate your curse and boon.]

The memory unfroze, and he saw Athela scurrying over to gather up the man's intestines, dancing back and forth and humming to herself as she did. She seemed so happy, and Riven realized sadly that it'd been a while since Athela had seemed so carefree. They'd both grown and changed with one another, but he wanted to see her act like she had in the beginning, back before she'd taken on the responsibility of being his antiassassin, before she'd seen him become the reincarnation of Gluttony. Back when she'd seemed so much more innocent and less burdened.

Watching her giddy, chittering laughter as she danced with the guts in her spider paws and looped it around to wear as a hat, a soft smile crept across his lips, and he began to approach her.

"Hey . . . Athela?" he said, kneeling down next to the large spider as she turned to face him.

"Yes, Master?!" she squealed, giggling to herself while hopping up and down in a macabre jig. "What is it that you want from this prominent princess?!"

He snorted in amusement. Yes, this is the Athela he liked, and the Athela he'd eventually grow to love. He placed a hand on her gruesome flesh hat and patted her a few times, making it more circular to look like a crown or tiara, if you could ever really call it that. "Mind if I help you decorate that hat of yours? I'd even like to make one for myself, if that's all right. Maybe we can do it together, yeah?"

Once again, the spider gave him a look of shock. "WHERE HAVE YOU BEEN ALL MY LIFE?! Of COURSE we can make intestine crowns together! Come, let me show you my artistic ways, and we can sing songs and chant by a sacrificial fire afterward, too! THIS IS GOING TO BE SO MUCH FUN! OH MAH GAWD, I CAN'T WAIT TO TELL MOM!"

Grabbing a small, bunched-up portion of the dead man's intestines, Riven rolled his eyes and sat cross-legged on the ground as he began to use Athela's threads to stitch them together in his best attempt at stacking them in a ring. And within the hour, he and his memory minion were laughing and joking to their heart's content while they each wore sloppy, bloody circlets that stank terribly.

But it was the most fun he'd had in a long time. Saving the memory for later to show the real Athela through their mind link, he was sure she'd have a blast at the somewhat sentimental time he'd spent with her fake self. And he'd be sure to make more fond memories like it, too.

[First Memory's Choice: Your soul lattice has gained a boon and a curse based on your actions.

If you'd chosen to eat the man's heart, you'd have gained his ability Create Shadowling while strengthening your soul lattice with Shadow energy, simultaneously gaining the curse of Neglected Minion, which would have weakened your soul bond with Athela and her access to Gluttony.

Instead, you have chosen to help Athela create a crown of guts. You and Athela have both gained the linked ability Twin Crowns of Flesh (Blood) (Tier 2), which is a position-swapping ability that comes at the cost of 50% health. This ability can be used anywhere, at any time, at any distance, as long as Athela is not banished to the nether realms with a temporary death. Your soul link with Athela has drastically improved in strength, and your soul lattice will reflect this. You have also acquired the curse of Famished for not eating the heart, which increases your gluttonous and vampiric hunger twofold. You will need to feed twice as often from here on out and will experience debuffs that are twice as bad if you aren't regularly fed.]

CHAPTER 30

[**Floor Forty: A Dark Delve Through Time and Space, Part 4**, is
about to begin. This is a repeat of Part 3. You have had many pivotal
moments on your path leading to power, and Elysium has created
a series of these moments that you can now replay with the knowledge you have gained. You may truly die during these tests, as your
abilities are set back to what you were able to do in the moment, and
every single action will provide both a curse and a boon for you or
those close to you in reality. Each test has multiple boons for you to
choose from, with disguised curses lurking behind each as a price.]

Riven's reality warped three more times, going through Floor Forty's parts four, five,
and six. Each time had a different memory, though they were certainly out of order.

The second memory was the replay of his argument with Allie, back when
he'd first learned that she had a slave harem full of thralls. He'd been so pissed
back then that he'd blown up at her, yelled at her about her morals, and had made
a huge deal about it in front of Mara and the others. He cringed while watching
the memory play out before he had to pick up at the end of the conversation,
where he was given the opportunity to speak his mind on the matter, now that
he knew what would come in the future. The memory's fake Allie and he had a
long, extended talk after that, and though he wasn't given a choice between two
options, Elysium judged him based on what he said along a myriad of different
possibilities.

Honestly? He'd told Allie that although what she was doing was wrong, he
had no room to judge. He told her that they'd likely both become monsters
given time, that they would both become mass murderers without a doubt, and
that he'd love her no matter what she did, even if he didn't necessarily agree with
her ideologies of forcing people into becoming thralls. It was a reminder of the
recent fight he'd had with his own demons who'd abducted the two drow, and
despite all that he'd become, all the people that he'd murdered and eaten, he
couldn't bring himself to force someone into losing their choice in the matter.
Even now. Even as ruthless and, in many aspects, evil as he was.

Thus, the second memory had given him the soul lattice boon of a direct connection to his sister called the Siblings' Pact. He felt it slowly beginning to form, stretching out across the cosmos as his soul reached into the void to touch her own, and he felt their souls intertwine. At its current state, it was still too flimsy to be a true method of communication, but he'd at the very least know where she was at all times. Hopefully he'd be able to improve it to the point of communication that he had with Athela, Fay, and now Azmoth. The curse of the second memory was Thrall Cap, which essentially limited his ability to create more than ten thralls. That would hamper his ability to create a blood farm from thralls, but he could always use normal mortals for part of the blood farm, and he wasn't big on thralls all that much anyways. Even with Genua, who he'd originally hated upon first capturing her and her people from Greenstalk Village, the offer of becoming a thrall had been something of a backhanded, spiteful attempt at revenge for her family's betrayal. He was surprised she'd taken the offer, was more surprised about how it'd turned out, and now he had an enormous weight of responsibility and guilt riding on his shoulders for what he'd done, despite it being Genua's choice. Probably because he now kind of liked Genua and who she was, particularly before her mind had taken a nosedive and she'd gone off the crazy-train deep end. She and her family had been absolute asshats for trying to kill him, though, so he didn't feel too bad about it. It was just enough guilt to remind him that, should he create more thralls, he probably shouldn't get attached to them. One time making that mistake was more than enough, and ten total thralls was beyond what he ever really needed, as the blood farm could just hold mortals he didn't like.

The third memory was the battle against the satyr warlord in Negrada's dungeon. It'd been thrilling to actually go through it again, and he'd torn that bastard limb from limb as he used incredibly precise strikes and his advanced knowledge of combat to completely avoid damage himself. It'd been a massacre, but it'd also brought up a part of the memory that he'd forgotten about until now—a piece of the memory that he'd suppressed early on but now found fascinating to experience again.

It was the part where he'd killed and eaten the young man named Ben after the boss fight, after his vampiric awakening and stricken hunger. Just before eating Ben he'd been given a choice to suppress his hunger, and Riven merely cackled while refusing, letting the hunger engulf him as he tore the mortal human limb from limb and ate him alive. It was just too . . . too thrilling to pass up. He used to think of that suppressed memory only as something to be ashamed of, when he was coping with what he'd become, but now he embraced it fully and savored the flavor of his victim's warm blood. This in turn gave him the boon of Embrace Your Bloodline, which added onto his Blood subpillar's soul lattice and allowed him to unlock various aspects of his vampiric heritage faster, as long as he continued to feed on mortals and thralls regularly.

The curse he had woven into his soul lattice was called Vampiric Abomination, which literally warned mortals that got too close about what he was even if they couldn't identify him and even if he had a disguise on. It would tell any mortal within five feet that he was a pureblooded vampire. That . . . that actually really sucked. He'd have to find a way to get around that if he ever wanted to travel the multiverse into other worlds in the future. For now, though, it wasn't anything to worry about. It'd just be a problem for FUTURE Riven to deal with!

Unfortunately, the sixth part of Floor Forty, the fourth memory instance, was a little more delicate.

[Floor Forty: A Dark Delve Through Time and Space, Part 6, is about to begin. This is a repeat of Parts 3, 4, and 5. You have had many pivotal moments on your path leading to power, and Elysium has created a series of these moments that you can now replay with the knowledge you have gained. You may truly die during these tests, as your abilities are set back to what you were able to do in the moment, and every single action will provide both a curse and a boon for you or those close to you in reality. Each test has multiple boons for you to choose from, with disguised curses lurking behind each as a price.]

Reality warped around him once again, but this time he was more of a spectral wraith than actually present in the flesh. Why that was? He had no idea, but that's how Elysium brought him into this memory, so he'd just roll with whatever the punch line was. He was now back near Greenstalk Village, back in Genua's old home. Back before Ethel and her family, her clan, had betrayed him. Before they'd called him a monster and pushed him over the edge toward a darker path. Little did they know, but they'd been the true catalyst for what Riven was today.

They'd done this to him.

RAT-TAT-TAT-TAT-TAT-TAT-TAT

The Gatling gun homed in on Riven's impersonator again, giving some of the holy warriors time to back up and regain their bearings.

Meanwhile, the man who had been manipulated with Silvertongue, pretending to be Riven, continued to stay still in his bindings. He grunted in pain whenever an arrow or bullet lodged itself in his mangled body, while Riven watched from the sidelines, hidden among the trees.

A clap of thunder overhead saw a gigantic white bolt of lightning fall from the heavens, crashing into Azmoth and making the demon howl in pain until finally the brutalisk fell dead to the ground as a smoking cinder of the creature he'd once been.

[Your minion Azmoth has died. He will be returned to you twenty-four hours after you pay the blood price for your minion. To resurrect

your level 31 infant Hellscape Brutalisk demon, you will be required to pay Elysium directly with a sum of thirty-one thousand Elysium coins. Simply will this transaction to happen and make sure you have the required payment to further this agenda.]

Silence overcame the clearing, with only the sounds of the wounded groaning or the smoldering corpse of the demon crackling.

Elder Bren, that old elf bastard, had sweat dripping down his face. He had to calm his breathing before steadying himself and walking forward to inspect the rune formation.

"Is he still alive?" one of the holy warriors called out, a human in Earth-made body armor that SWAT teams used to wear. Only he didn't have a gun; rather, he carried a broadsword under the summer sunlight that rarely touched the continent of Umbra in Riven's true reality anymore.

In fact, looking around from Riven's real vantage point, the Death-attuned lands looked unbelievably different from the sunny, green forests around them in this memory.

"The demon is dead; the vampire still lives," a husky voice called out from the woods, and the dozens of holy warriors that'd rushed forward to surround the captured target all got on one knee.

From beside a bush where the Gatling gun had been hidden stepped a handsome man who was easily seven feet tall. He had a thick, muscular build and a well-trimmed brown beard. His eyes were bright blue, and his hair was combed back with a thick gel. He wore plain brown robes, like those you'd see monks from medieval eras wear, and he carried nothing but a glowing white book.

"Prophet . . ." Elder Bren muttered before bowing in respect. "I—I didn't realize you'd come personally."

Prophet shot the old man a wary glance, then smirked. "Where else would we go? These monsters have driven us from our homes, just like they would do to you. I am glad you contacted us when you did—who knows what kinds of horrors they'd set upon you in time? Though we come from other worlds, I am glad we are of like minds on these Unholy abominations."

Elder Bren nodded eagerly, even enthusiastically. "The gods shun those who allow themselves to be corrupted by the dark. We would have dealt with it ourselves, but when we saw his might . . . we knew we couldn't do it alone. Thankfully we were able to use him against another mutual enemy of ours, as the orcs should be spooked into leaving these lands shortly."

Prophet raised an eyebrow, then grinned. "Oh? How'd you end up doing that?"

"Manipulating this man's heart with a pretty face." Elder Bren gestured to Ethel, who stood staring in the background, and Prophet laughed loudly.

Approaching the spot where Fake Riven was tied down and still barely breathing, Prophet came to a smug stop and glared down at the bound man.

Thorny vines still wriggled around the vampire, and his eyes were beginning to dull as blood poured out on the ground from numerous arrow and harpoon wounds. "Ah . . . the brother of the infamous bitch who ruined my life."

Prophet raised up his holy book, and brought it back to smack Riven violently across the face. The clap of noise caused Ethel and many of the other elves to wince, yet none of them attempted to stop him.

The big man brought his hand back yet again, gesturing to the two elf elders. The old men both stepped forward to join Prophet at Fake Riven's side, with Elder Preen cackling maliciously before he came to a stop.

"What an idiot. To think that you could take one of our own as a thrall? To think you could take my future WIFE as your thrall!" With a snarl, the lanky old elder brought his staff up and started viciously beating Riven across his face. The sound of beating flesh and cracking bone could be heard over and over again, with Elder Preen's wide, bloodshot eyes glaring down amid huffs and puffs of exertion.

WHACK-SMACK-BAM

Elder Bren eventually held up a hand, motioning for Elder Preen to stop. "That is enough. He is nearly dead, and I would have words with him before Prophet takes his head as a trophy to send back to this Allie girl."

Prophet grunted with folded arms. "Meh. I think I was enjoying that as Preen was."

Elder Bren ignored the other two laughing men and sighed when he looked upon the beaten, bloodied features of the man who'd saved their village. Bren stepped forward, lifting up Riven's hood to reveal a fractured skull and dimming eyes. "My boy. I am sorry we had to do this."

Fake Riven did not reply. He could not reply. He merely gave out ragged gasps for air.

Guilt surged in Bren's chest, and the old man gripped his cane more forcefully. He shot a glare at the other two leaders for their unnecessary cruelty, and then looked to the people around them. Both elves and humans alike had mixed emotions on the matter, but the vast majority of it was obvious—they were stares of approval. They approved of Riven's death; many of them even enjoyed the show, and Elder Bren couldn't necessarily blame them.

The old man rubbed his temple and turned his attention back to the fake vampire. He cleared his throat and began to say his final words to the dying man bound to the earth. "You may be wondering why your regeneration isn't working, or why your mana isn't coming."

Fake Riven only glared.

"It is because the runes of binding we have you tied down with sap your energy, my boy." Elder Bren tapped Fake Riven's head, right next to the open fracture of his skull. "Again, I am sorry we had to do this. But you must understand, though you may be a good man yourself, any that you turn would likely not be. To even acquire the Unholy pillar is a feat in itself that speaks to a person's misgivings. It warps people, changes them for the worse. That aside, as a vampire you are truly a monster. Whether or not you want to believe it, whether or not you see it that way, you survive on the blood of our people."

Bren turned around, calling out to Ethel. She, her father, Farrod, and her best friend, Senna, all approached from the crowd to gather around the dying vampire with looks of distaste and disgust.

The old man glanced down again with a fatherly smile. "Turning Ethel into a thrall would essentially kill her, Riven. You were willing to do that, to take her free will, to create a mind slave out of her to soothe your need to feed. A hunger that is justifiably needed to be sated, lest you go insane and kill everything around you. You and your entire species are an abomination, creation's mistake, and thus we could not simply allow you to leave. You are dangerous, like a cancer festering inside someone's body, and you must be surgically removed to mitigate any damage you could cause in the future. Do you understand?"

Fake Riven's gasps had turned into incredibly shallow breaths, and his eyes barely stayed open any longer. The man was on the very brink of death, and Elder Bren shook his head before drawing out a long dagger made of silver. He handed it to Ethel, who was then urged forward by her father.

"This monster wanted to feed on you, to bed you, to make you his slave," Farrod stated coldly, pointing toward the bound man on his knees in front of them. "Kill him. It is your right."

"Do it," Senna agreed with an excited nod of her head. "Just imagine the stories about you! Vampire slayer—doesn't that sound neat! You're literally killing one of the most feared monsters of our childhood!"

Riven, from his spot on the hill, winced at the words, even hundred yards from the site of the betrayal. Those words stung more than he'd like to admit, even over a year later. He'd truly liked Ethel and Senna, and Ethel's family. He'd thought the elves of Greenstalk Village would accept him if he helped them with the orc problem, and he'd been a fucking fool to believe it.

"Let's get this over with. I have a carnivorous bitch to send his head to," Prophet stated with an annoyed growl. "Come on."

Ethel glared daggers back at the incredibly tall man, then grasped the silver blade in her hand. It looked like she was internally battling with herself, trying to figure out if what she was doing was right. But resolve was soon set in her gaze and she stepped forward, her stump arm pressing Fake Riven's head back in line so she could see eye to eye with him.

Her nose wrinkled in disgust, and she managed to get out her words through clenched teeth. "I will never be anyone's slave. Especially not a bloodsucking monster like you. Did you actually think that I'd want to be seduced by something so gross? The mere thought of having you feed on me or use me in whatever other perverted ways you had in that gullible brain of yours is utterly revolting. You may be wondering about all those conversations you overheard when I thought I was all alone with my family or friends? All those looks of admiration? It was just a farce to get you to do what I needed you to do for my village. Thanks, by the way, for getting rid of those greenskin bastards. I can safely say I hate them a little more than vampires, but after one of your kind killed my grandmother so long ago, it's hard for me to compare accurately. See you in hell, creature."

Gross? Ugh. He hadn't remembered her saying THAT. He wasn't GROSS, was he?

That bitch was just plain rude.

The stunning young woman contorted her features with rage, and she plunged her dagger into Fake Riven's neck. Yanking his head up by the hair, she began to saw and cut—removing soft tissue bit by bit in a bloody mess until she finally removed his entire head.

The body fell limp to the ground, and Ethel brought the head up over her head for the entire village to see. She smiled a perfect, white smile on beautiful features that any man would grow weak in the knees for. She waved the head around to the cheers of elf and human alike, until, all of a sudden, an audible gasp was heard.

"FATHER!" Senna screamed in horror, and she dropped to her knees while staring in disbelief at the head in Ethel's hands. "REN!!!!"

Ethel dropped the head and immediately screamed in horror when she realized that the head she was holding wasn't Riven's at all, but rather that of her friend's father. The head rolled to a stop, and its red eyes opened wide with a sad and resigned smile on its lips.

Then it began to talk, and the voice coming out of Ren's head was Riven's own. His spectral body watched his younger self from on the hill, where they'd waited in ambush with Allie's forces silently circling like vultures. He remembered how hard it'd been to pull off this move, but he'd done it nonetheless, and it was something that haunted him even now in the looks Genua and her daughter Len gave him from time to time. Though Genua's looks were full of adoration, while Len's were filled with poorly hidden anger and despair for what he'd done.

"I had thought better of you, Ethel. The same goes for all of you here in Greenstalk, really." Memory Riven's breath shuddered one last time through a mere figment of Fay's magic still left in Ren's severed head before his words grew as cold as ice. The red eyes flickered to focus on Elder Bren last. "Old man . . . When I asked you not to do this, I was not begging for my own life. I was begging for all of yours."

With those last words spoken through Fay's remnant hallucinations, Riven's spectral form watched Memory Riven snap his fingers, and the barrels nearby detonated in explosions of red shrapnel. It was the beginning of the end of the old Riven and the start of something new.

Something much, much darker.

KABOOOM

Time in the copied memoryscape froze just as the bomb went off.

[Part 6, Fourth Memory's Choice:
Choose to amplify the explosion, making it large enough to kill Len, Genua, and many of the other elvish villagers that originally survived. This will provide you with soul-lattice pieces you can incorporate into each of their own souls, erasing the pain and memories of their past life and ingraining absolute loyalty to you while simultaneously providing them access to Gluttony's future evolutions.

OR, create a rift in this memoryscape and pull the fabricated version of Ethel into your own reality, thus saving her life. This version of Ethel is not the real one and is a homunculus, but it will act, behave, and look exactly the same. This version of Ethel will also completely believe that she is real, has the real Ethel's true memories up until this point, and will interact with her remaining family and you just as Ethel would have done after this event (should the real Ethel have been saved). This second choice will repair Genua's broken mind and will allow her to cope with her loss by returning her eldest daughter to her—or at least a figment of her eldest daughter. But it will also likely come with significant social consequences that should be obvious even at a glance.

Choose one and proceed to activate your curse and boon.]

CHAPTER 31

The meme Riven vividly remembered concerning the big-eyed alien *Star Wars* character on the spaceship, where he yells *It's a trap!*, came to mind as he read and reread the prompt for what he was supposed to choose between.

A trap between what was most beneficial and what he felt was the right thing to do. Between pragmatism and morals.

His heart thudded in his chest as his anxiety started to climb. He had more anxiety over being given this one single simple choice than any boss fight. The truth was that despite Genua participating in the act of trying to have him killed, betrayed, assassinated, call it what you will . . . he had very much grown to like her. He'd had a glimpse of who she was deep down before her mind had broken, and even now she retained a large portion of the person she used to be. She even seemed happier in this state of denial, not knowing about Ethel or her dead husband anymore. But he'd always asked himself what he would do if he could go back in time and change this one single act. If he could change what he'd done and not have killed Ethel somehow.

He still cringed every time Genua's remaining full elf daughter Len looked at him with that knowing accusation in her eyes. Knowing that he'd killed her big sister and not able to do anything about it. That one decision was without a doubt the most conflicting thing he'd ever done, looking back on his life, and the guilt had gnawed at him ever since. It wasn't wiping out an entire city to save Athela—he'd not known those people and Athela was worth far more, and he'd given the citizens a pretty quick albeit painful death by fire. It wasn't killing and eating random people when he needed to eat, because, again, he didn't know them, and they were a means to an end. It wasn't the innumerable people and creatures he'd killed ever since arriving in Chalgathi's starter trials at the beginning of the integration. No, it was the act of murdering Ethel that had taken top spot for the most disturbing action he'd ever followed through with. He'd known Ethel and had liked her as a person up until her attempt to kill him, and after getting to know Genua better, it'd made it feel all the more personal.

His actions had caused Genua and Len incredible amounts of emotional anguish and had led to Genua literally losing her mind. Perhaps she'd even known that it'd happen—maybe that's why she'd eventually agreed to become a thrall. But Riven hadn't known, and now he had to reap what he'd sown.

"Gluttony, I need your advice," Riven eventually said, having let the frozen image linger there with his decision waiting to be made.

Gluttony appeared beside him in the form of his usual demonic maw projection, a toothy black slit tearing out of space with tendrils of darkness leaking out. He didn't say anything, but waited for Riven to go on.

"Tell me," Riven began with a head tilt and folded arms, staring at the place where Azmoth's bomb was about to rip Ethel apart. "What is a homunculus, exactly?"

"They are artificial entities, or, in this case, an artificial elf. They do not age, and they must be upgraded by material means of vast wealth in order to ascend tiers instead of by means of insight."

"Do you think it would be cruel or a mercy to give Genua back a fake version of her dead daughter?" Riven raised a curious eyebrow. "Part of me believes that even if this did help repair Genua's mind, it would be a cruel joke if she ever found out that Ethel isn't actually Ethel. It may even damage her more. But what are the chances of her finding out? I'm torn between doing what I think is right by Genua and Len, trying to repair their family, but knowing that doing it this way would be repairing it under the pretense of a lie."

Gluttony was silent for a time and turned in the direction of Ethel to match Riven's posture. "Asking an original sin a question of morals is perhaps not the wisest thing to do."

Riven spluttered a laugh. "Perhaps! But wasn't it you yourself that claimed the Unholy and Holy foundational pillars and their subpillars did not designate between good and evil?"

"Yes. I did and I stand by that. I am just not obligated to act morally in most cases. I do what I want to do based upon what I need. And in this case, I see no benefit from the second option of supplying Genua with a new Ethel, even if she were real. In this case, she's not even that."

"Don't you think we owe it to our allies to help them when we can?"

Gluttony scoffed. "Do you forget the original reason why you killed Ethel and placed Genua in chains in the first place? Before you started to grow a friendship with her, she was complicit in trying to murder you. She would have gone back home and laughed with her husband and the village elders, laughed with Ethel over a dining room table about how they'd tricked the wicked vampire and brutally murdered him. They'd have told that tale as a generational legend among the people of their village for centuries to come, as folklore. Your mangled corpse would have had its head removed and your vampiric skull placed on a rack for Ethel's father to display on his wall. That, Riven, is the reality of it. Ethel does not deserve mercy. Genua is owed nothing—she is lucky to be alive and is paying off her crimes by service. If it had been my choice alone, we would have killed her and been done with it. But now that she is the mother of our child . . .”

Gluttony trailed off and let the message hang.

Riven nodded in acknowledgment. “Yeah. I get all that. I’m just feeling a bit guilty, and the more I look at myself, the more I realize that I’m truly turning into a monster. I feel like if I don’t give Ethel back, it’ll solidify the fact that I am one.”

Gluttony replied, “Nonsense, Riven. But if we’re going to play a game of morals, consider this: What happens if you do choose this false Ethel? What then? What happens when Len grows up, and realizes her big sister has remained the same age? Cultivation can put a stop to aging, but a fake Ethel won’t even be able to cultivate at all. It won’t take a genius to figure out what she is. Genua and Len wouldn’t just overlook this; your query about the pretense of a lie is correct thinking. They WOULD find out, Riven. The homunculus Elysium creates here would also find out that she isn’t even the original Ethel, and that alone would have lasting implications, even if you somehow managed to repair the broken relationship you and Ethel had before her timely death. What would that mean in turn? Wait, don’t answer that, because I’ll do it for you. It would mean that all the effort into repairing Genua’s mind would come flooding back in when she realized her real daughter was still dead. Len would be even angrier with you after finding out the same. The homunculus would be in a perpetual state of crisis because it truly thinks it is Ethel while the facts say otherwise. That doesn’t even take into account the other, more nuanced problems the return of a false Ethel would imply. So, in my opinion, the second option is only a Band-Aid prone to peeling off, ready and waiting to expose the wound once again. It is not a real solution, and I am amused that Elysium would even attempt to offer it in the guise of a prize.”

Riven didn’t like that answer. But he didn’t like either answer to this memory’s crossroads.

The first option wasn’t all that better:

[Choose to amplify the explosion, making it large enough to kill Len, Genua, and many of the other elvish villagers that originally survived. This will provide you with soul-lattice pieces you can incorporate into each of their own souls, erasing the pain and memories of their past life and ingraining absolute loyalty to you while simultaneously providing them access to Gluttony’s future evolutions.]

As it read, he was concerned that it was going a step too far. He didn’t want to erase their memories at all, nor did he want loyal mindless slaves out of the mother-child pair. Then again, Genua was already a thrall and had that loyalty aspect to her already, didn’t she? It was only Len that’d be affected, but what kind of person would he be if he ingrained absolute loyalty into a little girl who wasn’t even ten years old yet through some Unholy, cultish system fuckery? The only upside to this was providing them access to Gluttony's future evolutions, which was certainly a good one. But the overall package didn't vibe with Riven, either. Memories were what made up a person just as much as a soul did, and he didn't want to destroy them here.

"Gluttony, is there any way we can avoid erasing their memories, especially Len, while keeping your future evolutions?" Riven asked. "Assuming that this choice unlocks your evolutionary pathways, I'm going to go out on a limb here and say that you have something to do with this change directly. You'd be influencing them after all. Is that right? Can you modify it?"

Silence hung in the air between them for a time before Gluttony carefully chose his words. "You are looking at this from an external perspective, not an internal one. I see into your mind, Riven. You think that taking their memories takes what is rightfully theirs away and diminishes them as people. But if you were them, what would you want?"

Gluttony once again let the silence hang for more than a couple seconds. "Do you want Len to grow up with a mental scar that will affect her entire development, or do you want to give her a cleaner slate? You should want Len to be happy."

"It says that they'll lose the memories of their past life completely. That would include their memories of each other, Len and Genua. That is unacceptable. So are you able to tweak it to where they'll retain memories of each other? Or not? If you need to get rid of Ethel's memories to make them happier, then do it if there's not a better option."

Gluttony sighed, grumbled something inaudible, and grudgingly replied, "Yes. I will be able to do so, since my influence is integrated with the choice. But I do not think Elysium even intended for that to be part of the plan. I am rather convinced that Elysium only meant that the negative aspects of their past life would be removed from their memories to make them happier. If this is not the case, then I will intervene to preserve the memories on their behalf by contacting Elysium directly."

"You can do that?"

"Everyone can do that. Whether or not Elysium replies is something else entirely, but considering what and who I am, Elysium will respond to me. It is probably a small thing, but doable."

"Could you ask Elysium for another choice, then? These ones are ass."

"No, it would not accept and would only draw Elysium's ire. I would not make it a habit to try asking such things of Elysium, either, considering even the small and seemingly insignificant change to the first prompt. Elysium and I are certainly not friends—it imprisoned me and my kin for eons. The minor ask you are wishing for will likely cost me something personally, and you would not want to intertwine yourself in contractual deals with the multiverse's arbiter if you could avoid it. Believe me on that."

Riven fell silent, and he felt Gluttony's presence leave him.

Minutes passed.

Then hours.

Then half a day, until Gluttony's presence returned to his interior soul apparatus and a new message arrived.

[Part 6, Fourth Memory's Choice:

Choose to amplify the explosion, making it large enough to kill Len, Genua, and many of the other elvish villagers that originally survived. This will provide you with soul-lattice pieces you can incorporate into each of their own souls, alleviating the emotional anguish of their most painful memories from their past life and helping them understand why you did what you did to Ethel. Genua's vampiric thrall virus may have lingering effects to smother these memories and her mind will remain broken by the will of the virus to a large extent, but Len will be heavily affected by the outcome of this soul-lattice piece. Both soul-lattice pieces will allow Genua and Len to travel down a gluttonous evolutionary path, and you will have matching soul-lattice pieces connecting you to them that will increase the strength of your bond.

OR, create a rift in this memoryscape and pull the fabricated version of Ethel into your own reality, thus saving her life. This version of Ethel is not the real one and is a homunculus, but it will act, behave, and look exactly the same. This version of Ethel will also completely believe that she is real, has the real Ethel's true memories up until this point, and will interact with her remaining family and you just as Ethel would have done after this event (should the real Ethel have been saved). This second choice will repair Genua's broken mind and will allow her to cope with her loss by returning her eldest daughter to her—or at least a figment of her eldest daughter. But it will also likely come with significant social consequences that should be obvious even at a glance.

Choose one and proceed to activate your curse and boon.]

The second choice wasn't affected at all, but the first choice was far better now that they'd retain their original memories. He picked the first option without hesitation and gave Gluttony a mental thanks as he did as the memory returned into action and the explosion expanded beyond what'd been original proportions. Immediately he felt two new pieces of soul lattice lock into place, reinforcing his soul core with an additional layer of Unholy energy that was then reinforced on top of that with pieces of crystallized gluttonous Sin.

[You have picked Option 1. Len and Genua are now intimately bound to Gluttony's path and will inherit many of his powers as they grow in strength.

You have been granted the boon of Unholy Father, which gives all your children, adopted or not, a passive influx of your aura power and trickles of your XP gains.

You have been cursed with the Daughter's Vengeance and will be haunted by an aspect of Ethel's memories. This haunting is not done by an actual phantom, but rather by curse energy taking the form of Ethel, and when or where it appears will be up for it to decide.]

Allie lay in bed, black wings splayed out behind her and bare legs intertwined with Lahn's as his chest rose and fell in sleep.

He was such a good guy. She was lucky to have him. Luckier still that he'd forgiven her for the mistakes she'd made. She still hadn't asked him whether he'd slept with anyone else during their time apart, but if he had, she couldn't necessarily blame him. Regardless, she didn't want to know, so she wouldn't ask, despite the thought gnawing at her subconscious mind every now and then like a jealous little hyena.

The open window leading out to a balcony overlooking the guild hall's manor grounds let in a soft breeze and starlight from an unusually clear night sky, and the sound of servants bustling on the lower floors or laughing outside in the garden brought a smile to her face. Even the nearby cityscape of Brightsville could be seen, as her balcony faced north, and the city itself was filled with signs of nightlife, having grown into an absolutely sprawling landscape of Unholy and Death-attuned architecture. It was far different from the front lines in the hellscapes of Negrada and along Umbra's coastline, and was a nice change from the Abyssal Descent as well. Traveling through the Abyssal Descent had brought her closer to the core of Sin and had allowed her to transcend from being an angel of death to the Angel of Wrath, but in the end it'd been a tiresome adventure. She wondered when Riven would get back so she could apologize to him about her earlier outburst regarding that dark elf she couldn't remember the name of. She'd add it to the stack of people she'd apologized to since getting back. Even visiting the front lines herself to slaughter thousands of merfolk, ones that'd been harassing Retesh's fleeing undead refugees on pilgrimage to the promised lands of the Thane Necropolis, had done little to cool Allie's temper, though. And despite knowing she'd been in the wrong when speaking to Riven last, she still felt just generally angry. It was without doubt a side effect of being bonded with Wrath, just like Riven was having his own problems being hungrier and prone to devour things the longer he integrated Gluttony, but becoming easily enraged was a problem that she'd probably have to deal with forever. So she was doing her best to curb her enthusiasm for violence and lashing out and mentally checking off reasons why she was mad at any given time to make sure her emotions weren't out of place.

The thing she was probably most angry about right now, however, was likely legitimate. She still hadn't had any success finding Crendir and that stupid vampiric elder-god bloodline, and time was ticking down.

Pulling up the most recent notification and quest statuses about it, she visibly slumped, even being horizontally strewn across Lahn's bare chest as she read the words for the tenth time that week. The only thing that'd changed was the "APPROXIMATELY 45 DAYS," which had started at sixty-two days. But the commanders Amelia Deathfeather of Wrath and Tre'Zix of Gluttony were both on the case, and if those two absolute units and their clans couldn't figure it out, then Allie doubted she could do any better.

[<u>New System Quest UPDATE: Save Mara and Kathrine and secure</u> <u>the Fallen Vampiric God's Essence.</u>

Congratulations! You have completed half of this quest by saving Mara and Kathrine from death. You will not receive system prizes until the other half is completed as described below:

Crendir No-Name, a traitorous E-grade commander from the Blood Moon Requiem, has decided to take matters into his own hands concerning World Quest 4, Blood of the Fallen God. He is attempting to rob you and your planet of the fallen god's essence and opportunity. He is not a pureblooded vampire, but he has been given a means of temporarily disguising himself as a pureblood—becoming one of only a few on your planet who can benefit from drinking the ancient god's blood—and will be able to absorb it without issue.

He has already begun the absorbing process, which will take <u>approx-</u> <u>imately forty-five days</u> from now in total to complete. Crendir No-Name has been given a quest of his own that will reward him with extremely valuable prizes should he succeed—including a portal off Panu to anywhere in the multiverse if he successfully fulfills all his own requirements, INCLUDING AN ENTIRELY NEW ALTERNATIVE BRANCH OF THE BLOOD SUBPILLAR THAT WILL BE RESTORED BY ELYSIUM'S WILL SHOULD HE ABSORB THE BLOOD PROPERLY.

Stop him before he obtains this taboo power and leaves the planet, and secure the ancient one's blood for Riven, or destroy it entirely

if this cannot be done. Perhaps your brother, as a pureblooded vampire, will benefit if you manage to secure the ancient Blood subpillar alternative? Let the race commence.]

[<u>New religious quest dispensed: Destroy the Fallen God's Bloodline.</u>

You have previously been denounced as an apostate by the Blood God and have angered nearly all vampiric factions across the multiverse in doing so. You are hated by many and loved by few, the Blood God extends to you a new olive branch in light of recent events: Kill Crendir No-Name and purge the Fallen God's blood from the face of Panu entirely. Destroy all remnant artifacts of the ancient, alternate Blood subpillar, and you will be forgiven of your sins. Despite your ascension into Wrath's reincarnation, the Blood God will not tolerate allowing the ancient Blood subpillar alternative to revive itself by way of Elysium's laws. Destroying the ancient Fallen God's blood entirely will result with a gift of one planet to add to your budding empire, one of your choosing within the Blood God's domain, all additional slaves residing on that planet to rule over, devotion from any clergy of the Blood God residing on that planet, and all associated resources on said planet. You will also be labeled a Hero of Blood, and be given a short-range E-grade stargate setup for traversing between planets in adjacent solar systems should you choose to accept. Meanwhile, a crusade will be declared upon your faction and upon Wrath's church should you succeed in killing Crendir yet choose to allow this subpillar to exist.]

She grimaced at the threat the Blood God had dispensed. She wanted to do just the opposite of what the bastard asked just to spite the deity, but doing that would probably be unwise considering she had an entire legion of Blood Moon Requiem F-grade elites along with even a few E-grades that'd recently ascended on Panu under her banner. They wouldn't react well to her betrayal of the Blood God and would likely revolt if she did. So her current plan was to first find Crendir, kill him along with the Greed forces that'd helped him escape, and then somehow secure the bloodline to temporarily preserve it under the guise of trying to destroy it but being unable to. Wrath had already confirmed that destroying it completely would probably take time, so the excuse was viable, and she wanted Riven to at least have a choice in what she should do with it before getting rid of the thing entirely. But Riven came first, and if he wanted that bloodline, then she'd go to war for it in Riven's name. He'd have done the same for her, and he was the last real family she had.

Glancing up at Lahn's sleeping face, she put on a sly smile and pecked him on the cheek before unlacing her long legs from his and tucking him back in. Perhaps, if things went well, Lahn and his mother would also be family soon.

It was a pleasant thought.

Lahn only groaned and rolled over in her extraction from the covers of the bed, and she smoothed his hair out with a hand before lovingly kissing him again and writing a note to place on the nightstand so that he knew where she'd gone if he got up early. They had communication stones as well that they could talk through, but it was a gesture he'd already said he'd appreciated when she'd left a note the first time. So she made it a habit to do so now.

Putting down the pen, stretching, and going over to the closet, she pulled out a long, formfitting dress and withdrew her wings before donning a fur-lined coat with a hood. Not that the slight chill bothered her, but she wanted to remain inconspicuous. It'd been a long time since she'd actually walked through Brightsville—the last time it'd been to see the bone garden up on the highest tower's top floor. Perhaps she'd go there again just to see what kinds of progress the necromancers had made, or what kind of undead pilgrims were coming over from other worlds. Maybe she'd even attempt to go try her hand at that large stone cube with the shifting runes taken from Daskus, which Riven had obliterated many months ago. If she was right, it'd almost been a year since Riven had torched the place and he'd still not even tried his hand at the cube and its prizes a single time. That was despite the fact that it'd become one of the main attractions for Brightsville, outside the Unholy Elysium altar and the trading district that housed both the Negrada and Blood Moon Requiem trading communes. Or the Riven's Eye Wormhole that teleported one to the opposite side of the planet into Chicago's downtown, creating a massive trade network. Or the outlying dungeons that Gaia had helped cultivate in the forests where people could level themselves up and clear feral undead that spawned while harvesting herbs. Or even the portal leading into Negrada itself, where only the best guilds or official military units went in under mercenary contract to help fight enemy dungeons in the hellscapes. There were even combat tutors and opportunities to be turned into a vampire by the Blood Moon Requiem's commune in the trade district for people who showed significant promise or rare talents.

Actually, Brightsville had quite a few incentives and unique opportunities in or just around the city borders. She was rather proud to be what many on Panu's cortex called the Promised Lands for undead, or really anyone who was linked to the Unholy foundational pillar. Nowhere else on Panu could you find the kind of opportunities that the continent of Umbra supplied, and now that it was entirely under Thane Necropolis control, Brightsville had become the keystone of the empire among all the cities under their banner.

Giggling at how they'd kept the name Brightsville despite Riven's vows to change it to something more fitting for their capital city, she began putting on a pair of feminine leather boots and pulled up the Panu cortex to look for the cube's information. There was already a list of highlighted areas she'd been to or directly controlled, and she could access any forum group within her empire based on geographical location, though she could only interact with the outside world beyond the Thane Necropolis in the global forums because she hadn't been to many areas overseas. Since it'd been so long since even using the cortex, she opted to reread the basic information on the site without dismissing it out of hand.

[<u>Welcome to the Panu cortex</u>!

Here you will find forum categories and branching categories; you can scroll through subjects, post your own topics, acquire or share video feeds, create enemies or alliances, and even bargain for goods like a marketplace. Be warned that each has strict sets of rules, and you will receive a notification if your content is prohibited. Most prohibited material involves key events in the world of Panu or even in your local area, secrets of Panu that the Elysium administrator wishes to be found rather than publicly exploited, information released too early regarding worlds outside Panu, and spam content. Video feeds can only be uploaded by request. You must ask the administrator directly to upload content, and your request may or may not be recognized. Sometimes the administrator may also post video content even without an express request. In order to request video uploading, just mentally think of the time and place you want to upload and wait for a response.

<u>Please note that restrained or imprisoned personnel may not access the forums of Panu's cortex.</u> Forums extend only to places you have visited and guilds you have joined before with the exceptions of the main page discussion board and the world quest message boards, both of which are world-spanning and more heavily moderated. No forums outside key areas visited and guilds can exist other than Global Forums.

Feel free to select from one of the already categorized subjects, or you may use the search function for more in-depth selections of guild forums. Your options are as follows:
- **Main Page and Announcements (Global)**
- **Power Ladders, Guild and Individual (Global)**
- **World Quests and World Quest Ladders (Global)**

<u>OPTIONS for the Thane Necropolis:</u>
- **Brightsville, capital city of the Thane Necropolis**
- **The conquered dwarvish cities of the underdark: Charathigog and Reathian**

- The conquered elvish vassal kingdom of Tereen
- The conquered northeastern coastal cities of the Mayana Alliance
- The integrated kingdom of Dawn
- The integrated Golden Bull Sect
- The integrated western coastal provinces of Corpus Christi
- Bluefang, collective sprawl of the Greenskin Hordes
- The Unholy dryad communities Dungeon Alibast
- The Hellscapes of Dungeon Negrada
- The Silver Canyon Mining Reaches
- The scattered farming villages of the Central Plains
- . . .]

Allie stopped scrolling through the list and went back to where "Brightsville, capital city of the Thane Necropolis" was listed at the top. The list of grouped areas on her available Thane Necropolis locations was too long to care for, and each grouping had multiple settlements, locations, or cities. There were well over two hundred individual locations to pick from, and there was no way that Allie was going through all that just for curiosity's sake.

[Options for Brightsville, capital city of the Thane Necropolis:
- **General Forum**
- **Guilds**
- **Trade**
- **City Life**
- **Dating**
- **Upcoming Events**
- **Unique Features**]

She clicked on "Unique Features" and found what she was looking for.

[<u>Puzzle-Box Cube Labyrinth</u>: **This stone cube is a permanent fixture on the world of Panu, granted to this city by Elysium as a prize to the populace after the king of Daskus completed a difficult system quest with perfect marks. Afterward it was stolen and taken to the opposite side of Panu after Daskus was destroyed. <u>Rules</u>: The trials are formed by utilizing monsters, mazes, and puzzles with a real possibility of death. Only ten may enter an instance event at once; instance events that are not full may be entered by outsiders at any time as long as they are within the same tier of trial. Any number of instance events between different groups may be ongoing at any time. You do not require sustenance while inside the cube, you may only complete the Puzzle-Box Cube Labyrinth event up to three times with scaling difficulty and scaling prizes via attempt tiers one, two, and three, and**

you may leave the Puzzle-Box Cube Labyrinth instance events at any time—but only through the single entrance and single exit points inside. Leaving the instance event will forfeit all remaining attempts at completing this system event or collecting its prizes. To create your own instance event or join another's, just stand underneath the cube and focus on it while thinking "Activate."]

It shouldn't take too long to complete. Maybe she'd go for a stroll through the city first and then hit up the puzzle-box cube? Smiling excitedly and walking to the door, she turned back just one more time to make sure that Lahn was still asleep. Opening the door with a click and then shutting it quietly behind her, she turned around to start down the hallway leading to the lower floors when she came face-to-face with none other than Kathrine.

Princess Kathrine Vonsilla Crushada the Ninth hadn't been out of Riven's room for days now. To see her fully dressed and standing tall was a surprise to Allie, but she met the pureblooded vampire with a wide smile.

"Good to see you up, Kathrine," Allie said, coming over to embrace the other woman with a hug. "Are you feeling any better?"

Kathrine hugged her back and cleared her throat, sniffing once and adjusting her long brown hair. "Yes. I can't just let myself rot away in a cave all day for the next century despite what happened, so I decided I'd force myself to come out. Are you headed somewhere?"

"Yeah, I'm going for a walk around the city. Then I'm going to head to the cube in the trading district."

"The one Riven brought over with the internal labyrinth?"

"That's the one." Allie nodded. Seeing the look on Kathrine's face, Allie prodded, "Would . . . you like to come?"

Kathrine's features brightened, and relief swept over the hard lines that'd been there moments before. "If . . . if it isn't too much to ask, then yes. I was hoping for some company but don't know who to talk to since Riven is gone, and I don't know my guards all that well, even if they are from my parents' own house."

Kathrine gestured to the two soldiers in heavy plate armor stationed outside her door down the hall. "They're nice, but not the talking type."

Allie chuckled and locked her arm around Kathrine's before pulling the vampire along toward the spiral staircase. "Then off we go! I haven't explored the city in quite a while, and Lahn's asleep. It'd certainly be nice to have company! Maybe we can stop at a few street vendors for food on the way!"

"Do I need to bring my sword for the cube?" Kathrine asked hesitantly.

Allie paused just beyond the door to Riven's room and nodded. "Yeah, just in case. We probably won't need it if you just want me to do all the work, but if you want to participate, then might as well. It's always good to be prudent, regardless of the situation."

CHAPTER 32

Merriment was abundant. Laughter rose above the sounds of bustling crowds enjoying the nightlife of the city like a warm blanket, setting a safe, secure, and relaxed mood that was far different from when the city had initially transitioned into the multiverse. There was a sense of excitement, progress, and overall comradery, where Allie saw firsthand the results of her rule as displaced undead refugees were readily taken care of in well-kept housing establishments with ample food and minimal crime. Magical lights and neon signs from apartment buildings, bars, and nightclubs illuminated the darkness, and patrols of guards made sure the drunken fights that did break out were quickly subdued before the participants were taken to a drunk tank to cool off.

Smiling and waving at a little ghoul girl holding hands with her parents on a walk through the well-lit streets, Allie pushed through a thick wooden door underneath a lit set of torches and entered a half-filled pub. The establishment had a couple of vampires playing darts on one end, deathtouched enlightened elves alongside some flesh golems playing cards in one corner, and a mix and match of deathtouched enlightened humans with skresh divided between a few tables scattered around the room.

What was more interesting were the three tiefling demons, probably immigrants from Negrada, who were also playing drinking games with a Jabob demon. There was even a rare phantasmal woman strumming a guitar and singing in a ghostly, soothing voice onstage. It wasn't often you saw these species in Brightsville, but they were certainly present enough to not be an absolutely unique standout, either.

Walking through the pub and toward the bar, Allie stopped in front of a gruff-looking human bartender in a sleeveless vest and motioned him over from where he was polishing glasses. She raised two fingers and head-bobbed to Kathrine as the vampiric princess pulled up beside her. "Drinks for my friend and I. Whatever you think tastes the best."

The man put down a glass and reached under the bar to pull out two corked bottles of a glittering pink liquid with orange swirls. He placed both bottles on the bar and grinned while pushing them to the two women. "What's with the fur hoods and masks? You two are obviously pretty enough, no need to hide anything."

Hooded fur coats with Venice-styled Columbina masks that covered half their faces were enough to hide both royals to a point, avoiding immediate suspicion upon taking to the streets of Brightsville. Neither Allie nor Kathrine wanted to draw too much attention on their night out. It'd be the first time Allie had gone out into the city while hiding who she was, and she was eager to find out whether or not the nightlife scene she'd heard so much about lived up to expectations.

"It's just a fashion statement," Kathrine said with a wink, taking her drink, popping the cork, and sipping while sitting on a cushioned stool beside Allie. Eyebrows raising, she inspected the glittering liquid more closely. "Oh, this has something unique mixed inside. Essence of . . . something? With the blood of an immortal? The alcohol content is peak F-grade, too, not bad."

"Considering I couldn't identify either of you, I figured you're both pretty high level. First round is on me if you stay awhile—young women like you keep the men around hoping to get lucky," the man replied with a wink of his own, eyeing Kathrine's figure where the fur coat didn't manage to hide things. His eyes met hers and then shifted to Allie, who still wore a soft smiling expression while looking out the open windows at the people moving up and down the street. "A vampire and a . . . Eh. Not a ghoul, not human, either. What are you, lass? If you don't mind me asking?"

"I am an angel of death," Allie said nonchalantly, turning her attention to the burly man only briefly before clinking her glass with Kathrine's and taking a large swig. "This tastes nice."

The man's eyes widened. "Angel of death? There are only a few dozen in the entire necropolis. Did you happen to come over with the queen's entourage? The banished clan following the sin of Wrath?"

"Something like that." Allie's smile grew, and she let a single set of her wings extend from her back, black feathers glittering and causing a lot of heads to turn as they extended outward to touch the ceiling. She retracted them soon after and began to tap a finger on the table in thought. "I'm curious. Do you like this city, human? What do you think of Brightsville now that it's the capital of an Unholy empire?"

Still somewhat surprised, the bartender shook his head and let out a chuckle before leaning across the bar and putting his chin in his hands. "Ah, where to even begin. Yes, I love living here! It's one of the safest cities to live in across all Panu. I've made a profitable business here, the taxes are rather lenient, and I never have to worry about my family's well-being or persecution for our practices of black magic."

Allie did a quick once-over of the man and identified him readily enough. Jewelry like the identification ring on her left hand was becoming somewhat commonplace now, but just like the amulet the bartender himself wore, they could only identify things within a certain level range depending on the quality of the item.

[Level 16 Bartender, Human]

The man's level was only sixteen despite having a noncombat class, which probably meant he'd not strayed off to try different brews. That, or he'd failed to get any advanced ingredients for higher-quality drinks. He probably hadn't been the one to make the alcohol she was sipping on right now. Given that crafting classes leveled up differently than combat classes, she wondered what he'd been doing since arriving on Panu.

He probably just wasn't very driven. But she didn't necessarily judge him for that, because there were millions of civilians just like this man across her empire who only wished to live out peaceful, simple lives free of pain or grief.

"Your family practices black magic and you chose to be a bartender?" Kathrine asked in good humor. "Why?"

The bartender got up to get one of the off-duty vampire soldiers a drink of blood wine and quickly came back to continue the conversation. "My father is a warlock. He's actually a pretty good one, too, level 140. A founder of one of the adventuring guilds here, and he also runs a succubus brothel in the red-light district through his summons and a few other succubi that came over from Negrada. I never really had the talent for any of the Unholy magics, even though it's my only affinity, so I picked up a crafting class instead and help him run the business side of the guild and brothel in my spare time."

"Are there any incubus brothels around?" Kathrine asked curiously, a sly smile spreading across her lips. "Any good ones? My maid has been asking about them."

The man rolled his eyes and chuckled again. "There actually is one with a pretty good reputation called the Long Pole. I'm sure you can guess why it was named that, but everyone in the red-light district is very strictly policed and all the sex workers are treated very well. None of it's shady and unregistered sex work is illegal, so I wouldn't say any of them are necessarily bad."

Kathrine side-eyed Allie. "Hmm. I'll have to tell Cherna."

"Cherna is the blonde vampire I first met you with, right?" Allie shook her head and sipped on her drink. "It's been a while."

"Correct. She recently broke up with her fiancé when she found out he was cheating on her with a friend's thrall."

"I'd be pissed."

"She obviously was! But such is life—I can't say I really blame her for wanting to find an incubus to keep her company. Speaking of which, when is your brother getting back?"

Allie rolled her eyes. "Can we not talk about that?"

"Can't you just ask him? Didn't you very recently make some sort of soul connection?"

Allie glanced over her status information and read aloud for Kathrine's benefit.

[The Siblings' Pact (Trait): You and your brother Riven now have a direct soul connection, manifested through the dark arts of the Abyssal Descent. Currently it allows you to sense where your sibling is, but as time goes on this trait will evolve into a direct form of immediate communication regardless of the space between you two.]

Allie gave Kathrine a raised eyebrow and sipped on her drink. "So no, I cannot just ASK him when he'll be back. Athel— Ahem, I mean, his first minion has a stronger bond than even I do."

The queen of the Thane Necropolis quickly shot the bartender a glance to make sure he hadn't caught her almost-name drop. He didn't seem to be much the wiser and was pulling on a swig of brandy himself while listening in.

"Well, that sucks!" Kathrine shook her head with a dramatic, pouting sigh. "My family keeps asking about when we're having kids. Even though it's just a political marriage, I do like him."

"It is what it is," Allie said, waving her bottle in the air. "You'll be fine. He'll be back eventually."

Kathrine grinned and bobbed her head from side to side. "All right. Oh! Don't tell my parents that I'm out drinking like this—they'd be furious. I forgot to mention it. And . . . Would you want to go dress shopping with me?"

Allie's eyes lit up with excitement, and she nearly lunged across the bar to swat Kathrine on the shoulder. "We can go before the cube! I've been wanting to try on some new lingerie for Lahn's benefit, as a way to say sorry about you know what."

"How's that going, by the way?"

"Lahn's great. The most lovable guy I know." Allie smirked.

"Ugh. I'm so jealous. I wish you-know-who looked at me with even half of the romantic intent your man does!"

The bartender had slowly been raising both eyebrows and hesitantly commented, "Are you in an arranged marriage of some kind?"

Kathrine glanced back and shrugged. "Kind of."

"That's fucked-up. I'm so sorry. Can't you get your angel friend to help you out? Or are you one of the vampires from off-world? You know, from the requiem?"

"Yes, I'm from the Blood Moon Requiem. Our customs are slightly different from yours, but I guarantee you that this particular case is more of a benefit to me and my family than it is anything to be upset about."

"Don't you want to marry for love?" the man asked with a frown.

Kathrine laughed, putting a hand up to her lips. She shook her head. "Nobles don't marry for love, silly human. Not in our society. We marry for political gain and power as a duty to the house we're born from, and if we get lucky then love comes later. Plus, I already do think of the man I'm engaged to as a friendly acquaintance—I don't hate him or anything like that. If anything, he's rather pleasant to be around compared to most others, and he's not bad to look at."

That comment caught the attention of some of the other vampires playing darts, who shot her curious and simultaneously skeptical glances and muttered among one another while continuing to play.

The man nodded sternly. "Ah. So you're a noblewoman, then?"

"Yes. A handful of us came over when Elysium allowed our legions to defend the Thane siblings. I'm one of them. From a young age I always expected to marry for the benefit of my family, and I happened to get paired with someone who fits that bill. Now, could you pass me another one of those drinks?"

The man did as asked when Allie held up a finger to ask a question. "Do other humans like it here as much as you do?"

The bartender finished popping off the cork for Kathrine and gave Allie another once-over. "Can't speak for everyone, but there are lots of humans that still live here and are quite happy with their lives. Most of them are immigrants from the Chicago side of the Riven's Eye Wormhole, or crossed the ocean to get here like my father did when they heard the Unholy foundational pillar had a rooted movement on Umbra. The Thane Necropolis has drawn all sorts of people like my family from around the world, and the only ones that really give us much trouble are the vampires."

He head-bobbed to Kathrine before leaning back with crossed arms. "No offense, miss, but your people really don't seem to like humans much."

Kathrine giggled. "Yes, well, that is to be expected. It isn't that we hate you humans—we just view you as inferior creatures. As food."

"So I've been told." He sighed, shaking his head. "But the proclamation the Thanes made about blood donations from mortals has stemmed a lot of the hate we initially saw. Our restaurants actually pay to mix a lot of that donated blood into our food specifically for vampires—it makes life bearable for everyone when the vamps aren't starving and trying to eat us."

The bartender gave Kathrine a wink. "So no hard feelings."

Downing the second bottle, Kathrine burped and slid the bottle across the counter while gesturing for another. "I wouldn't have cared if you did have hard feelings. I'd probably just have eaten you. Now get me another drink; that stuff's good."

"You gonna pay this time? I just gave you each two free rounds because you're pretty, but you can't drink me out of house and home, either."

Allie laughed and opened up a coin pouch. "I've got it covered. How much?"

The bartender stroked his beard. "Three silver and five copper Elysium coins apiece for those drinks you've been downing, and fourteen copper apiece for anything on the lower shelf. If you want, I can even set you up with a gallon of that stuff in concentrated form for a gold piece."

Allie grinned, locked eyes with Kathrine, and pushed over two gold pieces along the wooden countertop. "Give us each a gallon. We'll take it for the road."

The crowd roared, and Allie roared with them while drunk off her ass as the twelve undead goblins raced squealing, fleshy pig creatures around a large obstacle course. Each of the mounts had a different-colored flag attached to its collar, and the betting odds changed by the minute depending on what the front-runner was.

"COME ON, BLUE! I HAVE FIFTEEN THOUSAND RIDING ON YOUR CHUMMMY LITTLE ASS!" Allie screamed, waving her half-finished gallon of pink and orange alcohol in the air. She almost hit Kathrine in the face by accident, but the drunk vampire princess managed to duck before falling onto an irritated bunch of kids on the row down.

"Sorry!" Kathrine said apologetically, stumbling back up to her seat while the parents chided her and the kids grumbled. "So sorry!"

"Get ahold of yourself, Kathrine!" Allie slurred, giggling and hoisting up the vampire with one hand while flipping a few coins in the direction of the kids as an apology. "You gotta stay upright if you want to keep drinkin'!"

Kathrine gave Allie a hiccuping glare, chugged another long swig of her own gallon, and wiped her mouth on Allie's sleeve. "Want to go before the crowds get big? I need to get to the Blood God's temple to drop off some stuff for my parents. Something about a new priest and whatnot . . . I can't remember really, but it's all in a nice little package so I wouldn't forget!"

She hiccuped yet again.

Allie scowled, not really a big fan of the Blood God, but glanced over her shoulder to where the race was still ongoing. Blue was almost in dead last, and there was no way she'd be winning anything anyways. "Bah! Fine. Let's go, but you need to make it quick, okay?! I really don't think that guy likes me much."

"Who? Is someone giving you an evil eye?"

"What?! No! I'm talking about your sucky-sucky god!"

"The Blood God?!"

"That's the one!"

"Allie! You can't call him the sucky-sucky god just because you're mad about being labeled a heretic!"

"I was labeled an apostate, not a heretic! And YES I can be mad about it!"

"They're basically the same, Allie! And for the record, I can't believe I'm friends with one; this entire situation is so weird to me."

"I'm the apostate here and what I say goes! Now hurry it up and move that pale ass, Kathrine! We've been drinking for six hours and it's well past two in the morning and we still need to get to the cube! Ohhhh, and uh, dresses, too!"

"Allie, you can't seriously be considering doing the puzzle-box cube while wasted!"

"Why not?!"

"Because it's dangerous!"

"Kathrine . . . Listen . . ." Allie slurred, leaning over onto the hiccuping vampire and ruffling her hair. "The only way to do puzzle-box cubes is to do them when drunk. It's law."

"Says who?!"

"The queen, bitch! Plus I'll have time to detox before that while we try on new clothes!"

Kathrine snorted a laugh, grinned eagerly, and started out of the row and down the stairs, avoiding a flying bag of half-eaten food when a drunken fight broke out between two bettors. She and Allie avoided a hastily moving guard on the way to intercept the brawling idiots, and then they began to make their way out past the refreshment lines and away from the goblinoid pig races. A few larger undead abominations, obviously intoxicated, ambled through the streets with one another and had to be avoided, but otherwise the crowds weren't all that bad and easy enough to traverse.

Kathrine gripped Allie's hand and pulled her along when the queen of the necropolis became too slow.

Drunkenly sipping on booze, stumbling through the streets and giggling to each other about what they saw or telling bad jokes, they were quite a mess. Allie hadn't ever had the opportunity to go out like this back on Earth, and she was having the time of her life. At most she'd been to a few underage house parties when she was younger, but nothing like this. This was great, and being so intoxicated was something she was already determined to force Lahn to participate in. She was actually wishing he was here and that she'd woken him up to come along instead of letting him stay in bed, but he'd looked so dang tired and had been too cute to wake up.

Passing between towering skyscrapers, businesses, and apartment buildings numbering in the dozens, the duo passed into a less crowded area of the city where the lights were dimmer and people were more subdued. Instead of boisterous laughter and drunken shenanigans, people smoked cigars and various plants from pipes while low-beat music played from open doors. Farther down the road, the beginnings of the temple district came into view where various clergy waited at the front doors to speak to passersby about their religions. Getting closer and closer, and ignoring the catcalls from various men on the street, Allie and Kathrine soon came face-to-face with the large gates of the Blood God's temple.

There were three prominent religions here in the temple district, with three bigger temples, and half a dozen smaller temples for local fledgling gods born to Panu when the integration started. These six other local gods were essentially baby gods and hardly a threat to anyone, but Allie had decided to keep them around and cultivate them, helping them grow by providing them followers instead of starving them out of faith. If anything, it was just to see if it paid dividends in the future. When gods were something akin to greater spirits that fed on faith and could provide blessings to the city, who was to say it was a bad idea other than the other already established gods and their clergy? No one would dare tell her she couldn't, because this was her damn city. Freedom of religion was a fact of life in the necropolis and protected by law, and the clergy of the various religions often competed to attract those looking for their own meaning in life while shooting insults at one another. The clergy were even reported in many news articles and recordings on the cortex to have thrown food or pulled mean and petty pranks on one another, like flooding each other's bathrooms or throwing foul-smelling concoctions at different temples while preaching. It was actually quite hilarious to watch, at least in Allie's opinion, and it'd even made something of a show for diners at the various restaurants with outer balconies to watch the priests and priestesses interact.

First and foremost of the three larger religions was the temple of the Scythe, which was by far the tallest. It looked more like a haunted tower than anything else and was staffed with a large assortment of various undead, with a statue of the grim reaper in a meditating position holding a large scythe over its stone lap. The large statue was built out of obsidian and smiled grimly at people passing on the street, and was actually built into the temple's entrance as people passed underneath the sitting monument to come and go. Souls swirled around the enormous tower in a spooky display of glittering lights, and unlike all the other temples where sermons could be heard inside, this particular temple to the Scythe was unusually silent as people came or went.

The second of the larger religions was a temple devoted to the combined worship of both Wrath and Gluttony, with the churches of both sins finding solace here considering their reincarnations were brother and sister. Neither sin was technically a god, but when they grew more powerful they'd be able to act in something of a similar capacity based on faith, or so Wrath had told Allie only recently. The implications of this new partnership were far more widespread than just Panu, but the only demons that really had access to the reincarnations directly were those from Negrada or those lucky enough to be contracted to summoners, warlocks, and black-magic wizards of various sorts. In fact, warlocks here on Panu had seen an uptick in the quality of demonic contracts available to them simply because of their proximity to Wrath and Gluttony, bringing even more of an incentive for people to come to Umbra in order to change their original affinities to that of the Unholy foundational pillar at the Elysium altar in the trade district.

The Unholy Elysium altar's ability to change people's affinities to Unholy opened a lot of doors for those who weren't content with the hand they'd originally been dealt. In many cases their affinities were also slightly higher for whatever pillars they acquired after their transition into the Unholy magic types, too, and thus government records had noted a significant increase in the number of warlocks and bonded demons living in Brightsville. The net result of all that had been the prompt construction of a temple to the two great sins, but instead of building upward, they'd built down, shaping an enormous, deep pit into that of Gluttony's maw with a stone depiction of the lion of Wrath guarding the entrance stairway leading down. The temple had been built into the ground for a massive fifteen, spaced-out stories and had numerous demons of varying species coming inside regularly to pray. Other than religious practices, the temple also held classes and day care for demon children, at Allie's request, and it'd almost become something of a school. Warlocks also often congregated there to help one another and their demons cultivate dark magics. Nearly half of the previously banished sins that'd been sent to the abyss with Gluttony and Wrath so long ago had taken up residence inside the pit. Allie herself had gone inside more than a handful of times since arriving back on Panu and had helped hastily construct the underground temple while Wrath gave insight on various religious matters, but she tended to avoid going there too often or too publicly because of how much attention it brought. Being worshipped definitely had its downsides when it came to crazies or religious nutjobs following you around trying to kiss the ground you walked on.

Last of the larger religions was the Blood God's temple, and it was staffed by more than a few vampires. They also had thrall servants, including a few legitimate thrall blood priests who'd come over from the requiem. There were also a good number of humans who supplied blood for the temple's practices in exchange for practice in the blood arts, with donations often rolling in from the Blood Moon Requiem itself. Many of the native-born vampires visited regularly, and it was the second-largest of the temples currently present in Brightsville with a large Gothic-style building that took up many hundreds of feet in diameter and height. Candles illuminated red-stained windows, and a stylized outer gate and a red teardrop made from rubies adorned the wall over the main doors leading inside.

"We've been expecting you, Princess Kathrine Vonsilla Crushada the Ninth." One of the elderly blood priests, a thrall with crimson tattoos very much like Genua's, stepped out of the shadows to bow slightly in her direction. The old man glanced warily at Allie a moment later when the proclamation caused ripples in the vampires worshipping inside, who turned heads to get a better look at the princess after the priest's announcement, and he sighed as he shook his head at Allie as if he was a disappointed old grandpa. "To think that you, Allie Thane, would have thrown away such a bright future in the light of our god for a lesser entity such as the Scythe . . . it is truly a crime against our people. But, as the sire of our order commands, we will accept you into our halls despite your transgressions against the faith. Do you intend to come inside and ask for forgiveness, Apostate? Or do you wish to remain outside as Kathrine finishes her business here?"

Sipping on her drink and almost sputtering at the way she was being talked to in her own city, Allie glared at the priest from underneath her hood and mask, not knowing how he'd even known who she was. She also didn't like the scowls she got from the vampires kneeling at altars she could see inside, and was all the more tempted to NOT destroy that fallen elder god's bloodline if or whenever she got her hands on it. Inside her, Wrath wanted her to strangle the very life out of the little pissant bastard, and she had to take some steadying breaths so that she wouldn't murder the man and start some kind of feud with the Blood God yet again.

At least, that wasn't the plan YET.

Thusly she ignored the priest and hip-bumped Kathrine to move along. "Go on. I'll wait here. I don't feel like going into that nasty place anyways."

The old man frowned at her words, and Kathrine sighed with an eye roll.

"You should really stop being so antagonistic. You did commit a grave sin against vampires at large, you know." Kathrine patted Allie's head with a drunk smile and held up her jug with another hiccup. "You wouldn't believe how angry many of the people back home were, but you have a chance to improve relationships if you find Crendir fast enough. I pray that you do. Either way, we have Riven to lean on as an important asset the Blood God wants on his side, and I don't think Riven will be betraying the Blood God anytime soon. So don't take the words of that old guy to heart—he's just pissy that you basically got away with murder and won't be punished for your actions. At least, as long as Riven doesn't become an apostate or heretic as well!"

Kathrine laughed at the absurdity of the idea and pulled out a parchment with a package out of her spatial ring before walking inside. "Be right back, Allie! Then you can take me shopping, and then to the cube!"

CHAPTER 33

Len frowned down at the red mirror and set aside the grimoire she'd been study-ing in her room to give her mother a very serious glare.

"Mommy, you need to make sure Iris is getting fed three times a day. Okay? It's important for babies to eat. Don't you forget!" She wagged a finger at Genua through her mother's Blood Mirror ability, their only means of communication while Mommy had been gone all this time. "And feed her lots of treats! Like cookies. She'll definitely like that!"

Genua smiled lovingly back at her elder daughter, red eyes twinkling with ill-suppressed and lighthearted laughter. "Yes, dear. I'll be sure to give your baby sister all the treats she wants until we get back and you can meet her in person. But I've got to go now, Kara already has her hands full with how much power that little baby has inside her! To think that she's so strong at such a young age! Ugh! Anyways, I love you, Len! Say hi to Tupper for me!"

"All right, Mommy! Love you, be safe!" Len gave a brilliant ear-to-ear grin and waved enthusiastically as her mother's ability peeled off. The red mirror used for communication turned into an ordinary one, and Len found herself staring back at her reflection instead.

Her eyes had become a brilliant purple color that literally radiated Sin energy whenever she got excited or upset, and two tiny white nubs of bone were grow-ing from her forehead ever since the system had notified her about Riven and Gluttony influencing her future path through their trait Unholy Father. She was otherwise still an elf . . . but was something of a hybrid demon, too? Her teacher and Fay's brother Tupper had been in awe when he'd first seen the change, but he'd said it was only something that'd benefit her. And Len was happy that she now matched her baby sister Iris's own look, even if Iris did have pink eyes instead of purple. It definitely didn't make up for what Riven had taken from Len after he'd killed Daddy and her big sister, Ethel, but it was a start. Len was still having problems coming to terms with the idea that Riven had replaced Daddy and that Ethel was gone forever. But as Mommy told her time after time, Riven had only been protecting himself and hadn't wanted to kill Ethel. He'd needed to, or so Mommy had said before Mommy's memory went bad and she'd forgotten about Ethel.

Was Mommy's head somehow sick? How did she not remember Daddy and big sister?

Len had contemplated that question for quite a while but had no real answer. Whatever the case, Mommy seemed very happy with Riven now, and Riven wasn't ever mean to Len. So she was trying her best to fit into this new life of hers and focused on making friends at school, or learning magic from Tupper. Tupper was . . . not the greatest teacher Len had ever had, but he'd been nicest to her while here and not many people outside the staff or guards were allowed inside the mansion. Riven's sister, Allie, was just annoying, and Len ignored her most of the time whenever Allie tried to talk to her, but Len did like the nice grimoire Allie had given her after getting back to Panu. Maybe Len would finally take Allie up on her offer for private lessons if Tupper couldn't help as much as she'd like. But she didn't want to take that option unless she had to, because of how annoying Allie was.

Whatever the case, she needed to master a few spells in the next year to impress her classmates, to prove to them that she was just as Unholy as they were now that they'd all turned into undead children. She'd even been getting made fun of for being a high elf up until just a few days ago when the horns and purple eyes came on and her race changed from high elf into a hybrid elf-demon thingy. They'd definitely have treated her better if they knew who her mommy was, or, as much as she hated to say it, if they knew that Mommy wanted Riven to be Len's new daddy. Who would make fun of her, then, if they knew the king wanted to make Len a princess?

The thought made her internally recoil, though, on an instinctual level, even if she was trying to combat that kind of reaction. She was still angry and very sad about what'd happened and didn't have an outlet for her emotions other than when she complained about it to Tupper.

Yeah. At least she had Tupper.

A knock at the door caused Len to startle, and she fell off the bed with a thud. Angrily getting back up and thrusting her balled fists down with a ***HUMPH***, she stomped over to the door and began to turn the knob. Who was up at this late hour to bother her so? Was it Tupper again? He was usually in bed by this time, and the servants and guards he lorded over didn't dare mess with her sleeping hours.

"Tupper, is that you?!" Len called through the wood and yanked the door open a moment later. Her eyebrows lifted in surprise as she stared upward, and she quickly recognized the man standing there as the boyfriend of that annoying Allie person.

Len pointed accusingly with pooched lips. "You're Allie's guy. Why are you here bothering me?"

Lahn, for his part, raised his own eyebrows in amused surprise and put his hands on his hips while leaning against the doorframe. "I couldn't help but notice that you're still up. The light in your room is still on, I could hear you talking to your mom through the door, and Tupper and I just finished some late-night snacks before going to bed."

He shrugged and looked down the hallway in the direction of the staircase leading to the kitchen. "Allie went off with Kathrine into the city and left a note, so I'll be up for a while waiting for the girls to get back. I figured I'd ask you how your magical studies are coming along. Need any help?"

Skeptically, Len gave the bigger old man a once-over and snorted before whirling around and heading to the grimoire on her bed. Imperiously, she came back and thrust the book into Lahn's arms. "That's what I'm studying, but I can't get any spells to work. I was learning how to do plant magic at first, but since I got these horns my affinities have changed to Unholy, Sin, and Blood. I've never been able to cast any magic at all, even before the change, but the academy sent over a special guy when Tupper asked them to and they said that my affinities are very, very, very, very high!"

A smile cracked her lips, and Len couldn't contain her excitement at the idea. "So my chances of making spells are SO good now! But I still can't do it even while reading this boring stuff. Can you explain it in a way that a kid like me could understand?"

Lahn seemed more and more amused the longer Len spoke, but she ignored it. The adults always thought she was funny for one reason or another, so she just took those looks as they came and tried not to stab the man in front of her.

Maybe she'd poison some more cookies and give them to him later if he didn't stop belittling her with those stupid smiles that the adults always wore.

"Sure thing, Len." Lahn waved at her to follow him down the hall. "Want to head to the library? It's better lit in there, and I can at the very least help you with the Unholy aspect of your teachings. I know a few spells myself since becoming an undead, and both Unholy and Death are pretty high up there for my own affinities right now. Sin and Blood, though—I won't be able to demonstrate any of that for you."

Len hopped out of the room and excitedly raced after Lahn with a giggle. "That's okay! I'm just excited that you can help. Tupper is nice, but he's kind of bad at teaching."

Lahn snorted a laugh. "Don't say that! You're being mean."

"What?! It's true! The last time we tried to go over the grimoire, he blew up a cauldron and had to get a healer for his face!"

"Seriously?"

"Yeah! And he's a demon! Aren't demons supposed to be good at magic?!"

Lahn scratched his chin and turned, descending the stairs to the lower floors as moonlight trickled in through glass windows. "I would think that most are, but maybe not. Anyways, don't let him know that's what you think. He's very much taken a liking to teaching you, and it'd break his heart if he knew you thought he sucked!"

Len giggled again and bounced down the steps after Lahn. "Don't worry! I'm not a meanie or a bully. I won't say a word! That's a promise!"

Riven's party continued following the abyssal spirit guide King and Queen Rantali had bought for them back on Floor Twenty-Two after he'd befriended their son, who had dropped out of the Abyssal Descent a long time ago now. Riven's eyes shifted over the new sets of traits, including both boons and curses. Unholy Father with Daughter's Vengeance, Embrace Your Bloodline with Vampiric Abomination, and the Siblings' Pact with Thrall Cap.

The dark energies were growing harder, denser, and more potent the farther they delved, and that meant his attempts at meditation were growing in productivity as he laced pieces of his soul lattice together like threads in a tapestry. While he continued meditating on Azmoth's shoulder as their group continued down a long spiral staircase to Floor Forty-Five, he could also clearly see the pieces of soul lattice responsible for the curses plaguing him. They were intertwined with other functions of the soul pillars and core, but he and Gluttony both had confidence that they'd be able to purge the curses in due time. It may take a while, perhaps even years or decades, but it was doable. And he certainly didn't intend to have a figment of Ethel haunting him for all time, or a Thrall Cap, which would be the first he'd purge due to his hard limit on ten thralls. Even though he'd been angry with Athela and Fay about lying to him, their idea about having a blood farm was a good one. Thralls' blood was better in both quantity and quality and synergized with his own if he had turned them. He also had the trait Enhanced Thrall Minions, which boosted their power, obtaining it here in the descent for Genua's sake. Considering he had four thralls in the making inside Fay's pocket realm dungeon, he would have four including Genua after cutting Luke's connection, having let Luke Blissfallen go on a quest for his nephew. Er, son? Grandson?

Definitely not a daughter, though. Riven was pretty sure it had been a male relative.

Damn, he should really pay more attention to these things. Luke would be pissed if he knew Riven didn't even remember what kind of younger relative he'd gone looking for, but regardless of who or what, Riven wished the old man the best. Hopefully he'd even see Luke and his remaining family sometime soon after getting back to Panu, assuming Luke's quest had been successful.

Gah, he hated meditating. He'd completely lost track, and Riven let his eyes open with a grunt and an annoyed snort, allowing himself to finally see the oncoming portal leading into the next floor just ahead of them.

"Weirdo ahead," Athela stated, landing next to him in a flicker of blood that formed her body within milliseconds. She pointed a long red katana down the stairway. "Other side of the portal, eating a bunch of other descenders. Kind of like you when you get hungry, but this guy is a lot more gross about it? Really strong aura when I got in close, too. Comparable to yours or that dragonkin Hatchmire. Be wary."

Riven's vertical third eye opened up with a deep-purple light across the center of his forehead. "Noted."

Athela disappeared in another flash of blood, Fay continued circling overhead on outstretched wings, and Retesh seemed to be snoozing on Azmoth's other shoulder with his bony legs crossed and his hands behind his head.

Did elder liches even need to sleep?

Riven directed his attention to the oncoming portal, and then beyond it. From their direct vantage point, it was hard to tell what was beyond the large mass of swirling energy leading to the next floor. But when he really strained his senses, he was able to pick up faint heartbeats and a steady thrum of tainted energy.

By tainted, Riven truly meant it. There was lots of Sin or Unholy energy around, along with all the other aspects of the dark arts. But this particular flavor of energy was . . . odd, in a way that he'd never seen before. It was like touching a familiar painted masterpiece, only to find that instead of paint, the picture was created from crayons. The mana seemed to want to leave or escape whatever entity it was bound to beyond the portal, but for some reason it couldn't.

Mentally signaling Azmoth to halt when the abyssal spirit guide stopped at the next portal's edge, Riven dismounted his large brutalisk and let himself float to the obsidian stairway below, lightly touching down and then creating a portal to shift right. He flashed ahead in a blur of shadow and appeared on the rightmost side of the swirling orb of energies to behold a truly mesmerizing sight opposite the descending stairway.

Though some may have found it sickening, it spoke to Riven in a way that resonated with his gluttonous tendencies . . .

Five crucified victims had been flayed and left on large beams of wood, each of the victims placed at the tip of a five-pointed pentagram. The victims were still alive, but their energies were visibly being drained into the center of the circle. Maws similar to Gluttony's own, but corrupted and burgundy in color, hissed and gnawed at the air to consume the energy in the center of the ritual as a lone naked man on the outskirts tossed in body parts.

Probably the body parts he didn't want for himself, considering the disfigured man was eating from a pile of deceased men and women of various races while performing strange rites under the green light of two large candles. He had sickly, unnatural green veins that bulged and pulsed every couple seconds across much of his otherwise pale-white body. Blood covered much of his front, splattered across his face, and his eyes were pitch-black. His jaw split down the center, creating a three-way mouth that was unhinged from its sockets and extending far more than what a normal human would be able to do as he ate various pieces off the corpses and absorbed their items into a spatial sack off to the side.

Upon seeing Riven, the naked man quickly stopped what he was doing and snapped his attention to where Riven stood watching about fifty yards away. When he spoke, his voice was crazed, high-pitched, and even gleeful.

"So the rumors are true! You're actually here; you've actually arrived! Oh my! Have you finally come to partake? I knew you'd be coming! I just knew it!"

Riven's eyebrows raised, and the purple eye across his forehead narrowed. He recognized these people, this crucified group, along with some of the bodies in the pile nearby. They'd been on the same floor where Allie had ascended into the Angel of Wrath and had been particularly strong if he'd read their power levels correctly back then.

Messenger's gluttonous maw across his chest gave a warning hiss when the naked, bloodied stranger stood.

But the stranger raised his hands and stepped back placatingly, gesturing to the flayed victims crucified to the wooden poles around the pentagram. "I've even prepared some of the best of the Abyssal Descent as a feast in your honor, oh gluttonous one!"

Meh. Riven wouldn't say they'd been even close to the best, but yeah, these victims had certainly been strong.

Riven continued staring, ignoring the people crucified nearby, and leaned on Jackal to inch closer with more than a little bit of curiosity at the forefront of his thoughts. "What have you done to create those figments of Gluttony? They seem very off."

"Oh! Oh, they are wrong! Yes, yes, I'm glad you noticed! As expected of a reincarnation! Hee-hee!" The naked man giddily hopped from one leg to the other in what seemed to be anticipation, giggling madly to himself while muttering under his breath. "That's actually why I've been waiting for you after I heard you were delving! I was hoping you'd help me figure out what I'm doing wrong. You see, I actually cultivate Sin more than anything else . . . In particular, a variant version of Gluttonous Sin twisted into the shape of my soul core. Who better to ask about where I'm going wrong? But it's my own brand, unique to me, and if I don't fix this little problem and get rid of the impurities before my soul lattice completely solidifies . . ."

The naked man shrugged helplessly. He held up his bloody hands as his split jaw snapped out to either side with a long, fleshy tongue snapping forward and back in. "Then this entire trek through the Abyssal Descent will have been a waste for me! And I've killed far too many people to get to where I am now without results. With the bottom of the descent so close at hand, I am aware that I'm running out of time. So if you would . . . Please, partake in this feast with me, and hopefully we can come to some kind of agreement! I have a lot to trade after feasting on so many. I'd have more, too, if that damned Hatchmire prick hadn't nearly killed me after I set off one of Elysium's tribulations for insights into taboo practices, which left me weak. That is the way of the strong, though—they take what they want when they can get it!"

Riven pursed his lips and tore his eyes off the odd stranger to inspect the snapping maws in the pentagram's center. Fay landed beside him and Azmoth stood a bit farther back. Athela was nowhere to be seen as he gestured to the middle of the ritual with his staff.

"This pentagram is a representation of what you're trying to incorporate into your soul lattice, as an external construct? Like an additional pillar, I assume?"

The man eagerly nodded. "Yes, yes! So insightful! So grand!"

Fay scoffed loudly and tipped her witch's hat to cover her eyes with a head shake, then yelped surprisedly when Riven playfully jabbed her stomach with the butt of Jackal.

"Yes, quite grand indeed," Riven mused while examining the ritual in greater detail and listening to Gluttony's whispers in the back of his mind. "And just for curiosity's sake . . . What happens if I don't help you, oh naked one?"

"Oh, that's easy!" the man replied with a genuine smile, black eyes turning into large orbs and expanding as his skull began to crack as dark tears trickled down his face. "I'll just eat you and hope to absorb some of Gluttony's power for myself! That's about as fair of a bargain as you can get, methinks!"

CHAPTER 34

Riven's eyes narrowed and began to burn a bright crimson as the air shimmered around him, red snowflakes slowly accumulating. The entire massive, unnatural stairway they stood on shuddered as he flexed his aura, void sky around them thundering with crackling dark lightning.

"The fuck did that bitch just say to me?" Riven asked aloud, not taking his eyes off the naked guy who'd threatened to eat him only a second ago. "Did I just hear that motherfucker right? Or am I going crazy here?"

The naked man had talked about how Hatchmire had tried to kill him, but he'd managed to escape. That alone meant this individual was rather powerful, but not being as powerful as Hatchmire also meant that he wasn't overwhelmingly more powerful than Riven, either. It also matched Athela's read on the guy's general power level.

Athela was the one to speak next over the thundering storm accumulating around them. Her voice was flat and cold. "Do you think it wise to insult a reincarnation like that? Especially when you desire help?"

A long black tongue slithered out of her mouth, licking her lips as red katanas emerged from her chest and six arachnid blades sprouted from her back.

Fay took to the air in preparation for a fight with a flash of neon-blue lights budding from her tail, Retesh took a back line with dozens of spectral undead gathering around him as his own power flared, and Azmoth's enormous frame spread its flaming wings with the war hammer drawn wide.

The naked man giggled through his split three-way jaw, and the pulsing green veins along his pale, bloody body began to vibrate. Black eyes blinking rapidly for a moment, he held up a finger and cleared his throat while stepping around the pile of corpses and beyond one of the crucified victims that surrounded the pentagram. "No need to be offended, dear reincarnation! If you just do as I say, then there will be no problems! I merely wish to . . ."

[Floor Forty-Five: The Black Garden]

* * *

Bardog paced back and forth with his large hands clasped behind his back amid a black landscape of strange flora, underneath a pale-white sun in an otherwise dark sky. The barbarian's horned helmet was slick with blood, even more so than his chest, arms, and two-handed battle-axe embedded in one of the teammates that naked bastard had tagged along with.

Once again, he glared out at the portal leading up to the previous floor. He couldn't go back up a floor without using a space-breaking ritual, and so he was stuck there thinking about his friends dying without him there to help. Bardog's empire had tasked him with making sure the five teams of delvers into the Abyssal Descent made it out intact, and Bardog had utterly failed after their most recent encounter. Arrogance had gotten the better of both him and his men. He was certainly strong, perhaps in the first percentile even here, but the true cultivation monsters of the multiverse that made it as far as he had . . . Many of them were impossibly strong for F-grades.

The strange, masked three-armed man radiating Sin, the twin princes of Vilheld, Charmar of Tactulis, Hatchmire of the First Draconic Fist, the lady formed from harvested souls, and, to his despair, the naked man with black eyes and the split mouth who'd called himself Caker. Just Caker. They were all titans among their same-tier peers, army killers and pillars of the Unholy path should they reach the higher realms of ascension. Those were only the ones he'd encountered, too, and it made him wonder just how many of these monsters existed here in the deep parts of the multiverse.

"How long until the ritual is complete?" Bardog barked at two of his teammates, the mages he'd brought along for his personal squad.

The mages held up a hand signaling three or four minutes.

That was three or four minutes too long.

Everyone else was tending to their wounds among the strange gardens of black plants and prepping to go back up after the way was opened, if it was even possible. The naked man, Caker, hadn't followed his team through the portal, likely knowing that the numbers game would leave him vulnerable. Despite that ugly bastard Caker being an elite among elites, even he would have a problem against the full might of all five of Bardog's teams put together.

Or what remained of them.

So Caker had very likely stayed behind to wait for another delving party to come by in order to ask for help, or the sick fucker was performing some of those disgusting rituals on Bardog's friends even as he stood there thinking about it. Bardog needed to get back up as soon as possible, and he was literally starting to itch with worry about the fates of his charges as he helplessly stood by and watched the flickering sphere where the staircase between floors forty-four and forty-five had dropped them off.

Suddenly, one of the mages shot to his feet and screamed, "EVERYONE, GET BACK!"

Bardog had absolute faith in the ritualist and immediately sprinted for cover without second-guessing the order. The same could be said for all the other members of their bloodied expedition, and that fact saved many of their lives.

The portal pulsed, and with a flare of crimson energy a figure cannonballed through from the other side. Caker, the naked madman, broke the sound barrier and emitted a shock wave as his mangled body ripped through the landscape in a spray of debris.

Bardog's eyes widened in shock, and he was about to call for an attack when another hooded figure blurred out of the portal in the next second with black lightning and rivers of blood roaring around his body like a cyclone.

Immediately the newcomer, a vampire with brilliant-crimson eyes, launched an enormous bolt of black lightning out of his skull-topped staff that ripped the ground apart in a direct line for two miles out.

Bardog had to cover his ears due to the destructive noise and felt frost accumulating on his body as the man's oppressive aura clamped down on the surroundings like a vise grip.

Caker, however, wasn't out of the fight. He took the destructive bolt of dark lightning with an outstretched hand in the crater his body had created and screamed with a mixture of pain and crazed glee as the flesh was ripped off his arm down to the bone.

But the flesh reknit itself quickly to form a fleshy spear off the mutilated arm, and the naked madman took a step forward as space itself warped. Caker lunged and thrust ahead, extending the point of his arm-spear a mile's length within the course of a second only for a flash-freeze effect to radiate off the vampire in a half sphere going forward.

The sphere made contact with the arm's extension, and Caker's arm shattered entirely with the madman recoiling back.

"YOU BASTARD! THAT WAS—"

Caker was interrupted by a trio of solid red lances wrapped in Sin and Shadow that left crackling tears in space like trailing ribbons. The three projectiles crashed into his chest, abdomen, and lower jaw, tearing out swaths of bone and flesh and sending him deeper into the crater he'd created with another cloud of stony debris being tossed into the air. The last strike nearly decapitated the madman, but not entirely.

Caker retaliated with an earth-shattering roar as his body ruptured on its own, sending streams of green and burgundy vines from tears in his flesh that roiled out toward the enemy mage. Tiny jaws by the dozens and then hundreds opened up at the ends of those vines and whipped around like seeker missiles as they closed in on the flying caster in the sky.

The vampire flicked his wrist and summoned four totems along with a thunderclap of power that produced thousands of spinning blades that screamed toward the vines like a hornet swarm.

Caker's attack barely managed to penetrate the oncoming cloud before being utterly shredded and smashed into a solid barrier of crimson ice that flashed into existence with the totems piling layers behind it as the maws began digging through.

Caker gagged, and then lurched forward as if to vomit, only to spew out a stream of acid that destroyed most of the oncoming blades as the ground between them shattered and melted in hundreds of explosions.

That was when Bardog noticed a large shadow covering the sun, only for a burst of propelling flame to erupt overhead and a huge figure's descent to follow.

CRACK

A building-sized flaming demon blurred from the heavens like an asteroid to shatter the realm below, with an enormous stone maul simmering with magma leading the landing. The attack caused fissures to tear open in the landscape for miles, smashing Caker's body flat into the dirt like a pancake. Caker tried to claw his way out from underneath the enormous maul while burning alive and screaming curses, only for a dome of fire to encompass the huge archdemon as the burning titan of metal and flesh let out an evil cackle.

The dome of fire caged Caker and turned the earth beneath them into a bubbling pit of magma, and one of four clawed hands crashed down onto Caker's squirming body, dunking it back into the magma and squeezing the life out of the man.

Caker's gurgling cries escalated into an unusually high-pitched scream before a shock wave of Unholy energy pulsed out in a pillar of green light, eradicating the giant's clawed hand as the flaming monster's eellike maws reeled around from his back to breathe fire onto the madman.

But Caker's spell had torn a hole through the top of the dome, and the bastard launched himself through it, only to be sniped with another one of those incredibly fast crimson lances wreathed in black.

The attack tore off another of Caker's arms, only for it to regrow even faster than his previous wounds had done, but he was sent spiraling into the ground yet again, where he hit some kind of invisible runic trap. The sigil, hidden until the man collided with it, flashed green and then set off a chain reaction of other previously hidden traps that all simultaneously exploded around him, ripping him apart over and over again as the offensive magic tried to annihilate him while his insane regeneration stopped it from happening.

After a solid ten seconds of explosions, a dull quiet settled over the battlefield as Bardog gawked at the exchange. Because there, standing in the rubble, was Caker, showing off his nude body where the last remnants of his wounds were rapidly sealing shut again. How was that even possible? The number of times Bardog had seen the man's intestines torn out, limbs ripped off, brain splattered, and bones shattered had been many dozens in that last exchange.

And just who were these people fighting Caker, anyways? Should Bardog help them?

Caker's laughter echoed across the stunned silence and through the airborne dust and debris. He pointed up at the vampire and called out, "This would have been a lot easier if you'd just talked to me instead of taking my threat as an insult! I was being honest—you don't have to die! I'll even forgive this little transgression of yours and not eat you if you just help me with my soul lattice concept! What say you, Gluttony? Surely you don't want to lose the host you only just recently found, right? I've heard compatible hosts for the original sins are quite hard to find, especially good ones. So don't make me kill the one you're in now."

Bardog's eyes widened in shock, and he looked again at the man hovering hundreds of yards off the ground with a swirling storm of black and red around him.

The vampire laughed, loudly, and it wasn't a fake one, either. It was a genuinely amused chuckle that turned into full-blown laughter as he doubled over in the sky, clutching at his gut. "You crazy bastards are always the most fun to fight!"

"You cannot win this!" Caker said during their pause, cracking his neck and grinning back at the laughing caster above him. He held up his hands to either side to show off his body. "As you can see, I am completely unharmed. It would be good of you to just accept my demand and help, would it not? There is no need for violence!"

"The fuck are you talking about, asshole?! You're the one who said you'd eat me first!"

"I only said I'd do that if you didn't help! You can't kill me, so do as I ask before I get serious!"

The vampire's laughter faded, and he scoffed audibly. "Well, you certainly need to work on your people skills! And threatening those more powerful than you probably isn't a good idea! It's blatantly obvious by watching you regenerate that you're drawing on the people you've eaten to replenish your damaged body, yes?"

Caker's smile became crooked.

The vampire's eyes flared with delight. "As I thought. It is just as you said! I, too, am of a gluttonous concept—it's not hard to figure out! I wonder just how many bodies you've stuffed into that little intrinsic concept core of yours anyways!"

The two remained silent after that for a time, until Caker's expression was replaced with a sneer. "Enough bodies to last me years of continuous battle, reincarnation. I have killed and consumed an entire world to get to where I am now, to ensure my continued growth. But the time for talk is over. I will kill you, and eat your corpse, and in the process will discover what makes Gluttony click. PREPARE TO MEET THE GRAVE!"

Both of his arms became rigid burgundy blades of flesh that pulsed with scattered Unholy lights. "You will regret not having taken my offer when I feast upon your corpse!"

Suddenly Caker wasn't there anymore, and a moment later he appeared behind the flying vampire while bringing both fleshy blades down on the caster's back.

A stream of flesh unwrapped itself off the vampire's body to take the form of an Arshakai demon. She withdrew her twin katanas in milliseconds to block both of Caker's blades, while six sharpened arachnid limbs whipped forward to impale and then truly decapitate the madman.

Caker's head reattached itself to his body in the next second, only to be met with a cursed fireball the size of a horse. He teleported again, only to appear within another invisible land mine that ripped open his spine before yet another bolt of green fire launched from the outstretched wand of a flying succubus burned away his recently regrown left leg. Then another cursed flame smashed into him, and then another, and another.

Caker created a wall of bones to defend against a rain of cursed energies, only for it to be smashed aside when the titanic flaming demon used a propulsion ability to barrel through the defensive spell. The maul's swing only barely missed its mark when Caker teleported again, but he was struck from the sky with another arc of black lightning. A brutal spinning kick from the Arshakai rogue then torpedoed him back into the ground, where the flaming giant trapped him yet again with another dome of flame and tried to drown him in the lava.

All the while, the vampire overhead was simply laughing.

Bardog's men on the other side had been butchered for the most part, but they did manage to retrieve five of the survivors that Caker had begun to crucify for a ritual that hadn't been finished. Half of those that'd followed him into the Abyssal Descent were dead, but at least he'd saved some of them.

Or rather, the vampire warlock and his minions still beating the ever-living shit out of Caker had saved Bardog's men. Even if unwittingly.

He'd taken up a position on one of the hills to watch the fireworks play out, and the battle had been going on for hours now. It was like watching an unstoppable force meet an immovable object, where overwhelming power met overwhelming resilience. Caker managed to strike back at the vampire numerous times throughout the fight and did some rather serious damage to the large tanking flame demon over the course of the battle. At least, Bardog thought it'd been serious damage, but the brutalisk wasn't showing any signs of slowing down or being in any pain despite the numerous scars of Sin energy and deep trench wounds along its body. If anything, the brutalisk had become invigorated with the fight, being able to smash and tear Caker apart bit by bit on repeat.

But aside from a few glancing blows against the flying warlock and the majority of the damage done to the front-line tank, Caker had been unable to land a single strike against the Arshakai rogue or the support succubus higher up. Whenever he did manage to get free of the brutalisk's grasp, the succubus's illusions quickly redirected Caker into optimal positions before the rogue snared and repeatedly stabbed or decapitated him. If he managed to break through the domes of flame the brutalisk produced, get past the rogue, and force his way through the illusions by flexing his Sin aura, the warlock himself would smack Caker right back down into another crater for his minions to pile on.

It was truly a sight for sore eyes. Bardog wished he could participate in this brutal display of violence, but the more he watched, the more he realized that both sides of this fight were miles beyond his own abilities. If he'd gone up against the vampire warlock, he'd simply be annihilated. And where he'd previously thought himself a possible match for Caker, Bardog now realized he'd been wrong. The madman simply regenerated anything and everything done to him, and Bardog was thankful that Caker hadn't pursued him onto Floor Forty-Five after the initial fight. It hadn't been cowardice on Caker's part—it'd simply been that Caker didn't find Bardog interesting or worthy enough to pursue.

The truth stung a bit, but Bardog had to face facts when watching the vampire pour millions of units of energy into abilities to attempt to subdue the madman, only for Caker to somehow still remain alive. He was like an ugly, vicious cockroach, and many of Bardog's men were taking bets on who would win this battle of attrition. Would it be the vampire and his immense mana pool that ran out first? Or would it be the seemingly endless source of regeneration, and, if Caker had been honest, the seemingly endless source of bodies that he'd harvested and eaten in the past for regeneration purposes?

Bardog still wasn't entirely sold on the idea that the warlock above them was actually a reincarnation of Gluttony—given Caker's little speech, the naked man was truly crazy after all—but then again, it wouldn't surprise Bardog all that much after watching the display of true might whenever the warlock raised his staff to attack. The landscape, once a pristine swath of valleys and hills full of flowering abyssal plants, was now a smoldering ruin, completely glassed for dozens of miles around them.

Hours turned into days, and days turned into two entire weeks before Caker started attempting to run.

When running didn't work, he turned absolutely feral and began cursing the team keeping him pinned here. Bardog couldn't help but let on a self-satisfied and shit-eating grin as he noticed the regeneration starting to slow, and as Caker's desperate struggles grew more heated, Bardog finally witnessed the last showdown.

An absolute barrage of blood, shadow, and sin tore Caker's body apart rapidly in a steady stream of mana that lasted for nearly five minutes straight. And when it was apparent that Caker didn't have much more to give, the vampire descended and began to eat the man alive as Caker's body still struggled to regenerate the scattered pieces of flesh that had been torn off his skeleton.

The crazed man's screams of anguish as he was eaten were all that Bardog had wanted to hear and more. It was priceless. With that, Bardog could leave with a clear conscience after knowing that the man who'd murdered so many of his friends was meeting a similar fate. But perhaps . . . perhaps it wasn't a good idea to stick around.

He didn't know how the abnormally strong vampire or his ridiculous minions would react to his own party, and it didn't take long for the remnants of the five groups to come to a unanimous agreement that they would be leaving the Abyssal Descent entirely when they reached the end of this floor. Within minutes they were headed off to where they suspected the end of Floor Forty-Five was located, and in only hours, they had left the darkness of the abyss entirely.

From another hilltop far away, Retesh the lich continued to meditate in a lotus position to the sound of prolonged violence.

CHAPTER 35

[Floor Forty-Nine: The City of Wandering Souls: Congratulations on making it to the second-to-last floor of the Abyssal Descent. On this and the next floor, you are unable to do damage to anyone else present and Elysium will strike down anyone who tries to harm you. While on Floor Forty-Nine, you will have access to unique vendors only found here, along with their extremely valuable E-grade growth items of immense power, godlike traits, otherwise forbidden abilities, taboo artifacts, and upgrades that you won't be able to find anywhere else as long as you have the necessary performance credits. This opportunity will never come again—choose what you wish to purchase wisely.

- You may only spend performance credits while here, though you may trade performance credits or items with other individuals who managed to arrive on Floor Forty-Nine. All of Athela's, Genua's, Azmoth's, Narg's, and Fay's performance credits have been given to you, their master.
- Total performance credits earned: 1,309,700

You may choose to move on to Floor Fifty: the Seat of Abyssal Power, at your leisure with but a thought after you spend at least one week on Floor Forty-Nine. There you will find an ultimate source of abyssal energy and will be granted a single opportunity to build your soul lattice under some of the most potent dark energies available to any F-grade. These energies are specifically cultivated to help F-grades ascend into the E-grade while building soul lattices. How you perform while finishing your soul lattice on the last floor, paired with how you performed on the way down, will determine your overall score and any additional prizes that the Abyssal Descent provides before you ascend to E-grade.

Lillith of the Black Skies will be freed from imprisonment when you arrive on Floor Fifty.

<u>Concerning your Chalgathi trial</u>**: Successfully completing the Abyssal Descent will result in fifty points. Completing in the top one hundred contenders will result in three hundred points. Completing this event in the top five contenders will result in one thousand points. Finishing first will result in three thousand points.]**

Riven materialized alongside all his minions, ALL of them, on a long, glowing, ethereal pale-blue road leading to a city made from spiritual plasma. Ghostly spires with distant lights of souls dancing illuminated the darkness, and there was no one else in sight beyond the ghosts and phantoms intermingling with the smaller specks of illumination.

His attention flitted to Narg, who he hadn't seen in many weeks now. The beholder demon's green skin looked sickly, wrinkled, and pale, and the orange central eye was dilated while all the others on stalks were closed. He drooled through razor teeth onto the glowing road beneath them and was unresponsive when Azmoth poked him with a foot.

"I will carry," Azmoth said, shrinking down and picking up the smaller demon in two clawed hands before coming over to stand next to Genua. "Lillith will know what to do."

Riven frowned at the state of his fourth minion but nodded in agreement. He didn't know what was wrong with the beholder, but it was very obvious that whatever bloodline curse had afflicted Narg still wasn't completely dealt with. "Yeah, Lillith will probably know what to do. Let's go."

Briefly walking over to Genua and nuzzling his nose up against Iris's face, he tickled the child and got her to laugh before moving on ahead while the elf thrall smiled behind him at a slow trot. There was no reason to rush anymore, and it would be down to how Riven performed on the very last floor while creating his soul lattice that really solidified whether he'd make the top spot.

Luckily for Riven, he kind of had a cheat. Gluttony would be helping him along the way, and Riven was curious about what kind of second class he'd get.

Kara Blackbow took in a sharp breath, coming out of Fay's pocket realm prison at the succubus's prodding, and the drow's fingers tightened into fists while her eyes went wide underneath her ranger's hood. "I can't believe I'm actually standing here right now."

Athela aggressively slapped her ass, producing a yelp, and then prodded her forward with a wink. "You can not-believe-it all you want, just keep walking! We have credits to spend!"

"Speaking of which, how many did you get?" Fay asked curiously, stepping in beside the other women and behind Riven as the warlock led the way up front.

Kara glanced hopefully down at a system notification and then dismissed it a moment later. "Twenty-two thousand, two hundred performance credits in total. Is that good?"

Fay winced a bit and adjusted her witch's hat after shrinking her horns down to the smaller versions that only protruded two inches from her forehead. "Well, Riven has over a million by a good chunk, but he's also not the norm here and has a combined pool between all his minions. So that's, like, six people total all pooled into his pocket for spending."

"It'll probably be enough to buy SOMETHING! We just won't know what that is until we find the vendors," Athela exclaimed, leaning into the drow and pulling her close while shooting the elder lich nearby a raised eyebrow. "Yo, bag of bones, how many performance credits did you get?"

Retesh didn't bother looking their way, clicking his staff against the ethereal road with every other step he took. "One hundred and ten thousand, five hundred performance credits, but as you said, we don't know if that's bad or good yet. It is to be determined based on what is available and at what prices."

The lich's skull flared with neon-teal flame from the eye sockets, and he began to pick up the pace to catch up with Riven in front. "I'm quite excited to find out. I've never heard of a vendor being able to sell traits, which implies that this will be a rather unique experience."

Inside the ghostly city was far, FAR more lively than anyone had anticipated. And it was full of a lot more than just ghosts and souls, even by the local denizen standards. Various demons and other undead called this place home, with a fair share of other mortal races oriented toward the Unholy foundational pillar. Surprisingly enough, there were a couple hundred other delvers there who were partying to their hearts' content while being under the direct protection of Elysium, and Riven certainly couldn't blame them after what it'd taken to get to this point. After talking with a few of the unusually happy drunkards, it appeared that you could stay here for up to five years, and many people from the last cycle of the descent's opening were actually still here for it. Many of them had refused to ascend into the E-grade in order to escape the reach of their faction elders or parents, and it was very common to find that most were prestigious scions that hailed from great powers of the multiverse. Here, though, with an absolute protection guarantee, they could do whatever they wanted until they were forcefully kicked out or they ran out of performance credits to spend, as it was the only thing the local vendors would take unless people wanted to trade among themselves. Performance credits drove the entire economy here, which became clear to Riven almost instantly as the locals threw themselves at delvers to offer services of many varieties.

The City of Wandering Souls had thus become a place of absolute debauchery. Drinking halls, bars, swingers' clubs, drug dens, gambling rings, and whorehouses were in abundance. And given the fact that Riven was exhausted from his own trek down, he carelessly indulged himself in much of it that very first day but made it very clear to everyone that they'd be out of here as soon as the mandatory week's stay was over with. He needed to free Lillith, build up his soul lattice, and move on to win Chalgathi's trial—if that was at all possible given the months he'd spent here and the likely massive lead his counterparts in the Chalgathi trials had on him now.

Nevertheless, he didn't have much of a choice in the matter and had some time to burn, and the first day was a lot of fun. He got incredibly drunk, lost a few games of cards to some cheating skresh bloke by the name of Steve, and rented a room in one of the strange ethereal hotels. Ordering room service, he was even able to let out the soon-to-be volunteer thralls from Fay's prison realm, which was a first. Fay had been unable to do so before now, and they weren't technically his minions yet, but the yellow-and-purple merwoman witch, along with the white-scaled draconic warrior and the half-ogre barbarian, all joined him at the dinner table as extravagant amounts of high-quality food were ordered with extremely minimal expense on the credit side of things. It appeared that Elysium wanted to reward those that made it this far, and the entire feast along with a side of alcohol and powdered amphetamine-like drugs was only eight credits in total. They then went to the equivalent of a theater to see a play, turned up at a dance club, and made friends with a few of the other delvers from some obscure shrouded-in-shadows origin empire that Riven's party didn't push for further information.

The group went back to their rented space for even more food, drugs, and alcohol before he passed out early when Fay and an extremely drunk Genua had basically force-fed him some green cider that smelled like oranges. It was great stuff, but damn, did it kick hard, and he couldn't handle staying awake after that.

The next day was another story entirely, though, when he woke up with a killer headache that throbbed like the dickens. He didn't know how many hours had passed, but he felt like it'd been at least twelve.

"Jesus Christ . . ." He groaned, rubbing at his forehead and blinking the bleariness from his eyes before pushing himself off the large bed where someone had tucked him in. Smiling at that fact and noticing that no one else was there, he carefully extracted himself from the room while shutting the door softly behind him.

The girls were nowhere to be seen, and Retesh was long gone, too, though he'd left his staff in one corner of the room near where Narg's body was still shuddering and unresponsive. Otherwise it was just his daughter, Iris, and Azmoth, there in the center of the main room.

Iris was currently watching the equivalent of television with Azmoth on a large fluffy couch, giggling and making baby talk while entranced by the screen on the wall.

"How's she doing?" Riven asked, plopping down next to the brutalisk baby-sitter with a slight bounce. "Oh, you are just so dang cute, Iris! I can't believe you're so adorable! Yes you are!"

Patting her head and taking the baby from Azmoth to hold in his own lap, he received a fist bump from the brutalisk, who stood up and went over to a large counter full of various foodstuffs on trays.

"Iris doing well, she very curious. About everything," Azmoth said, picking up four large steaks and inhaling the meat before moving on to a jug full of sparkling liquid. "Very happy baby. How you sleep?"

"I slept great, but I feel like I was punched in the head a few times."

Azmoth snickered. "Genua is funny drunk. I like her. She nice, but makes everyone drink more just like Athela, and she called Len three times. After you pass out, Fay puke in bathroom and Kara fall asleep on floor while I babysit Iris, but I like babysit Iris."

The large demon chugged the jug of liquid, wiped his face, and stole a large cake off the counter before sitting back down next to Riven and Iris on the couch. He gave a small piece of torn-off cake to the baby girl, who ravenously reached out and chomped down on the dessert before the brutalisk pulled back into a relaxed position. "Even Retesh get drunk."

"I didn't realize an elder lich could get drunk."

"It a spiritual brew. That what he say."

Riven smiled down at his daughter when her tiny hands grasped one of his fingers and began to play with her as she giggled in his lap. "Huh. Interesting. Well, we learn something new every day lately, that's for sure. Where are the others, by the way? They obviously got up before I did."

"You sleep long time, yes. They all very hungover and went to find potions before looking in market. They try to find vendors the notification talk about, where traits and treasures sold."

Riven bobbed his throbbing head, staring at the mounted TV where nothing less than some kind of kids' show was being aired. His jaw dropped when he saw that it was about a little ghoul kid growing up in an Unholy society of some kind here in the abyss, where his death-priest parents were teaching him how to sacrifice people to the Scythe.

This probably wasn't the greatest material for his daughter to watch at the prime age of only a few weeks old, but he didn't know how to change the channel and didn't want to look stupid asking.

A knock at the door sounded, and when Azmoth told them to come in, Riven saw his three soon-to-be thrall volunteers enter in a single-file line. The draconic warrior, merwoman witch, and half-ogre barbarian stood staring his way after lining up against the wall.

"You guys have a good time last night?" Riven asked, putting his feet up on a nearby coffee table to lean back and tickling Iris relentlessly. "I hope so, I had a great time."

The draconic nodded enthusiastically. "Yes, Master Riven. None of us have had even an inkling of freedom for until millennia, so participating in the festivities was certainly a boon to be cherished. Thank you for allowing us out of the prison so that we could participate."

The draconic bowed low at the waist, and the merwoman with yellow skin, gills along her neck, and purple hair clasped her hands in front of her before speaking in turn.

"It is truly appreciated, Master. Thank you for your supreme generosity."

She, too, bowed low, and the half ogre just grunted his acknowledgment, but nothing more.

Riven raised an eyebrow. "Is Zafima still inside Fay's dungeon?"

"Yes, Master," the draconic said, straightening his posture. "The drow prisoner is still undergoing her ascension into thrallhood and is strung up with chains from the ceiling inside Fay's realm. Because she is fighting the process, it is taking far longer than we who are willing."

"Is Fay still delivering my venom to you regularly, then?"

"Yes," the merwoman said, cutting off the draconic and stepping forward with an eager-to-please and ass-kissing smile. "We take it regularly, and the transition for each of us is going well. I will most likely be the first to officially enter into your service as a thrall, likely because I am the most powerful of us three, and I can already feel the changes overcoming my body as the vampiric virus empowers me."

The ogre snorted at her words but didn't appear to care much that the witch thought she was the strongest. The draconic warrior, however, hissed in her direction with a barely concealed snarl.

"Fay said it was you who was captured first, therefore you certainly cannot be the strongest!"

The witch seemed taken aback. "She said no such thing! How dare you try to make me look bad in front of our savior and master!"

"How dare you assume to be the best of us three when we've not even sparred a single time!" the draconic retorted with folded clawed arms.

The two started bickering like an old married couple, and Riven was thoroughly amused that these weaklings would care about arguing over who was more powerful or who was captured by Fay first. Then again, *weakling* was a relative term. They were each level 200 and would soon be flooded with power from his own bloodline as he made them into thralls, and level 200 even by itself wasn't anything to scoff at back on Panu. When the average level was somewhere around sixty for anyone with a combat class, Panu was still quite new. These three would doubtless be considered powerhouses back home.

Eventually it started to spiral out of control, though, when the draconic shoved the merwoman after she'd conjured an orb of basic Unholy mana, and Riven flexed his aura in warning before the two could come to outright blows. "Did any of you three get performance credits?"

The three soon-to-be thralls quickly stepped into line.

"No, Master!" the merwoman replied in a sickly-sweet singsong voice, dismissing her spell. "We didn't get any! I don't think the Abyssal Descent considered us as participants in the event, and probably for good reason."

The ogre acknowledged this statement with a confirmatory grunt.

Riven yawned and handed Iris over to Azmoth when the eager brutalisk gestured to hold the little girl again, and he smiled at how cute it was to see Azmoth—a child in his own right—being so gentle and protective of the baby.

"Well, do you three have names?" Riven eventually asked after a long silence where the three people stood against the wall without moving an inch. "Any names at all?"

The three glanced at one another, but none of them had an answer.

Riven sighed. "I'm assuming that's a resounding NO? As in, NO, you do NOT have actual names?"

"We can't remember them," the draconic replied nonchalantly, shrugging. "We were trapped in that blood-sea realm for eons, without bodies or people to communicate with. We have no idea what our names were back then."

"Perhaps you'd do us the favor of naming us yourself?" the merwoman asked, eyes wide with excitement and gills flaring. "I've been wanting a name ever since I came out of that dreadful place!"

Riven didn't think that was a bad idea. "Yeah, I can do that. But are you sure you'd not want to name yourselves?"

The half ogre cleared his throat, leaning against the wall. "We have already discussed this between ourselves and wish you to name us. Please, proceed."

"Are you sure?" Riven pressed.

He got three simultaneous nods.

"I'm pretty bad at naming."

Not a peep from the three ahead of him.

"And you're A-okay with that?"

Each of them nodded yet again.

Clicking his tongue and not putting more than a minute's worth of brainstorming into the effort, Riven nonchalantly named the three after each of their races. He pointed to the draconic: "Your name is LIZARD."

He pointed to the merwoman. "Your name is FISH."

Lastly, he pointed to the half ogre. "Your name is BRUTE."

He threw up his hands in mock celebration. "There! The three of you have names, congratulations! Now, if you don't like them, please let me know now. It's what I'll be calling each of you from now on, so if you don't mind them, better get used to it."

CHAPTER 36

Retesh stayed behind to watch over Narg and let the girls know where Riven had gone, but Riven had no intentions of just sitting around doing nothing while waiting. Plus, he'd strengthened his connection to all his minions while here in the descent. They could all telepathically communicate with him now, outside of Narg, who'd not been present on the floors where he'd gained such boons, and all of them had a general idea of where he was at any given time through the solidified soul links chaining them all together.

So, realistically, they were just as likely to ask him directly or even locate him on their own rather than ask Retesh after he'd left their rented room. He didn't know what they were up to, but he was glad to see that they were all getting along and having a good time. He could feel them a few blocks away and up a few floors in one of the skyscrapers, but Riven decided to let them do their thing and didn't head there directly given the extra time he'd be spending here anyways.

Meanwhile, Lizard, Fish, and Brute followed close behind Riven and Azmoth as the leading duo walked through the lower marketplace of the strange, ethereal city. They were eager to please and after beginning to talk to the three, Riven found that the three volunteer soon-to-be thralls had forgotten a lot about life in general. Questions about basic household items, clothes, where they were, and the taste of food were hot topics among the three, which led to Riven buying them a lot of different foodstuffs from stall vendors along their stroll.

The vendors were abundant enough, that was for sure, and they eagerly tried to get Riven, who was an obvious delver here in the descent, to spend his points at businesses owned by the locals by letting him sample small quantities of the street food for free.

"Iris seems to like it," Riven said, smiling and holding his baby daughter as she made a mess with some kind of icy, creamy, and very sugary golden paste a phantom had been selling in jars. It could only be described as a semiliquid cake, and Riven had already cleaned out a few of the jars himself before stashing a couple dozen inside his spatial bag.

It was important to have soft food for Iris anyways, since he didn't want her choking on anything, so he'd bought the vendor out entirely for the relatively absurd price of a couple hundred performance credits.

Fish hummed with delight and slurped from her own jar with a laugh. "This is amazing!"

"I can't say I remember eating anything this good before," Lizard chimed in, nodding his scaled white head with an open jar in either hand. "Thank you for the gesture, Riven."

Brute scoffed at Lizard with a large roll of his eyes and trudged along, already having eaten his share. "You can't remember eating anything this good because you don't remember almost anything at all, you dimwit!"

"Yes, yes, that's true," Lizard said, scratching the back of his neck with his tail. "No need to be rude, though! I'm just enjoying the moment, unlike you, you gluttonous troll thing."

"Can I hold your baby?!" Fish asked, and the merwoman jogged ahead to walk alongside Riven. "Please?"

Riven eyed Fish skeptically and shook his head. "Not to be mean, but not yet. After you three have actually become thralls, then sure. But until then I can't be entirely sure that I trust you yet."

"But afterward I for sure can?" Fish pressed eagerly, staring down at the baby girl in Riven's arms.

Riven nodded. "Of course."

"Great!" Fish fell back in line. "I can wait until then! I just think your daughter is adorable, so don't think I have nefarious intentions!"

"Oh, I don't! But safe is better than sorry," Riven replied, stopping briefly as a notification hit him.

[Your minion Athela has requested to utilize 292 performance credits for a purchase. Accept? Decline?]

[Your minion Fay has requested to utilize 311 performance credits for a purchase. Accept? Decline?]

[Your minion Genua has requested to utilize 197 performance credits for a purchase. Accept? Decline?]

Having more than 1.3 million credits to spend, he accepted each request and smirked to himself while heading toward the Ascended District, which was where all the really good stuff was supposed to be. Hopefully they'd found something good on their day out, as it was now obvious they were on a shopping trip with Kara.

Speaking of which . . .

He turned around and looked over the three soon-to-be thralls. They still wore the same clothes they'd come with after exiting that blood portal where

Riven had fought the clam, and none of them had any weapons anymore since Fay hadn't bothered taking what she'd called "junk" when originally abducting the three. Their clothes were rather worse for wear, too. In Lizard's case, he only sported boots and pants, while Fish wore a short, stained witch's outfit and Brute had on thick studded leathers over his pale-green skin.

They really needed some new stuff, and he didn't even know what their affinities were. If Narg was able to communicate and wasn't in a state of everlasting seizure, Riven would have also bought him some new things as well. But despite their attempts to heal the beholder demon, he didn't react to any potions or healing spells they had at their disposal, so he'd likely have to wait until they reached Lillith for insight. Truly disappointing, considering that Narg had missed out on over half of the entire Abyssal Descent along with associated rewards.

Maybe if Riven saw something he thought the beholder demon would like, he'd get it just in case. Riven kinda felt bad for the guy, as he'd been so eager to please on the earlier floors, like when he'd saved Nora from death at the hands of that burned titan chained in a lava pit.

"Hey, Azmoth, go ahead and accompany these three to a tailor or clothes vendor of some sort." Riven gestured at the poorly equipped Fish, Brute, and Lizard. "Ask the vendor how to send me a request if you can't figure it out by yourself and buy them a few outfits each."

Azmoth grunted the affirmative and pointed in the direction from whence they came. "I saw vendor with clothes in window back two streets that way."

"Thank you for your generosity, esteemed one," Lizard commented with another low bow, and Fish smiled in delight while doing the same. Brute just copied Azmoth's grunt with folded arms.

Riven waved them off and watched them disappear into the crowds, and seeing that Iris had fallen asleep after finishing her jar of sweetened paste, he chuckled and moved on ahead.

It was time to see what kinds of floor rewards were available to him with the given number of points they'd collected.

The Ascended District was in the very center of the ethereal city and entirely encased by a large pyramid-shaped roof. It was held up on a platform with each of the four corners supported by one of the downtown skyscrapers and was far less busy than Riven would have expected it to be. The only other customers here were other individual delvers or teams of delvers from what he could see, with none of the natives shopping here. There were natives working in the stores, though, which were far more ornate than anything found down in the lower city, but there were only four of these stores in total with enormous amounts of various treasures in each glass storefront. The interior of each was even larger than Riven had expected and was spatially expanded when he briefly looked inside the first of them, and just from the aura cast out from some of these objects, he could tell that he wanted nearly everything here.

"Morgana's Traits and Upgrades, Jitzi's Growth Items, Dao Taboos and Treasures, and the Skill Shop." Riven read the names off the signs hanging over each entrance and began walking back into the closest of them, Morgana's Traits and Upgrades, to begin his shopping trip.

The smell of familiar perfume hit him full force when Athela teleported out of the shadows nearby. "Hey, baby! How's the kid?!"

"Just in time," Riven said, handing Iris over to an excited Athela, who was making "gimme" motions with her hands. "Don't wake her up, though, she just fell asleep. Where are the others?"

He looked around the spatially expanded room, where an arched ceiling full of sprouting crystals illuminated various displays and shelves of goods while a handful of other delvers commented on or examined the goods with local employees.

"Still shopping!" she said, upbeat and leaning into him with a loving nudge as they walked forward toward the main checkout counter. "Genua's buying baby clothes again. That woman is obsessed, but I can't really blame her! Fay's trying out new lingerie she thinks you'd like, and Kara's wanting to buy a bonded pet. She can't afford anything on this floor, so she's exploring the less expensive options in the lower city."

"They sell pets here?"

"They do! Along with the necessary status-page changes for bonding, which is super neat, but that's all over in Jitzi's Growth Items. Whatever you do, don't buy anything until you've taken a look at all the goods in each of the stores. There's some very interesting stuff up here."

"What did you end up buying for yourself?"

"Oh, you know, some stuff regarding a tailoring profession down below where it's cheaper. I've been wanting to expand my skills after making that cloak for you!" She pinched the fabric of his Riven's Happy Birthday Cloak, which was shadow-crafted on the outside with a bloodsilk interior. "Stuff like this. You have your enchanting and totem-making, but I want to start making clothes and leather armor. It'd be so fun!"

"You'd have unlimited threads to use, of the same grade that you are."

"EXACTLY!"

Iris sputtered something in her sleep, and Riven playfully bopped Athela on the forehead for being too loud as she grumbled and glared his way.

Coming up to the desk under the sparkling crystal roof, the pair was addressed by a ghostly man at the counter who stood straight at attention with a larger-than-life smile. "Hello, prestigious scions! How is the young couple doing today? That's quite a cute child you've got there!"

Athela blushed, likely at the thought of having a child of her own.

Riven put an arm around Athela's shoulders and brought her closer. "Thank you for the compliment. I was hoping to get a list of your wares before deciding on what to buy—do you have any such list? Or, at least, categories of what you sell here so I can take a look?"

"We most certainly do," the ghost said, promptly producing a large paper scroll that he unfurled with a flash of light. Words began inscribing themselves onto the parchment a moment later in fancy stylized letters, and the ghost pointed to different categories. "Morgana's Traits and Upgrades deals in, well, traits and upgrades. You can literally buy traits from Elysium itself in the form of crystals that can be absorbed, which are stocked on our shelves. You can also buy upgrades for different aspects of your status page, including abilities and spells you already have, though if you want new abilities you'll have to find them over at the Skill Shop across the street. Just like the other stores here in the Ascended District, we are named after what Elysium has decided to store here for the best of the Unholy foundational pillar's younglings. You can see that there are categories based on the type of affinity, whether or not it's offensive or defensive or even combat related, and by what prerequisites are needed."

The ghost held up a finger. "Be warned, though, do not try to steal anything here. Though you may technically attempt to do it, you'll get a one-way ticket to obliteration and a permanent death if you get caught by any of our wards or employees."

Riven's eyebrows raised. "Elysium actually allows us to attempt theft? That's surprising."

The ghost nodded. "Oh yes, it's certainly doable, and some particularly skilled thieves get away with it. But yet again, I wouldn't recommend it. We're required to tell new arrivals about this opportunity, but know that any employee who catches someone attempting to steal gets a very large bonus in the form of performance credits, so we're inclined to report you to Elysium immediately for your quick execution—or worse—should any attempt be made."

Athela and Riven exchanged glances.

"Noted," Riven said, scanning the aisles filled with different colors and shapes of crystals and gems. Some were small, while other displays were the size of a person. "How about we just figure out what you have for sale and go from there? Do you mind helping us out?"

"Certainly," the ghost said. "Now, what is it you'd like to know? Do you want recommendations, or is there a specific subset of stuff you'd like me to help you look for as we go over our wares?"

It turned out the traits and upgrades were nothing to scoff at, and the list was incredibly helpful, as Riven didn't have to wander among a bunch of glowing rocks that he'd otherwise have to evaluate with his mana sense to get a feel for. It was a very lengthy list, from traits that would allow a person to gain additional experience from kills by 100 percent to doubling your minion slots and even being able to create your own baby gods if you managed to get ahold of the correct spiritual ingredients. The upgrade stones, on the other hand, were in one of two categories—very generalized or very specific. There was an upgrade stone that allowed someone to upgrade the spell Jogi's Potent Swarm of Flying Frogs, for example, which would create far deadlier killer frogs but needed that very specific spell in order to upgrade it. While the generalized upgrades weren't usually as potent, they could be applied to numerous things, like the ability to upgrade an ability of your choice by 20 percent. Or an upgrade stone that'd allow your cultivation to select a specific trait for the natural path of ascendancy, creating a version of the trait one or many tiers above the F-grade. There were even sets of upgrade stones that specifically targeted stats and would change a selected stat into either an affinity-based stat or an enhanced stat that would increase the efficacy of every single stat point you put into that pool. These crystals, gems, and stones, however, were all incredibly expensive, even for Riven, who by the vendor's proclamation had one of the highest performance credit pools they'd ever seen.

Jitzi's Growth Items was far different than Morgana's Traits and Upgrades. In Jitzi's Growth Items you could actually tell what you were looking at most of the time without exploring the spiritual or magical aspects of each item, and just as Athela had said, Jitzi's Growth Items also had pets. Apparently Elysium considered pets growth items? Riven really wasn't sure why, but maybe he was missing something here.

Large fire salamanders, drakes, dragons, griffons, shadow beasts, giant spiders, abyssal goats, nine-tailed foxes, void mantises, and hellsteeds were housed in the first rung of stables located on the left side, but they were all rather young and not fully grown. All of them were also top-quality pets, with incredibly potent bloodlines and serious potential for growth, and they came with an added bond slot for pets in your status page should you choose to buy. After that, it was far more surprising. Harpies, imps, humans, dwarves, elves, goblins, orcs, incubi, succubi, devils, ghouls, skresh, draconics, and many more of the enlightened races were imprinted with strange slave sigils infused with abyssal energies in the forms of pentagrams on their foreheads. They all, each and every one of them, seemed completely oblivious to their surroundings and did not interact with any attempt at speaking that Riven or Athela made, though two of them did make eye contact before they were beaten by the staff for their actions. When the staff were asked why that was and who these people were, the answer was simple: These people had been caught thieving, and instead of dying they'd sold their souls to the Abyssal Descent for another chance at life under a permanent slave contract via Elysium's apparently irreversible soul bindings. It was to the point that they couldn't even function without an owner, making their choice to steal a truly poor one that they couldn't just get out of if their original owner died. Many of them were actually prominent, or once-prominent scions themselves, though even more of them were delvers down on their luck not being able to afford the things they'd wanted to buy. They'd tried their hand at thievery and now paid the price, waiting here forever until someone bought them to remove them from this abyssal prison. What was even more interesting was that they didn't count as minions but filled the same pet slot that you'd get if you bought any of the animals.

After the stables and slave pens came the more typical items Riven would have guessed there to be in a place named after growth items. Swords, scythes, spears, shields, staves, armor, boots, trinkets, and jewelry were in abundance with seriously potent effects. There was an amulet that you could stuff the souls of your enemies into, and those souls would die in your place should you take a potentially fatal blow. There was a ghostly plasma scythe that couldn't be blocked by physical means and did direct soul damage. There was even a shield created from a dead elder god from a lost C-grade pantheon that'd been obliterated in a war with the heavens, and it still had some of that god's lingering soul fragments present within the shield.

Then there were the oddities. A living miniature star, a pot that could swallow light, a carriage made from the abyss. There were also a number of guild hall add-ons here that were technically growth items that'd become more powerful as you did and could not only bind to a guild hall but change the rest of the hall, too. This category interested Riven, as he'd been warned by Lillith that they may end up using that guild hall more and more frequently in the future. Athela had immediately latched onto a very pricey nether merging stone that'd allow her family, and Fay's family, to cross between their nether realms and even PARTIALLY merge their nether realms with the guild hall itself as an anchor point, and she made Riven promise to buy it with more than a little prodding. It even had three merge slots for three different nether realms, so he could potentially get someone else from the Church of Gluttony in on this, too.

Seeing how happy she got when he said yes was more than worth the money he'd spend, he was sure. And it'd be kind of nice to have the two demonic clans in and out of the guild hall anyways, providing protection for Iris whenever he was gone, if nothing else. Weren't their clans going to be extended family? It shouldn't hurt to have them around.

Leaving Jitzi's Growth Items behind and moving on to Dao Taboos and Treasures, Riven's aura sense was berated by tens of thousands of other auras emanating from various species of plants, natural crystal formations, keepsakes of long-dead cultivators infused with their insights, and different taboo treasures. He made sure not to make it too obvious as other delvers shopping nearby came and went, but he made particular note of all the taboo Blood-affiliated treasures that could help him better understand his pearl and the secrets it held. Many of these treasures would be great for a cultivation room he was planning on building in his guild hall anyways, and he marked down over a dozen of them that he would potentially buy for future use.

Finally, the Skill Shop was at hand. Grimoires, ability tomes, and skill scrolls were in abundance. Riven actually hadn't seen ability tomes and skill scrolls since early on in Negrada's dungeon before he'd become a vampire, and grimoires had been rare as well, with Fay's viper grimoire being one of the very few he'd come across over the past two years. The Elysium altar in Brightsville occasionally had a few of them pass through the available buy lists but they were always gobbled up in an instant, making it luck of the draw on who was able to get ahold of them. The trade communes of Negrada and the Blood Moon Requiem also provided a few different ability tomes or grimoires, but Riven didn't remember any of them ever having specifically provided skill scrolls to the public before. Or even to him, for that matter. Skill scrolls in particular were incredibly expensive because they automatically fused with a person's soul to provide a skill and were infused with the knowledge of a master craftsman who also happened to have knowledge of that skill. To be both a master craftsman, proficient in both enchanting and scribing, and then also have an ability worth a damn to spend years infusing your knowledge into a scroll for—well, it just wasn't done very often, even on a multi-versal level. But here in the Ascended District of the Abyssal Descent, there were dozens, many of which were Tier 2, Tier 3, and even some Tier 4 spells, miracles, and martial arts. One scroll in particular caught his eye, an Infernal ability that would allow him to summon his actual soul pillar into the world around him and create a cataclysmic explosion of hellfire as it dropped from the skies onto a targeted area. It was essentially a precision nuke, and using it would temporarily shatter his Infernal subpillar along with all the abilities associated with it until the pillar put itself back together again. Based on the descriptions, it was exactly what he was looking for in terms of extremely hard-hitting finishing strikes. He really only had Blood Nova for something like that, and it often was a harder hitter, sure, but didn't provide the amount of umph his entire mana pool could provide. This spell, though, could.

[Your minion Azmoth has requested to utilize 66 performance credits for a purchase. Accept? Decline?]

"Master." Azmoth pinged him through their internal link. "I finish basic clothing of Fish, Lizard, and Brute. We come meet you now."

"Good! Good, I'll see you soon," Riven replied, accepting the transaction for Azmoth while still going over the scrolls in the last store. Meanwhile, Athela rocked Iris back and forth on a bench provided by one of the local staff. "Athela is already here. Retesh and the rest of the girls are coming over now, I'll see you when you get here. We have some deciding to do on what we want to buy, because even with what the merchants claim to be an absurd number of points, I don't have nearly enough to buy all the things I think we need."

CHAPTER 37

Kara ended up using many of her points to buy a pet, just as Athela had said she would. It was an abyssal wolf puppy, and she got a binding slot to assert complete control over the creature as it grew up. With the ability to mold itself into darkness and temporarily forgo its physical form, the creature was mostly black with purple eyes and random patches of dark-purple hair. It was pretty mild-mannered and was cute enough that Kara ended up rather happy, especially considering it'd turn into a quite powerful specimen when it reached adulthood. She'd also acquired a Dao treasure from the same vendor. The treasure came in the form of a strange coin that had a vampire's depiction on one side and a werewolf's depiction on the other, but she hadn't elaborated further on the subject, becoming thoroughly embarrassed whenever Riven asked about it. She said she'd talk to him about what they were after all his shopping was done, as she wanted his opinion on a choice she needed to make. His eyebrows had raised at the proclamation, but despite his guesses, it could be anything, and he didn't push the matter further. For now.

Azmoth had returned after buying clothes for Fish, Lizard, and Brute, and Riven had okayed buying some basic combat equipment, too. Brute and Lizard now both had full heavy-plate armor sets made from gray metal, along with a respectable war hammer for Brute and a longsword-shield combination for Lizard. Fish had a new witch's hat plus dark-magic caster's robes and a new wooden staff that amplified her magic-casting abilities.

Retesh had used every single last point at Morgana's Traits and Upgrades to create unique minion slots for his undead, enabling him to enlist a few dozen superpowered, nonsentient but permanently undead minions that could level up with him. They'd remain soulless, but if they died he could still revive them eventually with the right conditions met. Trying this out, the minions he assigned to these slots automatically retained a 100 percent power boost without additional cost to Retesh, and they all were enveloped in large swaths of deathly auras that stood out among whatever other minions Retesh had on hand.

Riven, on the other hand, had to split his points up between himself and everyone else under his banner, but he had more than enough points to splurge.

It made him wonder just where he stood among the rank and file of those who entered this place, but he was told by multiple vendors that he'd find out more about his ranking whenever he entered the very last floor.

First thing he bought was a keep, a castle-like add-on for guild halls that he could attach at certain points. It had a bunch of unique features that would come in handy, like an additional layer of antiscrying as well as an alchemy lab and defensive measures against flying enemies. Riven still remembered the time that roc from Dawn had landed on top of his guild hall back in the day, and he didn't want anything like that ever happening again.

[Unholy Keep Variant (Guild Hall Add-On): A five-story, square Gothic keep with four additional towers at each of the corners. This keep boasts antiair measures, shields, and a variety of upgradeable add-ons. Currently created with D-grade stage materials, it is truly a marvelous home to dwell in for anyone in or below the same tier.
- **Four antiair towers that shoot rays of Unholy light at those labeled as enemies**
- **A backup power core to charge guild hall functions with potential for runic additions**
- **Dome shields that surround the entire campus of your guild hall**
- **+30 additional attendant slots for hiring staff with correlating rooms**
- **+15-mile additional exploration radius for attendants**
- **Enhanced homeward teleportation, allowing guild members to recall to the guild at half the normal time required**
- **Defensive trap wards and alarms for potential assassins**
- **Antiscrying wards**
- **Alchemy lab with reinforced walls]**

Given the taboo artifacts he'd be holding there, he thought it a pertinent thing to do. This was of course just a secondary measure, as the blood lake add-on for his guild hall that he'd already procured by defeating the Blueblood Precursor Clam should hide his blasphemous activities as well.

[<u>Blasphemous Enriched Blood Lake (Unique Guild Hall Add-On)</u>: A large portion of the Blueblood Precursor Clam's realm has been cut off from the Abyssal Descent and has been molded into a hyperdense, energy-rich cultivation resource for you to use. This lake will appear as a normal blood lake to any clergy of the Blood God and may also provide an ample environment for growing exotic Blood-affinity plants and Dao treasures. While meditating within or near the lake, the current Blood God will be blind to any taboo experimentations and objects, and abundant amounts of Blood energies will be

available to your call. **The Blueblood Precursor Clam, along with the leech swarms of the Abyssal Descent's Floor Twenty-Two, will reside within this lake and are disguised from being blasphemous creatures while they remain within or near the lake, and they will protect your guild hall with their lives should it come under attack.**

- **This add-on feature will be available to you at all times through any guild hall you own until used.]**

Next, and the most expensive item out of the bunch, costing him a whopping six hundred thousand performance credits, was the merging stone. Athela had requested it originally, but Fay was equally excited and had thanked him over and over again after he'd acquired it. Riven very much suspected he'd be seeing a lot of arachnids, incubi, and succubi walking around the guild hall and its grounds after this one, but it was well worth the happiness it brought his two minions. Most importantly, it added an additional series of layers of protection for his home and his daughter while he was away. Any future children he had would get that same protection while growing up.

[Merging Stone (Guild Hall Add-On): Place this stone onto the core of your guild hall to absorb it. After it is absorbed, you will be able to select up to three nether realms to merge with, allowing denizens of those particular nether realms to travel in and out of the guild hall wherever it may be at any given time.]

Next he'd bought a boatload of natural treasures in the forms of crystals, plants, and remnants of powerful beasts. The plants and crystals could be grown and would be going straight into his garden surrounding the tree where his friend Jose had been buried. They would not only help him cultivate just by meditating in their presence, but would also be a good source of crafting materials that would be reproducible as long as he kept a stern watch on their growth and waited long enough.

[Blood Lotus]
[Black Fang Flower]
[Drakin Crystal]
[Hellspawned Geode]
[Black Lagoon Vine]
[Wraith's Kiss Shrub]

Taboo cultivation treasures related to Blood were also present, but his suit's identification clause wasn't strong enough to pierce their veils. All he got were question marks when trying to figure out what they were—even the locals here on Floor Forty-Nine didn't know what they were selling—but they said that was normal for taboo artifacts and made it less dangerous for the buyers once they left this place. The only guarantee they gave was that those artifacts were taboo, and Riven had to figure out which ones had the Blood affinity in them. He took more than a few, as he didn't know when he'd next be able to get taboo Blood artifacts, and stuffed them into his spatial sack after making sure none of the other delvers there had seen him buy these particular trinkets. There was a small shield, a large ruby, a very sharp fork, of all things, a shriveled head, three shriveled fingers with a blue hue to them, and a vial of glittering golden blood. He'd work on figuring out what they did later.

Stat upgrade stones were a no-brainer for Riven, and he bought one for himself and for each of his minions. Only one stone could be bound to your soul core at a time, and they acted like spiritual anchors, modifying and enhancing one particular stat. He bought intelligence upgrades for himself, Fay, and Narg, an agility upgrade for Athela, a faith upgrade for Genua, and a strength upgrade for Azmoth. They wouldn't absorb immediately, but over the next month it'd give a decent boost to power for every single stat applied to the given stat category that'd been upgraded. Riven's intelligence would become Upgraded Intelligence, which made Riven scoff given the lack of creativity on Elysium's part.

The single spell scroll he obtained was called Orbital Hellstrike. This godlike spell was the same one he'd been eyeing on his first go-around in the Skill Shop, and Riven felt a bit bad about not buying any additional skills for his minions, but they were more than happy with the stat upgrade stones. Fay and Athela in particular had insisted he get it after seeing him drool over the scroll since they'd begged him to get the merging stone, and they'd felt it was only right for him to splurge a bit on himself instead of community items like the guild add-ons. This meganuke of a spell would add a final finishing blow to Riven's arsenal, and an extremely powerful one at that.

[Orbital Hellstrike (Infernal) (Tier 3): Rip out your Infernal subpillar to manifest it as a missile high above you. Call down a precision strike from orbit, doing immense critical Infernal damage to a single target and cataclysmic explosive damage to the surroundings for many miles. This attack temporarily shatters your Infernal subpillar and will disable all other Infernal abilities until the pillar re-forms in your soul core. The lower health your target has, the more damage this spell does.]

Riven was also able to buy two cures for his curses from prior floors. One would dispel his curse of Vampiric Abomination, which literally warned mortals that got too close that he was a pureblooded vampire. The other would dispel his Thrall Cap curse, which was the big one he wanted gone. Not being able to create more thralls when he wanted to would really suck if he actually did pursue the idea of having a blood farm, and he gladly shoved the credits out to get these cures. The Famished curse wasn't great, but it only made him hungrier, which he could deal with. The Daughter's Vengeance curse, however, was another story—it would cause him to be haunted by aspects of the now-dead Ethel's memories, but curing it cost him another additional natural treasure he simply couldn't afford. Daughter's Vengeance hadn't manifested yet, either, so it couldn't be too bad to experience occasional hauntings. Right?

Right?

He might be fooling himself, but a bit of psychological harm was a small price to pay. He could deal with it as it came, even if the hauntings would probably suck.

Overall he didn't get anything game-changing right now, but the prizes were all pretty good. He probably could have bought something truly grand if he'd focused on a single item and had been purely selfish in his ambitions, but the guild hall add-ons would benefit everyone. As would the stat upgrades and the natural cultivation treasures for his garden. So he had few regrets when he finally went into the last section he'd been holding off on, the area where slaves and pets were kept.

The slaves he completely disregarded. Riven didn't really want slaves—he already had an entire planet full of them back on the House Wraithtide homeworld of Luteski. He also had Genua as a thrall, three volunteer thralls, and one soon-to-be drow thrall that he was punishing on Kara's behalf. His blood farm was steadily coming along and he didn't see any benefit to buying people like that right now, given how many points each of them cost.

The pets? Well, that was another story. He'd originally dismissed needing any additional pets because although the ones he'd seen were good, they weren't something that he NEEDED when compared to some of the other things in these four shops. His mind had been changed after a talk with the people who worked here, though, who told him that the pets on the first floor that he'd initially seen weren't the best of what this place had. That was on the second floor of the shop above them, where they had some kind of ritual machine linked to Elysium, one that would feed a blueprint of a copied status page into the machine and Elysium would create a specific pet to match the descender. Thus he'd had to give the merchants of Jitzi's Growth Items a scan of his status page before going up. They'd originally told him to come back in two hours so they could feed the information through Elysium to create these creatures, citing a whopping one hundred and fifty thousand credits apiece with a five-thousand-credit viewing charge just to look. He'd decided to take that gamble and had ordered two of the creatures. So here he was, back at Jitzi's with his entire party in tow.

"We have your selections ready for you, young scion." The phantom merchant bowed with a flourish and proceeded to take them up to the second level along a spiraling silver staircase. "As asked, Elysium's ritual machine has generated two creatures that match your status page. Each creature will be linked to you as a pet should you choose to buy them, imbuing you with the two necessary pet slots not provided by your class. Like demonic and angelic minions, you can summon them from nether realms. Unlike your demonic minions with pacts, pets can and will die permanent deaths if an enemy strikes them down. Pets do not share experience with kills, so they'll have to level up on their own. They also have a lot more autonomy and do not need to stay if they are treated poorly. But a pet pact is beneficial to both sides because you can draw on each other's power in ways that demonic pacts do not do, so it is highly unlikely that they'd leave unless you truly give them a reason to do so. Especially these ones created here, where they are given an initial compulsion to serve the ones they were created for."

Riven was going to ask what the ghostly man meant by "draw on each other's power," but Fay sent him a mental nudge first.

"Pet pacts each manifest differently—each pact is unique," Fay said through their link. "You won't know how it manifests until you bind them, but usually it's a give-and-take agreement to work together that is somewhat reinforced by Elysium."

"Ah. Thanks, Fay, appreciated."

She gave him a knowing wink. Most warlocks never dealt in pet pacts—that was usually for classes like rangers or druids—so this was new territory for him.

The phantom merchant came to a large double door and placed a spectral hand on it. The door began to groan and creak. Screeching sounds of metal on metal echoed down the staircase, and the pungent smell of iron filled Riven's nostrils.

The single room inside was large and open to the dark skyline, with a strange series of metal rods, stone pillars, and an almost infinite number of layered, intricate, multicolored runes Riven didn't even come close to understanding along all of it. Even the walls and floor shimmered with the runic language of Elysium, and to Riven's knowledge none of it had any real foothold in any magic he'd ever seen. These layers certainly did not hail from the Unholy foundation, but rather gave off the aura of Elysium itself, such as when the tribulation had tried to strike him down from using Malignant Prophecy too many times. He'd not needed to use the prophetic powers often since then, but a chill still ran through his spine at the raw energy leaking from his surroundings.

Azmoth nudging him brought him out of his stupor, and he coughed to clear his head while following the trajectory of the phantom's pointing finger.

"They await your decision, scion of Gluttony," the phantom said politely. "If you deem them unworthy, you can always try again, but the cost will be another five thousand participation credits for another viewing. That said, I have not seen anyone come out of this place unhappy in the past five cycles. Elysium usually does a good job of determining what would be most beneficial and even provides an explanation as to why they were created the way they were."

Indeed, Riven could feel the auras of each creature from here.

The first was more obvious in what it was as they approached, but it was also the more intimidating one at first glance. It was a large red drake, the size of a school bus from tail to snout, with a wingspan slightly longer than that. Not as big as the drake he'd killed on Panu—this beast gave off a far more deadly energy and a confidence to match as it stared him down on his walk forward. Instead of scales, its outer skin was coated in a shiny, actively flowing layer of crimson fluid. Its features were sleek and sharp, with intelligent yellow eyes, and it had claws the size of his entire torso. Long, sharp spines with a frill membrane connecting them ran down the middle of its skull and partway down its neck, and a forked tongue snapped out between rows of jagged teeth as it began to grin devilishly at him.

A notification appeared.

[Elemental Blood Drake of the Descent, Classless: This level-201 E-grade creature was created as a prize pet for you and those who serve you, Riven Thane, upon entering Floor Forty-Nine of the Abyssal Descent. Made almost entirely out of blood from the fallen participants of the Abyssal Descent, this creature possesses a hundred bloodlines, with potential for awakening each of them. The common denominator is the concept of speed and mobility. The possibilities and rate at which this creature evolves are completely unknown and untested, but one thing above all is clear: This creature is incredibly fast. Currently clocking rates at over four thousand miles per hour, or nearly six thousand feet per second, this monster is far faster than the speed of sound at max flight and has incredible acceleration, making it one of the fastest monsters to ever exist within the Abyssal Descent. The blood along its body circulates to reduce friction from any liquid or gas it passes through, including air, further increasing its speed and reducing heat buildup along its body. The blood layer can also cover any rider for the same protective effect. This drake automatically regenerates any nonlethal damage after a short time and has inherited the soul and life experience of a long-dead drake from Universe 18 that Elysium deemed to be a compatible companion. Moreover, this pet bond will also grant Genua the same ability to summon it from its nether realm, allowing Genua to have a method of flight alongside the rest of your minions whenever traveling or fighting. Lastly, this monster has a single, potent offensive ability to utilize at this time. Please see the overview for the monster's details:

- **Elemental Blood Drake of the Descent, Classless (Legendary)**
- **Level 201 E-grade**
- **Body of Blood (Trait): Automatically regenerates any nonlethal damage taken after a short time. Your blood body's outer layer also significantly reduces friction while flying, increasing speed**

and buffering from heat buildup at higher speeds. This outer blood layer can be extended to any rider to keep them from falling off while also giving an additional layer of protection.

- **Red Breath Stream (Tier-1 Blood Martial Art):** Spray out a large stream of piercing supersonic blood at your enemies.
- **The Winged Lineage of One Hundred Scions (Trait):** You have taken on one hundred different bloodlines from fallen scions of the Abyssal Descent, each of which is based in speed. You gain a +200% bonus modifier to all Agility stat points. You are also able to unlock different aspects of your one hundred bloodlines and evolve over time as you grow.
- **Current Stats:** 2,984 Strength, 1,403 Sturdiness, 460 Intelligence, 3,000 Agility, 10 Luck, -6,553 Charisma, 611 Perception, 208 Willpower, 90 Faith

BINDING THIS PET TO YOUR STATUS PAGE AND SOUL WILL MANIFEST AS FOLLOWS: You will regularly help find potent Dao treasures related to blood for this drake's consumption, at least twice a year, and in return it will remain loyal to whatever cause you may have.]

Huh. Riven pulled up his own stats next. The monster's Strength stat tripled his own, Sturdiness was almost exactly the same with only a sixteen-point difference in favor of the drake, Riven's Intelligence was far beyond the drake's by about twenty-seven hundred points (not including his newly upgraded Intelligence stat, either), their Luck was exactly the same at a mere ten points—likely due to the cap on the Luck stat that couldn't be overcome unless particular conditions were met—his Willpower outmatched the drake's own by about eight hundred points, and both of their Faith stats were garbage and sub-one hundred points. Though the drake still beat him by a multiplier of ten in the Faith category, given its ninety to his nine. Charisma . . . Well, Charisma was quite negative for both, but his was far more negative than the monster's, which wasn't much of a surprise. The big focus for Riven was the difference in Agility, though, and he could see why it was considered one of the fastest creatures to ever visit this place at a quick glance.

He considered HIMSELF quite fast with an Agility of 1,228, while the monster boasted three thousand Agility, which almost matched his Intelligence stat, and that was without the 200 percent bonus modifier to Agility the drake would ever get. Right now, the drake was technically sporting a speed that would reflect nine thousand Agility points . . . which was just downright absurd. If he utilized his immense mana pool to further boost his speed through Blessing of the Crow or fed it into Messenger's thrusters, he might, MIGHT be able to match a decent fraction of that kind of movement, but he wasn't certain by how much. He only hoped it could maneuver well, though, because for a monster this size to have the same sturdiness as he did, that meant it probably couldn't take much of a punch. Riven usually blocked attacks with his magic and avoided up-close battles for this very reason, even with Messenger's armor on, yet the drake also had the ability to regenerate just like he could, too. So that was good—as long as it didn't outright get nuked by a hard-hitting strike, it'd be able to shrug off the attacks thrown its way.

- **Riven's Current Stats: 1,167 Strength, 1,387 Sturdiness, 3,183 Upgraded Intelligence, 1,228 Agility, 10 Luck, -51,058 Charisma, 414 Vampiric Perception, 1,054 Willpower, 9 Faith]**

He also wasn't sure why Elysium considered Athela to have a flying ability, as it dictated in the memo that one of its thoughts creating the beast was to help even out Genua's own mobility. Athela didn't necessarily fly . . . she could transform into a stream of blood and, erm, fly through the air so to speak if the technical definition of *fly* was used, but it couldn't be maintained indefinitely and it certainly wasn't fast enough to reliably use in combat. That was why most of the time whenever he took to the sky, she used that ability to wrap around his own body and launch off him like a springboard into her Arshakai form.

Either way, Riven was very happy with the beast and gave it a nod and a grin of approval, his gaze lingering on the frilled spines going down the top of its skull and neck before his eyes landed on the next of the two creatures.

This one was quite familiar in its form.

A skeletal soldier equal to his height in shiny red-and-black armor stood at attention, with crimson eyes blazing in its skull sockets underneath a horned metal helmet. A cape flowed out behind it between two bulky pauldrons, with a tower shield in its left hand and a large, flanged mace in its right, both made out of that same black-and-red metal. At first glance it appeared to be very similar to one of the summoned blood knights, or bloodstricken undead, he could summon from the Blood God's realm, though this one did have slight and very important differences from the others. The crimson symbol on its forehead just underneath the helm was not just a teardrop; rather, it was a pentagram with a five-sided star. Inside that pentagram's center was Gluttony's maw devouring the red teardrop, but the teardrop on closer inspection was also altered and more curved in its nature than what the Blood God now utilized for his own sigil. That held some significance, Riven instinctively knew, and he already had a few guesses as to what it meant.

[**Bloodstricken Undead, General Caltan of the Blood Legions: This level-207 E-grade creature was created as a prize pet for you and those who serve you, Riven Thane, upon entering Floor Forty-Nine of the Abyssal Descent. He is extremely skilled in melee combat, leading armies, and casting long-range blood miracles. He also has** an empowering aura that affects all allies within a large radius from his position. Nothing about this creature has been changed from his fundamentals, outside of the equipment he has been given upon arriving here and the sigil change on his forehead to represent his newfound allegiance. Bloodstricken undead are for all intents and purposes the property of blood gods and may only be commanded by their specific blood gods or those with a 100% affinity to the Blood subpillar. This general, upon gaining ranks and having acquired the ability to think for itself, disliked what the current Blood God was telling it to do. He disobeyed a single order and was cast down from the Blood God's service a few million years ago and banished back to the depths of the blood realm, buried there to linger in a cell . . . until now. He has had much of his soul core, associated abilities, raw power, and even multiple grades of his cultivation stripped from him to feed other pets of the current Blood God over the last few million years, but he retains his skills in leading armies and in battle with blunt weapons. Having achieved the rank of general in the order of the Blood Legions, Caltan also retains the ability to snatch control of other bloodstricken undead to hold under his banner. Foot soldiers and unthinking bloodstricken can be forcibly subdued and converted, while most sapient and sentient officers of the Blood Legion in service to the current Blood God will actively challenge General Caltan to one-on-one ritual combat if they encounter one another. The result will be that either he loses and is banished back to the blood realm, or he wins and is able to summon the defeated officer back to his side.

An E-grade general in the Blood Legion can control up to one thousand other bloodstricken. With every increased grade, the number of other bloodstricken General Caltan can control will also increase. This creature is oathbound by the Blood subpillar to engage in any challenge proposed by any other officer of captain, major, colonel, general, warlord, or hero general of the Blood Legion as long as they are within or lower than his own grade. Other challenges by officers above General Caltan's grade may be refused.

Though this creature has a very clever mind for battlefield tactics and the intelligence of most enlightened species, bloodstricken undead are pact-bound to remain as minions, summons, or pets depending on the situation and are built by the Blood subpillar in the blood realm to serve the masters who wield the pillar's power with at least 100% affinities. General Caltan is no different, but he only accepted the proposal to serve knowing you are meddling in the taboo arts of

the Blood subpillar and that you seek to unravel what the current
Blood God has hidden.

Please see the overview for the monster's details:
- Bloodstricken Undead, General Caltan of the Blood Legions
  (Legendary)
- Level 207 E-grade
- Blood Legion's Call (Tier-3 Blood Miracle): Drastically empower
  all affiliated bloodstricken undead and send them into a berserk-
  ing mode for the next five minutes.
- Battlefield (Tier-2 Blood Miracle): Create a battlefield on which
  you and those who identify as your allies can deal additional
  blood damage with every strike.
- Legionnaire Recruits of the Blood Legion (Tier-2 Death/Blood
  Miracle): Indefinitely summon a single unequipped bloodstricken undead beneath or equal to your level who is unaffili-
  ated and has not pledged to any of the blood gods yet. You may
  retain control of them indefinitely until they die or acquire an
  officer's title on their own within the ranks of the Blood Legion.
  Previously recruited bloodstricken who have acquired the ability
  to think for themselves and have thus claimed an officer's title
  have the opportunity to choose to affiliate themselves with you
  afterward for future summons.
- Sanguine Smite (Tier-1 Blood Miracle): Blast an enemy at short
  to midrange with blood energy.
- Red Flash (Tier-1 Blood Martial Art): Flash forward in a burst of
  crimson while dealing additional blast damage upon any physical strike.
- Make Sick and Bleed (Tier-3 Blood Miracle): An area-of-effect
  miracle, blasting divinity outward in a shock wave that throws
  opponents back before they begin to bleed from all their pores
  and does massive hemorrhaging damage over time. This ability
  does not work on mechanical, skeletal, or golem enemies.
- Mend Thy Bones (Tier-1 Blood/Death Miracle): Entirely restore
  and heal other bloodstricken undead at a mere touch over the
  course of a single minute.
- War's Baptism (Trait): For every dead enemy nearby killed by
  allies, you gain a small boost to all stats. For every dead enemy
  you've personally killed nearby, gain a larger boost to all stats.
- Three-Star Battlefield Commander (Trait): All Blood Legion
  units under your command will gain the ability to reanimate
  once within the hour before being banished back to the blood
  realm upon a second death if it comes too soon.

- E-Grade Blood Legion General: You are able to control up to one thousand other bloodstricken undead.
- Current Stats: 2,020 Strength, 2,409 Sturdiness, 277 Intelligence, 1,299 Agility, 1,008 Luck, -2,001 Charisma, 800 Perception, 463 Willpower, 1,686 Faith

BINDING THIS PET TO YOUR STATUS PAGE AND SOUL WILL MANIFEST AS FOLLOWS: You will pursue the reunification of the shattered pieces of the Blood subpillar. Straying from this path too many times in favor of the current Blood God's reign will result in the breaking of this pet pact.]

CHAPTER 38

"Do you know why you were brought here?" Riven asked the two figures in front of him, one towering over him while the other stood at about his own height.

The skeletal, bloodstricken general's red eyes flashed underneath his horned helmet, and he gave a slow nod. His voice came out crisp, almost frosty, like a loud whisper. "Yes. The better question is whether or not you will remain true to your path. Be it known that I am no slave, but I am willing to follow you to the end if you keep true to rekindling the lost facets of blood."

"Unquestioningly?"

General Caltan gave a curt nod. "My kind were made to serve the masters of blood. You are one such master, not lesser or greater than any other in the eyes of the pillar, and it is up to us officers of the Blood Legion to decide such things as allegiance between what options we have. With a 100 percent affinity, you are one such option, and you have already taken steps that directly oppose the great betrayer."

Riven's left eyebrow rose questioningly about the title of "great betrayer" referring to the current Blood God, but the bloodstricken undead in front of him shook his head when Riven gestured for him to continue.

"That is a very long story, my lord, and one I do not wish to discuss at this time. If you would permit me a stay of words, I will discuss such histories with you in the future." General Caltan lowered his head and planted his mace head-first on the ground. "Though if you insist, I will speak on it."

Riven hesitated, then shrugged. "Very well. But tell me, do you believe you're capable of serving me in the capacity Elysium summoned you here for?"

General Caltan didn't hesitate. "My lord, point me in the direction of your enemies and I will butcher them to the last. We of the awakened bloodstricken are ruthless machines bred for nothing but war, and I am among the best of my kin. I will not disappoint, should you choose to accept me into your flock."

Riven, satisfied, turned to the beast next.

The drake's bloody spines extended to greater lengths along the base of its neck when it saw it had Riven's attention, as if stretching. It then extended its wings to either side in a gust of wind and puffed out its chest, rearing up on its hind legs to show off its magnificent form before the large beast gave his own reply in a deeper, very masculine tone. "I, too, am aware of what purpose I now serve. If my new form pleases you, it is an honor to be given a second chance. Plucked from the grave from the sea of endless souls is something I'd never have deemed possible. I will hold true to the pact so long as you help me grow alongside you, and I beg you to allow me this chance."

No one else seemed to have anything to say, letting Riven do all the talking for the group despite him pausing to let anyone put in a word should they have an opinion.

"Elemental Blood Drake of the Descent . . ." Riven repeated aloud while reading off the drake's information screen. "We can't call you that every time we need to address you. What's your actual name?"

There was a pause. The drake seemed confused. "I do not have a name. Or, more accurately, it's been so long that I don't remember what my name was."

"Oh? How about Sanguine, then. It means 'bloodred' in my native language."

"If that is what you wish to call me, then I will gladly accept it."

Riven eventually gave them both a respectful nod and smiled while opening his arms in a gesture of acceptance. "Welcome to the club, gentlemen. It's nice to finally get some more guys around here—we were outnumbered."

Azmoth chuckled in the background and Athela jabbed Riven in the side, causing him to flinch.

"Does this mean you accept them as adequate prizes for the points spent?" the phantom merchant asked curiously, floating over to where Riven stood. "Are you finalizing the purchase?"

Riven nodded, and the drake in particular let out an audible sigh of relief as its large predator's muscles became visibly less tense. "I'll take them both. If the descriptions provided by Elysium are anything to go by, I won't be disappointed."

The phantom merchant put on a wide smile, bowed, and Riven felt two more pentagrams slice themselves into the skin of his chest underneath his other demonic markings. Messenger opened up to show his four demonic pentagrams, and now two more sigils that weren't pentagrams but were shaped into triangles with a drake depicted in one and a skeleton in the other.

[You have acquired two pet slots: Sanguine the level-201 Elemental Blood Drake of the Descent, and General Caltan the level-207 Bloodstricken Undead General, have been bound to these pet slots. Contractual agreements regarding Dao treasures of blood for Sanguine, and the pursuit of the taboo fragments of the Blood subpillar for General Caltan, will be further detailed in their status pages.
- **You are now able to summon these pets from their individual nether realms, but they can still experience true death despite being bound to a nether realm. There is no XP share between**

master and pet like there is with demonic contracts, and unlike demonic contracts you are able to push or pull energy, such as mana, stamina, and divinity, to one another through your pet contract's link.

- **Genua has gained Sanguine's mark just as you have and is able to summon Sanguine the drake at any time. Sanguine will treat Genua as an alternative secondary master to yourself.**
- **If General Caltan dies, you will lose access to any and all blood-stricken undead under his control.]**

Kara watched nervously from the back line as Sanguine and General Caltan were welcomed into the flock. Either one of them was equivalent to or better than many of the other top delvers here in the descent, with only the outliers at the top like Riven and Hatchmire casting a shadow over such bonds. General Caltan seemed a bit stiff but was certainly interesting as he met Riven's minions, and the drake was a beauty to behold. Majestic, even.

She was happy for Genua, who was obviously excited to get her own flying mount, even if it was technically Riven's elemental drake, and smiled when the elf thrall got up on Sanguine's back before being secured in place by the actively flowing outer layer of blood. Elysium's reasoning was solid, too, giving another one of Riven's minions the ability of flight so she could keep up with the group.

But where did that leave Kara? Kara wasn't able to fly.

It was obvious that Elysium hadn't considered her at all when bringing these two pets to the light. Kara was no heaven's chosen in the eyes of the system. A blood drake and an undead skeleton of that quality would tear her apart a thousand times over, even one on one. She smiled down at the abyssal wolf puppy sleeping in her arms and let her dark fingers flow over the silky-smooth black fur of the tiny creature. It was all she could afford after the token she'd bought, but despite it being weak right now, it was still hers. She'd earned it with her own points. She'd not even named it yet and probably wouldn't for a while until it developed a personality. In her culture, personality was important in naming pets, so she'd give it time.

Maybe she and her puppy were destined for a different path, even if she did want to keep up with the other absolute monsters in this group.

Pffft. Keep up? She wasn't even there now. More like catch up and THEN keep up, but that was a pipe dream at best. She'd survived only due to the kindness of those around her, and one way or another she was destined to follow them back to the world they called Panu. Why was she even going, though? What use was she to them? Outside of Athela, who seemed to be infatuated with her looks, Kara couldn't really think of a reason why they'd want her around.

"Are you okay?" Fay's familiar voice asked as the succubus touched Kara's shoulder with two fingers. "You look distraught."

Kara blinked and pulled her frown off her face as quick as she could, replacing it with a fake and flimsy grin as she came back to the world of the living. "Oh, I'm fine! Why do you ask?"

Fay truly was pretty. Kara was jealous and couldn't help but stare sometimes at the walking, talking pinnacle of beauty now standing in front of her. She'd heard that Athela and Fay had gotten into it a long time ago over Riven's attention, and Kara honestly couldn't blame Athela for feeling jealous or insecure about the blue-skinned babe in her witch's hat.

Fay, for her part, pretended not to notice Kara's blatant staring and pulled Kara into a one-sided hug while leading the drow woman away from the rest of the group as extended introductions continued. Coming to stand twenty paces out with at least a small amount of privacy, Fay reached down to pet the sleeping puppy's head.

"That's a real cutie you've bought." Fay giggled at the yawn the tiny creature made, and then turned around to face the party they'd distanced themselves from. "You must be proud to have gotten this far."

Kara internally cringed but kept the forced, polite smile nonetheless. "Proud isn't the word I'd use for it, but happy would be an accurate description. I'm happy all of you helped me."

"You helped us get here."

Kara rolled her eyes and gave Fay a knowing look tapping one boot against the ground. "Hardly. Half of the last stretch I was stuck inside your dungeon realm for my own safety."

Fay smirked, putting a finger to her lips as her long, slender tail flipped about lazily behind her. "Mmm. Yes, you were. That doesn't detract from your own part prior to that, though. You did what you could, and you weren't the only one put inside. Genua was in there, along with Iris, Lizard, Brute, Fish, and that prisoner we have. What was her name again? The one who tormented you?"

"Zafima."

"Ah yes, Zafima. She's not taking to becoming a thrall very well, but she deserves every second of the agony she's experiencing." Fay winked, then hip-checked Kara right where the token was in Kara's left pocket. "When are you going to ask Riven about that little gadget you bought? You were so excited to get it when we went out with just the girls."

Kara stiffened. "I still haven't decided on which path I want to take."

"But both paths coincide with that cute little class of yours, don't they?"

"They do."

"Then just choose the one that fits best!" Fay said, flipping a long strand of silky white hair out of her face. "I honestly didn't even know Elysium gave out classes like that. Truly interesting if you ask me."

Kara whirled on Fay with a glare. "You promised you wouldn't tell him."

"And I'm not going to!" Fay cooed, pinching Kara's cheeks like a mother would a child. "I don't lie to my friends! But Athela and I did have quite a laugh at your expense over it!"

Kara swatted Fay's hands away with a grumble and a huff. "I'm sure you did. If it were anyone else in any other situation, I'd laugh at them, too."

"Ah, don't be like that! It's adorable! We all think so! Genua was particularly enthusiastic if you do remember—"

"Let's not talk about that, please," Kara said with a growl, absentmindedly stroking the puppy's fur while Retesh the lich and General Caltan discussed which of them was a "better" type of undead, much to the amusement of Riven and Athela. How that'd come up as a topic for conversation, Kara had no clue.

Fay remained quiet for a time and eventually put on a pouting face while leaning into Kara with one elbow. "You think you're being left behind."

It was a statement of fact, not a question.

"Obviously," Kara muttered under her breath, barely loud enough for Fay to hear. "I've only just now found a place that I belong and am already struggling to remain. Genua even got a flying mount, but what am I supposed to do if I ever want to come along on another one of your adventures?"

Fay frowned. "Do you really feel like it's safe to accompany us into other places like this in the future?"

Kara nearly spluttered, and she felt a hot anger tint her dark cheeks a shade of burgundy. "I don't want to be safe! I want to be where I'm supposed to be! Where I'm accepted!"

Fay blinked and bobbed her head from side to side. "I get it. It wasn't all that long ago that I was in your shoes."

"How so?"

"I felt like I was holding the rest of the party back. I was the weakest link—I definitely was. I was pathetic, and there were millions of other demons just waiting for an opportunity to serve Gluttony's reincarnation in my place. In fact, the Church of Gluttony almost recommended to Riven that I give up my slot entirely and become something of a housewife to him instead, so that he could gain someone more competent than me."

Kara's eyes bulged in disbelief. "But . . . but you're an archdemon! You've been with him for a long time, right?! He wouldn't allow you to be replaced, would he?"

Fay snickered and shook her head. "Probably not. But it's true, I was on the chopping block, so to speak. Thankfully I honed my skills to an acceptable level, barely passing that bar, if I may add, so that Lillith and the rest of the church got off my case about keeping a slot. Anyways, what I'm getting at is that if I could do it, so can you. Even if it takes you a long time, it's definitely possible. Talk to him if you ever get the courage to do it, tell him what your class is and see what he says. At bare minimum . . ."

Fay pointed yet again to the token in Kara's pocket. "You should probably use that sooner rather than later. I'll try to take you with us in my dungeon pocket realm, and perhaps it won't work, but if it does, you'll find yourself back on Panu in the middle of a war. Being a drow is fine, but it is still a mortal race. Even Genua has ascended into something greater than a high elf. Before she became a thrall she had baseline skills in nature magics that could barely be called passing, if that. Upgrading your race to this degree is a rare thing indeed, and choosing one is going to be a decision you live with the rest of your life. Think about it, and if you need any insight, talk to Riven. If Kathrine were here she'd be even better to speak to because she grew up a vampire, but unfortunately she's not, so you'll have to deal with our resident half-baked vampire prince sex-muffin instead. He is rather lovable, though, a million times better than the last warlock summoner I had."

Fay innocently waved in Riven's direction when he looked their way, and smiled deviously at Kara when he looked away. "So which one are you leaning toward? You don't have to choose now, but I'm curious about your thoughts. Personally, I think we both know that the vampire option is the better one, given that you already have a pureblooded vampire here who'd be willing to turn you. Bare minimum you'd get a greater vampire class with his bloodline alone, and then the upgrade token on top of that may push you even higher. Maybe even pureblood if I'm guessing correctly. But then again, if you managed to find a potent bloodline for the werewolf side of things . . . that'd be rather unique. Who knows?"

"You really think Riven would turn me if I asked?"

"Of course he would. He spent three billion coins to keep you alive when he first met you—you're an investment now. You need to find a way to pay it off and this is a great way to make strides toward that. He may be my lovable, idiot boyfriend, but he's also Gluttony's reincarnation, and it would be sacrilege for you not to at least attempt to pay him back for the grace shown you as you are now—a very weak, filthy, dependent, and sometimes sniveling mortal. No offense intended of course. I like you and have high hopes for your future, but that's what you are right now."

Ugh. Kara didn't need to be reminded, and she gritted her teeth while firming her resolve. She hated what and who she was, and she owed more than a life debt to boot.

Plunging her hand into her pocket, Kara withdrew the token and let out a shuddering breath as she felt the power course through her body just at the mere touch. It truly was an incredible treasure, but which was a better fit? That had been the question she'd been mulling over since getting it, and it may very well be the ticket to her next power-up, a means by which she could finally catch up with the others. One side depicted a bat, while the other side of the token depicted a wolf.

[The Wolf and Bat Racial Upgrade Token: This token may be used only once and only by a mortal, and it dissolves upon successfully absorbing its power. This token applies one of the following, which-ever the user deems best suited to their needs:

- <u>Racial Upgrade 1</u>—Use this option to upgrade your <u>werewolf</u> heritage and unlock an additional three aspects of your bloodline. You must have VERY RECENTLY become a werewolf to use this token. Waiting too long after transformation from mortal to werewolf will negate the use of this token.
- <u>Racial Upgrade 2</u>—Use this option to upgrade your <u>vampire</u> heritage and unlock an additional three aspects of your bloodline. You must have VERY RECENTLY become a vampire to use this token. Waiting too long after transformation from mortal to vampire will negate the use of this token.]

Her hand closed over the token for the tenth time that day. If she could just muster up the courage to ask Riven to change her, then all would be for the better. If he said yes, that was. She thought he would, but would he prefer her as a werewolf or as a vampire? Where would she even get a werewolf heritage if that's what he wanted? Or was she overthinking this, and the obvious option of having such a powerful vampiric lineage was a no-brainer?

Probably the latter. It'd be stupid to try and find an equivalent werewolf heritage to Riven's vampiric heritage, right?

Unfortunately for her, just as Kara got the courage to pursue such an avenue on her climb to power, a new notification hit her full in the face and the world began to turn dark.

[**Congratulations on spending all your accumulated points. Now that you've done so, we want to welcome you to the <u>Floor Forty-Nine HIDDEN Challenge: NIGHT OF TERROR!</u>**]

CHAPTER 39

The room flashed and all the locals were gone. What had once been a splendid market was now wreckage, and time sped up, proven by a flickering candle on one of the walls as more teams were introduced into the instance event over the course of hours. They'd just pop in with flashes of light, probably after having tried to spend their points in the Ascended District if all things were the same between teams, and none of them were pushovers.

"ELYSIUM, YOU COCKSUCKING LITTLE SLUT! I THOUGHT WE WERE DONE WITH FIGHTING!" Athela screeched through their mind link since she couldn't talk out loud, an image of an enraged spider flailing its front legs against the bars of a jail cell flung through the group's shared mind. "THIS IS BLASPHEMY! A PRINCESS SHAN'T BE RESTRAINED LIKE THIS!"

"I thought it was too easy," Riven mentally murmured. "I guess this shoe fits better. But peak E-grade LEGENDARY monster swarms? That's crazy dangerous, even for us. Peak E-grade is level 350 to 399, isn't it?"

"Especially if we only get a single ability to use . . ." Fay agreed, worry obvious in her projected voice.

Riven's eyes flitted to Retesh and then Kara. Then to Sanguine the blood drake, and to General Caltan the bloodstricken soldier. Eyes were the only thing he COULD move here, and he wished he had some way to contact them, too, as more teams were pushed back into the instance from the once seemingly safe city.

Azmoth mentally snorted. "At least we don't fight other team here. That good."

"Yeah, that's true . . . it'd suck to be pitted against the Abyssal Descent's best," Riven agreed, eyeing the three dozen teams now stacked alongside them amid the wreckage of the market. "But they're definitely not going to be friends, either. It's obvious that some will just wait around for other teams to die so they can loot their bodies. I think we need to immediately go into hiding after this. Anyone have a good idea of where to go?"

"Agreed," Genua said.

Athela groaned. "We don't even know where the monsters are going to spawn from! Will it be right on top of our heads? Or around the city border? Fuck, Iris is still out!"

Indeed, Iris was actually in Genua's arms right at this very moment. Surprisingly enough, Fish, Brute, and Lizard were all out in the open, too. This floor must have different participation rules in it, otherwise they'd have been flung back into Fay's prison, right? Or did it not matter since they'd been out upon initiation of this event?

System shenanigans at their finest.

Wait. Even Zafima was out of the cell! What the hell was she doing here?!

[Fifty teams have been reached.
Here is a quick review of the rules for NIGHT OF TERROR!:

Ten thousand peak E-grade Legendary monsters have been randomly unleashed into the city's interior and surroundings. Hide, fight, or run until the new day begins eight hours from now. You may loot the dead but may not directly harm other living teams. Your direct offensive strikes will only affect the monster swarm, though friendly fire is still possible between teammates. Picking up spatially compacted

defensive structures, bottled spells or miracles, and barricades will be available and are noted by glowing orbs you can find all over the city.

What ability would you like to keep for this trial? Please choose one from your status page. You have sixty seconds to comply before one is chosen for you.]

Fay's voice cut through his mind like a knife, terrified. "Riven! It won't let me select my dungeon ability! I keep trying but it won't accept it!"

Riven's heart clenched at the realization of what that meant. Again his eyes flitted to the four up-and-coming thralls. No wonder Zafima had been pushed out: The event was refusing to allow Fay to contain them any longer, and that meant . . .

That meant Iris was in serious danger, as were they all. A swarm of this magnitude was something even Riven probably couldn't handle with his entire skill set, and they had to survive for eight hours?

His heart began to pound as the seconds ticked by and his team began to increase the pitch of their chatter among the minion bonds. Genua was becoming frantic at the realization, Kara wasn't included in the mental exchange but was visibly sweating, and even Azmoth seemed nervous by the way he kept starting a sentence only to stumble over his words.

This was not good. At all. For the first time in a long time, Riven was genuinely worried.

[Thirty seconds remain. Please select a skill to utilize during this eight-hour event.]

Shit.

Cursing his luck, Riven went over his skills.

- **Abilities: Profane Blessing of the Crow (Unholy/Blood/Shadow), Wretched Snare (Unholy), Silvertongue (Unholy), Bloody Razors → Storm Balls/Storm Razors → Gluttonous Storm Razors (Blood/Shadow/Sin), Crimson Ice (Blood), Blood Lance → Sniping Profane Blood Lance → Critical Storm Lance (Blood/Shadow/Sin) (Tier 2), Voodoo Doll (Blood) (Tier 2), Blood Nova (Blood) (Tier 3), Hell's Armor (Infernal), Blaze of Profane Glory (Infernal) (Tier 3), Riftwalk (Shadow), Gluttonous Sacrifice (Sin) (4,999 years until cooldown is complete), Black Lightning (Shadow), Legionaries of the Blood God (Death/Blood) (Tier 2), Ravenous Beetle Swarm (Sin), Farsight Banishment (Sin), Soul Clone Projections (Sin), Gluttony's Aspect of Demonic Heritage (Sin) (Tier 3), Twin Crowns of Flesh (Blood) (Tier 2)**

Shit again.

He was torn between three different spells. First and the most obvious was Critical Storm Lance, which was his fastest and longest-range ability and packed a rapid punch. His original Blood Lance had evolved twice over now.

Then there was Crimson Ice. The incredibly versatile skill had even been incorporated into his aura to an extent, but he could use it individually for both offensive and defensive purposes. He could even use it for utility purposes, but it was only mediocre at straight damage.

Last of the abilities he was considering was Riftwalk. Riftwalk was an amazing spell to help get away and would keep both himself and his daughter safe should he choose it, because he had enough mana to recast the thing for hours on end without stopping. He was only inhibited by potential cooldowns afflicting him if he chose to do that, but two more obvious problems were obvious with this choice: First was that he'd be left almost literally defenseless outside of his items and physical strength when it came to combat. Second was that he wasn't sure he'd be able to teleport the entire team accurately and all at once with their individual portals, and if they all used one portal to flee through then it'd mean a single-file line that could either slow them down or let monsters through in the attempt.

[Twenty seconds remain. Please select a skill to utilize during this eight-hour event.]

"Bloody Strings for me," Athela called through the minion mind link.
Azmoth was next. "Dome of Flames."
"Dreamwalker zone for illusions, since I can't pick the dungeon!" Fay said in a panicked voice. "I can't believe this is happening! This is so bad!"
"Elysium has disabled my ability to heal through my aura entirely," Genua said with an audible sneer. "I'll pick Sanguine Smite, then."

[Ten seconds remain. Please select a skill to utilize during this eight-hour event.]

Kara wasn't the only one sweating; Riven felt a trickle of it running down his face. Gluttony seemed absent for the moment, either unable or unwilling to give input.
Shit.
Shit.
Shit.
With his heart continuing to race, Riven picked his single ability and only hoped that he'd chosen correctly. And as the seconds ticked down to zero, in that last instant, a huge, clawed hand crashed through the pyramid roof above the destroyed marketplace and smashed into another delver in a splattering of blood. The guy never stood a chance with a strike that fast. The aura of the titanic

fleshy abomination that'd appeared there soared to new heights and began to weigh down on everyone present as everything around them sprang into action and the fifty teams began to flee or fight as roars from all around the otherwise abandoned city began to reach the sky.

[Riftwalk has been selected. You may begin.]

A different winged creature crashed through the near wall, a mix of eagle and snake, tearing through the streets toward them with wild abandon, and yet another monster that looked like a large floating puffer fish smashed through a different wall to start spewing acid in all directions. An unfortunate necromancer was caught up in the raining acid and let out a yelp before melting into goo within seconds.

A dome of flames roared to life around their team as Azmoth activated his ability, blocking falling chunks of the ceiling as the stone crashed and bounced off the defensive skill. Fay cast a dreamwalker zone to hide them from the eagle-snake beast rapidly closing the distance between them. The beast stuttered to a stop, confused by their sudden disappearance, and whirled to chase another team of delvers who were racing toward the nearest stairwell.

[Level 378 Venomous Guardian, Raptor Serpent. LEGENDARY. EVENT CREATURE]

Riven, meanwhile, kept an eye out for other creatures as the madhouse unfolded and Azmoth went to pick up the still convulsing beholder demon, Narg. Riven relaxed slightly when he saw that most of the forty-nine other teams were drawing the monsters away and out into different parts of the city as they fled. He did a head count and motioned for everyone to remain silent. He was absolutely sure that they'd be unable to stay here forever, but milking it for time wasn't a bad thing and he'd take what he could get.

"YOU BITCH!"

Riven heard a woman scream as he whirled around, only to see Zafima rushing at Kara's back with crackling Black Lightning at her fingertips. Kara was holding her wolf close and had her gaze locked on a distant battle, so it was doubtless she'd see it in time to react. Zafima the drow enchantress obviously still had a bone to pick with the other dark elf woman, and by the way she wore a crazed look of rage with lips curled back, he had little doubt Zafima intended to kill Kara even if it meant losing her own life in the process.

Riven immediately went for his staff to try and use Jackal's innate abilities as a way he could optimize his firepower, now that he was down nearly all his skills, but unfortunately Elysium wasn't having it. It appeared he really only could use Riftwalk even concerning his items imbued with abilities, as that was the only soul sigil on his pillars that activated upon command.

A flash of darkness ripped open in front of him and he imposed himself directly in between the two dark elves, colliding with the Black Lightning in an explosion of debris that ripped open a large part of his forehead and right upper cheek where Messenger's armor didn't cover. His right eye also got annihilated as Zafima screamed in anger, putting everything she could into the skill in an attempt to kill the other woman, and with Riven's abilities mostly locked down, all he could do was take the hit.

He was sent sprawling, slamming into Kara as she turned, and the puppy she was holding let out a loud yelp when Kara smashed into the floor.

"WHY WAS SHE THE CHOSEN ONE?!" Zafima shrieked, getting another bolt of Black Lightning charged up at her fingertips. "SHE IS UNDESERVING OF—"

CRUNCH

Sanguine the blood drake was the fastest to react. It snapped huge carnivorous jaws down onto Zafima's upper half, ripping her stomach open with huge crimson teeth while the drow enchantress let out muted screams inside its maw. Lifting the kicking and desperately flailing woman into the air as Black Lightning crackled out from the edges of the drake's mouth in her attempts to make it let go, Sanguine jerked the bitten woman back and forth like a wild animal would do to smaller prey. Opening up to chomp and crunch down again a few times over, squelching noises and garbled cries of pain were accompanied before the drake swallowed her whole with a gulp. Riven watched the bulge of her body travel down the drake's throat, settling in Sanguine's stomach moments later.

Riven's eye was already re-forming through his vampiric regeneration, and he took General Caltan's hand to pull himself up.

"Are you okay?!" Kara gasped, rushing over to him after making sure the puppy was all right, while the others looked on, knowing full well he'd be fine. "I . . . I can't thank you enough, again."

Riven brushed himself off and shrugged. "Don't mention it. Sucks that Zafima was let out by Elysium—that's a thrall down the toilet, but not much we can do about it now."

"He's fine!" Fay said, patting Riven's shoulder with a wink. "He's taken a lot worse punishment from a lot stronger people before. Those wounds will be healed up in no time."

Kara still looked worried but nodded with pursed lips and stepped back to give Riven some breathing room.

The tower shook as something huge smashed into the lower levels, and then three more impacts caused Riven to fall to his knees as many of the others did, too. A guttural roar from somewhere far below caused Riven's ears to hurt, and was accompanied by a loud snapping sound before the tower started leaning to the left. His eyes went wide, and his team began to slide that way as the tower began to fall.

Genua screamed with a crying Iris clutched tightly in her hands, but Sanguine lurched forward to catch the two in its claws. Crimson strings shot out from Athela in a weblike pattern the next second, rapidly catching their entire group and stopping them from sliding while the tower smashed against another skyscraper, mostly stopping its descent with a resounding *BOOM*. The pyramid-shaped ceiling buckled at the very pinnacle where it'd connected with another building, sending dust and debris billowing into the large chamber where the shops were located. Seconds later, the tower came to a grinding halt, tilted at a forty-five-degree angle.

Other teams that'd also stayed weren't so lucky to have someone who could stop their falling, and they quickly found themselves sliding down the sloped streets while being chased by various monsters that continued to appear through holes and cracks around the top floor. Riven saw a screaming orc shaman get swallowed by a giant leech, a ghoul warrior on the opposite side of the floor get impaled by a cross between a spider and a centipede before having his head ripped off, and a frantic dwarf woman get roasted alive with a belch of infernal power out of the mouth of a giant three-headed Cerberus.

Riven gave Athela a thankful thumbs-up, heart thudding in his chest. "Nice catch!"

The area around them flickered and shattered, and Fay abruptly vomited blood with a backlash of power as her dreamwalker zone's illusion splintered into a million pieces. The direct cause for this was probably the large, plated scorpion bearing down on them, with a mystical, glowing eyeball in place of a stinger, and the pressure it gave off was absolutely immense. Huge pincers snapped and crackled with gray and red chaos energies, and it nimbly clambered over the buildings with a hiss. Somehow, that eye had annihilated Fay's magic, and Riven could feel through their link that she'd also accumulated a very long cooldown. She wouldn't be able to use her single ability for quite some time.

[Level 362 Sight Bringer, Ashen Wastelands Scorpion. LEGENDARY. EVENT CREATURE]

A snap of sound and flash of gray light erupted from the eye at the end of its tail, and Riven opened a rift to swallow the energy bolt in a split-second decision. The rift's other end opened up behind his party and the scorpion's bolt completely bypassed his team, smashing into another monster instead and splitting open the bearlike beast in a spray of gore. Buildings were torn asunder under the power of that bolt, and Riven went pale at the thought of what would have happened should it have hit them.

A beam of supersonic blood erupted out of Sanguine's throat in response, blasting the scorpion backward and causing it to stagger. A follow-up from Retesh's staff sent a huge ball of neon-teal flames crashing into the scorpion's tail-eye, causing it to let out a shriek of pain and rage. The monster's reaction was so pronounced that Kara followed up a third time when it managed to recover, shooting one of the arrows Riven had made for her directly into its eye with a streak of red and black light.

Which was bullshit, in Riven's opinion, because why would her arrows work and not his staff? Was it just channeled abilities but not enchantments that were nullified?

He tapped his staff on the ground in a moment of realization, just to see for himself, and felt slightly better about the situation when he managed to activate Jackal's on-hit explosion in a puff of hellfire.

Thankfully the beast didn't seem to have more than one ability, either, and every time it opened its tail-end eye it was blasted, causing the armored scorpion to retreat. Despite this, their attacks were doing minimal damage to the monster and there were more enemies coming their way. Riven and party couldn't stay here or they'd die, which was precisely why he'd picked Riftwalk as his sole ability to get him through.

One hour into the event:

Lizard hadn't felt this alive in . . . Well, he couldn't remember. But it'd been a very long time. His white scales were drenched in sweat and part of his tail was missing, but he barely felt the pain through the flood of adrenaline.

Sparks lit up as claws met his blade, and his sword accelerated through sheer force of will to meet an opposite strike as he held off the beast attacking him so the rest of his team could go ahead. He'd even volunteered for this, and his draconic teeth gleamed in the dim light of the strange city as sounds of battle echoed throughout the landscape.

Rushing through the hallways of a large keep and following the rest of his team through the next rift portal Riven had conjured for them, Lizard side-stepped another claw strike from the six-legged cat. Rupturing Parry, his best and currently sole ability, connected with the far stronger cat's claws and created a moment in time where rebounding chaos would replace the enemy's momentum and explode backward. It had to be timed to the millisecond, not too soon or too late, but Lizard's past life had given him ample experience despite his memories still being fuzzy. It was akin to muscle memory, and he grew more proud of his own prowess with the skill every time he successfully landed it. But if he made even a single wrong move and triggered at the wrong time, he was done for.

The thrill of it was invigorating and exciting. He couldn't hope to kill the monster by himself, but so what? The fact that he was even successfully defending against such a beast that was both far faster and physically superior to him in every way was enough to get his entire team's heads turning his way in astonishment with every successful parry he achieved, sending off the sharp claws of the monster with a rebuffing splash of chaos stamina directly back into the cat's snarling face.

"LIZARD!" Riven yelled over the angry yowling of the large cat while holding the portal open with his right hand, extending his left hand out to where Lizard was batting aside the cat's attacks. "THROUGH! NOW!"

Another rift in space sliced cleanly through the air right behind Lizard's position, and Lizard didn't hesitate to fling himself through. He rolled to the floor right before the next portal where the rest of the team had already vanished and barely came up to parry yet another claw strike from the cat as it, too, tried to go through the rift in space.

A splash of guts and blood and a startled cry caused Lizard to snap his head backward over the backlash of chaos energy in his sword arm, and his eyes widened in surprise when he saw Riven's shadow portal trying to close over the half-through six-legged cat. Only the single paw it'd swung at Lizard with was all the way out this side, along with part of its chest, its neck, and its head. The portal had attempted to snap shut, but due to the endurance of the beast, it was having a hard time doing so and was instead sawing away at the innards of the monster. The portal was flickering and Lizard wasn't sure whether it would give out first and force the cat through one side or if it would succeed in Riven's attempt to decapitate the beast.

"I've always hated cats," Riven said, twirling his staff around in one hand and grinning under Messenger's mask where it covered everything under the bridge of his nose. "I've always been more of a dog person!"

BOOM

Riven swung Jackal directly into the cat's face with an explosion of hellfire, ripping off part of the cat's face. Blood sprayed out of the screeching, struggling creature as the portal continued to close down on its body like a razor-sharp vise grip, and Riven swung again.

And again.

And again.

[Jackal (Legendary Weapon, Vampiric Artifact, Sin Artifact, Gluttony Aspect, Sorcerer's Staff) (Evolving Symbiote): 1,812 average damage on strike with each physical strike dealing additional explosive Infernal damage.]

Lizard watched his master bash the skull of the trapped cat until there was nothing left of the cat's head but a roasted, smoldering hunk of meat at the base of its neck.

Grinning and pushing himself up to his feet, he raced through the portal with Riven in tow, closing it behind them as a huge armored centipede spotted them and raced down the hall in their direction with clicking mandibles and flaring red eyes.

Two hours into the event:

The wall crumbled like a ruptured balloon under the titanic humanoid that giggled and laughed while chasing them down.

Fish was flung off her feet and to the left, being yanked by Athela's red strings just in time to avoid the falling body of the cyclops. She felt her blood run cold as the spot she'd just been in was eradicated under the sheer weight of the giant creature, but she managed to finish casting another draining hex on the cyclops to slow it down significantly before Azmoth's equally enormous form barreled into the one-eyed monster.

Flaming wings and armored claws dug into fleshy skin, trying to find a grip as the far stronger and overlevered cyclops rolled around on the cathedral's outer grounds. A dome of fire burst out from Azmoth's body and collided with the titanic beast, sending the cyclops backward through another wall only for their opponent to smash a meaty fist into Azmoth's armored face. The natural armor coating the brutalisk buckled and gave way, splashing molten blood all over the ground as Athela screamed at Fish to wake up.

"WHAT IS WRONG WITH YOU WOULD-BE THRALLS?! STOP STOPPING AND MOVE!" Athela roared, slapping Fish across the face and pointing to where Riven was missing an arm and holding up another portal to span the length of a river of souls winding through the city's center. "AND DO IT NOW!"

Another skyscraper fell as an explosion from farther up caused Fish to startle, and she scrambled to her feet when a tiefling delver's corpse splattered onto the nearby stone road. "What about Azmoth?!"

Athela yanked and then shoved Fish toward the portal with a huff. "Azmoth is staying behind."

"But he'll die!"

The level-390 cyclops ripped one of Azmoth's wings off and tackled the brutalisk to the ground, taking a bite out of the archdemon before Azmoth managed to rake his claws over the exposed eye of the cyclops and caused it to scream. Even with the slowing hex applied, a portal trying to sever the cyclops' lower right ankle, and the barrage of death globes from Retesh, it was obvious the cyclops was going to come out victorious on this one as Azmoth was ravaged.

"And he'll be sent back to the nether realms in a day, what of it?" Athela whirled and jabbed a finger into Fish's sternum. "You, on the other hand, can't respawn. Don't be the one who holds us back, Fish! I don't want to have to tell you again!"

Three hours into the event:

There wasn't enough time, and the treasure spawned by the system that'd been meant to create a defensive bunker had been snatched by another team moments before arriving.

They weren't going to make it through the hive mind of wraiths swooping down onto his master's location, and even now, the team that'd gotten to the treasure first was literally laughing at their efforts to flee again.

But Sanguine was built for speed, and the knowing look the blood drake exchanged with Riven was more than enough. Sanguine, with Genua and Iris on his back, took to the skies in a burst of power as Riven and the rest of their group rushed through the portal.

Genua screamed and blasted one of the swarming wraiths from the sky in a flash of red, then another, and another, as Sanguine picked up speed and pumped his wings to accelerate at blinding speed. Rising up into the dark sky above them and with a swarm of wraiths at their back, Sanguine let out a defiant roar while unleashing a stream of hypersonic blood that sliced through a number of the wraiths before racing into the distance. Leaving a trail of crimson in their wake, Sanguine rushed into the clouds like a red comet to leave his pursuers in the dust.

CHAPTER 40

[Six hours have passed. Two hours remain. Twenty-three of fifty descent teams remain; 8,117 of ten thousand peak E-grade monsters remain.]

Black skies rumbled overhead with the crash of distant battles that echoed over roars from the streets. In front of him, a three-armed, green-skinned mutant man with a multitude of bloodshot eyes covering his body was whipping about another attack in a forward thrust that split the air with a scream of wind.

Caltan, formerly known as General Caltan, was at the forefront of their charge as his tower shield barely parried a scathing blow from an oncoming spear that nearly cracked the metal of his armor. He was sent rolling due to the strength of the much higher-leveled mutant warrior but regained his footing and used the momentum to swing his very large, flanged mace in an arcing uppercut. The weapon smashed back the three-armed mutant humanoid, and he pressed the attack with swift sidesteps utilizing his red flash.

[Red Flash (Tier-1 Blood Martial Art): Flash forward in a burst of crimson while dealing additional blast damage upon any physical strike.]

Out of all his abilities, this was the one he'd settled on. It was easily used in quick succession and let him compete with the much stronger and larger creature's repetitive spear thrusts. Not only that, but he was also able to amplify his own blocks, counters, and offensive strikes if he focused the skill into specific parts of his body instead of utilizing it as a whole. The exchange left his limbs blurring in repeated red flashes while the mutant, nearly 160 levels above him, was being pressed backward as their weapons clashed in a storm of metal blows.

Flipping over another spear thrust and spinning over the mutant's extended green arm, Caltan smashed the flat of his shield into the monster's body and swept the creature's left leg with his mace. Even so, levels didn't count for nothing, and despite Caltan outclassing the mutant in combat in every given way, he was doing little damage with each of his strikes that'd be devastating to anyone his own level.

Caltan sneered as much as he could with a skull for a face, smashing aside another spear thrust, and was then sent catapulting backward into another building across the street in a spray of dust and debris. He clicked his bony jaws together, cracked his neck, and pulled himself out of the collapsing building with sheer brute strength while bringing dislocated hip bones back to their original placements. He could see the floating orb of shimmering white light ahead and behind the roaring beast, the prize behind the curtain, and touching it would have lasting implications for the trial if what they'd seen of the other teams was any indication. Finally, they'd come across an unused bunker zone. Most of them were guarded by the more dangerous monsters in the event, bringing destruction to many of the teams that tried accessing them, but those that managed to reach one seemed to be getting various nondescript boosts that allowed them to hold their own or sequester themselves entirely for a time. Thankfully it appeared that this particular mutant wasn't all that strong despite being designated to guard this place.

Riven had even tried to teleport in to touch the sphere, but the area was quarantined and didn't allow teleport abilities to function inside a large radius, so Caltan had volunteered to take on the guardian monster alone while the others held off the three rather powerful werewolves that were on their heels. Even now he could hear the werewolves howling amid the clash of weapons and magic.

Genua and Sanguine were both long gone, having fled the hive mind of wraith oddities that swarmed the city streets in the central district. Azmoth had been banished. The Zafima woman had been eaten after her betrayal. Lizard and Fay were in terrible shape, both being carried by other people and sporting deep wounds from when they'd run into a lasher monster with serrated whips for limbs. Narg had never been able to hold his own to begin with, having been banished from the plane within minutes of the event starting. All in all it wasn't going too terribly, though, because unlike many of the other teams, they were still alive. Gluttony had played a small part in that to an extent, showing himself only twice to flicker in and out in large snapping motions when saving Retesh and Fish from certain death. In larger part that was also due to Riven's ability to teleport their group around, but with how frequently this needed to be done, even Riven's enormous mana pool was becoming exhausted.

Caltan's red eyes gleamed under his horned helmet, and the bloodstricken undead went in for another engagement when a streak of crackling black and red smashed into the mutant spear wielder's centermost eye.

The mutant howled and stumbled back, only for Caltan to capitalize upon the larger creature's pain and surprise with a devastating blow to its neck. A loud *CRACK* resounded out from the blow, but it still wasn't enough and he was flung back by the mutant's third arm only for another two arrows to lodge themselves into the beast's chest.

"I've got your back! The others are almost finished!" Kara yelled from the side street, and the drow archer notched another arrow. "It's almost dead! Let's do this!"

Caltan briefly evaluated the drow archer, snorted, and turned his red gaze upon the beast again. He let the next arrow slam home and took a spear strike sliding off his pauldron before crashing his knee into the mutant's gut, followed by a flash of blood that sent him backward to avoid a grappling maneuver. If the howling, enraged mutant managed to get its large hands around Caltan, the fight was over. His skill would mean little when it came down to a sheer contest of strength, and the beast would no doubt have far more of it given their level discrepancy.

Thankfully he was managing to outpace the monster, though, and after twelve more arrows and seven more bashes with his mace, the monster eventually fell dead to the ground with its brains splattered along the road.

"Good work, elfling." His deep, masculine voice projected out from his cracked armor as he started forward. "You are not as useless as the others deem you to be."

Kara simultaneously blushed in embarrassment and winced, not knowing whether to take that as a compliment or not. He had no time to explain it to her, either, and reached out and grasped the floating orb of shimmering white light. Just as the others rounded a corner of the last building, bloodied and bruised, Athela carrying the severed heads of two large werewolves, a notification appeared.

[You have accessed a spatially compacted defensive bunker zone. Activating this bunker zone will grant you either one hour of complete sanctuary from all harm or two hours of reduced enemy levels down to a flat level 201 for anything that enters the zone. Which do you wish to select?]

He didn't even need to think twice. They were only a little over five hours into the event, they needed to reach eight hours, and their party could easily handle a bunch of level 201s even if they were still ranked as LEGENDARY. Caltan selected the second option, and the street erupted into a showering of white-hot light.

Pillars lurched skyward almost instantly and a domed ceiling of solid metal began forming from the cooling light, settling into shifting black and purple hues that radiated the truths of the abyss. Caltan actually saw Riven stumble when an obvious epiphany hit him like a sprinting bull, but Athela tugged the warlock toward the bunker zone shortly thereafter and the trance was broken. There were already more enemies closing in, and despite the obvious frustration on Riven's face, probably for having lost much of the insights into the Dao of the deep places of the multiverse, he needed to get into the relatively safe area beyond the pillars and underneath the dark dome ceiling.

"Two hours?" Riven said, panting as he hit the ground with both knees and slid to a stop underneath the bunker zone. "Two hours of level 201s? We can hold this place. That's doable, right?"

He continued panting, his soul core giving off obvious fluctuations of a very strained Shadow subpillar, producing pockets of black spots that flexed in and out of existence around him in the air.

Caltan lowered his gaze to his new master and nodded while pointing his mace to a building in the back half of the zone. "We will be able to handle it. The monsters that enter this place will be significantly weakened, and we will have the advantage. Go, you need rest. You've been producing rifts constantly for almost six hours now. Take the injured into the building and use what potions you have to settle your soul cores."

Riven glanced over his shoulder at the large flaming turtle and the bone golem lumbering toward their position before breathlessly using Jackal to push himself to his feet. "I just informed Genua through my minion link that she and Sanguine could find refuge here, but they're being followed by that wraith swarm."

"Still?"

"Still. Retesh, create another skeleton cannon from these corpses and set it up."

The tired lich nodded in Riven's direction, already heading toward the mutant that Kara and Caltan had slain. Fish and Brute were picking clean the bodies of dead delvers nearby, unceremoniously flinging their spatial rings and amulets into sacks.

Retesh grunted at the two beasts coming toward them on the road. "It'll take me another few minutes to create the cannon since my last one wasn't able to be recovered at all, but the construct will certainly amplify my death globes. Please cover me while I work."

Athela finished shoving a wincing Fay into Riven's arms and dropped Lizard off like deadweight along the building's interior before coming to stand beside Caltan and the others. She stared at the approaching flame turtle and bone golem with raised eyebrows. "If their levels are reduced inside this place, we'll be fine. Look."

She pointed.

Just as she did, and within a thousand feet of the zone they now inhabited, the monsters running their way began to shrink slightly, and their auras were significantly diminished. Caltan watched curiously as their enemies began dropping levels by the second, from 381 to 356 to 304 in seconds. The monsters stopped reducing their levels at 201 but didn't seem to notice as they continued plowing toward them with renewed ferocity the closer they got.

Kara didn't waste any time, notching one of the arrows that replicated Riven's Critical Storm Lance, and fired twice in a row.

They all watched in muted silence as the streams of red and black hissed through the air, exploding on impact with a devastating force that shattered the bone golem entirely and stunned the turtle in one go. Another arrow hit its leg, and then another hit its exposed neck before the beast dropped like a rock into the street.

They all turned to look at Kara, then at each other, as large smiles widened across their faces. Kara seemed mighty pleased, and for good reason. She was easily the weakest one here, even between Fish, Lizard, and Brute, the would-be thralls. Yet she had just taken out not one but two of the monsters that'd so recently been peak and LEGENDARY-rank E-grades. Even with upgraded arrows, they were being launched from her own bow and her own fingers, so it'd be her stats that influenced the projectiles.

"So, on that note, I'm going to go heal Lizard and Fay," Riven said with a relieved laugh. Wincing and turning around, he began dragging the half-dead succubus along with him to the building where Lizard already lay on the ground groaning. "The potions may take a bit considering their damage. Be on the lookout for Genua and Sanguine. They should be here any minute."

The abyssal dome covering their bunker zone was working wonders, and for the first time since the event started, they were finally able to have some breathing room. Despite the monsters not being absolute pushovers, they were still all barely E-grade, and regular level 201s just couldn't match the raw power of Riven's elite group even with Azmoth gone. One for one, any monster that entered the zone was easily matched. But most of the time they didn't need to be and were promptly handled with overwhelming force with a systematic battle formation after everyone had been healed.

General Caltan, Lizard the white draconic, and the half-ogre Brute were the front line in Azmoth's absence. Sanguine would sometimes join them in melee but usually kept to the sky and utilized his supersonic blood beams to annihilate things from under the dome's shadow. Brute in particular was a heavy hitter in close combat, using an ability called Sledgehammer that made enemies literally explode whenever his spiked fists met flesh. Brute was something of a pugilist, though he was also familiar with various melee weapons when Riven had asked.

Retesh had manually constructed a skeleton cannon that amplified his deathly orbs and was wreaking havoc from the midline on an elevated rooftop along with Kara, who shot arrows at whatever the lich didn't manage to blow up, and Genua, who was using her miracle Sanguine Smite to crush things at a slightly closer range than the other two.

Athela and Fay were on overwatch, creating diversions or dealing with the more stealth-oriented adversaries together. They'd been working together rather well over the past months coming down the descent, and their teamwork was only getting better as Fay hid Athela's movements with illusions even more than what Athela was usually able to do on her own, and that was saying something. Simultaneously, Fay would also blind the minds of the incoming monsters with similar projections, making them rather easy prey for the Arshakai demoness.

Lastly, Riven was in the back line and looking out a window while holding Iris in his arms, with Fish the yellow-skinned merwoman standing beside him in a shredded witch's outfit that was barely there anymore after she'd been mauled so many times. Her wounds were gone at least, but she looked rather ashamed of herself at having been nearly killed. Riven would divert enemy attacks, redirecting them through portals as a support and sometimes managing to decapitate enemies while closing rifts around their heads, and Fish would utilize her draining hex to rapidly slow down and weaken enemies for the front line to finish off whenever they came too close.

Bodies of fallen creatures lay splattered and slain by the hundreds, creating small hills of corpses all over the bunker zone, and every other minute a new one—or even several—would show themselves to mindlessly assault their team's position.

"You have a very cute daughter. Eh, I know I say that a lot," Fish commented, seemingly infatuated with Iris as the little girl played with a small doll the women had made for her earlier on this floor. "I just want to have a daughter like that someday."

"Perhaps you will," Riven replied, smiling and raising his staff to create another portal that opened and snapped around the head of a flying dinosaur-like creature, decapitating it in a spray of blood right after it flew into the bunker zone's influence. "I didn't think I'd be a father anytime soon, but that's what I get for sleeping around."

Fish raised an eyebrow. "Do you regret it? Having a child with your thrall? I thought vampires looked down on that sort of thing."

"Absolutely not. I'm glad Iris was born," Riven replied without hesitation, but his eyes flitted to the image of a familiar, enraged high elf in the corner of the room that only he could see. The figure of Ethel screamed at him from the beyond before disappearing the next moment like she'd never been there to begin with. "I sometimes regret how Genua and I started out, but I've put a lot of thought into it and think it was for the best. It's a long and complicated story, that one."

"She thinks she's your wife and is infatuated with you. Will I have similar thoughts?"

"Doubtful. The vampiric virus doesn't necessarily work like that—it just shapes your mind to better serve the vampire who changes you. For Genua in particular, her mind broke under the virus's influence in order to cover up her lingering resentment after I murdered her husband and eldest daughter. You, however, don't need to cover up old memories of resentment. It's highly likely that you'll retain your entire being and just see me in a more positive light that influences you to pursue my ambitions."

He patted Iris's head and smiled. "Have you given any thought to what kind of husband you'd like? There are merpeople back on Panu, if they suit your fancy. But they're also at war with Retesh's faction, so it's highly likely we'll be going to war with them, too."

Fish shrugged indifferently, casting a few more hexes on some large venomous lizards heading toward Caltan and Brute. "I haven't thought much about it, but if you're willing to let me pursue relationships outside my thrall contract, then perhaps I'll try to find a werewolf to date. The ones that fought us earlier were rather attractive before Athela took their heads, and I wouldn't mind having one to come home to."

"What would a werewolf and a merperson even produce as offspring?"

"I do know it's compatible. I can't entirely remember how I know, but I have a very strong feeling that I've seen or heard about that particular combination working out from a faint memory of my past life."

Riven tilted his head to the side, trying to envision what a baby between a fish and a large, muscular werewolf would look like. "Hmm. Werewolves can transition into a human form, right?"

Fish held out her hand and twisted it from side to side. "It depends on if the werewolf was originally human or not. If it started out as a human, then yes. If it started out as something else, it reverts to whatever that was, but it will retain some of the lycan characteristics, too. Usually in the form of fur, fangs, a tail, something like that. It just depends on how potent the lycan side of the bloodline is."

"I see. Kara actually got a token to become either a vampire or a werewolf. She's deciding now, to my understanding."

"I know, she showed it to me when I mentioned my recently acquired infatuation with werewolves." Fish chuckled dryly. "Unfortunately she would not give it to me, but that is to be expected. She's rather insistent on impressing you with the transformation. Do you have a preference in what she chooses?"

Riven shook his head, watching Sanguine and Athela split apart another group that tried to sneak in off the left side of the zone, this one large, carnivorous goat men wielding axes. "No, I don't. I'll be happy either way."

"I heard you almost ate her once."

Riven raised an eyebrow, and slowly turned to look at the merwoman. "Who told you that?"

"Kara did."

"She knows?"

Fish shrugged. "She said it was right before I arrived and shortly after you unlocked a part of your vampiric bloodline. Ring a bell?"

". . . Yes, she's right. I just didn't know she knew."

"Don't take it to heart, Riven. You didn't eat her, and she's firmly indebted to you in more ways than one. She's anything but angry and just hopes to please."

The two of them paused and turned their heads in the direction of another descent team racing toward their location with a trail of enemy monsters chasing them down. Only three of the other team were left, with the third and slowest of them falling to a bloody death when a massive, clawed hand crashed through a wall to rip him from this life. They were all tieflings, and the two remaining men were absolutely terrified as they smashed face-first into the bunker zone's outer perimeter.

Riven winced, as it was obvious the first fleeing tiefling had broken his nose, and utilized mana to emphasize his voice so the two tieflings could hear him. "The bunker zone won't allow other teams inside. Go find another one."

"LET US INSIDE!!!" the second tiefling shrieked at the top of his lungs, pounding on an invisible barrier that sealed off Riven's team from the other. "LET US INSIDE, PLEASE!!!"

Riven projected two rift portals and used the shadows to pull the two tieflings out, narrowly getting them out of harm's way before the descending monsters pounced. "I would if I could, but I can't! You two need to run! Now go!"

Retesh, Genua, and Kara had already begun firing on the monsters the tieflings had led into the zone, and Fish was busy slowing them down while the front liners shifted positions to match the two dozen oncoming enemies.

Athela flashed inside the building behind Riven's back, quickly killed another stealthed mutant, and vanished again as Riven gave her a mental thumbs-up. The room he'd chosen as the back line's holdout was connected to the rooftop the midline was now settled on, but it was one floor above them and also had a reinforced back door where Athela's webs had created a lattice most enemies wouldn't be able to get through. Even if they did, they'd certainly alert the arachnid assassin—the dozens of bodies behind Riven's position were more than enough of a testament to that fact.

The tieflings continued to scream for entry, begging Riven's party to adjust the barriers so they could enter, but they stopped ignoring Riven's warnings and made a run for it shortly after when they realized that the monsters outside the bunker zone were still coming on hard. Despite the small bombardment from Riven's midliners, the farthest-most monsters that hadn't entered the influence of the bunker zone were still as strong as ever, and it took a lot more to even scratch those bastards than anything that entered the circle of death created by their abyssal dome above.

CHAPTER 41

The tusked humanoid beast reared up to its full height, spitting out debris from its bloodied mouth where it'd slammed face-first into the stone after lunging through a misdirected rift in space. "I WILL TEAR YOUR BONES FROM YOUR BODY, VAMPIRE CHILD!"

It flipped its hands outward and formed a steepled cross with its sausage-like fingers, channeling chaos energy into its next attack that crackled along its skin.

Riven raised an eyebrow and put his hands on his hips. "What is that, like, a gang sign or something?"

"CALL OF THE CHAOS RIPPLE!" the tusked humanoid snarled, and the ground shattered in a wave of pulsating chaos directly in line with Riven's position.

Riven slammed his staff down into the attack's trajectory and dispersed the shock wave with a radiating boom of flames on contact with Jackal's skull head, smirking at the beast's piss-poor attempt. "Here, it's my turn! Strangling mouths of a thousand black holes!"

The air around Riven's enemy became speckled with dozens and then hundreds of tiny rifts that opened and closed down onto the monster, shredding him from all directions and in different trajectories. Sprays of gore were splattered and sent spewing out of the tiny rifts' other ends, and the beast fell dead to the ground in a heap of splattered body parts.

"Strangling mouths of a thousand black holes?" Athela said, coming over to lean against him with a snort and a laugh. "What are you trying to do, bore us to death with your poor naming schemes?"

"Cultivation novels always have naming schemes like that. Don't you know? You read a lot of Earth's old literature in the nether realms shortly after bonding with me, didn't you?"

"Well, yes, but I didn't ever read any cultivation novels. They had those back on Earth?"

"Oh yeah! Lots of talk about young masters killing each other and chi and whatnot."

"What's chi?"

"Basically a type of energy, equivalent to mana. The important part is that they ALWAYS named their attacks things like Death From a Thousand Viper Strikes or Glory of a Billion Blazing Suns! They'd shout it out while doing the move and maybe do some cool martial arts, too."

Athela did not look impressed. "So, Strangling Mouths of a Thousand Black Holes was your cheap naming imitation of conjuring a bunch of riftwalks, even though you didn't need to say it out loud?"

"I did it for style points!" Riven said defensively. "You wouldn't understand, okay? Just let me have my moment now that we're in a relatively safe area and not surrounded by monsters nearing level 400!"

Relatively safe was the key there. It was nowhere near safe, which was why Genua and Fish were currently on full-time baby duty to make sure that Iris didn't get hurt.

Athela gasped and smacked Riven upside the back of his head before pretending to threaten him with one of her katanas. "You take that back RIGHT NOW! I'm the most STYLISH one of this bunch, you hear me?!"

General Caltan's figure blurred left and his mace smashed another gigantic snapping turtle, sending the creature spinning out of the bunker zone like a torpedo from hell. The rest of the battlefield was much the same, though they had changed locations since the first bunker zone they'd acquired.

Riven's group was maintaining a rhythm, defeating wave after wave of enemies until the abyssal dome had run out of time for utilization. But that same tiefling party of two that his company helped earlier in the night were able to wave Riven down at the very end of the last remaining hour, into another defensive bunker zone that allowed up to three teams inside instead of one, but otherwise the zone was very similar to the monster level suppression that General Caltan had grabbed.

Aside from the two tieflings and with only fifteen minutes to spare, Riven hadn't hesitated to claim the third team slot and promptly got to work defending the bunker area along with the two tieflings and the other team he hadn't met yet.

The tieflings, it turned out, were both swordsmen and pretty damn good ones, but then again, they had to be in order to make it this far in the descent. They didn't bother introducing themselves after their initial shouts to grab Riven's attention but merely went back to work killing the monster swarms that continued barreling into their position with renewed vigor now that the time limit was almost up. The monsters had become crazed, forgoing all strategy or self-preservation in favor of ending the remaining delvers now that the end of the event was approaching. The heat was figuratively turned up and everyone was absolutely exhausted. Some were even badly injured and were essentially deadweight that needed to be protected until they got potions or healing.

But protect them they did.

The other team that Riven hadn't met yet were a full delving team of five, though unlike Riven's team, they didn't have any minions to bolster their numbers. They were men from a demihuman species with fox ears and tails, four of them being spear users while the last was a dark mage, and were incredibly agile, armored by a strange assortment of Unholy-attuned plants. The plants were flexible but sturdy enough to take hits and were quick to repair themselves with infused mana, which Riven saw on multiple occasions. It was quite fascinating, as he noticed the plants seemed to be rooted to the demihumans' bodies after a hard blow from a monster claw exposed the layers underneath.

That plant armor in particular caught Riven's attention, and it made him wonder if he'd be able to find plants with similar properties somewhere down the road. Because if he could utilize such specimens in his enchanting and totem-making . . . that led to an entirely new branch of item creation.

[The final five minutes are all that remain. Eighteen of fifty descent teams remain; 5,983 of ten thousand peak E-grade monsters remain.]

Riven went all out with his remaining mana as the monsters continued sweeping in, tidal waves of dark tears through space redirecting or snapping down around enemies to eviscerate them.

[The final three minutes are all that remain. Seventeen of fifty descent teams remain; 5,111 of ten thousand peak E-grade monsters remain.]

A loud *BOOM* radiated across the city, and a building was toppled under the powerful strike of another delver that Riven didn't recognize. Shock waves of hellfire eradicated other buildings and monsters alike as the human torch used an enormous claymore bigger than Riven was tall to rip apart enemies even outside a bunker zone.

Riven gawked at the sheer power behind those strikes. It appeared that the other delvers had the same idea to let loose now that they didn't need to conserve their power. Even now on the horizon, a red sun began to rise to signal the coming of a new dawn in this strange place, but still his gaze was glued to the rushing madman whose features were unidentifiable due to both shrouding enchantments as well as the flames covering his features. Riven had thought his own power something to be proud of, but whatever or whoever was able to go out and slaughter numerous level-350-plus monsters outside the bunker zones was simply beyond him.

It made him realize just how big the multiverse really was, and that though he was strong, there were people that still probably outstripped even him.

[The final two minutes are all that remain. Sixteen of fifty descent teams remain; 4,622 of ten thousand peak E-grade monsters remain.]

To the far left and down a straight road within Riven's line of sight, yet another delver had taken up the flaming man's challenge. This person was a cloaked human woman with auburn hair who slammed an obsidian staff into the ground and unleashed a devastating tidal wave of Shadow-attuned energies that shattered an entire city block instantaneously, along with all the other monsters coming for her team. The beasts around her exploded in a blossoming flower of blood and shrapnel that was sent flying for miles in all directions, even over Riven's own head due to the force of the Shadow magic unleashed.

Then an Azag hive mantis burst out of a tower to unleash a furious assault on an armored dragon, shattering the level-362 dragon's skull in a burst of immense killing intent with bladed arms wreathed in . . .

In something.

Was that some sort of Depravity energy?

That's what it felt like. But it looked odd, not maintaining any color at all and having properties that warped the air around the mantoid's blades as it sliced and diced through the dragon with immense amounts of rage. Perhaps the dragon had killed one of the mantoid's teammates? He couldn't see any other reason why that dragon had specifically been targeted in the last moments while flying by.

Thus Riven would have stood slack-jawed, realizing that not one but three of the other delvers here obviously outclassed even him, and it made him sad that he'd not met these people.

Yet, at least. Perhaps in the future that may change, but it also gave him an inkling of what the wider multiverse was really like. He may be special in his own ways, but certainly wasn't alone in that category. There were others just like him, or in some cases even more dangerous. It was something to keep him on his toes at the very least.

[The final one minute is all that remains. Sixteen of fifty descent teams remain.

All abilities have been unlocked. You are now able to damage and kill other teams to loot from. All living monsters have been removed from the floor.

A truly unique D-grade treasure box containing the power of a single wish—within reason and grade—has been highlighted by a pillar of light in the city's center. The last person to be touching this treasure box upon the countdown's end will be allowed to leave with the prize.]

The monsters vanished into clouds of mist, their cries echoing one final time before disappearing altogether. The bunker zone around them shattered, and there was a moment of silence as all eyes turned to a pillar of deep-purple light that smashed down into the street a half mile away.

A wish, within reason and grade. That could mean a lot of things . . . and if it was here at the end of Floor Forty-Nine of the Abyssal Descent, a prize to be contested by the best of the Unholy pillar? There was a statistical chance of zero that this wish was something that Riven could pass up.

But he hesitated. Despite the other teams immediately carving their way through the city toward the beacon of light like mad hounds on the scent of blood, Riven had also registered the other words of warning Elysium had let off. They were now able to kill and loot other teams, teams that'd bought from the same prize shops on Floor Forty-Nine that Riven had. They were all essentially loaded with goodies ripe for the taking, and even in his peripheral vision he saw another team down a ruined back alley get assassinated by two rogues in quick succession. Shadows burst from the walls, and they were dead within seconds while only one of them had the time to let out a horrified scream.

All his teammates had similar thoughts, and the air was tense around them as Riven's group, the two tiefling swordsmen, and the five demihumans stood at an awkward distance away from one another amid piles of monster bodies.

Riven checked his skills and grinned as a sparking shaft of solid blood encompassed by Black Lightning and Sin formed in the air above him. He then turned around with another mana pulse and launched the Critical Storm Lance behind them.

The two-story building there was blown apart with a scream as one of the flanking assassins had his brain plastered along the flying rubble, his body torn apart instantly as his teammate quickly fled in a blur of darkness.

One of the tiefling swordsmen sheathed his weapon and held up his hands, taking a step away from the narrow-eyed demihumans and in the direction of Riven's team. "My brother and I want no part of violence. You already helped us once. Let us help each other again and avoid violence while making it to the next floor."

The sounds of battle erupted farther into the city as two of the more powerful delving teams clashed. In particular, Riven saw the mantoid and the fire-bathed man go at it with immense amounts of energy radiating off their bodies in a flurry of strikes between claymore and mantis blades.

Athela shifted into her drider form in the next second, becoming large and bright white as icy flowers bloomed across her skin and a crystalline maw ripped open where her humanoid and arachnid bodies connected at the front. She glowered at the demihumans threateningly and crackled with both Fae magic and Sin, her huge, sharp legs slamming into the stone road as dozens and then hundreds of crystalline spiders began crawling out of her maw as she prepared to fight.

The tieflings were no threat. Riven could feel it in the way their hearts thudded in their chests, and the genuine looks of appreciation they'd given his team earlier when they'd been helped out of a tight situation. But these demihumans . . .

Riven wasn't so sure.

Lizard and Fay had been mostly healed of their injuries but were still not in great condition, with Fay in particular looking rather worse for wear with a large gash across one wing. Retesh had damaged his mana channels and was having a hard time casting, and the teal glow in his eye sockets flitted from Riven to the demihumans with an audible gritting of his teeth. Nor had any of his zombie minions survived the floor debut. Caltan, Brute, and Athela seemed ready to go, though, while Fish, Genua, and Sanguine stood protectively over Iris clutched in Genua's arms.

Riven felt mana pull on his identity with some sort of skill and felt the ability fail as the men opposite him tried to get a read on what his class was. One of the demihumans shot his companions an obvious and questioning glance, silently asking whether or not they should attack, but the entire group of fox men took a rapid set of steps back as Riven's aura skyrocketed to the heavens. Red ice immediately coated their surroundings and a storm rumbled above them as Gluttony's maw flashed behind Riven's head.

Riven raised an eyebrow as he summoned the power to his call, mentally poking the great sin, who'd remained dormant the entire time during this trial until now. Riven's third, purple eye across his forehead also ripped open, giving his aura an additional boost that caused the windows that were still intact on nearby buildings to shatter simultaneously.

"I was locked down by Elysium" was Gluttony's audible response to Riven's internal question, and so Riven turned back around to stare at the five potential enemies dressed in plant-based armors not far off.

The demihumans were now wide-eyed and shocked, almost as shocked as the two tieflings who'd dropped down in prostrated positions of worship, and they immediately summoned a series of boosting skills that snapped around their bodies like blankets of Unholy stamina and mana. Their muscles pulsed and their own auras beat back at Riven's attempt to suppress them with small amounts of success. They were obviously reassessing their odds now that Gluttony had shown himself and they felt Riven's aura to its fullest, and despite not being anywhere close to pushovers, they lost the metaphorical dick-measuring contest and decided to back out.

"We will leave. Do not pursue us," the lone mage of the demihuman group called out, slowly backing away as his fox ears twitched from side to side and a semitranslucent wall of shadow began to separate the two groups. "Let us part ways amicably."

Forty seconds were left on the floor. The treasure box was being fought over this very moment and was currently in the hands of the flaming, claymore-wielding man as he was chased throughout the city by both the mantis, the shadow sorceress, and numerous others that fought and killed one another to get ahold of the wish given out by Elysium.

"Why let them go?" Brute asked with a snarl, spitting in the direction the demihumans ran as the wall of shadow evaporated behind them. "We should have gutted them and been done with it to take their bags of holding. They likely have very profitable goodies to plunder!"

Riven gestured for the tiefling men to stand, not looking their way and instead focusing on the fighting farther into the city. "Because fighting would have taken more time than it's worth. Let the tieflings live and form a defensive ring. Sanguine, to me."

The drake immediately scooped Riven up onto his back with a swift, fluid motion as the blood layer around his outer body swam up Riven's clothes to lock him in place.

"I'll go with you—" Athela began, but she was cut off with a quick snap of Riven's fingers.

"No, you're the most powerful one here aside from me. You stay here and watch Iris." Riven pointed to his daughter. "And protect the others. I'll only be taking a chance at the treasure chest if I get a clean swipe, otherwise I won't risk it. Wish me luck."

Athela was about to protest, but Riven was already launching into the air with a swift and powerful flap of Sanguine's wings. The drake let out a roar, and in a burst of power they were skybound with the buildings of the cityscape blurring beneath their intense acceleration. Although he wouldn't say it out loud, Riven wanted to test his mettle against the other three delvers who'd stood out above all the others in the last minutes of this trial. And above everything else . . . there was one very particular wish he wanted from Elysium. One that he wasn't sure Elysium would be able to grant—in fact, it probably wouldn't be able to bring Jose back from the dead, but he had to at least try.

If there was even a small chance, he'd take it.

The treasure box was easy to follow, and interestingly enough, it exchanged hands more than once even in the five seconds it took for Sanguine to get within Riven's projectile range. Towering auras of truly grandiose proportions rocked the city as the three outliers Riven had noticed earlier went to town in an attempt to claim the treasure box for themselves. They were all so fast that each action was interpreted in milliseconds, but each time a skill of any kind made contact with the treasure box illuminated by purple light, it'd be transported into the hands of whoever had landed the hit, regardless of whether that ability was offensive in nature or not.

An enormous explosion blasted the mantis backward first, flinging the creature through three buildings and covering the delver in magma. That explosion in turn smashed into the box the Azag hive cluster representative was holding, and the inflicted damage to the box transported it to the flaming man with the claymore. He turned to run in the opposite direction, only for the flying shadow witch with auburn hair to send a pillar of darkness crashing into him from the sky above with pinpoint accuracy, obliterating the street around them. He let out an angry scream as he was buried a hundred feet deep into the ground, and the shadow witch obtained the box a second later before being smashed aside by a whiplike tongue when the Azag mantis tried to get the box back. The mantis delivered energy blades swiping out through the air, wings buzzing and mandibles clicking viciously while engaging the flaming man as fire incarnate burst from the ground like a volcano to smash aside the mantis while simultaneously locking down the witch's flight with a cage of fire in the sky. The mantis doubled back and deflected two swings of the sword with its own blades before spewing acid at the treasure chest in the flaming man's off hand, obtaining the box yet again, only for the shadow witch to rip herself out of the mantis's shadow to blast both of the other competitors in the face with a reverse flash-bang of black light that sent them reeling in pain.

Dodging, strikes, projectiles, and movement abilities were utilized a dozen times per second between all of them—all the while they were unable to fully penetrate each other's defenses while simultaneously trying to get ahold of the box and break away. Those other participants that were foolhardy enough to try and interpose themselves were quickly mutilated and butchered, but these three were at a hard stalemate as the seconds ticked down.

That was, until a fourth massive aura entered the fray.

CRASH

The three original combatants were entombed in a cataclysmic swath of Crimson Ice as a large red blur shot through the air like a bullet. The ice was dissipated immediately along three different locations, but by then the box was already in Riven's hands.

Thankfully he was also riding an absolute unit of a racehorse, so to speak. To quote Elysium's description of Sanguine:

[Currently clocking rates at over four thousand miles per hour, or nearly six thousand feet per second, this monster is far faster than the speed of sound at max flight and has incredible acceleration, making it one of the fastest monsters to ever exist within the Abyssal Descent.]

The air felt like hot knives tearing into Riven's body as the acceleration increased, even through his armor and the blood layer of Sanguine's body encompassing Riven to reduce friction. They shot out into the sky, the large drake pulling up to avoid a lance of darkness that nearly ripped him in two.

Riven countered the flying shadow witch pursuing them with a roaring storm of Black Lightning and red frost that shattered the otherwise silent abyss above them, but the witch traveled up through the storm's Black Lightning with her Shadow affinities and landed on Sanguine's back with a snarl.

"THE WISH IS MINE!"

She lunged with a wand slamming into Riven's back, but Riven turned to deflect the wand, then her primary staff, and barely avoided another burst of deep black imbued with some kind of sharpness-related Dao that he didn't quite grasp. The darkness did split Sanguine's shoulder, though, and the drake let off an enraged scream as Riven smashed his staff into the witch's face with an explosion of flame.

She deflected with a quickly formed barrier and went in for another burst of darkness, only to meet a swath of Sin-afflicted beetles that poured from Riven's mouth like a tidal wave. The witch screamed in anger and riftwalked out of the way while swatting at the beetles with darkness-infused jabs, cursing loudly at Riven from her position in the back.

It was just in time for the abyssal sky to light up with the sun exploding overhead, only for its full weight to come bearing down on Riven's position like a magnet. The attack was simply too large to avoid, taking up a bigger surface area than the city itself did, and Riven's eyes widened in shock as the gears in his head rotated on overdrive to figure out what to do. He couldn't let that attack hit—his teammates were still in the city and the entire area would be eradicated if he didn't meet the attack head-on.

Growling and gritting his teeth, Riven's body burst with a storm of black and red that roared to life behind him. Blood and Shadow met fire in a monumental clash of titans, and the shock wave blew Sanguine off course to careen into a building. Riven and Sanguine tumbled through the top two floors and through an outer wall before the drake regained flight, but by that time Riven realized he'd lost the treasure box to the flaming man.

Only seven seconds were left.

"SHIT!"

He urged Sanguine back into the sky, and the drake quickly ducked and wove around energy blades the mantis threw their way while pursuing the flaming, claymore-wielding thief. Curling his fingers and utilizing the Snipe function of his Critical Storm Lance, the world seemed to slow as his vision vastly improved.

WHOOMPH

A streak of Blood, Sin, and Shadow tore space itself apart as Riven infused all he had into the attack. Streaming ribbons left crackling lightning in their wake as the projectile knocked the box out of the flaming man's hand right before the mantis got to him, and Riven found himself holding the box yet again as he cackled triumphantly and flipped off the other treasure hunters.

"CATCH ME IF YOU CAN, MOTHERFUCKER— UMPH!"

The shadow witch slapped him out of his seat with a strike of dark lightning, sending him like a smoldering comet into yet another building as he skidded across the fifth floor and out the side wall in a shower of stone.

"COCKSUCKERS!"

Three seconds to go.

He shifted his position in midair, feeling the beginnings of a riftwalk forming through the shadow witch's mana patterns, and grinned. He reoriented her own spell, adjusting the magic to change the output location to end directly in front of him, and his grin turned devilish as she appeared in front of him with a look of absolute shock at not having come out of her rift in the correct direction.

BAM

Riven's spiked knuckles took the pretty woman right in the nose, breaking it with a crunch and causing her to fumble the treasure chest and drop it.

Riven summoned a large platform of blood underneath his feet at an angle to push off and launched himself down toward the falling chest, catching the box in the next instant with an expanded Wretched Snare as the blades of a mantis shimmered in the light of a fiery being only ten feet behind.

Riven's three glowing eyes widened in horror as the mantis blades searched out his neck, beginning to pierce a weak spot in Messenger's armor and into Riven's skin.

But then the end of the floor came to be as the red sun fully made light of the dawn, and Riven was only left with a shallow stab wound in his left carotid artery that quickly began to seal up after an initial burst of bleeding. All his friends were with him on a lonely platform floating through the abyss, with large crystals of various Unholy colors shifting in the darkness to give slight illumination. And in the middle of them was a crystal with Lillith inside, where the famous demoness was held in stasis . . .

Only now the crystal holding her was beginning to melt.

[Floor Forty-Nine's hidden trial has come to a close. Eleven of fifty descent teams survived.

You, Riven Thane, are the last person to hold the D-grade treasure box containing the power of a single wish. This wish will be within the realms of D-grade only and may be accessed only while holding the orb contained within this treasure box.

Congratulations on making it to Floor Fifty: The Seat of Abyssal Power. Here you will find an ultimate source of abyssal energy and will be granted a single opportunity to build your soul lattice under some of the most potent dark energies available to any F-grade. These energies are specifically cultivated to help F-grades ascend into the E-grade while building soul lattices. How you perform while finishing your soul lattice on the last floor, paired with how you performed on the way down, will determine your overall score and any additional prizes that the Abyssal Descent provides before ascending to E-grade.

Lillith of the Black Skies will be freed from imprisonment now that you have arrived.
Calculating your overall score now . . .
Calculating additional prizes . . .]

CHAPTER 42

[Calculated score: 2,498,665 points
Your current cycle ranking: 9

The final points distributed will be based on your ascension into E-grade. Please ascend to E-grade and complete your soul lattice in order to get your final score and ranking. You may leave the Abyssal Descent at any time once you have a rank that you deem acceptable to claim your end prize, and you will receive the points that are associated with said rank even if it falls or increases in ranking after your departure.

Current Top 10 Scoreboard for Abyssal Descent:
Rank 1: 3,721,184 points, Lumis Breathfallen, Priestess of the Flaming Lagoon Cult
Rank 2: 3,458,818 points, Cragstan Razorbeak, the One Who Walks Unseen, Reincarnation of Sloth
Rank 3: 3,444,001 points, Nix'El'Tok, Basilisk Butcher of Integration Planet Tophrus in Universe 78
Rank 4: 3,096,660 points, Brotukek, Azag Hive Champion of the Horned Wing Clusters
Rank 5: 2,934,224 points, Hatchmire Felwing, Son of Overlord Felwing of the First Draconic Fist, 137th Heir of Universe 9
Rank 6: 2,899,911 points, Zulu Partinsans, Prodigy Student of the Night Witch Covens of Universe 20
Rank 7: 2,708,803 points, Drakscar Red-Tooth, Warrior of the Fifth Devil's Hellspire
Rank 8: 2,689,999 points, Ozompic Brathi, Scion of the Skullbreaker Hordes
Rank 9: 2,498,665 points, Riven Thane, Thirty-Sixth Prince of the Blood Moon Requiem, Reincarnation of Gluttony
Rank 10: 2,633,456 points, Atidi Pox, the One Who Has Lost His Mind, Grandson of the Chaos Pillar]

The platform was many miles wide and studded with towering spires of crystal infused with black magics of all varieties. It was like a forest of solidified power hovering in a sea of nothingness, and the silence when not speaking was nearly overwhelming.

"I was honestly unsure that all of you would make it out alive," Lillith said, sitting cross-legged next to Riven at the edge of the crystal-laden platform as the two of them stared into the abyss. Glancing sideways as Riven closed the notification screen, she patted his knee in approval. "You did well to get this far relatively unscathed. I am sorry I did not anticipate Elysium's move to trap me here, and I would go so far as to say that I owe you my life now. I would have been imprisoned here forever if you hadn't come."

Riven snorted absentmindedly, feeling the absolute black around him trying to seep into his very soul. The potency of the ambient energies was incredible, and being here on the lip of the drop into nothingness made him feel like he could reach enlightenment just by sitting still.

"You've done me solids before—you saved Allie. You owe me nothing," Riven said matter-of-factly, red eyes shifting to meet the black ones staring back. "And Gluttony never would have let you remain here. Even if I'd failed, he would have sent someone else to get you eventually."

Lillith grinned slightly and pushed a small bit of crystal off the platform, watching it fall endlessly into the darkness below until it disappeared from sight. "Perhaps. But don't you think it's time to meditate?"

"It is time," Gluttony said from beside them, ripping out of space itself to appear before them with a hungry and excited growl to his voice. "I have been preparing the second class we discussed for close-quarters combat . . . and I have a new body for us to share as well. It will be nothing less than a masterpiece."

Riven had no doubt that Gluttony was right. The original sin had been working on this class since the beginning of their descent, and from what he could tell, Gluttony had been fixated on getting some remnant of self-governance through this second body without imposing on Riven's own path and power. They'd still be bound but would be able to act independently from each other if Gluttony's attempt went according to plan, but it would also need a very large amount of input from Riven as well. Riven was the keystone to even allowing it to happen because he was the one that would be required by Elysium to ascend, so letting only Gluttony go ahead with the E-grade soul lattice construction would not only fail, but would likely result in a tribulation that could kill Riven to make Gluttony start over from scratch.

Meanwhile, Riven would also need to strengthen the foundations of his current class or even upgrade it depending on how far he could push it. He'd need to push it far enough that he could claim the top-ranking spot on the current ladder, otherwise, if what his mother had said in that vision many floors ago was correct, he'd likely lose out on the Chalgathi inheritance and would need to flee Panu altogether. That was solely based on trusting the same mother who'd abandoned him in childhood, but he saw no reason why she'd lie about this, as she, too, had the gift of Malignant Prophecy.

Which in turn had given him the idea to force Malignant Prophecy into action during this attempt at creating the soul lattice, boosting it to a perfect version that would fit not one but two classes. And doing so would, again, likely lead to some form of tribulation, as he would probably accumulate a lot of malignancy points from doing something so tremendously influential toward his future. And if that wasn't enough, tribulations usually happened between grade advancement anyways . . .

Long story short, he probably had at least one and possibly three tribulations headed his way. Or perhaps just a very hard and compounded tribulation with the strength of multiple tribulations other people would experience.

Not a good thing, but he wasn't balking now.

"Give me some time. Azmoth only just respawned and the Narg situation still hasn't been corrected, either," Riven told Gluttony and Lillith, still thinking about how he was going to go about doing this. "I've given a lot of thought to how I want to proceed, but now that it's finally here, I want to review everything thoroughly again before I take the plunge. You won't die if this fails, Gluttony, but I will. I am not scared to proceed, but I wish to collect myself and be mentally ready for what is to come."

Gluttony, for all his excitement, gave a grim mental nod of acceptance and disappeared, while Lillith remained silently staring into the dark expanse before them while all the others prepared in their own ways behind them between crystal spires on the platform.

Picking up the box that he'd set aside after getting here, Riven opened the chest to reveal a glimmering orb radiating multicolored mist. To his incredible disappointment, this system wish had not been able to bring back the dead. In part this was why Riven was so solemn at the moment. Jose was never coming back . . . but then again he should have known better if Elysium couldn't have brought back the real version of Ethel in the trials on prior floors. Instead it'd given him an option to bring back a copycat of Ethel . . . so a D-grade treasure, even if it was a wish from the system, likely couldn't do so, either.

Or perhaps that was just hindsight thinking.

[D-Grade Wish (System Event Gift): This wish will be within the realms of D-grade only. Ask Elysium and it may provide.]

Totally nondescript and originally a letdown, he'd now come to think it was a godsend—with limits.

Riven wouldn't look a gift horse in the mouth. Despite his disappointment in not getting Jose back, he could think of a couple different ways this wish might be used. And he'd even experimented with it to see just how far the wish could extend by asking Elysium itself.

This wish could not kill someone, but it could displace them. The wish could upgrade skills or traits to a better version of themselves, or it could even create a new skill based on something he came up with, but it could not create an all-powerful skill. It could not stop tribulations from occurring and couldn't create his soul lattice to perfection for him, but it could give him additional insights into how to do it himself. The wish couldn't stop the integration quests on Earth, but it could give him avenues to a far easier time completing them. Then, he'd even discovered that the wish could take a part of Panu entirely and move it into another world. In particular he'd asked Elysium if it could move the continent of Umbra to another planet, and Elysium had answered yes—as long as the continent was at an average of D-grade entities or below, it could transfer Umbra to a world of similar strength and danger.

Imagination really was the key with this wish, and he was treating it now as a lifeline in case they failed to conquer Panu before the integration ended. Moving his budding civilization off-world if need be was truly something that gave him some peace of mind, but it certainly wouldn't fix all his problems, and he didn't intend to lose Panu to others, either. The wish would only be used in extreme situations and only when in absolute need, because he might need it for another dire situation in the future, only to be found lacking if he used the wish too early.

"I will again attempt to figure out what is wrong with Narg, as I have insights into his family's curse," Lillith eventually said as the silence dragged on. "I will also make sure that the others who are not undergoing their own attempts to seclude themselves yet will leave you alone. Good luck, Riven, I'm sure you'll do very well."

It was finally time.

E-grade was on the horizon, close enough that he could almost touch it.

Wandering the miles-wide platform until he found a large cave buried in the crystal formations, Riven secluded himself and began to set up a cultivation formation.

Bringing out numerous Dao treasures he'd acquired over the course of his descent and on Panu alike, the ones that hadn't been more oriented toward his minions that he'd handed out earlier, Riven laid them out in a circle. Plants, metals, even weapons and armor with auras infused into them that he'd taken off other delvers, and various trinkets he'd collected were arranged to cycle between the different types of affinities he used.

Sin- and Blood-affinity treasures were most prevalent, but treasures oriented toward the Infernal, Death, Unholy, and Shadow pillars were all present as well. Using blood magic to create a large pentagram on the floor, he then created different runes in the air similar to how Gragle the gnome had created graphics in the past.

The runes in the air twisted and turned, forming complex codes as Riven did his best to emulate the system skill Gragle used to make such complex concepts while holding them steady. Riven had to redraw the three-dimensional formations multiple times over the course of five hours, as they kept collapsing, but eventually he got it down to where a very crude version of a graphic had remained stable in the air around the pentagram before building layers upon it with strings of mana. He could also tell that the environment here was key in helping prop up his desires, allowing him to press on with the ritual with far less resistance than what would have been possible outside the deeper abyss.

For his graphic wannabe: The concepts of Re, Vo, and Tin were utilized like the conceptualized X, Y, and Z axes in describing a three-dimensional space. The concepts of Nun and Zika were utilized to represent orientation and affinity of a power source, and in this case it wasn't a singular power source, but all the affinities he meshed with and their associated pillars. Zika, in particular, being the intent behind it, was hard to keep in check as his intent was to ascend into the next grade while drawing in power from his surroundings for fuel, which was the purpose of this crude pseudo-graphic he'd constructed in the first place.

Gluttony helped him keep the formation stable as he added the second and third layers of the graphic onto the top. The pentagram hummed with power as droplets of blood began to float up from the ground. The air around Riven shimmered in the darkness of the cave's surroundings, slowly swirling with different runic sigils as they interacted with one another and merged, only to split again at random before merging with different parts of the graphic and the individual enchantments making up each part.

It wasn't until he took out his prized blood pearl, literally ripping it out of his chest and soul aperture, that he realized something was strange.

[Trishard Blood Pearl (C-Grade Blasphemous Blood Artifact): This relic has condensed the affinities from three of five paths the subpillar of Blood may take and has been impermanently bound to you, Riven Thane, as its new wielder. This item is shielded from the Blood God's farsight, detection, and scrying abilities and will be viewed as a normal Blood artifact by all but the most powerful of his Blood clergy, Blood precursors, and the bearer of this item. This item holds long-lost and buried secrets of the Blood subpillar and is marked as an extremely taboo artifact by the current Blood God. Study and meditate on this item for further insights into powers now lost to all but the dead. +200% bonus to Dao insights regarding the Blood subpillar while meditating with this item in hand. Large amounts of blood mana of any type may be stored inside this Trishard Blood Pearl, and it creates ambient blood mana at a steady rate to either be used as stored mana or to be used to change environments. This item may be stored within your soul space at will. Must naturally be of 99% Blood affinity or more to properly wield this item.

- **Supercharged Blood: Take an additional thirty seconds**

of channeling a Blood skill through this item to create a supercharged variant. This skill is incredibly potent, and overuse may damage your mana channels.

- **Within this item, secrets concerning the <u>Supreme Path of Red and Black Domination, the Supreme Path of Blazing Azure Creation (Taboo)</u>, and the <u>Supreme Path of Gold and Silver Stairways (Taboo)</u> are present but hidden. Unlocking these secrets to their fullest will add additional splitting pillar growths from your baseline Blood subpillar within your soul realm.]**

When he set the pearl down in the center of the pentagram, it easily began influencing the surrounding graphic and fused its will with the path Riven wanted to undertake. However, it also began pulling at the bonds in Riven's soul core that connected him to his minions.

Furrowing his brows and mentally tracing the lines of power that the pearl had wrapped its tendrils around, he found them: Genua, Azmoth, Fay, and Athela were being incorporated into the ritual of ascension.

But they were only the first layer.

Narg was incorporated into the second layer of the formation as the pearl shifted the bond a layer higher than the others. Iris, who wasn't even a minion, was also found before the pearl crawled up a similar link, one of birthright. The red vines of the pearl quickly reinforced the karmic link and then continued reaching out further to incorporate other people, too.

One by one, they came.

Fish came next. Then Lizard, and then Brute, linking rather quickly due to Riven's blood circulating through them while they were still undergoing the thrall transformation.

Surprisingly, the pearl began bypassing some of the others on his team, ignoring them completely. Sanguine the drake and General Caltan were left out of the ritual, examined and bypassed by the pearl as it perfused the connections of the others. Retesh was much the same, being seen and bypassed by the pearl's influence like he wasn't even there. It tried to travel along the Siblings' Pact that connected him to Allie, meeting resistance, but it couldn't penetrate the veil of the abyss and resolved itself to settling for what and who was present here on the platform.

Most surprisingly of all, when it found Kara, the pearl added her to the first layer.

From what Riven could tell, the pearl was utilizing blood ties, though he couldn't figure out why some went into the first layer while others went into the outer second layer. His demonic contracts were bound to him inherently with blood magic through the system itself, forcing them to obey his commands like they were his own limbs. Iris was his daughter, so his blood ran through her. Genua was a thrall made from his blood, and the three soon-to-be thralls had his blood running through them, too. Kara had been injected with his blood a single time, back when he'd been going at it with her during that foursome involving Fay and Athela.

He almost wanted to stop the process right then and there in order to somehow share his blood with others in the group—namely Retesh, Caltan, and Sanguine—but the process was already underway for whatever the pearl was doing, and he felt like if he stopped the process now it'd irrevocably harm whatever the pearl had started. The room was beginning to shake as a rumbling thunder echoed and cracked through the abyss somewhere overhead above the cave he now sat in, and Riven's eyes began to glaze over as the red light from his pupils began etching itself along the black Sin sigils tattooed along his body.

The tattoos then began to peel off his skin, floating into the air around him as an echo of Gluttony radiated throughout the cave.

"You must take the first steps," Gluttony called out as Riven's glowing red gaze went ballistic with rapid flitting motion to trace the patterns he wanted to imprint on his soul. "I will then manifest the pieces I need as you form the base layer, just like we discussed. Do not falter."

Riven gritted his teeth as he felt a pulse of white-hot pain course along his spine, and with a mental command he began to force the ambient magics of the abyss into his soul like a shot of pure adrenaline. His back went rigid and he let out a hiss as the world around him blurred into a myriad of colors. The graphics in the air vibrated and hummed, and his soul was laid bare as the constellation of his inner realm took flight to hover in the air above him and in between the ritual sigils all about.

The pillars of his soul core surged, each radiating their collective light around the brilliant white soul core in the middle. Fractals representing his skills were highlighted along these pillars and the inner core in turn, becoming more condensed as the high-grade ambient energies of the abyss around him fed their growth.

The pentagram and ritual formations drew in power from the abyss even faster, helped along by the Dao treasures laid out about him, and one by one many of the treasures began to shrivel and fade away into ash as their potency was decimated to fuel his ascension.

Riven considered brute-forcing a Malignant Prophecy to take place right then but decided he could go a little bit longer. The less time he used it the better, considering just how influential it would be on his future and the number of points he'd no doubt rack up, so he pushed back the edges of gray permeating his peripheral vision and maintained a clear head while grasping at nearby soul connections.

And the connections each snapped into place like jigsaw puzzle pieces within mere seconds.

Athela's connection came first, along with a depiction of the demoness, and the ritual's domain flashed brightly before tethering to Athela's projection with a thin but firm cord of light.

Another tether lashed out, smashing into the forming projection of Azmoth's figure and sinking into his chest.

Fay's image came next. Then Kara, Genua, Narg, Iris, Fish, Lizard, and Brute.

Ten soul tethers chaining images to Riven's core. They came together, twisting around one another to form an intertwined rope that led upward like a spire. At the same time, his soul pillars began to sprout threads and bridges among one another. First it was dozens, then hundreds, and then tens of thousands of threads that wove together as his soul lattice began to grow at an astronomical rate.

BOOM

The entire cave and all the crystal formations around Riven rumbled as energy gathered far above. Almost immediately after that, Riven felt ten additional tribulations roar to life as the dark skies overhead split with blinding light that illuminated even the dark cave he was in.

[WARNING: You are undertaking an ascension into the next grade. Prepare for a tribulation to test your resolve. Should you fail, you will have your cultivation ripped from you and you will possibly die.]

Riven's eyes widened as he realized that he was involving the others that the pearl had touched, bringing them both power and danger without their consent. Even he hadn't known this would happen, and he felt Gluttony become agitated with similar worries as something foreign and almighty set its gaze upon the platform Riven's friends and family now sat on.

"No. This tribulation is mine, not theirs."

Riven reached up a hand, and his soul screamed as he tore away the cave's ceiling in an explosion of force that sent high-grade crystals teeming with power spiraling out into the abyss. He continued to reach, pulling on the ten swirling vortexes over the miles-wide platform and yanking their attention to him, showing Elysium that it was he and not they that had called down the system's judgment.

Immediately the vortexes of multicolored light rumbled toward him, merging and condensing over his position to create a far greater tribulation than the one that'd been there before.

But Riven had expected no less. And now was only the gathering stage . . . he wasn't even done with his lattice yet. Elysium would not test him until it was complete . . .

At least, that would have been the case under normal circumstances. But he needed his soul lattice to be perfect, as his entire future would be built upon the foundations he laid down right now. And he had Gluttony's plan to complete, creating a second class in direct contestation with Elysium's rules.

Gluttony's maw split his soul aperture with a resounding ***CRACK***, tearing off pieces of each of his soul pillars to create a sister core made of black sin instead of his original brilliant white.

[WARNING: You are undertaking a taboo form of ascension. Stop immediately or face punishment in the form of a tribulation.]

The surroundings around him slowed and faded to gray. It was now or never.

[Malignant Prophecy has activated. WARNING: HIGH LEVELS OF MALIGNANCY POINTS WILL BE DELIVERED DUE TO ACTIVATION AT A KEY CROSSROADS SUCH AS THIS.

Desired action: Extremely high-tier manipulation. Current Willpower stat: 1,054. Sufficient Willpower to perform desired action. Performing this act will put your Malignant Prophecy on cooldown for significant amounts of time. Do you wish to proceed?]

"Yes."

[Desired action: Create a perfect soul lattice and ascend to E-grade. Malignant Prophecy's three options are as follows:
- Option 1: Redistribute the tribulations back to your soul bonds and divert Elysium's judgment. Azmoth will be crippled for two years, Fay will lose the ability to bear children, and Brute will die. Iris will grow closer to the Gluttonous Dao of Sin. Then you will be guided on how to empower your Path of Red and Black, before less focus is cast upon the rest of your soul lattice. This will increase your affinity for Blood up to 102% and your affinity for Shadow to 98%. Your split into two classes will result in a second demonic body for Gluttony to pilot. Chance for success: perfect.
- Option 2: Utilize Orbital Hellstrike to rip out your Infernal subpillar to directly skewer Elysium's tribulation. This will temporarily cripple your Infernal subpillar, but you will regain use of it within a month. When it comes back, your Infernal subpillar will have been infused with the powers of the abyss and will increase your affinity for Infernal to 99%. Each of your connections will be strengthened and have large increases in their own affinities. Your split into two classes will result in a second demonic body for Gluttony to pilot. Chance for success: extremely high.
- Option 3: Command the abyss to eat Elysium's tribulation through Gluttony's image, allowing the abyss itself to incorporate the aspect of the Great Maw for a short time. The resulting implosion of abyssal energy intertwined with Elysium's tribulation storms will resonate with you and will spread through your tethers into those connected to you. This

will permanently damage your ability to summon your demonic minions to you through nether portals quickly, and they will have to be summoned through ritual means from here on out, though everyone tethered to you will undergo significant upgrades to their base stats and to the potency of their skills. You will also upgrade your soul lattice in a way that significantly improves your storms and Path of Red and Black. Your split into two classes will result in a second demonic body, but Gluttony will be forced to undergo a period of hibernation throughout the entirety of the time spent in E-grade in preparation for the next step. This additional class and additional demonic body will be yours alone to pilot simultaneously, allowing you to live two lives. Meanwhile, Gluttony will be able to utilize this opportunity to create a true avatar of his original body when he returns, a replica of what he was before the fall of the sins came to be eons ago. Chance for success: medium.]

Riven felt the pulse of shock radiate through Gluttony as soon as the prompt appeared.

[Desired action has been selected: Option 2.]

CHAPTER 43

His eyes blazed red and Gluttony's essence condensed, fusing with Riven's soul pillars as they, together, made for their ascension. The gray world around him shuddered as the images of his vision that he'd just witnessed began to fade.

[Option 2: Utilize Orbital Hellstrike to rip out your Infernal subpillar to directly skewer Elysium's tribulation. This will temporarily cripple your Infernal subpillar, but you will regain use of it within a month. When it comes back, your Infernal subpillar will have been infused with the powers of the abyss and will increase your affinity for Infernal to 99%. Each of your connections will be strengthened and have large increases in their own affinities. Your split into two classes will result in a second demonic body for Gluttony to pilot. Chance for success: extremely high.]

[<u>Your manipulation of fate has gained you—</u>
<u>Your manipulation of fate has gained you—</u>
<u>Your manipulation of fate has gained you—</u>
<u>Your manipulation of fate has gained you—</u>
<u>Recalculating.</u>
<u>Current total Malignancy Points: 279]</u>

[WARNING: You are undertaking a taboo form of ascension. Your path will now be tested for legitimacy.]

The crystal cave around him shattered into millions of pieces in a thunderous roar of power. The strike lit up his position on the platform with immense amounts of tribulation energy that blasted down at him in quick succession. Fire and lightning caressed him as he screamed in pain, testing his path and his fate, the crucible being far greater than the first time he'd endured it back on Panu. Even more of it was gathering overhead as Gluttony expanded out from his soul aperture around Riven's ritual setup as he floated in the middle of it, lighting up even the darkness of the abyss as the sky began to flare with multicolored light.

CRASH

Another arc of lightning, this time far larger than the previous ones, descended to smack him like a disobedient child. Riven's eyes were seared from their sockets, exploding instantly as the defensive treasures he'd placed into the ritual graphics and pentagram began to wither and burn due to overexertion.

He felt his soul core begin to crack and shatter and felt more than he heard Gluttony scream in his own fresh wave of agony as the sin tried to keep their souls united and tried to keep Riven alive.

CRASH

He felt his right arm rip off.

CRASH

Another bolt of multicolored flame and lightning violently eviscerated him and tore a piece of Messenger when the armor attempted to swallow some of the energy, exposing Riven's charred and bloody chest. Riven's blood magic flooded his surroundings as a storm of black and red pulsed and crackled, fighting back and channeling through the pearl clutched to him in melted fingers, and Jackal only barely managed to block yet another blast of energy before the staff splintered slightly down the middle.

Riven's eyes had regrown and his arm had reattached itself by now, and his face warped in shock. He felt the damaged staff's soul begin to fade and quickly flung it out of the ritual like a comet, saving it from being utterly destroyed as he endured two more attacks, just as the vision had predicted would happen.

He began to follow the next step of the prophecy, pulling on his Infernal subpillar when the skies lit up a bright white and Elysium's might descended on him in a way that he had not foreseen.

Something had changed from the vision.

This wasn't supposed to be happening.

A brilliant golden blade containing the secrets of the angels was torn from a hole ripped open in the abyss to expose the cosmos, burning white-hot with the fury of the heavens and power that raged against the abyssal sin of the environment. The blade was so large that it threatened to decimate the entire miles-wide platform he and his team now resided on. It looked akin to the blade of some lost and vengeful god, with its wrath and ire directed at him.

[If Gluttony wishes to walk among your kind with naught but a soul tether, then you will be forced to show Elysium you can contain the Great Maw's hunger even when not intimately united. Should you fail, you will die. Your path will now be tested.]

Riven barely had time to react and his hands dug into his chest to literally rip out a piece of his flesh as a sacrificial offering. The spell then exploded open with a supernova of flames as he frantically screamed the incantation for Orbital Hellstrike: "OFFER MY FLESH AND SOUL TO BURN AWAY MINE ENEMIES!"

[Orbital Hellstrike (Infernal) (Tier 3): Rip out your Infernal subpillar to manifest it as a missile high above you. Call down a precision strike from orbit, doing immense critical Infernal damage to a single target and cataclysmic explosive damage to the surroundings for many miles. This attack temporarily shatters your Infernal subpillar and will disable all other Infernal abilities until the pillar re-forms in your soul core. The lower health your target has, the more damage this spell does.]

Riven immediately lost the ability to channel any of his other Infernal abilities.

His Infernal soul subpillar tore off from his aperture and manifested within the physical realm, a crackling and seething testament to the power of the hells. It was the size of a skyscraper and set the very air around it aflame, sending waves of heat digging into the landscape and protectively encircling his teammates as the descent of heaven's might barreled down like a torpedo through the darkness. Hell met heaven as the spire of Riven's soul met the golden-white sword manifestation, and the backlash was immediate.

The place where his Infernal subpillar had been torn off his soul core flashed white-hot inside his internal realm as the abyss itself burned with a mix of heavenly and hellish Daos, encompassing his very world in flashes of red-orange and blinding white-gold.

Was this truly what tribulations were supposed to be like? It was nothing like his first and only one before this incident.

GASP

Gluttony's presence disappeared into the Sin pillar while Elysium's tribulation tore into Riven's inner realm.

Riven doubled over as the heavenly Dao began to permeate his other pillars. The Sin and Unholy pillars reacted particularly violently inside him, like a body's response that tried to fight off an invading disease. His skin began to flake off and his vision began to swim with darkness despite the waves of light illuminating the platform from far above. He puked blood, vomiting profusely as he began to feel himself die . . .

Only for his tethered soul connections to strengthen him.

His soul core that had begun to shatter was held firm by threads that wound their way across his lattice, even forming new connections as the threads began to rapidly grow between the different aspects of his soul like a massive spiderweb

Athela was the first as her link to him was the strongest, but the others began to help soon thereafter. Though given that his child was too young to know what she was doing, and the beholder demon wasn't even awake, it likely wasn't intentionally done. Rather, it was probably the symbiotic connections he'd formed through his blood pearl that were now soaking in energy from the other souls to help support his otherwise imminent collapse. Azmoth, Fay, Genua, Iris, Kara, Narg, Fish, Lizard, and Brute were all there, too, and in turn, they each received a piece of enlightenment as his soul lattice was built with little pieces of them inside it.

And yet . . . it was still not enough.

The truths of the heavens still tried to claw and mangle his insides, both in the physical and soul realms. It burned and clawed like a vicious predator, trying to eradicate all signs of the sin that was its anathema. The closer to Gluttony it got, the more it tried to rip him apart. Riven's body spasmed with different energies that battled for control as he unleashed everything he had, using the ambient mana of the abyss to feed his need for more power despite the tremendous reserves he'd already built up. And it was still not enough even then.

He began to feel his bonds take damage as the circulating heavenly judgment tried to crawl out beyond his own soul to burn away at the tethering strings. He felt their pain and their horror as they, too, began to burn from the inside out.

But in his darkest hour, as he began to watch his friends and loved ones burn away, something inside him rose to meet the challenge . . . and it wasn't what he'd expected.

Malignant Prophecy spontaneously activated . . . again? Riven wasn't sure that was really what was going on, but the world turned gray, then back to a normal hue, then to gray and back again. This repeated seven more times in quick succession, causing the realm around him to stutter and stop every other second until it finally came to a standstill. He saw a piece of the Blood subpillar flake off like a candle in the night, floating above his cracked soul core with a brilliant red hue, before it flared brightly and vanished, bringing along with it all the heavenly Dao infused into his soul. His vampiric bloodline expanded and then began to shatter like glass dropped onto pavement.

[As a pureblooded vampire, you have come to embrace your predatory heritage. Your soul has drunk in the Blood of Heaven, an aspect of Elysium's tribulation, and has managed to suppress it at the cost of Malignant Prophecy. Within the Blood of Heaven, the <u>Supreme Path of Gold and Silver Stairways (Taboo)</u> has been touched upon.

- **You have gained the LEGENDARY vampiric bloodline expansion of <u>Heaven's Bane</u>, increasing the potency of your Unholy powers and all related powers, while your resistance to Holy powers and all related powers has increased. These changes are permanent. These changes apply to all your current blood tethers and the individuals connected to your soul, imbuing them with many of your own vampiric powers. Soul lattice constructions**

will be easier to complete for these tethered souls. Small racial
evolutions for these tethered souls are now available, and all will
bear the mark of Gluttony to draw upon his power.

- Malignant Prophecy's lineage has overexerted itself to save your
life. Malignant Prophecy has been temporarily damaged and will
be crippled upon arriving at C-grade.]

[Soul lattice construction is underway. Your path has been deemed
acceptable. Keep Gluttony's tendencies contained or suffer a worse
tribulation upon the next grade.]

Tears silently streamed down his face as his body twitched in agony.

The tribulation energy left the abyss in an instant with that last ominous
threat from Elysium, leaving a smoldering wreckage where Riven's cave had
been, and the tattered remains of his body and armor were evident to anyone
that had opportunity to look. His hair was singed clean off, one of his teeth was
missing, his body was a mangled mess, and there was a smoking hole in his chest
where his pillar had been torn out. Only some of his wounds were healing, but
very slowly, yet despite this he didn't feel sluggish.

If anything, the new class that he and Gluttony were now focusing their
attention to create was at the forefront of his mind. The tribulation might be
gone, but he still had a single chance to create the soul lattice properly . . .

The lattice continued to build layer upon layer, threads interweaving with
one another like the strings of a tapestry, and like a master artisan, Riven began
to paint the idea of what he wanted into the very being of his inner realm. Piece
by piece, he put it together with Gluttony's help . . . until he passed out from
exhaustion and entered into the world of dreams.

Riven's eyes fluttered open, and his head felt like it was going to pop due to all
the notifications that blasted through his vision. He could barely tell that there
was sunshine overhead amid a blue, cloud-speckled sky, before the holograms
rapidly snapped over one another in a layer of screens.

[You have ascended into the E-grade. Your soul lattice has been
constructed to maximize pathways and pave the way for your soul
skeleton, your soul core has been enlarged and reinforced, your energy
reserves have been reinforced, and your stats have been reinforced
and are now level 201. Primary class, Warlock of the Malevolent
Storm, remains unchanged. Secondary class, True Incarnation of
Gluttony, has been granted. Gluttony may now manifest in a separate
body of his own at certain times with strict conditions, focusing on
melee combat, and will be equal level to your own. If his gluttonous
tendencies are not controlled through your soul tether to him, you

will be targeted for elimination by Elysium to curb the potential destruction of your bonded Original Sin.

Heaven's Bane, Legendary Vampiric Bloodline Expansion, has influenced the bodies of you and your soul tethers. Your Infernal subpillar absorbed an abundance of heaven's energy as well, turning it and cannibalizing the energy of the tribulation to boost your Infernal affinity to 99%. Your soul tethers of Athela, Azmoth, Fay, Genua, Iris, Fish, Lizard, Kaya, and Brute have all gained potency for their own powers and significant resistance to heavenly powers, and they have been given slight changes to their appearances. Narg has undergone significant changes and has fully evolved into an Abyssal Eye Beholder.

Malignant Prophecy is now destroyed. Regaining Malignant Prophecy can only be done in the C-grade step of soul development, and even if you manage to regain it, the bloodline will be permanently damaged.]

[All of your party has reached E-grade. You have obtained the current number-one ranking spot for this round of the Abyssal Descent. Your party has exited the Abyssal Descent and each member has obtained a permanent boon of a +20% amplifier to all stats. You have also unlocked a branching pillar off the subpillar of Blood: The Supreme Path of Gold and Silver Stairways (Taboo). Alongside the Path of Red and Black, you now have two of the five branching paths of the Blood subpillar.]

[Jackal has been severely damaged. Messenger has been severely damaged. Your pet General Caltan has summoned an additional seven bloodstricken undead and has gained authority over them. Your party in the Abyssal Descent has been disbanded. Kara and Iris have successfully been transported in Fay's pocket realm dungeon back to Panu and into Chalgathi's trials. Retesh and Lillith have been returned to Umbra. Congratulations on your successful descent through the abyss; it is a challenge not many complete and even fewer complete so well.]

[Riven's Quest 2 of the Altars of Despair and Hope:

The Abyssal Descent, a monumental event that only happens every three hundred years involving the best of the younger generations bound to the Unholy pillar, has been successfully completed in first place. This results in three thousand points for your Apocalypse Beasts event.

There are twenty-one registered cultists.
- Seven Chalgathi cultists, six Chubin cultists, and eight Nekra cultists

There are nine registered noncultists entering this event.
- Three Chalgathi noncultists, four Chubin noncultists, and two Nekra noncultists

Total event points already accumulated: 3,216. Ten thousand event points are needed to leave. You are now in eighteenth place over-all. Netithi Bluskish, level-205 Naga, Apex rank, Champion of the Kraken, and a Chubin cultist, is in first place at 8,762 event points. No participants have managed to leave the Altars of Despair and Hope. Yet.]

Gragle was a drunken mess, and for good reason. The situation here in this strange land of mix-and-matched pieces of the multiverse that'd been brought together for an apocalypse beast event, of all things, was just getting out of hand. The battles between cultists and noncultists were now involving not just his home base of Outpost Number 84 that'd been scraped off his old world by the hands of the system, but they involved dozens of other cities just like his own, locations of interest used for system quests, cities that were forced to pick a side. Regardless of which they chose, it always ended in one disaster or another. In this place, a dead participant was only temporary—the blasted cultists and their counterparts just kept respawning to attack again.

Gragle and his people, on the other hand . . . Well, they couldn't respawn. And given Riven's intervention on their behalf, Outpost Number 84 had been designated firmly in the noncultist territory, which had put a large target on their backs with Riven gone. They'd lost hundreds of people to hit-and-run attacks despite bunkering up, constantly being terrorized in the night by the cultist side or the cronies of other factions that'd been subdued by the cultists, and that'd continued until Nora Lang had shown up again.

He'd only briefly met the small Asian woman a handful of times before she and the others had left on that months-long trip into the abyss. But he'd not even recognized her in the beginning . . . He'd thought she'd been another monster sent by the system or worse. Only that she recognized him . . . and despite having apparently lost her mind to madness and the screaming voices in her head, she'd protected him.

And she'd made life a living hell for the cultists.

Ever since her return, she'd gone on a campaign of bloodshed and butchery, actively seeking out all cultists with a gleeful vengeance as her legion of shadows with crooked smiles violently ended many of the cultists many times over. She'd become known as public threat number one to the enemy, and to those cities and states that'd come here and had been subjugated by the cultists—well, many of them simply didn't exist anymore. Down to the last woman and child, Nora had butchered them all while laughing merrily to the insane tune in her head. She'd told Gragle about it once upon a return trip to rest, though she barely ever did rest and more likely came to gloat about her violent victories. Each victory she achieved slightly decreased the enemy side's accumulated points, though she was becoming increasingly frustrated lately due to her inability to pinpoint the naga at the top of the food chain. She'd since joined the APEX ranks on her own planet and had fought the naga multiple times when trying to intervene in his system quests, but every time ended in either a draw or the naga's escape. Netithi Bluskish, one of Greed's new pawns, was anything but incompetent and had even almost killed her twice. His latest retaliation attempt had been to somehow drop an ice drake on the home Nora was sleeping in, which happened to be in Gragle's home on Outpost Number 84, and the resulting fighting had ended in the deaths of two dozen citizens.

What was even worse was that he'd been the pinpoint of people's ire for it. Who would dare yell and scream at Nora, the madwoman wielding immense power on a quest to help suppress the other contestants for whenever Riven got back?

No. They didn't yell and scream at her; they were too scared. Instead, they yelled and screamed at Riven's other acquaintances—namely Gragle.

Gragle sighed deeply, staring into the amber liquid of his mug while using a stubby finger to rotate and swirl the liquid in gentle waves. His eyes were heavy and his breathing labored from the intense alcohol use, but he was tempted to keep going despite being in a heavy state of inebriation.

"When do you think this shitshow is finally going to be over?" the barkeep asked for the fifth time this month, smoothing over a glass with a rag and glaring in Gragle's direction. "Warden Zuk says that—"

"I don't care what Warden Zuk says!" Gragle huffed, spitting off to the side and nearly falling over with the effort of it due to all the alcohol he'd drunk. "I've told you a billion times now, Mark! I don't know when the event will end! You people keep coming to me to ask when all I've ever done is help just a handful of the noncultists with enchantments and gear upgrades! I don't have the answers, so stop asking me!"

The skinny human bartender scowled deeply at the shorter gnome and put down the glass he'd been polishing to give Gragle a mouthful—when he suddenly went rigid and paled. Everyone else in the room did the same, and the talking abruptly died to a hushed whisper, so it got even the drunken Gragle to turn around for a look.

There, standing in the remnants of what had once been immaculate gluttonous armor, with a staff that had a split down the middle and crackled with spontaneous uncontrolled energy secondary to damage, was a familiar man.

"Hello, Gragle," Riven said, limping forward and sitting down on a stool next to the drunk gnome. Riven signaled the barkeep to get him a menu and slowly lowered his bald, charred head to the wooden countertop. "I'd say it's nice to be back . . . but it appears that I still have a lot of work to do. First thing about that would be to get a fresh repair on my gear. So . . . if you wouldn't mind, I'd like to talk business."

ABOUT THE AUTHOR

Ranyhin1 is the pen name of Trent Boehm, author of Elysium's Multiverse, an apocalypse LitRPG he originally released on Royal Road. A lifelong lover of fantasy, Boehm is also a science nerd, Dallas Cowboys fan, and wannabe gym rat. He hopes one day to pursue writing full-time.